ALEX GARLAND was born in London in 1970. He has written two novels, *The Beach* and *The Tesseract.*

W F DEEDES is a distinguished journalist who joined the *Morning Post* 70 years ago. He fought in the war and was a Minister in the Macmillan government before returning to the *Daily Telegraph* where he still works, reporting regularly from war zones and writing a weekly column. He is said to be the inspiration behind Evelyn Waugh's *Scoop* and is the Bill of *Private Eye*'s 'Dear Bill' letters. This is the first time he has written fiction.

TONY HAWKS has written two books, *Round Ireland with a Fridge* and *Playing the Moldovans at Tennis*, both surreal adventures prompted by bets. His third book, *One Hit Wonderland*, will be published in June 2002.

IRVINE WELSH As well as writing the novels *Trainspotting, Filth* and *Glue* and *Macabou Stork Nightmares*, Irvine has written story collections *Ecstasy* and *The Acid House* and a play, *You'll Have Had Your Hole.*

VICTORIA GLENDINNING has written biographies of many literary figures, from Jonathan Swift to Anthony Trollope to Vita Sackville-West. She has also published two novels, *The Grown-Ups* and *Electricity*. Her third novel, *Flight*, will be published in 2002.

GILES FODEN was born in England in 1967. As a child he moved with his family to Africa, where they lived until 1993. His books include *The Last King of Scotland* and *Ladysmith*. His new book *Zanzibar* is published in 2002.

ANDREW O'HAGAN was born in Glasgow. He is the author of *The Missing* and *Our Fathers*, a novel shortlisted for the Booker Prize and the Inpac Fiction Award.

THE WEEKENDERS

The Daily Telegraph, *who commissioned this book, will be donating the royalties to aid work in the Sudan.*

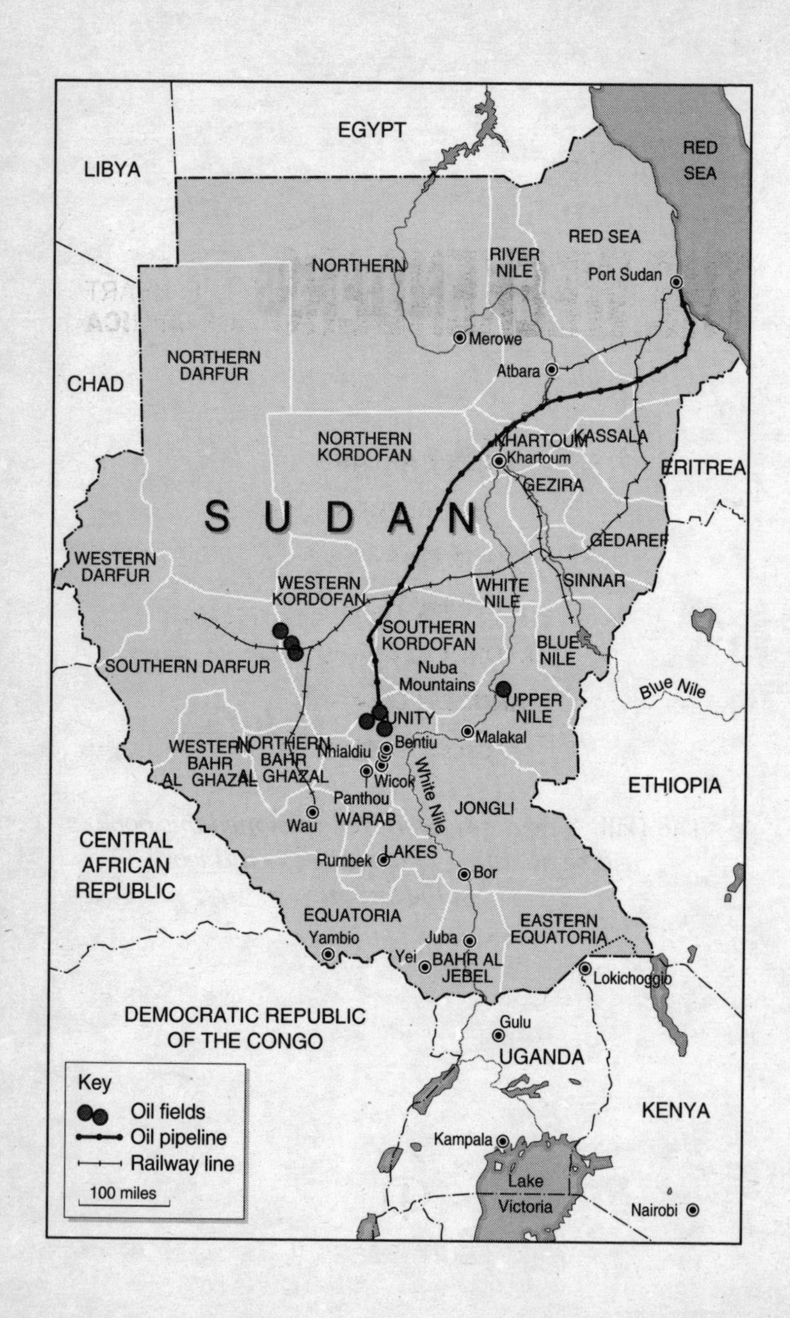
EGYPT
LIBYA
RED SEA
RED SEA
NORTHERN
RIVER NILE
Port Sudan
Merowe
Atbara
NORTHERN DARFUR
CHAD
NORTHERN KORDOFAN
KHARTOUM
Khartoum
KASSALA
ERITREA
GEZIRA
SUDAN
GEDAREF
WESTERN DARFUR
WESTERN KORDOFAN
WHITE NILE
SINNAR
SOUTHERN KORDOFAN
BLUE NILE
SOUTHERN DARFUR
Nuba Mountains
UPPER NILE
Blue Nile
UNITY
Malakal
Bentiu
WESTERN BAHR AL GHAZAL
NORTHERN BAHR AL GHAZAL
Nhialdiu
Wicok
Panthou
White Nile
ETHIOPIA
Wau
WARAB
JONGLI
CENTRAL AFRICAN REPUBLIC
Rumbek
LAKES
Bor
EQUATORIA
EASTERN EQUATORIA
Yambio
Juba
Yei
BAHR AL JEBEL
Lokichoggio
DEMOCRATIC REPUBLIC OF THE CONGO
Gulu
UGANDA
KENYA
Kampala
Lake Victoria
Nairobi
Key
Oil fields
Oil pipeline
Railway line
100 miles

THE WEEKENDERS

TRAVELS IN THE HEART OF **AFRICA**

ALEX GARLAND

W F DEEDES

TONY HAWKS

IRVINE WELSH

VICTORIA GLENDINNING

ANDREW O'HAGAN

GILES FODEN

EBURY PRESS

First published in Great Britain in 2001

11 13 15 17 19 18 16 14 12 10

First published by Ebury Press
Random House, 20 Vauxhall Bridge Road, London SW1V 2SA

Random House Australia (Pty) Limited
20 Alfred Street, Milsons Point, Sydney, New South Wales 2061, Australia

Random House New Zealand Limited
18 Poland Road, Glenfield, Auckland 10, New Zealand

Random House South Africa (Pty) Limited
Endulini, 5A Jubilee Road, Parktown 2193, South Africa

The Random House Group Limited Reg. No. 954009

www.randomhouse.co.uk

A CIP catalogue record for this book is available from the British Library

Cover design by the Senate
Text design and typesetting by Textype

ISBN 0 0918 8180 3

Papers used by Ebury Press are natural, recyclable products made from wood grown in sustainable forests

Printed and bound in Great Britain by
Bookmarque Ltd, Croydon, Surrey

Contents

Acknowledgements

The *Daily Telegraph* would like to thank all those who have been involved in the making of *The Weekenders* and given their time and creativity free – our special thanks go to Bill Deedes, Alex Garland, Andrew O'Hagan, Irvine Welsh, Victoria Glendinning, Tony Hawks and Giles Foden for writing such fascinating pieces. Thanks to Sue Ryan and Abbie Trailer-Smith at the *Telegraph*, to Andrew Nurnberg, and to all those at Ebury who have put in a huge amount of time and effort, in particular Jake Lingwood, Sarah Bennie, Helen Everson and Anthony Heller. Thanks to Martin Noble and the lovely people at Bookmarque and Textype.

FOREWORD

It is often said of newspapers that we have a short attention span. Disasters cease to make the headlines after the first dramatic exposure. Media fatigue sets in as the months go by and, save for the occasional dramatic development we pull out, leaving the aid agencies to get on with their work.

But for some journalists the story remains with them long after it is written and there is a need to find another way of telling it. The war in Sudan ceased to be news a long while ago. Bill Deedes, the doyen of journalists became increasingly frustrated at how little the outside world knew of what the Sudanese people had to endure from a war that has been a constant and ugly part of their lives for most of the last 30 years. Over lunch one day in his favourite Italian restaurant we discussed how the world has no clear picture in its mind of what it means to be a perpetual refugee, to be constantly fleeing from danger, to have no schools for the children, to have nowhere that can be called home. And we discussed how little political will there was internationally to help with a solution.

Before the coffee arrived this book was conceived. It would raise money for the Sudan, but more significantly we wanted to break the long silence that has lingered over this war.

This is not a charity book in its conventional sense; writers were not being asked to dash off a chapter in the comfort of their homes for a worthy cause. They were being invited to go to one of the most extraordinary and inaccessible places on the planet – for the war has ruined Southern Sudan's infrastructure – and engage with a previously unreachable war.

The writers included in *The Weekenders* went to the Sudan to do what writers have always been interested in doing: replenishing their imaginations with new experience. They would be exposed to the white heat of the unknown and the unknowable. They would be confronted with violence, desperation, poverty and also with courage, endurance and faith.

The new generation of British writers are sometimes accused of being hedonistic, of being wholly taken up with questions of materialism and enjoyment and popular culture, at the expense of any real interest in the economic or political affairs of the world.The Weekenders disproves it. The writers enthusiastically immersed themselves bodily as well as intellectually in this project, hopeful that what they wrote would chime with a new generation who may be familiar with the books but not the world of Graham Greene, Evelyn Waugh and Joseph Conrad.

Each of the authors is master of his or her genre – and each had to step out of their different but similarly exclusive worlds. Irvine Welsh, the druggy sub-culture of Edinburgh; Alex Garland, the hip thriller; Victoria Glendinning the biographer of other centuries, Andrew O'Hagan the insightful chronicler of contemporary lives. Bill Deedes, a journalist for seventy years, wrote fiction for the first time in his life and Tony Hawks sought to write a song with a Sudanese tribesman. Only Giles Foden did not travel with the group. His contribution was invited later as someone whose experience in Africa would add a different dimension and was written before the dreadful events in America on September 11.

The views, both overt and covert are entirely their own and all the characters in the fictional stories, are just that. But if the writers have vastly different backgrounds, political views and writing styles, they had no trouble in seeing the venture as a joint one, an opportunity to put their skills as writers and their enthusiasm to an end they couldn't quite be certain about. Most grew certain during their trip, as Bill had done before them, that the Sudan would not leave them.

Some people may ask how could we assume that we would have anything to add, in the way of understanding, to such a complex and horrifying situation. All I can say is that we felt bound to try, and that the writers went to the Sudan with some care, each with a mind to stretching themselves and engendering debate.

The Weekenders is testament to what will happen if you draw traditional commitment out of new experience: these are pieces by writers who are not up on stilts, not writing by remote control, not dreaming colonial dreams from afar, and not dictating the way ahead from a position of fear. *The Weekenders* shows what happens when you take writers back to where writers work best – on the ground, wandering away from their own lives, with no clear sense of where they're going or what they might find.

Susan Ryan
The Daily Telegraph

R.S.S.

ALEX GARLAND

GABRIEL and I called them the Professor and the Architect. The Professor, because he had earned a doctorate in Egypt. And the Architect, because he supervised much of the local rebuilding work.

We hadn't seen them for several days.

Their absence was unusual. We were used to seeing them regularly around the grounds of the school. Many years ago, they had been students here, and since their return to Rumbek, they were often found wandering around the empty classrooms, discussing how those classrooms might be returned to their former state.

As, one day, Gabriel and I hoped to be students at the school ourselves, we valued any time spent in their company. They would tell us stories about how things used to be, which suggested how things might be again.

So their unusual absence concerned me. The Professor and the Architect were old; it had been nearly half a century since they were students. I began to worry that one of them had fallen sick, or both of them had fallen sick. I even began to worry that they might be dead.

This sense of death grew stronger as the days passed. Often I found myself in the teak plantation. I would lie in the scrub, in the dust, on my back, troubled by the heat but too tired and lost in thought to move. And from the many conversations I'd had with the Professor and the Architect, two kept coming back to me.

The Professor saying: 'In general, women are weaker than men. If a baby is shot in front of a woman, she weeps. But a man does not.'

And the Architect describing the day he returned to

Rumbek Secondary School after the town had been retaken from the Northerners: 'The first place I visited was my old classroom. I walked directly to it. And when I saw it, I almost wept.'

Between these two statements, I felt they were describing how I should react to their deaths. I would feel sad, perhaps close to tears, but I would retain my self control.

This, I think, is reasonable. I am between fifteen and sixteen years of age and I would expect to behave more like a man than a woman or a child. After all, there are soldiers who are younger than me. And if one of these young soldiers were killing you, and you closed your eyes, you could not distinguish their actions from those of an adult.

In their case, it is a matter of self-preservation. In my case, it is a matter of self-education. I would hope that, from my speech, you could not distinguish me from an adult. Perhaps if you close your eyes now, you will hear an adult talking.

Many years ago, the British decided that southern Sudan needed a secondary school, as a complement to missionary schools whose only real purpose was the propagation of faith.

A competition to site the school was launched between the various governors of the regions. They were required to argue why their district would be preferable to all others. In Rumbek's application, the governor gave practical considerations, such as the town's accessible location and its supply of resources and livestock. But he also detailed the town's unique quality of tranquillity, which would be ideal for the function of study and education.

Rumbek's was the winning application. The school was built on the outskirts of the town. It lies off the main road, at the end of a path which is lined with mango trees: a collection of long, low buildings.

It was here, standing at the head of the mango tree avenue, with yellow dust coating my feet and ankles, that I spotted the Architect after his absence of several days.

The distance was too great to make out his face, but I could not mistake his slim silhouette. He was standing at the far end of the avenue, his head tilted upwards, looking at the faded lettering above the school's entrance arch. This posture was familiar to me. On the school premises, the Architect spent much of his time examining the buildings. Sometimes this was to assess their damage, to see if there was any hope of repair. But more often, he was simply remembering the way the buildings had once been, in the years he had been a student here.

Surprised to see that my fears were unfounded, pleased that my sense of death was misplaced, I set off immediately towards him. But I had only taken a few steps when he set off himself, heading through the short passageway to the front courtyard, then turning right to disappear around the corner. Rather than call out, which would have been impolite considering the difference in our years and status, I picked up my pace.

When I reached the courtyard, I saw the table from which the headmaster had once conducted open-air assemblies. And I saw the abandoned truck that sat stripped behind the headmaster's table, and the armoured personnel carrier with deflated tyres and open hatches.

But I didn't see the Architect. I had not moved quickly enough. He had already disappeared into one of the several buildings and passageways that provide exits from the courtyard.

It was impossible to guess into which of these buildings or passageway the Architect had vanished.

Rumbek School is vast and mazelike, with not simply the one courtyard I have already described, but several, which interlock around classrooms and dormitories that once accommodated a thousand pupils. And the maze extends further, because a school of such scale required supporting architecture. The teachers, and auxiliary staff, and vice headmaster, and headmaster all needed to be housed. Showers and toilet facilities were necessary, as were kitchens and eating areas. Space was set aside for recreational activity. Two churches were provided, one Catholic and the other Protestant.

With so many directions in which I might try to follow the Architect, but with no clue as to which to take, I chose to walk straight ahead. From the bright sunshine of one courtyard, to the dark shadow of a passageway, then into bright sunshine of another courtyard – the largest in the complex.

Apart from its size, this courtyard was notable for three things.

First, the number of empty bullet casings that lay scattered on the ground.

Secondly, a wall, which had been built by the Northerners around the yard's central fruit tree. Nobody knows why. It is too low to deter a fruit thief. Perhaps it was built to create an area in which senior army ranks could have a shaded place to take tea.

Thirdly, another Northern construction: a small, red brick mosque.

The Professor stood a few metres from the mosque; compact, dark, shimmering in the heat that rose from the ground. I was surprised to see him, in the same way I had been surprised to see the Architect beneath the entrance arch.

Beside him, only a short distance away, was Gabriel.

Gabriel was always recognisable at a distance because of his long T-shirt, which hung so low over his small body that it entirely covered his shorts.

They weren't talking to each other. The Professor was looking towards some point behind the mosque, with his back to me, but Gabriel was facing in my direction.

Having seen and then lost the Architect, I wanted to run towards the Professor, to ensure that the same thing didn't happen again. But I hesitated. Halfway over the distance between us there was an open well, uncovered, wide enough to swallow a vehicle and deep enough to lose it forever.

I was wary of running in the vicinity of this dangerous pit. If I were to fall inside, there would be no hope of recovering me. Others have died in this way. During the battle to recapture the town and school, many wells became contaminated by corpses.

So instead of running, I waved to Gabriel. I thought that if he waved back, the Professor might turn and see me, then wait for my approach. He might even be pleased to see me, just as I was pleased to see him. An idea had occurred to me. Perhaps, from the Professor's point of view, I was the one who had been missing for the past few days.

But Gabriel did not wave back. Not only that, but a moment after my wave, the Professor set off walking, just as the Architect had done, and seconds later he had passed behind the mosque and was out of sight.

I crossed the courtyard until I was close enough to Gabriel to speak without raising my voice.

'Gabriel,' I said. 'Why didn't you wave back? Didn't you see me wave?'

Gabriel shrugged. 'I thought you were waving hello. I could see you walking over, so I waited here.'

'Yes, but ... ' I frowned, looking past the mosque to see where the Professor might have gone.

Gabriel narrowed his eyes. 'I don't know why you're angry,' he said.

'I haven't seen the Professor for several days, and I wanted to talk to him.'

'I thought you were waving because you wanted to talk to me.'

'If I hadn't seen you for several days, of course I would want to talk to you. But I've seen you every day. We've spent all the past days in each other's company. And now I've missed both the Professor and the Architect.'

Gabriel shrugged again. 'If it's the Architect you want, I just saw him heading towards the dining rooms.'

We walked together, Gabriel accompanying me because he had nothing better to do.

I wasn't really expecting to find the Architect at the dining room. As I have said, the Architect's chief work was the renovation of buildings, but the dining room was beyond repair. The structure had no roof, and the walls were badly damaged. And, even if the Architect had been feeling nostalgic, it was not a pleasant place to stroll around. Local children had chosen the concrete floor as their toilet. It was impossible to walk unless your eyes were directed at the ground, and the smell was fierce.

Sure enough, when we reached the dining room it was empty. The only figures to be seen were sketched on the walls – karate-kicking figures between lines of graffiti, drawn in charcoal by bored soldiers.

'Are you sure you saw the Architect heading this way?' I asked Gabriel.

Gabriel shook his head. He didn't answer because he was using the bend of his elbow to cover his nose and mouth.

'You aren't sure you saw him,' I repeated, hardly bothering to hide my frustration.

'No,' he replied, muffled. 'I saw someone. But now, thinking back, I'm not sure it was the Architect. It may have been someone else.'

'I see.'

'In fact, yes, I'm sure it was someone else.'

I might have spoken irritably to Gabriel again, but at the moment he admitted he had not seen the Architect, I saw the Professor. First out of the corner of my eye, as a stocky shape glimpsed through one of the dining room windows. Then, as my head turned, seen clearly, framed by the rectangle of stonework, striding quickly towards one of the dormitory halls.

This time, I was taking no chances. I ran towards the exit in a series of leaps, landing neatly between the scattered clumps of faeces. Then I ran around the outside wall of the dining room area.

But turning the corner, I saw that again I had been too slow. No one stood where the Professor had been. The yard was empty.

For a moment, I was disappointed. Then, across the yard, a shadow seemed to slip inside one of the dormitory doorways.

The doorway led to a room that is pockmarked with a thousand bullet holes. There are bullet holes everywhere. The bullets casings lie in the dust, and the holes are in the exterior walls.

But in this room, the holes are on the interior walls. The concentration is so heavy that in many places, whole areas of plaster have broken away.

I have found that if you stare at the holes, patterns emerge. You identify a stitch of bullets from a single burst. The stitch shows how the recoil of the weapon has pulled upwards, slanting from left to right. You can see how, as a person was shot, the gunner struggled with his aim.

The only surprise would have been if the Professor or the Architect were inside this room. But they were not inside. And my mind had returned to its original fears: that the Professor and the Architect were dead.

I wondered if perhaps I had been following only their ghosts.

Standing motionless, my feet warmed by the concrete floor, I began to think back. I remembered that although Gabriel claimed to have seen the Architect, he later said he had been mistaken. I remembered that he had been very close to the Professor beside the mosque, but had not seemed aware of the older man's presence. I remembered that the Professor had shimmered from the heat rising from the courtyard ground, but Gabriel had not. And I considered the elusiveness of the two men. That repeatedly, just as I was about to catch them, they would slip away.

The idea that I had been following ghosts disturbed me. I became lost in thought, as I had been while I lay in the teak plantation.

I have little idea how long I had been standing in the room before Gabriel appeared, or how long he had been with me before I noticed him. But I suspect it was quite some time, because when my eyes focused on Gabriel, he seemed as preoccupied as me.

Eventually, he said, 'I found them for you.'

In Rumbek School there is beauty, with its tranquil atmosphere, and many courtyards, and mango trees. There is also horror, with its contaminated wells, and abandoned tanks, and execution cells. These two things, the beauty and horror, are usually in conflict with each other. But not always.

A few minutes' walk from here, there is another room where bullets have left a mark on the interior. But these are not on the walls. They are on the ceiling.

Here, a group of Northerners were trapped as the rebels mounted their final attack. And when the rebels clambered on to the roof, the Northerners fired up at them, punching hundreds of holes in the corrugated asbestos. Through these holes, the light of the sun fires back.

The room is otherwise lit only by its doorway, and that doorway opens only to a short covered passage. So aside from the bullet holes, there is almost perfect darkness in the room – and perfect darkness if you have just stepped in from the bright outside.

Walk from outside to inside, and look upwards, and you will believe you are looking up at the spread of stars in a night sky. Then look downwards, or to the walls on your left and right, and you will see that the constellation continues. Because where the sun comes through the bullet holes, it burns a precise light spot where it falls. And now you find that you are not so much looking up at a constellation, but standing inside one.

As Gabriel had said, the Professor and the Architect were inside the constellation chamber. And – now I regained my capacity to be surprised – they were talking about me.

As I had previously considered, they were under the impression that I had been the missing person over the past few days. In their walk around the school, they had been attempting to search me out.

My pleasure was twofold. First, to see them before me so fit and well, and secondly that I could introduce myself and put their concerns to rest.

I walked towards them, and when they did not break off their conversation, I coughed.

This did not provoke a response, so I spoke. I said, 'This is strange. To think that you were looking for me, when all this time I have been looking for you.'

They ignored me. So I spoke again. This time I said, 'Here I am.'

Then, when they continued to ignore me, and left to search around the defence trench that circled the school, I followed them, and stood directly in their path several times, announcing my presence even more loudly than before.

And finally, when they began to talk about checking in the old teak plantation, and also voiced their mounting fears about the location of Gabriel, I stopped and allowed them to walk on ahead.

Much later that day, close to sunset, but not so close that the mosquitoes would be swarming, I sat with Gabriel a short distance from the Professor's house. Outside the house, the Professor and the Architect were discussing measures that would need to be taken. The teak plantation, they agreed, would need to be marked in some way. The only question was how, given the size of the area.

'Mines,' the Architect said more than once, 'are a terrible problem.'

The Professor did not need reminding. Only last December, a boy was blown up and killed on a clearing in the centre of Rumbek Town. And now it had transpired that the teak plantation was one of the most heavily mined areas in the vicinity, given that it offered protection to any forces closing in on the school. Which, at the time, was being used as a barracks.

It made me sad to hear their conversation. One of my most treasured stories from the Professor and the Architect had been a description of how, in earlier years, the teak plantation had been a favourite haunt of the school's students; a place where they could relax and escape into quietness, and study beneath the shade of the trees. The description had entirely captured my imagination and had made me keen to seek out these qualities for myself.

You will remember that I asked you to close your eyes, and I explained that if you did so, you would hear an adult speaking, not a boy. Now, if you open them, you will be reminded that I am, after all, between fifteen and sixteen years old. Not an adult at all. My voice is an illusion of my education.

It is unfortunate that illusions only stretch so far. An anti-personnel mine, of the sort that might be found in the teak plantation, would destroy the leg of an adult. But a boy could easily be killed, as the blast reaches beyond the knee or thigh, and into the stomach. And if another boy, seeing his friend's injury, attempted to help, he might be injured too. Even if he took care to follow the path, tread where someone else has been, his foot could stray in the panic and anxiety of the moment.

A smaller boy, shorter than me, could be killed outright by such an explosion. In this way, the shorter boy would be saved from a further ordeal that might last several days.

As the evening drew in, the Architect returned home to take his shower and eat dinner. But even after his companion had excused himself, the Professor remained outside. He turned his chair so that it faced the direction of the school's old tennis courts, and rested his hands on his lap, and despite the mosquitoes, barely moved for the next hour.

It was strange to see him sit so still. I imagine he was

remembering a match that had once been played on the courts, perhaps in the early morning of a Sunday, when many of the students would have travelled home for the weekend, and the temperature was cool.

A Small Mission of Enquiry

W F DEEDES

WILLIAM Oldfield stepped out of the shower, wrapped himself in a bathrobe and moved towards his evening clothes, his thoughts on the evening ahead of him. A dinner party at Mrs Solomon's apartment promised the best of food and wine, and serious company. At least some of the guests would have noticed reports of the speech he had made 48 hours earlier to the United Nations General Assembly in New York. It had received a good press. Drafted by a talented young man in his Ministry of Foreign Affairs, it was designed to establish where his country stood on the issue of human rights. 'Let every nation know ... ' 'Oceana stands by its word ... ' 'It is for us to show the world ... ' The speech ran on phrases like that. The young man, Septimus Foyle, was friendly with one of the President's speech writers in the White House. He'd learnt the formula.

So William Oldfield anticipated an enjoyable few hours. He was not particularly vain, but it was good to know that he would be a centre of attention at Mrs Solomon's party. People, ignorant of the existence of Septimus Foyle, would say nice things about the speech. And Mrs Solomon's butler mixed the best of dry Martinis. It would be a good evening.

'Well said, Minister,' remarked someone behind him, as he stepped into the cavernous hall of his hostess's apartment. There was a murmur of assent. 'It needed saying, William ... ' The British Ambassador was among the guests. His brief nod of greeting and approval carried authority. It doubled the pleasure of sipping one of the redoubtable Martinis.

Some 24 sat down to dinner. Mrs Solomon was never

one for protocol. So Oldfield found himself between her first husband, who had been brought in at the last moment to make up numbers, and a girl with pale hair, dark eyebrows and a determined mouth. Like most politicians, Oldfield had a well-developed sense of wariness when encountering strangers at dinner parties. It warned him that his dinner table companions might well not be foremost among the cheerleaders. The girl had a personable young man on her right. So Oldfield spent the first course listening to a complicated story from Mrs Solomon's first husband about a fraudulent bookmaker at a recent race meeting. It had been this husband's propensity for gambling – with Mrs Solomon's money – that had terminated the marriage. After the settlement, they remained on friendly terms.

When the venison arrived (hung for just the right length of time, he reckoned), Oldfield heard the girl's voice.

'You've been speaking in New York, haven't you? Who writes that stuff for you?'

Though loosely on guard, the Foreign Minister was startled.

'You didn't approve?'

'Since you ask, I thought it was humbug. But don't let's talk about it. Enjoy your dinner.' It was said in a kindly rather than peremptory manner.

'But I'd like to talk about it.' Oldfield managed a warm smile. 'Your views interest me. What's wrong with human rights? Where's the humbug?'

There was a pause. Oldfield saw that his companion was making up her mind whether to abandon a dangerous conversation or pursue it.

'There's nothing wrong with human rights,' she said carefully, 'if countries practise what they preach.'

'And we don't?

Sly smile. 'Not "we". I'm not Oceanic. I was born in Kenya.'

'And Oceana does not observe human rights in Kenya; is that what you are saying?'

Oldfield was beginning to savour the conversation. Arguing with a woman at dinner parties was sometimes like playing daily-drop tennis with a very young niece. You made a hash of it. This girl was hitting the ball firmly over the net. Somehow it made it easier. Those eyebrows ... were they natural, he wondered, or did she darken them for effect? She laid her knife and fork across the unfinished venison and looked straight at him.

'You're familiar with Sudan?'

'Long way off. Not unduly.'

'You know about the oil there?'

'I know they have found oil,' said Oldfield slowly. 'I believe they now have a pipeline to Port Sudan, and the oil is moving up there. They'll make some money, which will be welcome.'

'Did you know Oceana had an oil company there – Phoenix, I think it's called? Did you know about the people who have been hounded out of that oil zone? That oil is making human rights a joke!'

The small set of traffic lights Oldfield kept working in his head moved swiftly from amber to red.

'You've seen all this?'

'No, but I know it's true. I have a – well, a friend. He's a pilot, works for a charter plane company. He's seen it all. He's seen them, thousands of people driven from home to keep the oilfields secure. And your oil company in the thick of it!'

Ah. Oldfield felt a faint surge of relief. So it was a boyfriend ... this was *his* story ... . He turned to her with an indulgent smile, well designed to convey the knowledge he had acquired about the unreliability of boyfriends. She caught the smile and its meaning. Unexpectedly, she patted his sleeve. 'I've bullied you enough. Enjoy your pudding ... .'

Smart lady, Oldfield reflected as his driver delivered him home. She would have foreseen the consequence of halting the conversation at that point. He glanced at the card in his pocket which listed engagements for the following day, and pencilled in at 8.30 am 'HS', the initials of his principal private secretary, Harry Stevens.

Surprised by an early buzz of the bell in the private office, Harry poked his head round the door. 'Harry, I want a short paper – and I mean short – on Sudan.'

'Yes, Minister. Any particular problem?'

'We have a company working on the oil out there?'

'I believe we do, Minister. I'll check.'

'I want to know what's going on up there, with the oil. There's talk of fighting, people losing their homes.'

Harry Stevens rapidly ran through in his mind the list of guests at the previous evening's dinner party which Mrs Solomon had submitted to the office. He guessed, wrongly, that the British Ambassador had been talking to his minister about Sudan. Hadn't there been some condominium there with Egypt and the UK? That was it. Harry had a golfing friend in the British Embassy. He'd know.

'Get the African department on to it,' said Oldfield. 'I want to know what's happening.'

'Yes, Minister.'

In the bar next door to the Mess at Lokichoggio air base on the Kenya–Sudan border, Ken Wilton was sipping a Coke. Tomorrow was a flying day. Every day was a flying day. His companion, Steve Hartley, also a pilot with the charter company, was eyeing, but not drinking, his gin and tonic.

'Flights are off – you know?'

'No, who says?

'Security. Bad reports from western Upper Nile.

Gunship ran amok south of Bentiu. Three villages burning. Now they're on the run.'

'But it's medical stuff. We have to deliver my load. They've had nothing like that up there for three months. It's needed, like hell it's needed.'

'Too bad. But the flights up there are off. There'll be no one on your strip there to take over the stuff. You'd better check with security.' Wilton scowled at his Coke as if it were hemlock. Then, apparently addressing his glass: 'I sometimes wonder what we're in business for. We're supposed to be flying food, medicine, relief to people on their last legs because of an unending bloody civil war. We do it for both sides – both sides for God's sake. Not for Sudan People's Defence Force, not for Government of Sudan. For both fucking sides! But only one side decides whether we can fly or not ... it's crazy. Government of Sudan rules OK ... mad, mad, mad, I tell you.'

'Have another Coke,' said Hartley consolingly. 'You can break training. You're not flying tomorrow!'

Ken Wilton shook his head, got up and moved towards his small cabin. Feeling a need for distraction, he pulled a letter out of a satchel and, for the second time that day, puzzled over it.

Ken, dear, thanks for your birthday card received this day. Look, there's going to be a change of plan. I've had enough of being fat cat in this PR business. It's like running an oyster bar when there's a war on. What decided me, I met the incredible Oldfield. Foreign whatever? Dinner with Rachel Solomon. We handle her personal publicity. Passed on – unattributably, I swear – what you told me about the oil business. He seemed surprised! He's clueless. Ornate but clueless. Nothing will come of it. So I've decided, I'm moving. I'm going freelance. My friend

Daphne was looking to get some journalists to do pieces in the Sudan but she's having a baby now. She's suggested I pick up where she left off. Will keep you posted. Penny.

There is no moon tonight. What little light there is comes from the stars. The long stretch of bush north of the airstrip is silent as the grave. You have to listen intently for the slightest sound of movement. It takes time before you realise that the bare ground is occupied – by people. Most of them are lying down. Only a few shadowy figures are moving about.

On the distant horizon to the West, there is a faint glow from the embers of a village that had burned to the ground two days ago. Slowly the mind pieces it together. That was a village. Where are the 900 occupants? Some of them are the shapes faintly discernible around you. Two days ago they were a village. Now they are displaced people. Everything they possessed has been destroyed. They have only the rags they wore when the firing started. But why so silent? Not even the small children are murmuring. 'Rachel weeping for her children ... because they are not?' No, the suffering of the people of Sudan has become inaudible. These are people nobody hears.

Fuma and his sister Matilda are lying close to their mother under a tree. When the helicopter gunships are prowling, trees seem to offer security. Even in darkness, it seems safer under a tree. Fuma is thirsty and has a pain in his stomach. But his thoughts about the fire in the village two days earlier take over from bodily wants. They had left everything behind them, and had run for two miles. There had been a little food in the village, dropped a month earlier, which they were sharing. Here there was nothing, except berries on trees and no water. The river ran half a mile away and the water was bad. There was nothing else to drink, so you drank it, leading inexorably to diarrhoea. As if she sensed what was passing through Fuma's head, the mother's arm tightened round him. He was only six years old. Matilda was older. She was thinking about their father, of whom she had seen little in her short life. He was always away somewhere, engaged in the war. They seldom wanted when he was with them. He was resourceful and strong and loving. Now he was ... where? Matilda blinks wet eyes. But where ... ? Her mother's arm draws her closer.

William Oldfield tapped the sheet of paper on his desk and looked across at the deputy head of his African department. The head of the department was in South Africa. His deputy, Sam Wyvern, was the sort of man who would be a deputy all his life.

'You've read this paper?'

'Yes, Minister.'

'Plainly it comes to this. Government of Sudan struck oil. They've leased concessions – one of them to our own Phoenix Energy Inc.'

'A private corporation, Minister.'

'I dare say. But under our flag.'

'Yes, Minister.'

'And hand in glove with the Government of Sudan ... '

'So it would appear, Minister.'

It was GOS that granted the original concession to Pluto Corporation, who later sold the rights to Phoenix.

'Does that concession lead to Phoenix taking a hand in defending the oilfields, so getting involved in the fighting? That's the point. That's what I want to know. It seems this oil lies on the slippery border between north and south Sudan. Yes?'

'That's my reading of it, Minister.'

'Where there's been fighting for years.'

'Off and on for 40 years, Minister.' Wyvern was shaky on policy, but sound on facts.

'This paper says oil has made the fighting worse. The South disputes the North's right to the oil, because the North has shifted the border. It also thinks that oil will help the North to buy more weapons and so sharpen up the attack against them. That's why the South sees the oil as a target. And the North, which sees it as a vital source of revenue for a poverty-stricken and war-ravaged economy, defends it. The conflict is driving everyone out of their home anywhere near the oilfields. Scorched earth. Human rights denied. That's about it, isn't it?'

'I think you put your finger on it, Minister.'

'And an Oceana company in the middle of it. That's where we're vulnerable. Supposing a newspaper picked it up?'

Much earlier that morning, Wyvern had spoken on the telephone to his departmental chief in South Africa. Good civil servants can usually anticipate the route their masters will take.

'Minister, you might wish to send a small mission of inquiry. To report quickly.'

'So that if anything got out, we'd have a bit of cover?'

'Just so, Minister.'

'We'd need the right inquiry. I don't want a report that rubs our noses in it.'

'If we pick the right chairman, Minister, we can get the report we want.'

'Get the office to call Lawrence at Queen's University.'

Mr Justice Lawrence, recently retired from the High Court, was supplementing his pension with modest fees as an occasional lecturer in law at Queen's.

'Philip, you busy?'

'Yes, very.'

'I want you to go to the Sudan for us.'

'Most certainly not.'

'Philip, I have always thought our predecessors in government were wrong-headed about honours and awards. What I have in mind for you, if you'll help us, would look well in an evening dress.'

'And what have you in mind?'

Oldfield outlined the plan.

'Impossible.'

'And legal fees are payable, at least to the chairman. Say, $5,000 on the brief and $1,000 a day.'

'That would be generous.'

Oldfield breathed a sigh of relief.

'I'm grateful, Philip. Talk to my office about whom you want to take with you. I'd suggest a couple of assessors. We'll find the secretariat and have a good man draft the report. We'll fly all of you first class to Nairobi. There's a Cessna Citation jet we keep around for this sort of job. That can be at your disposal.'

Oldfield glanced at the paper on his desk. 'Unless you'd sooner start from Khartoum. You'll want to talk to both sides presumably.'

Ken Wilton had acquired the knack through many emergencies of knowing when to sleep with one ear and half an eye open. He received the go ahead just before five in the morning.

'Looks like things are opening up a bit on western Upper Nile. Flights are cleared for Nhialdiu.'

'Say again.'

'Nhialdiu. It's pretty close to Bentiu. Seems like MedAID have, or had, a pitch up there. The strip's not great, they say, but it's enough. They badly want medical packs. Food too, I guess. But MedAID are talking medical.'

'OK.'

'We think it's best to fly via Rumbek. Sniff the air from there. If it smells OK, go right ahead.'

'Will do.'

Three hours later Wilton was taking off from Rumbek. Fifty locals, heedless of the hot, choking dust that Wilton's plane flung at them, had gathered to watch his departure. By contrast, there seemed nobody on the short runway at Nhialdiu.

'There should be an MedAID truck around,' they had told him. No sign of any truck. Then very slowly, through the hazy morning, spectres moved towards him. On most of the desert landing grounds, the plane got quickly surrounded. If it was carrying grain, there was a welcome prospect of gleaning. Whatever it carried, it kept hope alive. Anyway, it was an event in a day of otherwise unbroken monotony.

The spectres drew closer. For all his experience in all conditions, Wilton's spine prickled a little. He glanced at James Ngor who had flown with him to give a hand with the stores.

James's face was expressionless. 'These are Dinkas, I think,' he said slowly, 'who have run from fighting and have lost their homes in Bentiu. There's been no flying to these parts. They've had no food in a long time.'

'They look in a poor way,' said Wilton curtly. 'We'd better talk, find out what's going on here.' A dozen of the spectres were now close to them. The group, mostly in rags, included two small naked children with flies round their mouths. Wilton addressed himself to the group. 'We've brought up medical supplies,' he said in the most reassuring tone he could manage.

There was a terrible dignity about these people. A woman of about 60 suddenly broke the silence and, speaking through James, said in barely audible tones, 'There is no food here. I cannot climb Cuei trees to pluck the fruit on which people are surviving. Two of my children who are grown men were killed in the fighting before we fled. I have no one. How could they kill my sons?'

There was silence for a moment or two, broken by a younger woman's voice: 'Where do we go? Everywhere there is fighting. We are abandoned, without help. We have no homes, all we possessed stolen. For our children who are hungry, there is nothing ...'

She looked steadily at Wilton, who resorted to action. 'Let's get some of this stuff out,' he said harshly to James, who began to open the plane's side lockers. Opening up the plane usually created a stir; people on the strip moved up to lend a hand. This time nobody stirred, but others in the middle distance were slowly joining the group in front of Wilton. He caught the bizarre impression of people waking from a long sleep.

An elderly man addressed himself to James. 'It is good to have survived but now we have nothing, as you can see. Our homes were burned. Some were killed. My daughter lost her child. She had to run, for two days she had to run, like all of us. The baby was born dead. Now her only child is sick. Water is bad. Many children are sick because water is bad. You have brought medicine perhaps for these sick children? They have little to eat, only berries off the trees and leaves of water lilies. But they must drink. We want something to go in the water and make it less bad.'

James translated this steadily. He had been in Sudan for four years. He understood the war, though he never talked about it. He also knew a certain amount of what had been going on around the oilfields.

There was a fair crowd closing in on the plane now. Wilton had learned the value of letting people in these conditions tell their story, but it was time to move on. James hauled the big brown cardboard boxes out of lockers on the plane's side. There was no trolley to put them on. Wilton began to look round for someone who might take the packages into safe custody. There were invoices to sign, but that would have to go. He felt inadequate. If only his plane had food on board. Still, they needed the medicine.

While James unloaded, aided by a couple of young men who had stepped from the back of this desolate group, Wilton turned to the elder, who had addressed himself to James, and whose English was just intelligible. It was, said the elder, the children who troubled him. They knew nothing of the war and its causes. The oilfields, only an hour or two's walk away, which had led to some of this death and displacement meant nothing to them. It was so cruel, His people, the Dinkas, had come to peaceful agreement with their old enemies, the Nuer. They had signed a peace. When Dinkas fled to western upper Nile, the Nuer community had helped them to settle and to build homes. Now it was different. Homes had been burned down, and villages reduced to black heaps. Nobody could be hosts, for they had nothing to offer. For some now, only death offered hope of less pain, less hunger, less fear.

'We need to get moving,' said Wilton to James, who had somehow obtained an illegible signature on the invoices. He climbed into the cockpit, ran a practised hand across the instrument panel and set the single engine running.

At the small hut which served as an immigration office at Lokichoggio, Wilton encountered the senior security officer.

'I need to check with you before our 6.30 security meeting. It's bad?'

'No,' said Wilton, 'worse than that.' He paused. 'There's one hell of a lot of very sick people up there, and some of them are going to die – soon, embarrassingly soon for us. Where was Lokichoggio, where were the aid agencies, where were our planes when they started to dig the graves – those strong enough to dig, that is?'

'You've had a bad day?'

Wilton laid a hand on his colleague's arm. 'You know it better than I do. The oil's on stream. So stakes in this war have got bigger.'

'So?'

'It's led to huge displacement. That's what we've got there. They were glad of the medical stuff, by the way. Some will live a little longer ... .'

'And then?'

'God knows.'

Wilton raised an arm to his friend who was waiting, which signalled, 'I'm on my way'. Then, scratching his head: 'This was never a religious war, like they said. You know that. It's a war about assets, isn't it? Who owns what. There was never all that much to fight for, but they've fought for it, off and on, for 40 years. Now there's oil, a lot of oil – and who owns it isn't at all clear ... that's it, isn't it?'

Mr Justice Lawrence took a swift look round the British Airways lounge at Gatwick North. He had developed a mild attack of security-phobia since accepting William Oldfield's commission. A fee of $5,000 on the brief and $1,000 a day left a faint sense of indebtedness and conspiracy. William Oldfield's minute to him had been clear enough. He was to report as he found. But a long life in Justice had taught him not only to read the brief but to sniff the air. What the hell was a large Oceana corporation doing siphoning oil out of what was in effect a battlefield? Oldfield had been explicit on that point. 'They may be independent, but they wear our flag. So what they're doing might be seen out there as done in the name of Oceana.'

Lawrence knew the right questions to ask a witness.

'Am I reporting privately to the Foreign Ministry or for publication?'

'You're reporting to me.'

'For publication?'

'That might depend,' said Oldfield.

'On what I find?'

'On what you find. Yes.'

Ken Wilton was waiting on the tarmac for Penny when she stepped off the Nairobi/Lokichoggio shuttle. He picked up her heaviest bag and moved towards a waiting land cruiser.

'I'm pleased to see you, but puzzled. What's the plot?'

She fumbled in her bag, took her card from a small case and thrust it at him. Wilton read:

Penelope Howard, Freelance Journalist, Sudan Specialist, Lokichoggio, Kenya.

'But there's no press here just now. After 40 years of this war, they've lost the scent.'

'But there's going to be press here – and television.'

'Why?'

'Ken, you're being slow. It was you who first told me about the oil here, about Oceana's Phoenix being caught up in battles round the oilfield.'

'Sure.'

'And I told you, I passed some of it on to a dinner table neighbour, who happened to be Oceana's Foreign Minister. His response to what I told him was appalling. He went on eating. So later I called my pal Daphne who's an old Sudan hand. She said she had some information about this, and that she would let me have it. Ken, it's much worse than you said.'

Wilton halted the vehicle outside a well-built *tukul*.

'That I am ready to believe, but what can *you* do

about it? Here, by the way, are your temporary quarters. Lad who lives here is on long leave in UK. Showers in that block, loos adjacent.'

Married for six years to a Scottish beauty, Wilton unfashionably had no designs on Penelope Howard and aimed to establish the point diplomatically. No white mischief here. They had come to know each other because Penny, before being head-hunted to run a PR business in Oceana, had nursed sporadic ambitions to become a pilot.

She eyed the temporary quarters, which looked cosier than she had expected, and suddenly felt cheerful. 'Ken, let me reassure you. I'm not chasing wild geese. I have, I can tell you, got more or less lined up the *Daily Monitor*, Channel 7 and *Metropolitan Magazine*. They're sending people here. I'm here to meet them. I'm showing them what there is to see. OK?'

Ken Wilton pulled her bags out of the land cruiser. 'I suppose so. But what are you showing them? Flights around Bentiu have been off for quite a while.'

'We'll find a way. Thanks for getting me this far.'

'When you're settled in, ready, relaxed, come to the bar before supper and meet some of the boys and girls. Incidentally, I think we'll keep this plan of yours quiet for the time being.'

Penny nodded.

'By the way, I'm afraid the shower's cold but it's refreshing. See you there.'

They met an hour later. Most of the company seemed to be drinking Coke. 'I'd like a G&T,' said Penny firmly and took stock of her companions. The males wore the livery of their profession – shorts, trainers or desert boots, heavy-duty open-necked shirts. The women were more varied. Penny suspected they took more pains to bring a curtain down on the day's work by dressing up a bit. It was a time of evening stillness, a slowing down of tempo. The first planes went out at first light. For some, it had been a long day. The trees were still, the flies lethargic. Dusk fell quickly and lights came up. The warm evening suddenly entered the veins of someone who had left Oceana's chilly spring behind her. Penny hugged herself a little, and glanced around her, then tapped Wilton's arm.

'Don't look now. But at two o'clock there's an old boy in a tie and a smart suit, who looks serious. Who he?'

Wilton glanced to his right. 'No clue, never seen him before. People move in and out of here all the time.' He paused. 'But I can tell you who his companion is. He's our chief security officer.'

'Please, oh please, no more starving black babies!'

Sarah Tamach, features editor of the *Daily Monitor*, looked round the company with what she supposed was a disarming smile, in case someone found her remark distasteful. The *Daily Monitor* was holding its weekly 'futures' conference.

'We know about your allergies, Sarah,' said the foreign editor. 'But as I read it, this story is not altogether about starving babies. It's more about the oil they've found in Sudan and the trouble it's creating.'

'Not very sexy,' said the home editor, who had an item of his own to propose. It was a 2,000-word interview with a former prostitute in Rome, now living in Metrojam, Oceana's capital, who wanted to become a priest.

'Not sexy, agreed,' said the foreign editor, 'but mildly scandalous.'

'How so?'

'Simply from what I've heard, one of this country's largest independent corporations may be caught up in a new war to defend Sudan's oilfields.'

'City pages, why not?' suggested the magazine editor. 'That's the place they understand oil.'

'It could be an exciting tale,' said the home news editor, 'if to my certain knowledge that war hadn't been running for 80 years.'

'Forty, as a matter of fact,' said the foreign editor.

They turned to other items. The Italian prostitute who wanted to become a priest got everyone's vote. There had been a public inquiry into wife-beating.

'It's more prevalent than people think,' said the associate editor (features) darkly, who beat his wife regularly but who saw all life in terms of features. A top baseball player had confessed to being a transvestite.

'I'll tell you what,' said the foreign editor, as the meeting was breaking up. 'I'm not wild about this Sudan tale; it could make a nasty hole in my budget. We've got a good stringer in Nairobi now – Basil Blaby. He can take a sniff, and we'll only follow up if the scent's good. OK?'

'Pics?' said the picture editor, who had not spoken yet.

'You've got a million Sudan pics in that library of yours ... '

'Most of them starving black babies ... ' said Sarah Tamach, who disliked the foreign editor.

Raymond King, chief security officer at Lokichoggio, had commanded a good regiment before he left the Army. Sitting outside Lokichoggio's bar, he felt on sufficiently easy terms with a retired judge to raise the subject of dress.

'You've been in Khartoum a few days, I gather. Down here, we tend to dress casually. Best not to look conspicuous. You could drop the tie. Scuffed desert boots fit best here.'

Philip Lawrence laughed. 'You're right. Fact is our benevolent Foreign Ministry threw in a dress allowance. I felt I owed it to them to wear one of their suits.'

King ran his eye over the judge's well-pressed light brown jacket and trousers. 'Were they impressed in Khartoum? I'm surprised they saw you at all. They've got a strong hand, now the oil's running. What had you to offer?'

'I wondered too. But they're on their best behaviour. Now the oil's running at last after a lot of setbacks, some of the world showing interest, and they need stroking .... The war led to Khartoum being isolated. Now, because of the oil, Khartoum is being courted – and they like it.'

'Yes, but you weren't looking for oil concessions. You were heading an inquiry into how far fighting for the oil has created big hell up there.'

'Not quite. I'm not sitting in judgement on Khartoum. They don't deny they're defending the oil. Confidentially, what the Foreign Minister wants is a report on whether or not our people, Phoenix, are lending a hand to Khartoum's military. That's the red light for him – if a big Oceana company is linked to what amounts to ruin for a lot of Sudanese civilians in the area.'

'He's thinking what the press might do?'

'He thinks, as I do now, that it's an unsafe position. It's a faraway corner of the world to most people, but if a newspaper or television producer suddenly got on to this and related it to Oceana's well-known stand on human rights, it'd look bad. We tend to lecture the world on human rights – and not all the world enjoys it.'

'Who else is up there?'

'With the oil? Jantia and Neesandula.'

'Just them and Oceana.'

'Correct.'

'I get the drift,' said King. 'And now you're going up to the oilfields? We don't often go that far from here.'

'I saw advantages in approaching the oil from here rather than Khartoum. They offered me an "escort". I prefer to go without an "escort".'

'Right. But that Cessna jet of yours won't work. The air strips are pretty tight up there. You'll need to fly in one of ours. How many are you?'

'Two assessors with me. Three staff.'

'Six. We can do that. Last man up that way was Ken Wilton. He was rather shaken by it. You ought to have a word with him?'

'You'll arrange that?'

'Sure.'

Penny found a scribbled note from Ken Wilton under her door.

I'm off on a 3-day trip early tomorrow. If you can make breakfast in the canteen at 7, I have news for you.

'I don't reckon,' said Ken when they met for coffee and fruit juice, 'that I am betraying confidences. So I can tell you there's someone else up here hunting your fox.'

'Not the old man in a tie I asked you about? I thought he looked fishy.'

'The very same.'

Penny raised her dark eyebrows. 'Who is he? What's he doing?'

'He's a retired judge called Lawrence and he's out here with a small party sniffing the air for Oceana's Foreign Ministry. Maybe that dinner with Oldfield bore more fruit than you supposed.'

'Balls! But I'm confused. How do you know all this?'

'Because I've got to take him around. He wants to get up to the oilfields, for which the jet the Foreign Ministry lent him is useless. When I return from this week's trip, I'm taking him and his pals up there for a day or two.'

Penny's mouth tightened. 'Whitewash! That's what's behind this, if what you say is true. He's Oldfield's stooge.'

'He doesn't look like anyone's stooge to me.'

'Rubbish. Of course that's what he's here for. To produce some alibi for Oldfield if anything leaks out about this.'

'Have it your way. How's the hunt at your end?'

'I've seen the *Monitor*'s man in Nairobi. He's only their local stringer but he's new, bright, keen to distinguish himself. He's coming up next week. Channel 7 and *Metropolitan* are talking dates. They'll be here soon. I'm drafting a brief for them out of reports that aren't confidential. Can we get big scale maps up here?'

'I doubt it. I'd rather, by the way, you kept the judge to yourself. He's temporarily my responsibility.'

'What exactly does he want to do?'

'Look round the oilfields, talk to the Phoenix people – 48-hour job. Khartoum, surprisingly, have passed him in.'

'It's crazy, isn't it – here's you carting Oldfield's stooge around so that he can coat the thing with whitewash. Here am I trying to find people to report the truth ... .'

Ken Wilton felt it was a moment to swallow the remains of his coffee. Their breakfast table was beginning to fill up. 'It is a crazy world. *Au revoir*. I'll be back Saturday. Penny, please don't forget what we've agreed.'

Sarah Reinberg, executive editor of *Metropolitan Magazine*, was paid $300,000 a year, plus generous allowances, and was generally rated to be worth the money. As well as being a successful editor, she was popular with junior staff, who studied her dress style with interest and her reading glasses with fascination. The glasses came in a variety of styles, all of them expensive. The reason for this extravagance was unfathomable. A good-looking executive of 43, it was reasoned, may well feel shy of wearing glasses. 'Men seldom make passes at girls who wear glasses,' as Dorothy Parker had put it. If so, why draw attention to them? Or did she use them for effect?

The office accountant, Sidney Brine, sitting uncomfortably in front of her desk, felt convinced they were used for effect. In most top-brass offices, he thought resentfully, people got up from the desk, ushered someone of his standing towards armchairs and made them feel at home. He felt far from home.

He said in a subdued voice: 'Sarah, I need to have a word with you about this item on your future estimates of $12,000 for a feature about the Sudan war in the oilfields.'

'No problem there,' said Sarah, looking at him intently over the top of her glasses. 'I can itemise it. I've got best-selling author Christina Callaway on this job at cheap rates – $5,000 – she knows the Sudan backwards: her first husband was in some service there. That's why she's happy to do it for a pittance. We're sending a top photographer with her, of course – but he's one of our own. We've allowed $5,000 for the air fares, another $2,000 for accommodation and incidentals. Nothing extravagant. Well within budget, OK?'

'Yes, of course. OK on that side of it.' Brine shifted his seat and opened a small file in his hand. 'But it's something the Board raised at the monthly meeting yesterday. As you know, Board members see these estimates. They read your short summary of what is proposed here.' He paused, glanced at Sarah Reinberg who appeared hidden behind a gigantic pair of spectacles. 'What the Board thought you should know ... what they asked me to discuss with you ... perhaps I might put it this way: were you aware that *Metropolitan*'s holding company, Global Investments Inc., have an interest in Phoenix oil?' Brine put slight emphasis on the Inc., as if to suggest it was a little joke they might share together.

One of Sarah Reinberg's gifts was knowing the power of silence in certain situations. At the close of Mr Brine's statement, she tipped her head back slightly, as if she had misheard what someone was telling her, and said nothing.

Mr Brine, finding the ball back in his court, stared defensively at the reading glasses. Diplomacy was clearly lost on such a woman. There was nothing for it, he reasoned doggedly, but to assert such authority as the Board vested in him. 'So, you will see, the Board was confident that you would see ... certain difficulties arise over this particular assignment.' Sarah stared at him without moving her head.

'Are you serious?'

'Well, I'm afraid I am. You will readily understand the Board's position. It cannot reasonably allow one of its publications to attack a company in which it has an interest.'

There was a further silence. Then Sarah Reinberg got up from her desk and inclined her head. The interview, Mr Brine realised, was over. He gathered up his few papers, then felt compelled to break the silence. 'It's awkward, I know. I'm sorry ... .' Sarah Reinberg made a slight movement of her head again. Hastening back to his office three floors above them, Mr Brine felt a cordial dislike for her.

Penny Howard sat in her temporary office and began to piece together her story ideas. There was a rap on the half-open door and Ken Wilton walked in.

'Ken! You're back! How was it?'

'Not bad. We're back early. Judge Lawrence seems in a hurry to get back home. It's the effect Sudan has on a lot of people.'

'To slosh on the whitewash! I know.'

'I'm not so sure. It was a fairly dramatic encounter up there. I don't know it all. Naturally, I didn't attend the sessions Lawrence and his team had with the oil people, mainly with Phoenix's executive chairman, Harding Kingsmill. A tough nut, I gather. But I'm friendly with one of Lawrence's staff. We used to play rugger together. He let me see the minutes he took. They're surprising. You've heard only half of it. The helicopter gunships go off their pads! Part of the contract!'

'Part of the contract?' Penny wrinkled her distinctive eyebrows. 'In what way?'

'Well, they're operating in a conflict zone, and the speculation is that they're cooperating with the government in defending the oilfields and pipelines. To the government, that means keeping people away from oilfields. Hence, all the displaced people. You had it right. Congratulations. What's been happening at your end by the way?'

'Not much, maddeningly. I called *Metropolitan* day before yesterday. Sarah Reinberg – she's the woman I dealt with – has resigned. God knows why. Her PA, whom I hardly know, isn't talking. "We'll stay in touch," they kept saying.'

'And?'

'The *Monitor* were sending a man from Nairobi. I've met him; he was coming up here next week. Now he's suddenly been sent off to Ethiopia.'

'There's a famine there.'

'I dare say. There's a bad famine anywhere near

Phoenix, too.' Penny tried to keep the bitterness out of her voice and failed.

Ken Wilton looked at her anxiously. 'Look, try to get this in proportion – see where you started. You reckoned the suffering caused by the push for oil was wrong, and you determined to do something about it. You didn't know there was going to be a judge on the job .... And what's more – I've seen the minutes ... they're doing a running draft report ... I've seen that too. What d'you want? For the world to know what's happening here. The judge and his men are going to tell the world what's happening here.'

'Ken, grow up! You think Oldfield is going to tie this noose around his neck and jump. The hell he will! This judge is on contract. He'll fulfil his contract!' Penny got up from her chair, stood with her back to a filing cabinet and looked straight at Wilton.

'Listen,' she continued, 'as far as I am concerned, this is failure of a mission. The *Monitor* has pulled out of it, isn't interested .... The *Metropolitan* – I was really counting on them. Christina Callaway was just the job. She loves this place. Now the magazine has lost its editor. Channel 7 – 1 called them yesterday. They've got budget problems ... want to come back in three months' time. Half these people will be dead .... And it gets worse. I'm putting the story ideas together – but who's interested? I've wasted my time – and yours. I'm staying on awhile .... But I've failed, I know that ... you know that. Ken, I'm going to ask a favour.'

Ken Wilton, moved out of professional caution by this outburst, nodded his head. 'Such as?'

'Ken, I want to go up there, I want to see some of this for myself. It's legitimate. I need a sight of the action, if I'm going to keep the world informed. You going up again? I want to come with you, I want to see the worst of it.'

'Well, I'm not going to the oilfields, if that's what you want. The judge had special permits for that. No one else has.'

'But that scene you described near the oilfields, where villages had been burned. I want to see for myself what apparently no one wants to know.'

'I'll need to check the flight schedules. We don't have total control over these flights, as you know. Where do you want to go?'

'I want to see these displaced people, see how they live, see what it means – home gone, all possessions gone, families blown apart. I read reports about it. I need to see it ... .'

Ken Wilton thought back to his own recent experiences. 'It's bad up there. I believe they've had some grain up there, but so many people are moving around, there's never enough – of anything.'

'It's important to me, Ken – I've reached a point now when I don't trust anyone except myself – and you maybe. People die, people are dispossessed ... this war was simmering down. Now the oil's blown it up, it's obscene. The bloody news media doesn't care, isn't interested. The judge is out here to get the Minister off the hook. So where do we go?'

Wilton shrugged. 'I think you are being hard on yourself. You make me half sorry I started you on this trail.'

'Well, you'd better be in at the finish. Let me know about flights.'

They left soon after first light two days later. 'You can thank MedAID for this,' Wilton said, as they signed out of Loki. 'We couldn't put a Buffalo or a Hercules down on the strip I'm heading for. But this MedAID stuff is light, vaccines mostly, and they've someone up there now to take it over.'

It was a clear morning, wonderfully cool before the sun got up, with a light wind blowing. Penny climbed into the co-pilot's seat. The faithful James sat behind with boxes round his feet. No other passengers were coming their way that morning. They flew at around 9,000 feet.

'About 90 minutes,' said Wilton through the intercom. 'I'm coming down at Panthou to contact our people there, then straight on to Wicok.' On the approach to Wicok, he circled once to keep people off the airstrip, then dropped the plane down on a small stretch of desert. The heat struck at them as if someone had opened a furnace door. There was nobody on the airstrip, but a small open truck was waiting close to the track. A young man wearing the insignia of MedAID and several days' growth of beard stepped out and strode towards the plane.

'Franklin,' he said, extending a hand to them both. 'I'll bring the truck alongside so you can unload.'

'Where's everyone got to?' asked Wilton, recalling his last visit to these parts.

'Hard to say. There's so many living mostly off the land, they tend to move suddenly. We'll go to our clinic, where there's some gathered, make further inquiries there.' They drove half a mile through the scrub, and entered a clearing. A small crowd of women, nursing babies and accompanied by small children, were gathered under a large tree. In a makeshift shelter, three MedAID workers were engaged in dishing out small supplementary rations to mothers whose babies appeared to qualify, either on a weight-for-height basis or an upper-arm measurement. To Penny's inexpert eye they all looked likely to qualify, but about one in five mothers were being turned away.

'We run this place,' Franklin explained. 'We get the stuff up somehow, flights permitting, and hold a clinic when possible. There aren't a lot up here today. They've all been on the move again. It's been a bit desperate up here lately. This lot panicked when your plane came in just now. There was a gunship running through here a day or so back. They're jumpy ... .'

Penny watched the MedAID examiners for a while, wondering how they contrived to look so calm and patient in the fierce heat. One or two of the babies looked beyond saving, even with a supplementary ration. Then she moved over to where the women sat with their babies awaiting their turn. At first she felt as if she were being intrusive. All of them were in rags. Some had come a long way for this slender chance and were plainly exhausted. Most of them seemed to be staring into the middle distance and took no notice of her. Penny was seized with the uncanny impression that she had suddenly become invisible. She shook her head. It was this terrible heat.

She passed one woman who was not staring into the middle distance. She was looking intently at the baby which lay in her arms. With a flash of intuition, Penny guessed the baby was dead. She moved towards the woman who looked up at her with a quick imploring glance. There were two younger children, both naked, standing there, still and solemn. Some intimation of death, it seemed, had passed through them like an electric current.

Moved more by instinct than any process of thought, Penny crouched down beside the mother, ran her fingers round a tiny shrivelled arm. It was a gesture of pity, for there was no pulse to feel. Then she slipped an arm round the woman's bony shoulder, looking back at her tearfully and shook her head. The woman sat quite still and stared at the child in her arms. There were no tears, no cry of emotion. Penny rose and stepped away, feeling the need for five minutes by herself.

So this was how it ended. Here was the final seal on her mission of mercy. That look from the mother! Indelible. God, why had she embarked on this mad endeavour? She blew her nose and walked slowly back through the heat to Wilton, who was helping James to lift parcels off the truck.

William Oldfield shook Judge Lawrence warmly by the hand and directed him to the sitting room corner of his ample office. There was coffee on the table and Sam Wyvern of the African department was hovering in the background.

'Welcome back, and thank you, Philip. You've done a splendid job.'

'You've read my report?'

'It's on my desk. We're working through it now.'

'Working through it? You mean changing it?'

'Nothing to speak of, Philip. A few drafting amendments. There are one or two points of policy ... .'

'Such as?'

'Sam, fetch the report out of my desk. Second drawer on the right.'

Oldfield riffled lightly through the 60-page document. Some passages had been sidelined in red.

'Well, here we are, for example. Your report reads: "Two things are certain. First, the gunships which have attacked villages south of the river flew to their targets from airstrips in the oilfield where Phoenix are operating. This is known to Nuer commanders in the South and is one reason they are targeting oil facilities."'

'That's true.'

'Yes, but you go on to say: "Secondly, it is a prominent perception of the southern Sudanese that Phoenix, 'the Oceanan oil firm', is closely linked to the Government of Sudan, economically, politically and militarily."'

'That is also true.'

Oldfield turned a couple of pages. 'Then we come to this passage, where you quote a local official from

Nhialdiu as saying: "Civilians, cattle, children have been killed, homes burned. We don't think we are included in the human rights of the world."'

'Well, they don't. That's a fact.'

'Philip! Where do you suppose that leaves our declared policy on human rights?'

'So you want to doctor my report?'

'Not "doctor", Philip. We never do that. Simply align one or two passages with declared policy, that's all.'

'And you think that will win the day?'

'We may hope so.'

Judge Lawrence leaned back in his comfortable chair and instinctively brought his finger tips together, just as he had done years earlier when sentencing men to prison. He also adopted a more formal style of address.

'Minister, I must tell you I wrote this report in the knowledge that there were others beside myself taking a serious interest in what is happening in these oilfields and ...' – the fingertips pressing more closely together – '... could make trouble over it.'

'But your mission was entirely confidential.'

'So it was. You misunderstand me. The inquiries to which I refer are from a different source altogether.'

'What source? To whom are you referring?'

Judge Lawrence, having strayed into judicial mode, decided on the line he once took with juries who had plainly failed to get to grips with the evidence. 'For reasons of her own, a young journalist has sought to enlist the interests of the international news media in the situation prevailing around the oilfields and this country's involvement in it.'

'You met her? Who is she?'

'No, I did not meet her. My information came from the man who accompanied me on the flight from Lok:. The jet you were kind enough to lend me had to be ruled out for certain journeys. The man was friendly with the girl and knew of her intentions. He thought I should know.'

'But who is this girl? Why are you telling me this now?'

'I saw no need to tell you. I was satisfied that my report covered all the facts. We had nothing to fear from any independent inquiry. Only if we withhold certain facts do we become vulnerable.'

Oldfield turned to his principal private secretary who had joined them. 'Have you seen any press reports about this?'

'No, Minister.'

'There wouldn't have been,' said Judge Lawrence evenly. 'The media people were expected to arrive after I left.'

'And you have no idea who this woman is?'

'None. The man declined to name her, said only that she seemed to have her knife into you ... .'

'Into me? But how extraordinary.' Oldfield paused, searched his memory for likely assassins. The dinner party! Those black eyebrows. Men like Oldfield remember slights more readily than compliments. He pressed the bell. 'Oliver, do we by chance keep a file of those lists we get from hosts before parties?'

'Yes, it's a police requirement.'

'Bring me this year's file.' Oldfield thought again. 'No, look up Solomon – in March, I think. Bring the list.'

The list gave names in alphabetical order, but not the placement. Oldfield scanned it rapidly. 'Trouble is, none of us knows the name.'

Most of Mrs Solomon's guests were easily eliminated. 'Dulcie Trumpington? She's an actress, isn't she? Can't be her. Penny Howard – ring a bell with anyone?' As he uttered the words, Oldfield suddenly remembered the place card on his right. He had felt moved to glance at it after their differences, but had then put it out of his mind. Now it was back.

'I do have to say,' said Judge Lawrence, quick to perceive his advantage, 'that if my report does not square with the facts, and someone else reports what the facts are, I'm in the soup!'

'And if we publish the full report,' added Oldfield drily, '*I* am in the soup. How can we square some of this stuff with our stand on human rights?'

Judge Lawrence reverted to his judicial mode. 'I don't think you have much choice.'

There was silence.

'If this report goes out as it stands,' Oldfield said slowly, 'there will be a call for my resignation. You can bet on that.'

Another, longer silence.

'That could well be,' said the Judge.

A Song for Sudan

TONY HAWKS

KENYA AND BEYOND

As I headed for Heathrow Airport, I had only a smattering of knowledge about the African country I was about to visit. I was aware that it had been a British Colony which had established its independence in 1956, and that it had been ensnared in a bloody civil war since 1983. I also knew that although the war seemed to be drawn along the battle lines of Arab Muslim north v African Christian south, there were as many as twenty different sub-conflicts going on within it, mostly of a tribal nature, which complicated the issues still further.

At the airport I met my fellow travelling companions by the desk for the Kenya Airways flight to Nairobi. These included fellow authors Victoria Glendinning and Irvine Welsh, and a journalist and photographer from the *Daily Telegraph*. Oddly, I was the only one of us who was checking in a guitar. Maybe the others weren't that musical.

There was, of course, the possibility that I was the only one who seriously wanted to have a go at composing music with a Sudanese tribesman. My reasons were sound enough. I'd recently returned from a trip to Nashville, Tennessee, where I had learned that songwriters regularly work with different people every day, quite often with writers they had never even met before. These guys were professionals and didn't need the comfort of cosy friendships in order to plumb their creative depths – they could produce ideas on tap. I myself had taken part in this process and found it a surprisingly interesting and fruitful one. What now interested me was whether you could take this idea a step further, push it to the limits even, by attempting to collaborate not just with someone you'd never met before, but with someone from an entirely different culture. Perhaps I could discover if music really was the international language, and if it was, learn what notes you had to play if you wanted to say 'more muesli, please'.

During the long flight I read some more about UNICEF's work in the southern Sudan and discovered that as well as basic humanitarian aid to the innocent victims of war, it had a more long-term goal of showing the benefits of peace to a people who had only ever seen conflict. However, it does rather say something about me that I got most excited when I discovered that UNICEF's deputy executive director was called Karin Sham Poo. I studied her photo to see what her hair was like, and was relieved to see that it was presentable. With a name like that, the poor woman really had no excuse for a bad hair day.

When we landed in Nairobi we were collected and driven across the city to Wilson Airport, where we were to take an internal flight to Lokichoggio in north-western Kenya. As we sped through the bustling capital, I looked out of the side window of the minibus, mainly because it was preferable to looking ahead. Our impatient driver was weaving in and out of traffic with a wanton disregard for the rules of the road or, more importantly, my safety. It seemed a great irony that although we were about to head into one of the world's war zones, statistically this was probably the most dangerous part of our journey.

Nairobi was not a pretty sight. Occasionally we'd see glimpses of jacaranda trees and areas of green parkland, but for most of the drive we were surrounded by huge lorries coughing out pollution by the carbon monoxide-load, tatty concrete tower blocks, crumbling advertising hoardings, and a tense and overcrowded population scrambling around in search of the next Kenyan shilling. In the more salubrious areas, the properties came with the neat trimmings of barbed wire and security cameras. Nairobi is, after all, a very violent city. We heard about the all-too-frequent practice of *car-jacking,* in which the driver is held up at gunpoint, bundled into the boot of his own car and driven miles out of town and dumped by the roadside, at which point the assailants make off with the vehicle. The poor victim is left to walk home, having involuntarily become an expert on the design and contents of his own boot. I decided that there must have been occasions when the car-jackers became ambitious and went for a bit of minibus-jacking. It was the only plausible explanation I could find for our driver's refusal ever to allow his vehicle to become stationary.

Wilson Airport, we soon discovered, was one of those which had been designed to make the nervous flyer feel positively suicidal. Since this was an airport which specialised in short flights to unpopular destinations, the airlines evidently saw no need to supply any aircraft which had been built since 1950. The airstrip was dotted with antiquated flying machines with which goggles, leather hats and long flowing scarves would not have seemed out of place. The presence by the side of the runway of the burnt-out wreck of a plane, from what could only have been a previously unsuccessful landing, did little to inspire the confidence of the waiting passenger. Perhaps they might have tidied that away, I thought to myself, as I viewed its scarred remains while moving beneath the tired-looking propellers of our own sixteen-seater plane. I drew a deep breath as I readied myself to climb aboard and entrust my life to a couple of strangers in faded uniforms, chatting together up in the cockpit.

The flight was actually less scary than I had imagined it might be. There is something rather soothing about the open-plan layout of these aircraft. Every time there is a slight wobble you can simply look forward to see the pilots' reaction before deciding on yours. If they are still playing Scrabble then you feel pretty comfortable that everything is OK; however, if they are shouting 'Shit! Shit! Shit!' and desperately composing notes to their loved ones, it's probably a good idea to fasten your seat-belt and devote a quick couple of minutes to your relationship with God.

As we flew, Kenya sprawled beneath us. The land appeared to have been cultivated in an ordered manner and with the benefit of old colonial money. The healthy greens suggested that 'irrigation' to the farmers was not just a tricky four-syllable word, and the straight lines of fences and hedges implied that the fertile land had been divided up between the wealthy and the privileged. I firmly expected the landscape to change dramatically once we crossed the border into war-torn Sudan. However, the particular burden that *its* people had to bear was a massively corrupt government. I'd been told that a group of academics had recently collated enough data to publish The Top Twenty Of Corrupt Governments, Kenya making a strong showing at number nine – although how can we be sure they didn't use back-handers to buy their way into that position?

After a brief flirtation with some small mountains, which happily the pilot noticed before I had to point them out, we landed on what appeared to be an airstrip in the middle of nowhere. All around it were huts, tents and compounds resembling army barracks. This was Lokichoggio. Until the crisis in Sudan, it hadn't really existed. Until then the land had been occupied by the nomadic Turkana tribe who conducted themselves in the fairly decent manner of wandering around raising livestock while occasionally indulging in cattle-rustling against their neighbouring tribesmen, the Toposas, in southern Sudan. With the arrival of the Western aid agencies and the setting up of the camps which constituted OLS (Operation Lifeline Sudan), most of these tribespeople had descended on this area, drawn by the lure of money, material items and an easier lifestyle.

When we finally dumped our bags inside the highly secure compound, some of the dangers which this situation had created were explained to us by Ruben, a member of the security team.

'The problem,' he began, 'is that a lot of the Turkana people see all this food and aid arrive here and then watch it being airlifted into southern Sudan. This is frustrating for them because a lot of them are hungry and they could really use it themselves. The situation is made worse by the fact these people hold a large number of illegally acquired firearms so this means that in the surrounding area there is a great deal of highway banditry, armed robbery and rampant night firing.'

Mmm, this place sounded nice. I could spend time here.

'Why can't you pacify them by giving some of *your* aid to them?' I asked, rather intelligently, I thought.

'I wish it was that simple,' replied Ruben, 'but that would be going against our remit. We have to spend the money on exactly what it has been donated for. If we started syphoning it off elsewhere we could be accused of getting involved in internal politics and not doing the job we were sent here to do, which is to offer humanitarian relief to the innocent victims of war in southern Sudan. The Turkana people should be receiving aid from other Kenyan aid agencies and indeed the Kenyan government, but it never seems to materialise.'

Well, I shouldn't imagine you get to ninth in the corruption chart by handing out aid where it's due.

'So it's probably not a good idea to wander around outside the camp after dark?' I wondered out loud.

'Let's put it this way. This year alone, there have been 37 shooting incidents in and around Lokichoggio. Eighteen people have been killed and 19 seriously injured. We tend to encourage our OLS staff to stay in at night.'

I had to admit, a nice early night did suddenly seem very appealing.

Following our rather sobering meeting with Ruben, we were now led into another small conference room where a man called Patrick Fox briefed us on the security situation in the southern Sudan. Patrick just had to be an ex-army man, someone I imagined fellow officers referring to as 'a thoroughly good chap'. It was somehow disappointing that he didn't begin each sentence with 'Right men, now pay attention ... ' but somehow this was implied in his tone of voice. As well as updating us on the state of the war and pointing out the areas of the country where we were most likely to be bombed, he passed us each a security *aide-mémoire* which, among other things, outlined how best to behave should we be taken hostage. Being someone who's always anxious to act with decorum in every social occasion, I took a moment to study the instructions in detail.

1. Obey orders.
   (This made sense to me. Especially if my captors had a gun and I didn't.)
2. DON'T speak unless spoken to.
   (Absolutely. Being too chatty might get on their nerves.)
3. DON'T whisper to fellow captives.

(Sensible. I'd always been taught that it's rude to whisper and the chances are my captors would have been taught the same.)

4. DON'T look captors in the eye.
(Bit of a surprise this one. I would have thought that looking away from them would have made one appear shifty, but there you go.)
5. DON'T offer suggestions.
(Fair enough, although I would have been tempted by the suggestion, 'Why don't you untie us and let us go?')
6. DON'T argue, threaten or draw attention to yourself.
(Couldn't agree more. This is no time to start carrying on like a spoilt child.)
7. DON'T make any sudden moves – ask first.
(I'm a bit dubious about this one. Can't see much point in asking 'Could I make a sudden move please?')

Patrick explained that I was going to be air-dropped into a place called Yambio, in the Western Equatoria region. This had been given a Security Level of Two. Level One was a *Normal Operational Situation* but alas, this didn't exist in south Sudan at the moment. Level Two was a *Medium Operational Situation* which meant that we would have to make radio contact with the Lokichoggio base twice a day, and only make day trips from our base. Level Three was a *Tense Operational Situation* which meant radio contact three times a day and no travel outside base. Finally, Level Four meant that you had to get the hell out. Basically, hang on somewhere safe until a UNICEF plane came to airlift you to safety.

'It is extremely unlikely,' explained Patrick, in his soothing public-school delivery, 'that the security level of Yambio will become a Level Four while you are there. It has been firmly in control of the rebels for ten years. Unlike many of the populated areas in the south which are regularly bombed, it hasn't been on the receiving end of any shells for some four years. Any questions?'

'Yes, what's the music scene like in Yambio?'

This, unfortunately, was the question which I didn't have the courage to ask. I felt it would have trivialised all that had gone before, and besides, I suspected that it wasn't an area where Patrick was likely to have any great inside knowledge. Most of his life had probably been spent briefing people who had more than guitars as their first line of defence.

Following Patrick's security briefing we were taken to a huge warehouse and briefed on what aid was going where, then it was off to the radio room for a briefing on operational procedures, before finally being led to a courtyard in the centre of the camp where, along with the rest of the staff on the camp, we were briefed on the latest security situations throughout the southern Sudan. Goodness, more briefs than Marks & Spencers. I was now one of the world's leading experts on how to run an aid operation in a war zone. I felt over-qualified for someone who only really wanted to strum a guitar in a mudhut with a mildly interested local.

One evening in the OLS camp in Lokichoggio is enough to alert you to the fact that a long stay here might be quite tiresome. Two main factors worked against it, the fact that going out in the evening might result in death, and that staying in was deathly boring. Having eaten supper and sat around in the bar, I felt I'd pretty much exhausted all the available leisure options. I'd heard whispers that aid workers created their own entertainment by indulging in a fair amount of '*tukul* hopping' (*tukuls* being the little straw huts which workers slept in), but I didn't feel up to any of that tonight, and anyway I needed to channel all my remaining energy into putting up my mosquito net.

Back in Blighty the doctor had told me that the mosquitoes in this part of the world packed something of a malarial punch, so I was going to take every precaution I could. I'd already gone through the trauma of deciding whether to take Lariam or not. According to government health sources, Lariam is the only drug which offers you decent protection against malaria in this part of the world, but unfortunately it is also the drug which, when you announce that you are taking it, causes people to take a sharp intake of breath, shake their heads and list all the horrific side effects which it has induced in them, and all of their friends and loved ones. After much deliberation I'd opted to take the bloody stuff but thankfully, thus far, I'd suffered no ill effects. I'd taken the pills once a week and I'd followed all the instructions on the box. 'Keep Away From Children' it had said. Well, I'd certainly done that. Apart from brushing past one in a supermarket, I hadn't been near a child for weeks.

However, there still remained the risk that I might fall victim to one of the possible side effects listed on the accompanying leaflet. The most common ones were sickness, dizziness, vertigo, loss of balance, headaches, sleepiness, diarrhoea and stomach ache. Less common ones included unusual changes in mood or behaviour, feelings of worry or anxiety, depression, feelings of persecution, crying, aggression, restlessness, forgetfulness, agitation, confusion, panic and hallucinations. As if this wasn't enough, it went on to list the possibility of visual disturbances, ringing in the ears, co-ordination problems, shaking of the hands and fingers, changes to blood pressure or heart rate, palpitations, skin rash, itching, hair loss, muscle cramps, joint pains and loss of appetite. As far as I could see, they might as well have put a sign on the side of the box saying:

WARNING, THE EFFECTS OF THIS DRUG MIGHT BE CONSIDERABLY WORSE THAN MALARIA

I woke in the morning, relieved to find that I hadn't been bitten by any mosquitoes or attacked by any disgruntled gun-wielding Turkana. Consequently I was fighting-fit and ready for the next leg of this somewhat elongated journey. This involved climbing on to a yet still smaller aircraft, a six-seater Cessna Caravan which was going to whizz us to our destination at a top speed of 140 mph. In two and half hours' time the pilot would land us on a mud airstrip hewn from equatorial rain-forest. All feelings of fear were superseded by those of importance, because I knew that presidents and billionaire businessmen did not dilly-dally with Jumbos. No, the rules were clear; the smaller the plane, the more consequential the passenger. I looked around me and saw that for some of my fellow passengers this sense of buoyed vanity was not enough to dispel all concern about the journey ahead. Sue, the *Daily Telegraph* journalist, had a pallor and grim demeanour which suggested she was fully aware of what the results of being important had been for Buddy Holly, Glenn Miller, John Denver, and Payne Stewart *et al.* I attempted to offer her a comforting smile, immediately realising that the fear-stricken are not easily consoled by such feeble gestures of support. To her, mine could have had the air of a sadistic smile which was revelling in her suffering, while smugly welcoming the hideous fate which was about to befall us all.

Unlike commercial passenger aircraft which provide a one-sided, port-hole sized aspect of the journey, Cessna Caravans offer excellent views simply by virtue of being so small. Seated as I was, directly behind the pilot, I was afforded a full panoramic vista of the southern Sudan, which I soon discovered to be a little disappointing since it was so uncompromisingly flat. Perhaps the only relief in these parts was humanitarian.

After the plane had been in the air for about half an hour, both the pilot and co-pilot took out newspapers and began reading. I looked round to see if Sue had been privy to this potentially distressing sight but thankfully she was either asleep or had passed out. Of course, there was no need for alarm. Since all sides have agreed not to shoot down any UN aid planes, there probably wasn't much piloting to be done until the little muddy airstrip appeared on the horizon.

I began to read the newspaper over the pilot's shoulder (a first for me, although I intended to force my way up to the captain's cabin and do it on every flight henceforth) and I saw an alarming story of how a group of angry women had stormed some slum dwellings in Nairobi, smashing up equipment they believed was being used to create illegal alcohol. As a result of drinking this intoxicating brew, eight people had died and many more had been blinded. It seemed that the womenfolk had decided that enough was enough. I made a mental note to ask for a bitter lemon or a lime and soda if I ever found myself enjoying an evening out drinking in those parts. It would be a good opportunity to appear rather magnanimous:

'Tonight, Tony, we're going drinking in the slums of Nairobi. Wanna come?'

'OK. I'll drive if you like. I don't mind taking the car and not drinking.'

'That's very selfless of you, Tony.'

'Think nothing of it.'

Forty minutes before we were scheduled to arrive in Yambio, the countryside beneath us changed, becoming surprisingly lush and verdant. Unlike most of southern Sudan, Yambio County is a tropical rainforest characterised by tall trees as well as some savannah grasslands. There is plenty of rainfall, and fruit and vegetables are in good supply. All this was clearly visible from the sky and it made for exciting viewing. I looked down on the miniscule mudhuts and the tiny moving black figures which represented the first glimpses of civilisation, and I felt a rush of excitement. The simplicity of what was below me was somehow humbling. I was hovering over a part of the world which had not been party to the development of the one which I inhabited. What was I going to discover? How had life here been affected by its isolation from people and progress?

Soon Yambio's muddy airstrip appeared on the horizon and the pilots, who thankfully had finished with the papers, fiddled around with buttons and nobs in preparation for landing. I felt like a kid in an amusement arcade watching a video game over a bigger kid's shoulders. Of course, the difference was that we were involved in a game where if we messed up we couldn't just put more money in the machine and have another go. I glanced at Sue who didn't appear to need reminding of this.

We hit the mud at what seemed like enormous speed and wobbled a little. At once I became aware of how important it was for the airstrip to have been properly maintained. Had the wheels of our aircraft hit a small rock then we would have been tipped clean over and we'd have become another set of aviation statistics. However, there was no such calamity, just a smooth and successful touchdown. I felt like applauding. I'd been on a charter flight to Spain a few months previously and had been delighted to find a good proportion of the passengers had been unrestrained enough with their emotions to be able to applaud enthusiastically following the successful landing of the aircraft. Of course, if one takes the time to analyse their actions, what those passengers had really been doing was applauding because they weren't dead. (I'm pretty certain that's also why people applaud at the end of Neil Sedaka concerts.)

As the Cessna Caravan's propellers made their final transition from a whirring blur into gently spinning blades, the cabin door of the Cessna was thrown open and we were hit by a wave of equatorial heat. We had landed in the southern Sudan. I stepped out on to the red soil of the airstrip and into a war zone.

I was ready for anything though. After all, I had my guitar with me.

Stand by me

The first few hours in Yambio did not promise much with regard to the accomplishment of my personal mission in this country. The political figures who had authorised our entry into their territory had organised a complete itinerary for us, nothing of which involved any allotted time for musical collaboration. Instead we were to be whisked from place to place in order to be shown how responsibly their society was spending the aid money of which they were grateful recipients.

We were driven to the first of these rather formal meetings in a four-wheel drive with the letters U and N emblazoned on its side, clearly marking us out as benign and well-meaning sorts. Whether we'd been displaying the distinctive bright blue letters or not, most would have known our identity given that the UN were the only ones with any vehicles at all in this area. Ten years previously, many northern inhabitants would have been driving around on these mud-tracks which served as roads, but they had been forced to flee when Yambio had been 'liberated' by the SPLA, and with them had gone all motorised forms of transport. Once 'set free', Yambio, which had never been much more than a relatively under-developed market town, suddenly had to adapt to a life with all its former supply lines cut off. Like it or not, it was back to subsistence living for its inhabitants, just as it had been before the opportunistic British and Egyptians had first arrived a century or so earlier. A derelict petrol station, with rusting pumps and crumbling forecourt, served as a faint reminder of their prosperity, and the shell of a burnt-out bus bore grim testament to how these former overlords had been removed.

I looked around me and saw nothing but decay and neglect, which would have made the place feel like a ghost-town had it not been for the ant-like procession of villagers heading for the main market square, eager to trade whatever they could manage to carry there. These people were extraordinary. Each jet-black face, whether male or female, young or old, displayed a mysterious combination of intensity and warmth, of gravity and accessibility. Occasionally my intrusive stare would be returned with one of an even more penetrative and inquisitive nature, amazed no doubt, by my whiter than whiteness. After all, they didn't see many of my type, one of the few advantages of being entrenched in a bloody civil war being that you are spared adventurous backpackers from Oz parading up and down the main street in search of the Youth Hostel. From time to time I waved to one of my co-starers, and on each occasion I was greeted with a huge toothy smile followed by self-conscious giggling. Happiness appeared to be all around us. A little odd. These people had suffered greatly, so why weren't they showing it?

I sat by the van window, spellbound by the magic of the women outside who went about their business with such nonchalance, displaying the skills of circus performers as they strolled with huge baskets of vegetables balanced on their heads. I suddenly felt genuinely excited and privileged to be here, reaping the rewards at last of the exhausting journey.

Presently we arrived at Freedom Square, so-called, I assume, because of its freedom from any similarity to conventional squares. It was little more than a knackered old football pitch where desperate grass fought a losing battle against the elements. Beyond it was a single-storey building which looked like it was as familiar with maintenance as an alcoholic's ex-wife. This, we were told, was the Commissioner's Office.

Inside we were lectured on the Sudan's recent history by a confident and prosperous-looking man who introduced himself as Pascal, the Minister of Agriculture. After an initial gracious preamble, his expression hardened and he began to outline some facts which he obviously felt we needed to know.

'The suffering of the last 53 years has been caused by Britain,' he declared with a sudden severity.

I glanced out of the window and saw two moody teenagers pacing around with guns, watching our building.

'Our people,' continued Pascal, with more than a hint of the ruthless dictator about him. '... Our people have been killed like flies since the British deserted us to the Arabs.'

I felt a momentary shudder of fear and quickly reminded myself of the hostage procedure, taking care not to look anyone in the eye while I did so. Being on the receiving end of all this anti-British rhetoric, I wondered whether it might not be a bad idea to have an Irish accent ready.

'Ah Jeez, now there's a ting Pascal, 'cos if it wasn't the Brits who shafted us too!'

It was a relief to discover that instead of having us arrested, the Minister wound up his speech and introduced us to the Commissioner, a more frail, modest figure whom he referred to as 'His Excellency'. This was the first time in my life that I had been in the company of a 'His Excellency', the closest until now having been the Fixtures' Secretary at the tennis club (the difference between the two being that this one was more humble, and you didn't have to kneel before him).

'You are most welcome visitors here,' began the Commissioner, who I assumed was distinct from most 'His Excellencies' in the world in that he didn't have any laces in his shoes. 'I hope that you enjoy the programme that we have arranged for you.'

His Excellency then outlined this programme which he and his colleagues had gone to considerable trouble to arrange for us. To me though, it sounded extremely dull, and unlikely to bring me any closer to any Sudanese musicians – although I realised that this probably wasn't the best moment to point this out. Lunchtime, however, after a visit to a school, an agricultural college, and then a teak plantation, was.

'They're treating us like visiting politicians,' I moaned as we tucked into an unexpectedly wholesome meal back on the compound. 'They seem to think that we're more important than we are. Can't we tell them that Irvine wrote a novel about heroine addiction and I hitch-hiked round Ireland with a fridge?'

Talking to the powers that be had been a success and two hours later we were taking a gentle stroll to Yambio's market, chaperoned by three locals who were there to oversee our safety rather than provide us with propaganda. Rather optimistically I was carrying my guitar, ever eager to seize an opportunity for collaboration, should the moment arise.

'Please, I can take that for you?' asked Justin, the most enthusiastic of our chaperones, pointing to my guitar.

'No, it's OK, I can manage,' I replied, eager not to replicate any of my colonial ancestors' desire for native servitude.

'Please, let me take your guitar,' urged the fresh-faced and eager Justin, oblivious to my concerns.

'It's all right.'

'No, I take.'

'Oh well, if you insist.'

I handed him the guitar, for a split second wondering rather shamefully if he might run off with it as soon as it was in his hands. Instead he smiled meekly and alerted us to the fact that the little path we had taken had now brought us once again to Freedom Square.

'Is there a bar anywhere in the town?' asked Irvine, his accent sounding all the more pronounced and incongruous in this environment, although to my ears the nature of the request did seem to lend itself to the Scottish brogue.

'Yes, there is one,' replied Justin.

'Great,' declared a beaming Irvine.

'Would you like to go there?' asked Justin naïvely, presumably not having met that many Scotsmen to date.

'I most certainly would,' replied Irvine without hesitation.

'OK, I take you there.'

Justin looked to me to be in his early twenties, a neatly turned-out young man who definitely took great care with his appearance, despite wearing Western-style garb which was palpably not his size. His outfit was far more likely to have been a handout from an aid package than the product of numerous return visits to a clothing store's fitting room. I smiled to myself, momentarily warmed by the thought that all those clothes-filled binliners that we dump on the doorsteps of aid shops really do have a life beyond the two old ladies who first sift through them. It was nice to know that Justin and his like could return them once more to the cutting edge of fashion.

Justin's Christian name was exactly that, a Christian name. Sure he was one of the Azande people from the southern Sudan, but he was a Christian, so he'd been given a name which made him sound like he came from just outside Esher. That's how it worked. He led us along the narrow mud paths, past a constant stream of energetic and eager villagers who were each as fascinated as the next by our extraordinarily pale skin. Soon we reached a point where the mud-tracks widened and became the closest thing to a set of crossroads that this part of the world could offer. Ahead of us there was a dilapidated shack with a sign outside which read: KABASH'S INN. Irvine beamed and led us inside where we discovered that its inn-like characteristics didn't stretch much beyond a few tables and chairs. The bar was little more than a counter with a few bottles stashed behind it. African music blared from an old music-centre which was powered by a solar panel which lay in the sun on the porch outside.

'What a terrific idea,' observed Irvine, pointing to the contraption which was eagerly harnessing the sun's rays.

'Yeah,' I replied, 'although it must be a bit of a bummer if it gets cloudy. Presumably the music stops.'

'Hmm,' responded Irvine thoughtfully. 'Maybe that's why you don't see many of them back home in Scotland.'

The beers were ordered easily enough but there was a problem when it came to paying for them. Since the only economic connection the southern Sudanese had with the Khartoum regime in the north Sudan was funding an armed struggle against them, Sudanese currency was not readily accepted. We'd been told in Lokichoggio that US dollars were what locals were after but we were now being asked to pay in either Kenyan or Ugandan shillings, and none of us had any. Perversely we were in the embarrassing situation of being unable to pay for a drink in a region where we were supposed to be the providers of aid. The owners of Kabash's Inn were giving us suspicious looks. Maybe they were expecting one of us to tip them the wink, tap our noses conspiratorially and say, 'Let us have the drinks for free and we'll sort you out with a nice tractor, OK?'

I couldn't understand why they weren't mad keen for our American money.

'Justin, why are they waving our dollars away?' I asked.

'Because you have too much,' he replied.

It seemed an odd moment to pass comment on the economic injustices which meant that we probably had enough spending money in our pockets to feed an entire family here for three years.

'What do you mean we have too much? We're trying to redistribute some of our wealth here and they won't let us.'

'It is that you have only twenty-dollar bills. They cannot give you any change – they do not have any dollars.'

'Oh, I see. Well, tell them not to worry about change. We will buy everybody here a drink and they can keep any of the money left over.'

Justin got to his feet with a twenty-dollar bill and explained this proposal to the tall, thin lady who seemed to be running operations. The marked change in her expression suggested that this arrangement was not a disagreeable one. In fact she had quite a spring in her step as she reached for the beers from the solar-powered fridge.

'You're lucky to have bottled beers,' we were told as

they were delivered by the beaming proprietor. 'Yambio is near the border so they get goods like this from Uganda. If we'd taken you to some other places in the southern Sudan you wouldn't have had luxuries like this.'

The beer hit its mark and it felt good. I looked at Justin who was drinking like a naughty teenager, not normally allowed alcohol.

'Are there many musicians here in Yambio?' I asked, making a token effort to get my visit back on track.

'Yes, there are many.'

'Could you introduce to me some?'

'I think so, yes.'

I was quickly growing to like Justin. I felt there was room for our relationship to develop beyond that of would-be composer and guitar carrier. But that would have to wait. As we got to our feet to head off for a stroll around the market area, Justin made a dive for the guitar and held it to his chest like a mother might a small child. He wasn't yet ready to relinquish his new-found role.

There is an urgency and earnestness about market-places in the third world which sets them apart from anything we experience in the West, such is the importance of each transaction. I found myself quite enthralled by the vibrant atmosphere of this one, bustling as it was with the irresistible energy of traders with an indisputable vested interest. Many had walked miles to sell their wares, the proceeds of which would provide food for their children and next of kin. Little wonder that emotions ran high and that shopping was done at volume and with passion.

Expectant merchants sat cross-legged on the dusty ground, their particular specialist fruit, vegetable or spice spread out before them for the passing shoppers' perusal. Little money seemed to be changing hands, the barter system understandably being favoured in a land where economic stability had gone out of the window the day the bank had been blown up. As I watched a particular deal being struck, I became somehow envious of the simplicity of it all. As someone who has always been too lazy or stupid to have ever properly grasped how money *really* works, there was something irresistibly gratifying and somehow romantic in watching a bunch of bananas being exchanged for some grain. And not a reward card in sight.

What impresses me most about the barter system is the way it excludes outside influences. The value of the currency, in this case bananas and grain, cannot be decided by anyone other than the buyer or seller. Its value is entirely subjective and therein lies its beauty. Unlike in our system where the worth of our currency is often decided by the actions of financiers in the City or on Wall Street, no decision on a distant trading floor can alter the value of those bananas to their owner. Better still, the problem of counterfeiting never raises its ugly (and almost identical) head. After all, who in their right mind is going to forge a banana? Apart from anything else it's bloody difficult, and the equipment needed is expensive and only available over the Internet (www.forge-a-banana.com). Certainly, the presence of forged banknotes within our society has led to the most annoying practice of the staff on supermarket checkouts holding our twenty-pound notes up to the light to check the validity of their watermarks. I deeply resent this, and whenever it is done to me I pick up each item of shopping from my trolley and hold it up to the light, in a similarly untrusting manner. Frankly, if they think my twenty-pound note is dodgy then I'm hardly going to head home with my groceries until I'm absolutely certain that they haven't tried to fob me off with some counterfeit Shreddies or Marmite.

'Why don't you give them a song here, Tony?' came Irvine's suggestion, rather jolting me from my profound thoughts on world shopping.

'What? Here in the marketplace?'

'Yep, right here. Why not? I reckon you've got to put yourself on show. If you want the Sudanese Paul McCartney to come out of the woodwork, then he'll have to know that his John Lennon is in town.'

Fortunately I was tuned into the same wavelength as Irvine, and his irrational logic made perfect sense to me. I knew he was right. My instinct was telling me that if I wanted to make something musical happen here then I would have to take the initiative, and so I asked Justin to hand me the guitar. I began taking it out of its case and a crowd immediately began to develop. Well, why wouldn't it? One of the white people was producing a strange-looking instrument from a bag, and it looked like he was going to begin playing it.

An expectant throng gathered before me and I became suddenly very nervous. I was about to make a performance for which I was totally unprepared. I still had absolutely no idea what I was going to sing. And once I'd decided on it, how would it be received? Would my actions be offensive to the local culture? Maybe producing a guitar and singing uninvited in the middle of the market might be a great insult? Would I be arrested, reported to the commissioner, or worse still, completely ignored? The butterflies whizzed around my tummy more than they had done for years. The odd thing was, I liked this sensation. Masochistic though it may have been, I found this feeling of discomfort reassuring in that it was confirmation that I was stretching myself, and not settling for the comfortable, easy life. These were the moments that stopped life being boring. Here, with an audience of fifty or more south Sudanese villagers assembling before me in expectation of something special, I knew one thing. I was alive. (I was hoping still to be that way at the end of the song.) And that is not a feeling to be underestimated.

How do you choose a song in a situation such as this? I was denied the *Here's one that everyone will know* option, one of the few benefits of the civil war having been shut off to sounds like 'American Pie' or 'Streets of London'.

Quite why I elected to go for 'Stand By Me' I can't really remember, but I strongly suspect that it was because it was the only song I could think of at the time. As I played the introductory chords there was a buzz of anticipation among the fascinated onlookers. There I was, the white man beneath the jacaranda tree as dusk fell, strumming away much like a busker on the London underground. Except that I was much more of a novelty here. Extremely special, in fact, in this location and against this backdrop. I drew my breath for the first line, and with my heart pounding I launched into song. Nothing could have prepared me for what was to follow.

'When the night has come and the land is dark ... .'

With the first line of the song barely over, my audience fell about laughing. Not gentle tittering or embarrassed giggling but full-blown guffaws and hysterical side-slapping. These people were, to use the vernacular, pissing themselves laughing. It was not quite what I'd expected, and a little bruising for the ego. What made matters worse was that the response of the locals was so unusual and in itself so amusing, that Irvine and the rest of our party also began to lose themselves in laughter. My singing had never produced such mirth before, even while performing a comedy song when that had been the intention (more's the pity). It was so disconcerting that it felt pointless to proceed with the song, especially since none of it would have been audible above this mirthful and overwhelming cacophany. The sound must have been carrying for miles around, confusing humans and frightening the wildlife.

After having vamped on the same chord until the laughter had subsided (it may have only been a minute but it seemed much longer), it was time for the singer to resume the song, albeit with an entirely different set of expectations.

'... and the moon is the only light you'll see.'

More hysterics, this time slightly tempered by general exhaustion from the first outburst. I elected to continue regardless, and by the time I'd made it to the first round of 'Stand by Me's, the listeners' laughs had dwindled and become smiles which occasionally broke into the odd titter. By midway through the second chorus there was something approaching complete silence and there was definitely room for suspicion that the sounds I was producing were genuinely being appreciated. Then I made a mistake. I had come to the section in the song where a long solo begins and I was faced with the choice of either humming it (not really an option, I mean how hysterical were they going to find humming?) or thinking of something else. That something else was to have a go at a spot of audience participation. I began to sing a round of choruses without guitar accompaniment, urging my audience to get involved by raising my arms above my head and clapping, much like desperate old rockers do at the conclusion of their regular comeback gigs. Instead of recognising this gesture as an invitation to share in this memorable performance, my fans regarded me with confusion, before a bold few took this as a cue to burst into a round of applause. The rest followed. My music was now drowned out by an audience applauding enthusiastically, regardless of the fact that I hadn't yet finished. This time the sound was too much to fight against so I had little choice but to throw in the towel and wind up proceedings with a bow. On seeing this new signal from me, the crowd at once ceased applauding and began watching me with interest to see what I would do next. Thus, the conclusion to my epic performance was greeted with complete silence. Well, almost. If you listened carefully you could just hear the sounds of a small group of white people desperately trying to suppress laughter.

'Thank you Yambio, and good night!' I exclaimed in ironic homage to the old rocker.

The suppressed laughter of the white people erupted into loud guffaws.

It really was turning into quite a busy day. I mean, hadn't I done enough already without getting involved in a game of football? I suppose I would have said no, had I not still been reeling from the shock of the singing experience.

'Why don't you and Irvine join in with the game?' we were asked.

'Because I'm wearing these silly sandals,' I'd replied.

'Yes, but most of them are playing barefoot, look!'

I looked and I saw. Freedom Square was now hosting a spirited football match which was being contested between two youthful teams, most of whom were happily competing without any footwear. It didn't matter though, because the soles of their feet were as tough as old boots. Considerably tougher, as it turned out, than my designer sandals.

Irvine and I were quickly assimilated into proceedings. The addition of one more player to each team didn't make much difference when there were 17-a-side already. A hundred or so excited onlookers were watching a game which was being played in a competitive spirit even though ultimately it was little more than a friendly kick-around. It was just bad luck that the only player on the pitch who had failed to grasp the meaning of the word 'friendly' was the one who had chosen to mark me. When the ball first came to my feet, I attempted to control it with my back to goal before laying it off to one of my teammates. However, before I could do this, I felt a shooting pain in the back of my calves as my legs were scythed from beneath me and an opponent's body shot out from underneath my feet, taking the ball with it.

I collapsed on the rock-hard ground in an uncomfortable heap. I had just been the victim of a Sudanese tackle from behind (they don't come any worse, check with FIFA if you don't believe me). Then I heard a familiar sound. I did not recognise it at first, still being a little dazed from the severity of the tackle and subsequent tumble, but I knew it, I definitely knew it. What *was* it? Ah yes, I recognised it now – hysterical laughter. Of course! My fall had been the funniest thing the crowd had seen in their lives to date (their presence at this game meaning that this lot had missed out on my earlier singing) and the obvious response was to shriek with laughter. To call these people uninhibited would be a gross understatement. They were producing the kind of sounds that most of us could only make following dangerous levels of drug consumption. Their readiness to explode with such demonstrative expressions of mirth was remarkable, not least given the hardship and suffering which recent history had forced them to endure, but it was personally a little disappointing that I should be the one who seemed to instigate these emotions, especially when I'd been attempting to do something serious.

The game continued, and so did my marker – with the same unbridled ferocity. Perhaps Pascal, the Minister of Agriculture, had explained to this lad exactly how badly the British had messed things up around here, because there was scant evidence to suggest that he saw me as someone who was in the region to help his community. After being on the receiving end of a fifth bookable offence, I decided that it would be dangerous to carry on, or else one of the crowd would have almost certainly died laughing. I limped from the pitch to huge cheers, and with every possibility of being promised a testimonial match late next season. I slumped to the ground on the sidelines, nursing my wounds and cursing the aid organisations. OK, I thought, they might do sterling work in the area supplying engineers, teachers and doctors, but would it hurt to ship out the odd referee as well?

'Would you like to do anything this evening after you have had your supper here?' asked the impeccably mannered Justin, as we arrived back at the gated compound, which was home for the duration.

'Is there anything happening in town?' asked Irvine.

'Well, many of the villagers will be going to a big public showing of a video. Also there is a bar we could go to later,' said Justin, almost too eagerly.

'Going to both those places sounds good to me. Anyone got any other suggestions?' offered Irvine to the rest of us.

I didn't have the energy to make my suggestion, which was probably just as well. It was a little violent in nature, and Justin probably didn't know where that footballer lived anyway.

'Don't worry, just keep following me,' called a concerned Justin. 'They have saved spaces for us.'

He was leading us through a mild version of an angry mob, made up of villagers who were struggling to gain entry into the big straw hut which was housing tonight's video show. Rather embarrassingly we were now being ushered past them like VIPs. I felt uncomfortable with this. We had only wanted to come here to see what the locals did for entertainment, not to deprive them of it. I tried to point this out to Justin but by the time I could make myself heard, we had already been crammed inside, along with a good proportion of Yambio's population. These excited viewers were huddled together on small slithers of wood which acted as benches. They were transfixed by the blurred moving pictures emanating from a large TV at the end of the hut, but theirs was not a passive appreciation. If they saw something they liked then they cheered, and if they saw something of which they didn't approve, then they made suitably disapproving noises. Nobody seemed in the least bit concerned about the dialogue, but that didn't matter given that they were watching one of those third-rate American action movies where you're better off not hearing what the actors are saying anyway.

We settled into our 'reserved seats' which afforded us an excellent view of a wooden pillar and, in the distance beyond it, the left-hand side of the video screen. As Justin was returning from some discussion with the man in charge of the VCR, the video screen suddenly went black. The noise level immediately tripled as viewers rose to their feet, waving their fists and bellowing abuse in the general direction of the video operator.

'What's going on?' I asked Justin as he rejoined us.

'They are putting something on especially for you,' he replied.

'Justin, we don't want that. These people were in the middle of enjoying a film.'

'It is OK. They do not mind. You will like what we show you.'

'What is it?'

'Dancing.'

'Oh. What kind of dancing?'

'They are dancers from the Congo. You will like them. They are all buttocks.'

'What?'

'You watch. Their dancing – it is all buttocks.'

Justin was wrong on that score. We didn't like them, in fact I think we actively disliked them. One male dancer, who clearly fancied himself a fantastic amount, was wiggling his buttocks in the foreground, while a bevvy of dubious Congolese beauties did the same just behind him. This man, who appeared to be leading proceedings, was by no means the best dancer and I guessed that the only reason he was at the front was because it was his camera that was filming it all.

'It is good, isn't it?' said Justin, looking around for confirmation which never came. 'These dancers they are all buttocks.'

He was right about the buttocks, but less accurate when it came to them being good. He'd definitely made an error of judgement there. Any top-notch dancer will tell you that wiggling your buttocks just isn't enough, but nobody seemed to have told these dancers that. The music, though rhythmic, was not much better than the dancing. It was being relayed through poor-quality equipment and was distorted and barely audible. After ten minutes of trying to smile approvingly, my facial muscles began to tire and I had to say something.

'Justin, how long do these dancers go on for?'

'Oh, for a very long time. They are very fit.'

'Yes.' I took a moment to ponder my next question. 'And how long *is* a very long time exactly?'

'Maybe an hour.'

In the Sudan it may well have been courteous for a guest to have allowed himself to be 'entertained', but I felt there was need for some protestation for five good reasons:

1. It was very hot.
2. I was perched on an uncomfortable slither of wood.
3. There was a pillar in the way of the screen.
4. Everybody else wanted to watch another film.
5. A Congolese man's gyrating buttocks were making me nauseous.

'Justin, can't you get them to put the other film back on?' I suggested, as persuasively as I could. 'It isn't fair that their enjoyment has been interrupted.'

'It is OK, they do not mind,' he replied with an insouciant smile.

'They do. They mind. Take a look at them.'

Justin took a moment to do exactly that, and must have noted something which had escaped his attention before, because he jumped to his feet and headed off to provide the video operator with a new set of instructions.

Five minutes later we were struggling to make our way out of the hut, freeing up our slither of wood for the bottoms of more enthusiastic devotees of action movies. The trip to the video show was over. It may not have been the most successful of outings, but for me it had been something of a personal triumph. No one had laughed at me.

The next place Justin led us was a small bar which bore more of a resemblance to someone's house, and one which had clearly been opened especially for us (I guess not having anything smaller than twenty-dollar bills can open doors for you in this part of the world). A lady emerged to take our orders, looking rather like we'd just got her out of bed.

'Why don't you try some Sukusuku?' Justin asked me. 'It is the alcohol which they make here in Yambio.'

'Er, no thanks,' I replied unadventurously, 'I think I'll just stick to a bottled beer.'

'Why don't you just try a little?'

I remembered the newspaper reports detailing some of the horrific consequences of Nairobi's home-made alcoholic beverages.

'Thanks, but no. Not tonight. Really, thanks but no.' I felt like a prim convent girl refusing a kiss.

'It is strong, but it is good.'

'I'm sure it is, but I'm happy with a beer.'

For the second time in the evening I was being rather churlish with regard to the hospitality which was on offer, but ultimately I was comfortable with my decision. It wasn't very British, but by my reckoning it was better to risk appearing rude than to go blind or die.

'Justin, tell me about your family,' I requested, just after I'd ordered the considerably safer option of a beer.

'I never knew my father,' he explained. 'Nobody talked about him and I think perhaps nobody knew who he was. My mother died when I was two days old. I was brought up by her sister but she died when I was twelve years old and then I had to remain alone.'

'And how did you manage?'

'I had to absent myself from class so I could go and try and find work to get money. It was a condition which forced me to get married. I am 29 years old now and I got married in 1991 but this was too early for me.'

'How could getting married help?'

'A wife could at least contribute to looking after me and help me to complete my studies. Women have many techniques for getting money here. They can brew beer which they can distill and then sell. They can cultivate the garden and plant some things which can help get money.'

'So you married for money, not for love.'

'I married on a condition basis,' said Justin rather shiftily, almost sounding like a politician. 'Once you have a wife she can help you in different things.'

I knew that in the past a woman had been considered to be of such value to the Azande people that marriage was usually contracted by the gift of about 20 spears by the bridegroom to the family of the bride. I wasn't sure if this tradition was still observed but I was aware of what trouble I'd have over here, having carelessly let my spear collection dip to as low as six (two of which were slightly damaged and buried somewhere in the loft). I also knew that girls here married very young, sometimes being betrothed only a few hours after birth, presumably to someone who'd been very careful not to throw their spears without being sure of their safe retrieval. Polygamy was also practised – this being the rather unfair system in which a man can take as many wives as he wants. It had been common for nobles to have taken so many wives that there hadn't been enough to go around and other men hadn't been able to marry, regardless of how many spears they'd managed to accumulate. What a bummer.

I learned that Justin's wife had been 14 years old when he married her and that now she had given him two healthy children. Unfortunately she was suffering from appendicitis and was in the hospital awaiting an operation.

'The doctor will not operate,' he explained. 'She is anaemic and she has to build up the strength of her blood. It is difficult for me right now because I need to find the money to bring her the food which will build up her blood, and the hospital already is expensive. You have to pay for the admission card, and then for the bed and for the person who washes the bedclothes. On top of that you have to pay for the operation.'

'It seems that things are tough for you, right now.'

'Yes, I think that I am unlucky.'

'*Have been* unlucky,' I corrected him.

'What do you mean?'

'You *have been* unlucky.'

'I don't understand.'

'We have an expression where I come from: "Tomorrow is the first day of the rest of your life." '

Justin looked blank. I did my best to explain to him and he nodded as I did so, but I knew that it was one of those nods you do when you haven't understood – you know the ones – when you're just nodding because you can't be arsed to have the person try and explain again. It had been a long day for all of us and people were getting worried that we weren't back in the compound.

And so it was that we finished our beers like naughty children who had stayed out too late, and we jumped into the school bus to head home. As we alighted at the compound, I shook Justin by the hand.

'Thank you for looking after me,' I said.

'It has been my pleasure.'

'Perhaps tomorrow you could take me to the hospital to visit your wife.'

'I will arrange it. No problem.'

'Goodnight.'

'Goodnight,' he said with a wave, before adding kindly, 'sleep well.'

MALARIA AND PADLOCKS

I awoke in my tent in the morning, having obediently followed Justin's instructions to sleep well. At breakfast, the day's schedule was finalised. As a group we were to visit a girl's school, before splitting up and doing our own thing. I had elected to spend the day with Justin, cycling around the mud tracks and among the *tukuls* of Yambio, getting a real feel for the place and hopefully visiting the home of a musician with whom I could set up some kind of writing session.

'What kind of music are you hoping to write?' asked Sue.

'I really don't know,' I replied honestly. 'Hopefully we'll end up with a fusion of Sudanese tribal music and good old-fashioned pop.'

Silence around the breakfast table. I guess everyone was trying to figure out what kind of a sound this might be, and indeed, whether anyone would really want to listen to it.

'I suppose I'm really more interested in the process than the actual result,' I said, feeling the need to fill the embarrassing silence which had suddenly descended over the table.

'Well, at least you're going to have a go,' offered Irvine, supportively.

At the girl's school we were greeted by the headmaster who led us into the large dusty courtyard which lay beyond the narrow, single-storey building which constituted the school itself. The building, we were told, only really served as an administrative centre, most of the lessons taking place beneath the surrounding jacaranda trees. The headmaster explained that he was unhappy about this and longed for classrooms, but for me it all seemed so romantic. I remembered being stuck in a dingy classroom suffering double-geography lessons with Mr Baxter.

'In our society we don't sit under trees as much as we ought to,' I said, trying to be profound.

Just as I was beginning to regret the pretentiousness of my remark, we were interrupted by one of the most beautiful sounds I'd heard for a long time. At the far side of the courtyard, a large gathering of children had begun singing, and they were doing so specifically for us – a song of greeting:

'*We are happy, we are happy to receive you.*'

The voices were shrill, but extraordinarily musical, and the sound cut through the air with a great power which arrested the senses. The meter of the song was complex, the singers occasionally pushing a beat rather than singing to the uniformed rhythm of a metronome. They accompanied their singing by gently clapping on the downbeat, providing a crisp percussive energy to the performance, actively driving it along. At once we all stood still and watched intently, mesmerised by the joyous sounds emanating from these 150 or so girls whose ages must have ranged from five to fifteen. Then, remembering the nature of my mission here, I quickly produced my minidisc recorder from my bag and moved towards the girls to begin recording this spectacular aural treat. These sounds, I knew, could be sampled and incorporated in any future musical composition I might produce as a result of this visit. Adjusting the levels on my small machine and pointing my microphone towards the children, I must have appeared like a strange alien who had infiltrated their world. And in some ways, I was.

We were treated to four songs in all, the lyrics mostly being English but nonetheless difficult to comprehend given only the approximate pronunciation of the words. Of the discernible lyrics, my favourite was the simplest:

'*Number one, number one, we are number one.*'

I liked to think that after I had used the technology of 'sampling' to incorporate their voices into three and half minutes of commercial pop, then 'Number One' is exactly what they'd be – the proceeds from the smash hit providing classrooms not just for this school but for every one in the region. Oh, how I dream.

'Are you going to be all right on that thing?' I was asked as I wobbled around on the bicycle which Justin had just wheeled into the compound.

'I haven't done this for years,' I said, displaying all the authority of a child whose father had just released his supportive hands from the bike's frame for the first time.

'Are you sure you know what you're doing?'

'Yes, it's all coming back to me. You don't forget this. It's just like riding a bike.'

Bicycles, I've decided, are brilliant things. They don't cough pollution into the atmosphere, and cycling them gives you excellent aerobic exercise. Not only that, but when in motion they are pleasing on the ear, and they neatly obviate any need to place trust in garage mechanics. Along with the pumps for fresh water supplies and the introduction of medical vaccinations, these little contraptions had to be one of the more valuable contributions which foreign aid had provided. Yambio's muddy, bumpy tracks were packed full of a furiously peddling population, most of whom were sporting large grins. It made quite a contrast with the expressions of car drivers, whose stress levels force them towards the obscenity of 'road rage'. Where I was right now, perched on my neat little saddle, the prospect of witnessing any 'bicycle rage' did indeed seem distant.

'Do people have padlocks for their bikes?' I asked Justin as we pedalled our way up a busy artery which was leading us to the hospital.

'No, there is no need. People do not steal.'

This I liked. The concept of a padlock-free society. I asked Justin if there was any crime at all.

'Yes, there is a prison.'

'And who is in it?'

'People who have taken others' lives. And adulterers.'

Immediately I thought of our overcrowded prison population in the West and I wondered whether our town centres would have room for anything other than prisons if we counted adultery as a felony.

We cycled past roadside (or, more accurately trackside) traders, who were selling seeds, herbs and fruit. To most of these merchants, the sight of a white man on a bike was most unusual, but it was funny, too, and while some smiled and waved, most of them laughed heartily. I should have expected as much. Although I wasn't singing or playing football, I had another act up my sleeve as a trick cyclist, and that could still get the punters rolling in the aisles. Never before had a combination of pedalling and sweating caused such unbridled laughter, but then not everyone had my comic timing. As I listened to the shrill sounds of the laughter reverberate through the trees of the surrounding rainforest, I resigned myself to the fact that whatever I did here was going to be the source of immense amusement, unless of course I'd stood on a box and delivered my stand-up comedy routine. Ironically that probably would have left my audience stony-faced and confused. (Tragically, it wouldn't have been the first time.)

'We turn right down here for the hospital,' announced Justin, braking suddenly to avoid overshooting the turning.

After a hundred yards of narrow path we found ourselves dismounting in a courtyard which was full of people seated in the shade of its four large trees. They were silently and patiently awaiting treatment, with an air of resignation about them, many not being able to afford the limited medicines and treatments which the hospital could offer. Justin led me into one of the four shacks which surrounded the courtyard and into a sparse room which served as a hospital ward, the complete absence of medical equipment meaning that the sick people were the only clue as to its identity.

Visiting any hospital is a humbling experience primarily because it invariably involves seeing those who are suffering when you are in a relative state of good health yourself. This one, however, left me with a new feeling of numbness. Although a Norwegian aid agency provided assistance to operations here, there seemed to be little evidence of it anywhere in the immediate environs of Justin's wife, who was perched on one of the few beds in the ward. Many of the patients simply lay stretched out on the floor. The pungent smell of sickness momentarily threatened to overpower me and I had to work hard to stop myself from retching. As she was introduced, Justin's wife shook me weakly by the hand and tried to smile. Two things were immediately clear to me – she was in pain and she needed help. I felt frustrated at my powerlessness and after a brief and stilted conversation with her, I decided that enough was enough.

'I think we should go now,' I said uncomfortably, turning to a dulled Justin.

'OK.'

Just for now, there was nothing more to say.

'I will show you where I live now,' announced Justin, as the motion of our bikes began to revive the senses which had been deadened by the hospital visit.

An eagle circled above a banana tree, and the sun's rays smothered us like a gigantic hot towel. I wobbled on my bike as I took a sip from my bottle of water. A group of young girls giggled. I felt better. The world of suffering was five minutes behind us now. Time, the great healer, was already working its wonders on me, but I just wondered what it might do for those whom we'd left stretched out on the hospital floor.

The twenty-minute cycle to Justin's home involved the negotiation of a labyrinthine sequence of twisting, bumpy, pot-holed paths among which Yambio's dwellings were dotted. These constituted a circular plot, around which four or five mudhuts were neatly arranged. I was afforded a unique glimpse of another world as I peered into these primitive domiciles. Mothers toiled, very often weighed down with a baby or two strapped somewhere about their person, and children were playing. Ah, the children – how delightful they were. The Azande are an attractive race with good bone structure and an open and welcoming physiognomy, but their kids are just stunning. Barefoot and beautiful they ran, beaming and joyous among the *tukuls*, oblivious to their dubious destinies. They smiled and waved at this strange pallid onlooker, who felt privileged and exhilarated to be seeing what was unfolding before him, like he'd been allowed to step into the past. Apart from tattered Western clothes everything was as it would have been for centuries. I imagined myself to be one of the first white explorers, except that I was going to be a benevolent one who wasn't going to foist his religion and culture upon the people. I'd just give them a bar of melted chocolate and then move on.

'This is it,' called Justin to the explorer behind him. 'This is where I live.'

We dismounted in the middle of the charming and well-kept ring of tiny mudhuts and I was invited into the furthest one on the left. Inside this small circular space which was presumably the reception area, we took a break from the power of the afternoon sun. Justin offered me a refreshing drink but I refused, fearing that my stomach might not have the requisite fortitude to withstand an onslaught of Sudanese water. I felt it unlikely that 'Yambio Spring' had compared that favourably in tests alongside Evian, Perrier, Highland Spring and the rest.

'How many people live here?' I asked, pointing to the four other huts which were distributed evenly around the neat little plot.

'Me, my wife and our two children, and my wife's two sisters and their three children.'

'So there are nine people in this small area,' I said a little hesitantly, unsure of my maths.

'Yes. Nine. But it is OK.'

'Why aren't the husbands of your two sisters here?' I asked, half expecting him to tell me that they'd been killed in the conflict.

'They left Yambio when it was liberated by the SPLA. We think that they have gone to one of the neighbouring countries but I have no way of knowing where they are.'

'Why did they leave?'

'They are refugees of the war.'

I questioned Justin on this subject for a further five minutes but failed to get a satisfactory answer as to why his brothers-in-law had fled. It would have to remain one of the mysteries of this complex war, but whatever the uncertainty surrounding the reasons for their disappearance, the real victims of it were skipping around just outside. The children.

'Justin, did you fight in the war?' I asked.

'No,' he replied, 'I did not have to because the chief knew my position.'

'What do you mean?'

'The way we find our soldiers is not done politically

and we do not have subscription. When the army need support then the commanders call on the chief and he does the recruiting. If you are a father and he has already taken one of your children to fight, then he will not come and take another. If you have two or three then he will take one. For me, the chief knew that I was an orphan already, and he will not take me today because he knows that there would be no one to look after this family.'

Had Justin been lucky? It was a difficult call. His circumstances had meant that he'd avoided being a part of the horrific dehumanising atrocities of war, and yet he'd been denied the love of a father or mother, or even a surrogate step-family. His had been a solitary struggle into adulthood. And here he was as an adult, entertaining the inquisitive white visitor in his front hut.

'When would be a good opportunity for you to introduce me to a musician?' I asked, rather abruptly changing the subject.

'I think it would be better to do it tomorrow.'

'Is that not leaving it a little late? I only have two more days here.'

'Tomorrow is good because there will be musicians everywhere. Tomorrow is the tenth anniversary of our liberation from the Khartoum government. There will be a party all day and musicians will be a big part of that.'

'So you could introduce me to some and we could see if anyone was interested in writing with me the following day?'

'Yes, this is not a problem.'

'So what shall we do now?'

'I think that you should meet Randolph.'

'OK.'

This sounded good to me. I'd always liked the name Randolph. It conjured up images of a rather plump and warm individual with a propensity to giggle without much prompting.

This Randolph fulfilled my expectations in terms of his weight only, because he turned out to be a rather serious individual, heavily involved with the SRRA (Sudanese Relief and Rehabilitation Association). Outside his *tukul* we shared a conversation which was almost drowned out by the all-too-frequent crowing from a nearby cock.

'What does the SRRA do?' I asked him, after just having declined another refreshing drink.

'The SRRA is an organisation which has been set up to monitor human rights abuses,' he began in a rather ponderous and pleasingly Randolphish manner. 'We organise workshops and seminars to try and re-educate people in this region.'

'What kind of problems are you addressing?'

'Well, there is the soldier who goes away for a long time. He is not paid, so he is vulnerable to activities related to human rights abuse.'

'Being things like what?'

'Raping,' he said rather solemnly. 'The soldier is entitled to rape.'

'According to whom? The army?'

'According to the situation that is facing the soldiers. Because they are away from home. This, however, is a situation that we wish to change.'

'What other abuses are there?'

'Well, not far from here we have people marrying children. The cattle-keepers look at their children as a source of income and they may sell their daughters to an old man who has a lot of money. This we also want to change.'

'Is it working?'

'We think so, but we have a lot of work to do.'

Randolph could only have been in his late twenties

but he appeared to have the wisdom of a much older man, his manner at this moment not being unlike that of a chief who was sharing an audience with another dignitary. I decided to quiz him on something which had begun to fascinate me in the last few days.

'Randolph, the people here seem very happy, in spite of the difficulties. Why do you think that should be?'

'The British came here with the intention of educating us through religion, but they didn't do enough. What they did was give us four years and after that they left us to the Arabs who were far better educated and with many more resources. Now, they use our riches to enrich themselves.'

Randolph, it was becoming clear, had all the skills of a politician. He was taking this opportunity to tell me what he thought I needed to hear rather than honouring me with an answer to my question.

'We are growing through this war,' he continued, still failing to address the question of happiness, 'and, of course, we are ending our lives in the same war. Unless the international community intervenes and creates a forum where we are able to iron out our differences with the Khartoum government, then the war will go on and on and on.'

'I hope you find peace,' I said as I got to my feet, indicating my wish for the meeting to end.

'I hope you enjoy tomorrow's celebrations,' he offered with a meaningless shrug as he shook my hand.

'I will,' I replied, confident that this would indeed be the case.

I couldn't have been more wrong. I awoke the following morning with a fever and an aching body. I couldn't move. I lay there, hurting, not just physically but emotionally, too. This was nothing short of a disaster. Instead of meeting Sudanese musicians, I was going to spend the day in the same manner as it had started, wretched and bedridden. How could this have happened? I'd been so careful not to drink the water and I'd eaten pretty much the same as everyone else, and yet something had reformed my constitution. Damn.

The concerned visitors to my tent offered their sympathy, along with an array of unsuitable medicines from their personal first-aid kits.

'How do you feel?' each one would ask, as they stooped to enter the tent of the sick one.

'Awful,' I replied, shortly before the visitor offered their theory as to why I'd ended up feeling that way.

'Maybe you overdid the cycling in the Sudanese sun.'

Yes, maybe I had done, but frankly that was an irrelevance now and all that mattered was that I felt crappy. Too crappy in fact to tell people how unwanted their theories were.

The worst diagnosis was yet to come, and it was given by a local doctor who'd been summoned to my tent after having been spotted making his way to the tenth anniversary celebrations. He made a brief examination and asked the same old routine questions which are so basic that they do leave you wondering why doctors spend years qualifying, instead of just a couple of months.

'I am afraid that you have malaria,' he finally declared, almost triumphantly.

'But I can't have malaria,' I replied in disbelief.

'You have all the symptoms,' he said, reaching into his bag. 'You should take a course of anti-malarial tablets.'

'But I don't have malaria.'

'I see. You have decided this, yes?'

'Yes, I have decided this, yes.'

The doctor made his way from the tent and I heard

the short exchange which took place outside.

'So, Doctor, what do you think?'

'I think,' he replied, 'that the patient has malaria. The patient, however, does not.'

I had pretty good grounds for doubting this medic. Not only had I been taking the anti-malarial drug Lariam, I was also pretty certain that I hadn't actually been bitten by a mosquito, and anyway, even if I had, I'd definitely read somewhere that malaria takes a minimum of nine days to develop after you've been the reluctant recipient of the bite. Even in my present state of delirium I knew that this quack's maths were suspect.

Malaria or not, my visit to this place was pretty much over. The spectacle of Yambio in celebration was to remain unseen, and its musicians would play without the scrutiny of my watchful and opportunistic eye. In the distance I could hear the sound of drums and occasional gunshots, but unlike my travelling companions who had departed to immerse themselves in this rich cultural experience, I was left in my tent to sweat profusely and wallow in the damp sheets of self pity. Occasionally I'd break the monotony by throwing up.

Damn.

'How are you today?' asked Justin, having returned from ferrying the others into Freedom Square.

'Not good, I'm afraid.'

I explained my symptoms and was more than a little frustrated by Justin's response.

'I think that you have malaria.'

'*I don't have malaria!*' I shouted, foolishly squandering precious resources of energy.

Poor Justin looked a little hurt, but not like someone who'd just made a mistake. It was as if my quick outburst had made him even more certain of his diagnosis. Flying off the handle and denying that you have malaria is probably one of the more recognisable symptoms of the disease.

'Here,' he said, offering me a glass of water. 'You must drink lots of this today.'

I was touched by Justin's concern. He stayed with me for a full half hour, mainly just sitting quietly, but occasionally uttering some quiet words of commiseration. I was in too much discomfort to offer any responses. At one point he leaned forward and pointed to my guitar which was leaning rather forlornly against the bed.

'May I play?' he asked.

'Do you know how?' I managed, with a groan.

'Yes, I learned it in the church.'

I made an attempt at a nod in the direction of the instrument, and Justin picked it up and began to strum a rhythm and sing a few lyrics, presumably in his native Azande dialect. It was not bad at all, and he clearly had a reasonable guitar technique (although from his singing you might have thought that he was the one with suspected malaria, not me). I was suddenly struck by the irony of the situation. Here I was, a man who had made it his mission to find someone in Yambio with whom he could collaborate musically, and as it turned out, the very person he had charged with finding this potential co-writer had turned out to be precisely that man himself. There was probably a moral in there somewhere, but I was definitely too ill to work it out. In my present state all I could do was listen to Justin's lilting renditions, and lament the belated discovery of his musical prowess.

'Justin, that was very nice,' I said, when he had finished the song. 'Now please could you pass my bag over to me?'

He did so, and I rummaged around in it until I found my wallet.

'Here,' I said, thrusting some dollars in his direction. 'This is for your wife's operation.'

Justin looked at the money and then gently leaned forward and took it.

'Thank you. Thank you Tony,' he whispered gently. 'This will make things much easier for me and for my family.'

I had been considering making this gesture from the moment I'd seen his wife suffering quietly in the hospital, but until now I'd not wanted to unbalance our relationship with such a gesture. For me, it was not a huge amount of money – no more than the cost of a meal for two back in London – and yet I knew that here, on the front line, it was going to make a huge difference.

'It is my pleasure,' I said. 'I hope that things continue to get better for all of you.'

I had been anticipating this moment for some time, and it felt good finally to be doing some giving. Something in me, however, had expected this to be a warmer and more emotional moment. In spite of Sudan's heat and the warm-hearted nature of the transaction which had just taken place, there was a cool atmosphere in the tent. It was difficult to fathom.

I was still awake at 4 am, and it wasn't just my relentless fever which was keeping me awake. The people of Yambio had decided to rub salt in my wounds by partying into the night. The distant sound of drums seemed to mock me as I lay there wondering what exciting opportunities would have been opening up for me had I not been ambushed and assaulted by this wretched fever. I longed for the snugness of my own bed, and for all the familiar comforts of home. I knew only too well that for all the positive observations I had made about life here – the laughter, the sense of community, the lack of cars or padlocks, the stress-free simplicity of life – there were much better places in which to fall ill. Unlike the unfortunate occupants of the hospital and those waiting in the courtyard outside it, three different aircraft were soon going to whisk me to a place where I could feel cosy and unwell, instead of just unwell. I reminded myself how lucky I was. Yep, I felt like shite, but I was lucky.

Justin came to my tent in the morning.

'Are you feeling better today?' he enquired, sensitively.

'A little.'

He ambled over to the far side of the tent and looked down at my belongings which were untidily strewn all over the ground.

'This is very fine,' he said, picking up and studying my camera. 'We cannot get these here.'

There was a pause. He looked uncomfortable and a little restless.

'What's the matter?' I enquired.

'Do you need this camera?' he asked.

'What do you mean?'

'This could be very helpful to me in finding money for my family.'

'How?'

'There are people in Yambio who would like to have their families photographed. I could take their pictures and sell them the photos.'

'But where could you get the film developed?'

'This I would have to do in Uganda. But I have ways of getting this done.'

What a palaver, I thought. Personally I would have waited until 'Snappy Snaps' had set up in Yambio.

'There is a problem, Justin,' I said after a moment's reflection. 'I really want to take pictures documenting my journey back to England and I need the camera for that.'

'Oh.'

'I'm sorry.'

'It would be very helpful to me and my family.'

'Justin, I'm sorry but I need it.'

I didn't actually need it as much as I was making out. I could easily have got duplicates of photos taken by my fellow travellers, but I was confused by what I felt about this latest request. Hadn't I already helped Justin enough? Wasn't he being a little greedy here? After all, I'd paid for his wife's operation. I needed time to think about this one, and in my position of supine immobility, I had plenty of time to do just that.

But time, as it inexorably does, ran out.

'So Tony, what a bummer you being ill,' sympathised Irvine, as we stepped from the minibus on to the red mud of Yambio's makeshift airstrip. 'It means you didn't get what you wanted from this trip, did you?'

'That's not necessarily the case,' I replied, tapping my minidisc player which was hanging round my neck. 'I have the girls from the school singing. With the technology of sampling I can do a kind of collaboration with them.'

'A collaboration which they know nothing about?'

'Yes.'

'That's the best kind of collaboration, if you ask me.'

There was a short delay while twenty or so villagers unloaded what looked like a tractor engine from the waiting Cessna aircraft. Still feeling well below my best, I sat down in one of the seats which had been removed from the plane, and waited for the first leg of the journey back home to begin. When Justin approached me I thought that he was going to thank me and wish me a pleasant and safe return journey.

'Tony, I know that you said before that it would not

be possible,' he began. 'But I wonder if you have been able to change your mind?'

I shrugged, implying that I did not know what he meant.

'Do you think it might be possible for me to have your camera?' he asked, almost in an apologetic whisper.

My heart sank. I had forgiven Justin his previous over-zealousness in this matter but now his persistency was beginning to make me question my whole relationship with him. Had Justin had an agenda from the moment he took my guitar from me a few days before? What had his motives been for visiting me in my tent and generally looking after me? Did his bold request stem from a genuine need, or was he something of a chancer?

I had a strong feeling that I should be firm with him and refuse his entreaty. But then again, another part of me didn't want to be mean. Didn't I have a responsibility to help this man and his family? After all, one of the reasons I'd accepted the offer of this trip to Sudan was because I'd wanted to make a difference, and here I was with a real opportunity to do exactly that. How could I be sure that the root of my uncomfortable feelings wasn't linked to my own ego, and that what I'd wanted was for this man to have been so moved by my initial gift that he should have felt too humble to have broached the subject of another?

'Justin, if I give you this camera, are you certain that it could improve things for you and your family?' I asked, when the expeditious soul-searching was over.

'Yes.'

'And you can really get the film developed in Uganda?'

'Yes.'

'In that case, I want you to smile while I finish off this film with pictures of what you looked like immediately prior to becoming the owner of a new camera.'

And so the final photographs I would shoot with this camera featured a man grinning from ear to ear. I didn't even need to get him to say 'cheese'.

Heathrow was cold and unwelcoming. It seems that the hotter the climate of the country from which one has begun one's return journey, the more damp, grey and blustery the climes provided by England's awaiting airport. That's just the way it is – it's some kind of unwritten law of nature. Personally I blame New Labour.

The last two hours of the journey had left me restless and confused. The reason had been the conversation I'd had with Abi, the *Telegraph* photographer who'd been with us for the duration.

'You know you said how wonderful it was that Yambio was a town with no padlocks?' she'd said. 'Well, I noticed when I was taking pictures at Justin's home, that he had a padlock on one of his *tukuls*.'

The revelation had sent my mind racing. A padlock? What did he have to lock away? Hadn't he told me there was no theft in Yambio? I became worried that I'd been duped into giving to a kind of southern Sudanese 'Del Boy'. Well – he had a lock-up, didn't he?

I began to wonder if I had engaged in the wrong kind of giving, and I devoted my thoughts to this matter as we completed the final leg of our retreat to the land of a million padlocks. It now seemed clear to me that giving is something which should be done on a daily basis to those all around us, in terms of time, consideration and love. The problem is that in certain situations we give carelessly and, by so doing, we unwittingly upset the gentle economic balance of a society. For instance, back in the bar in Yambio we had paid for our beers with a twenty-dollar bill and this had immediately begun to alert the greedy and opportunistic in the community. As a direct consequence of our 'generosity' another bar was immediately opened especially for us with a view to enabling us to be generous once again. How much of this money would have filtered through to the rest of the community?

If we'd stayed in Yambio, and if we'd soon been joined by hundreds of tourists like us, then how long before we'd have created a new affluent élite who fed off our wealth, exploiting the town's resources and caring little for the old way of life which had supported their society for centuries? Our gesture had looked generous, but it had been too easy and much in the manner of over-indulgent parents who don't spend enough time with their kids, and then shower them with expensive presents to assuage their guilt. Time and love, those are the greatest gifts of all.

I concluded that I shouldn't have given Justin my camera. Giving it had been largely a selfish act. I'd wanted the power of feeling like I was making a difference, and I'd wanted to bask in the glory of the gesture. My motives hadn't been dishonourable, but they could have been channelled in a more mature way. There were people who understood better than I how to distribute wealth in these parts of the world – people who had experience, who knew what does and doesn't upset a society's gentle equilibrium; people who were already in place – drilling boreholes for fresh water supplies, supplying vaccines and handing out bicycles. I'd have been better off helping them instead of giving Justin a leg up into the murky world of African entrepreneurialism. No, I shouldn't have given Justin my camera, for all the above reasons. Oh yes, there was another reason, and although it may not have been as profound as the others, it was valid nonetheless. If I'd hung on to my camera then I wouldn't have had to go straight out and buy another.

In the splish-splashy wet gloom of a grim Heathrow morning, I made my weary farewells and jumped in a cab which would soon speed me to the warmth of a familiar bed where I could nurse my ersatz malaria.

'Gor, you look brown, mate,' declared the cabbie, chirpily. 'You been somewhere hot?'

I wasn't yet ready for the inane banter of the cab conversation, so I offered a deliberately abstruse reply which would guarantee a peaceful journey.

'Time and love, those are the greatest gifts of all,' I offered devoutly, already seeing a furrowed brow forming in the driver's rear mirror. 'And I am going to give a song, sung by some lovely schoolchildren.'

It had worked well. The cabbie was now genuinely scared of me.

'Hmm,' he mumbled nervously. 'Where do you want to go?'

'Wimbledon. Oh, and if you pass a camera shop ... '

Fish River

ANDREW O'HAGAN

Our sun is a pot of golden fire in a world without end our escort and our judge. All the hours of our lives we witness the passing of the sun.

In the old times, long, long ago, it shone for the mothers of our grandmothers, and also for our neighbours, whose spirits come walking now in the shadow of the sun that is always the same. Each day it moves across the sky. When the sun is gone, we sit beside fires, we laugh, we drum and we speak in the night, we laugh and we sing when nothing remains, but always we long for the warmth of the sun and the same old love.

There is no moisture. The slave train is coming from the north and it is not far from here. We cannot see the train nor hear it but we feel its movement. This is not the time for rain or for grass growing in the field. What we smell is fire. Out there the cattle bend in the day's heat. The smell of fire comes over the wind. You will not see our children asleep in the arms of time. The train may come today.

Geng Kuack Athiang takes his hands from his knees and makes a hole with them to look at the Jesus. It is only another yellow day in the middle of his hands. Geng's arms are covered in dung-ash and the sky is blue as Geng smiles and unfurls his legs in the dust so dry at this hour. He wears a shirt that came from the centre for vaccinations. 'Texas Instruments.' The words are faded to nothing now only specks of paint. Geng strokes the words on his chest with spread fingers.

On the ground in front of the boy there is a stub of pencil and a school jotter. There are sums and words on every square of the paper. Geng sits with a group of children under the shade of a Kuel tree at the centre of the village. He puts his hands into the dust until they grow cool. There is no movement in the leaves of the village tree. There is no sound, only the smell of burning comes on the wind as Geng opens his mouth and laughs, the yellow of the Jesus in the middle of his hands. In the village of Wargeng the Dinka believe in the Jesus who died on the cross. Our children are learning the story of salvation under the Kuel tree. But this summer of guns is long: in the village of Wargeng we know to eat hope with the millet and the sorghum.

'Out of the sky death comes in oil drums,' the teacher says, 'and we must beware of evil. Out of the White Nile danger comes in many forms. It comes with noises.'

The children sing the national song. The teacher is proud of the singing and the children standing. There is peace in the way they sing and they are smiling and the Kuel tree is still and the sun is always the same. The children rub the ashes on themselves. Out in the desert, beyond the cattle, Geng can see herons crossing the air. A cow moves in the distance. I know the boy wonders how it would be to hold a rifle.

He puts up his hand. 'Child,' says the teacher.

'The story of the donkey and the wolf and the fox,' says Geng, 'can you tell this story?'

The teacher wears a white robe and he draws in the dust with a stripped branch. Lifting the branch over his head he curls his arms around it. He smiles at Geng and nods at him so the other children look round at the boy. 'Geng Kuack Athiang,' the teacher says, 'the story is for you to tell. The others will listen. Stand here under the tree and tell us the story of the donkey and the wolf and the fox.'

The Kuel tree is in fact several trees that have joined together over the years. A palm tree has been uprooted by the growth of the Kuel and made one with it: the trunk is the thickest to be seen in any village. Geng stands up against the warm bark of the tree and he smells the fire coming on the air and the dwellings of Wargeng are loud now with singing and talking in the afternoon. The boy thinks of his dead cousin Bol Bol Makiew who loved to tell stories in the night with the stars over the fire. Geng felt afraid against the tree but he took courage thinking the story might go into the hearts of his brothers. Geng touched the words on his T-shirt and stamped his foot to begin. 'It is told that a donkey lived in the old times,' said Geng, 'when all things spoke in the same language.'

As the boy begins speaking, the teacher wonders silently if there is whisky or guns in the distance. He wonders if the large bird across the desert can hear the voice of the boy under the tree and envy him. Teacher feels the village is being looked at. In this country every grain of sand is an unmoistened eye. Yet the boy who remembers goes on with his song. The schoolchildren gather at trunk of the tree in the shadows and soon there is a love of Geng's voice singing his song under the same sun and the same sky.

'The donkey was very hungry all summer long. He was very thin. He became just skin and bones. He was about to die. And just in time the rain came and the grass was green to the horizon. There were flowers in the grass and all was healthy and green as far as the eye could see. The donkey went into the grass and ate it and never looked back at the village. He enjoyed every minute of his time there, the grass was so green and so healthy, and the donkey so hungry, he stayed in the field with every flower until he was strong and fat, eventually forgetting how near he had once been to death.'

As Geng speaks teacher collects the books. There is little left of the pencils. Outside one of the nearby huts a rooster squawks and flaps, then comes the sound of women singing on the other side of the village. As Geng tells the story he can see the women becoming one with the vapour in the distance over the place of the cattle and the planting. He will always remember the shape of the women, cloths wrapped around them, with jars on their heads, walking past the cattle nuzzling the ground. The women of Wargeng are forbidden from touching the animals.

'One day the donkey heard a whisper of feet behind him in the grass. He looked around to see a hungry wolf with a mouthful of sharp teeth sloping through the grass. Eventually the wolf was only a spear's-throw from the donkey and the donkey knew the wolf wanted to eat him. The fat donkey ran and ran; he ran as fast as he could but the wolf was always behind him. At last the donkey ran into a muddy swamp and got stuck. The wolf thought he had finally got the donkey and he followed him into the swamp. A few yards from the donkey he got stuck also. He tried to go back but found he could not.'

Geng is shaking both hands and stamping his feet as he tells the story. The dust rises. The more he tells of the story the more he puts out of his mind the same heat of the day and the sound of the women going in the distance. The story was everything and everything was the story: Geng himself was the story, and as he stamped his foot he became a thing of words, the flesh and blood of speech.

'Then Abul Hussein, the fox, came wandering by. He was a very wily fox and he knew how to trick everyone. Abul Hussein was clever but he was wicked; he knew how to get the better of other animals, and he looked at the stuck pair with his slow eyes. "Oh Abul Hussein!" said the wolf, "things are very bad for me. I find myself in a bad situation."

The fox was at his worst. "What is this bad situation?" he asked the wolf.

"I am stuck here," said the wolf, "I tried to catch and eat the donkey but I am now stuck here, as is he. I cannot get back to the road."

"The worst is still to come," said Abul Hussein. "The sun will soon rise and the mud will dry and catch your legs. The farmer will come to look for his donkey and he will bring his gun." When Abul Hussein said this the wolf cried out and then it died of fear in the marsh. When the sun came up the farmer did come looking for his donkey. He found it in the marsh, half-eaten, with a dead wolf stuck in the marsh behind it. The farmer was upset but he skinned the wolf and made a good coat of his skin.'

Under the sun and the Kuel tree Geng stands and smiles at the clapping of his schoolmates, and out there, in the desert, the herons cross the air of the afternoon. The women have disappeared from view.

The railway line from Khartoum into the southern reaches of Sudan is not used for most of the year. From north to south, it runs past green rivers and dusty villages, where people speak in different tongues and live with the same fear.

Early each year a hundred or more Government bandits board the train and head into the south. Many more ride on horses beside the slow-moving train, shooting and waving swords, drinking from bottles, making war cries. You can smell them coming.

In the afternoon Geng's mother and some other women had gone out of the village to collect baobab fruits and eakuadhai grass. They knew the train was near. They had gone in fact to collect these foods in preparation for a long journey. The village was about to be abandoned for the season. They knew the train was coming from the north.

Geng's mother was out beyond the field with others. They sang as they walked and they could feel the sun and see the dust rising over the trees and still hear the chanting of the schoolchildren behind them in Wargeng. It only faded when they were a long way off.

The Arabs ride out from the train. They go for miles from the train with their guns ready and madness in their eyes. This afternoon, the day Geng's mother and her neighbours walked over the plain, a group of forty or more Arabs descended from the wavering horizon and the women of Wargeng crouched around their jars under the hot sun. Many of the men on horses wore black and some had military uniforms and they wore cloths. They fired guns over the heads of the women and one of the women who ran with her jar was shot in the side and she lay bleeding. Several of the jars lay broken with water seeping into the sand. Four of the men took Geng's mother and they tore her clothes. One of them made his horse crouch on the ground and two of the men lifted Geng's mother on to the back of the horse. They tore off her beads. They spat in her face. Each of them raped her over the back of the horse with the bone of the saddle digging her back. They spat on her again at the end and they tied her hands behind her back. Around them the other men did these things. The women's screams went into the air.

Geng's mother woke on a moving train. There were women and children from many villages loaded into a metal wagon smelling of oil. From inside the train the women could hear the roaring of the men outside. They heard the hooves of the horses padding the sand. There was a pot of dirty water sloshing over the floor of the wagon. Geng's mother put her hand into the pot and rubbed wet fingers over her swollen tongue.

'I do not know the name of the one we should ask for help,' said Geng's mother to the woman bleeding in the dark beside her. The woman had been whipped and her nose was broken. She was hoarse with thirst. 'The baby Jesus Christ,' said the woman as she lay in her ripped coverings.

This was told to us. This is the story of our village and all that was said and all that happened. All our voices are bound together in this story of the end of Wargeng. My name is Arou Deng Arou. I speak with the voices of all. And now you must translate as it pleases you. I sing the song of my ancestors and praise the beasts which live as we live and die in our midst. I will tell the stories as they are told to me and as they now are expected of me under the sun and in the eyes of the Jesus. Let all words be unshakeable as the tree.

Some of the soldiers who captured the women of Wargeng came to the village that day to kill us all. Many of the children had ran with their mothers to the next village and some had gone to hide in the bush. Geng Kuack Athiang ran from his dwelling and climbed the Kuel tree when the gunshot started. The Arabs arrived on horses and they shot the people running. Geng could see his neighbours lying in the dust with blood pouring or their legs. The screams of the village people rose in the air and seemed to Geng to shake the very leaves of the tree.

The men on horses made cries in Arabic. Geng crouched among the boughs and looked at the cattle on the horizon. He wanted to praise the cattle and also to cry to them for help. He asked that they come from the fields with milk for the dying. Geng looked at the cattle and begged for their help. He could see some of the villagers running with the cattle in the smoke and the sound of gunshot. They were trying to collect the cows and run with them to another place. They prayed to the cows. From the branches of the tree Geng beseeched the cattle in the same way but also he mumbled the words of a prayer to the Jesus taught to him by the Christian Brothers. He tasted fire and blood as he gripped the tree.

Some of the Arabs tied their horses to the shell of a truck burned the year before. The horses made cruel and sickening noises. Some of the new huts were already ablaze and Geng could see the cattle running, and see that some of the village men behind them were lying on the ground. In the distance he could hear people screaming in Arabic. He remembered his mother. When Geng turned his cheek on the warm bark of the tree he could see Aher Arol Aher, the oldest man in the village, making his escape on a bicycle. The boy knew he was going to the next village to bring the men with guns to fight the Arabs.

The huts burned. Geng could hear voices shouting 'You are dogs! You are bitches! We will kill you foolish dogs on the ground!' The Arabs stripped the clothes from one of the cattlemen and made him stand beside his burning house. His son, a tall school friend of Geng's named Thuc Mawien Deng, went to his knees, and he begged the bandits to spare his father. His red eyes were flooded with tears. He turned them up to the sun. And then he looked at his father who was quiet and ready. 'If they kill you and drop your body somewhere,' said Thuc Mawien Deng, 'we will find you and bring you back to be buried among us.' The boy's father kept his eyes steady in front as the Arabs danced around him and the horses brayed in the smoke. 'I am proud to be buried at home with my father and my mother,' he said. One of the Arabs came running with a rough boulder and he pushed the cattleman into the dust and beat his stomach with the boulder until he was dead.

Geng Kuack Athiang saw this from the village tree. He could not speak and yet he struggled not to shout and so he licked the bark of the tree in his nervousness. Gunshot and screaming surrounded him beneath the tree. Geng closed his eyes. He knew his mother was out with the other women collecting fruit. Had they managed to hide from the Arabs? Was she safe in another village and thinking of him now? From the tree Geng heard a motor vehicle and he could see through the leaves that the SPLA men were entering the far end of the town and that they were already firing their rifles. The Arabs had rounded up the women and children of Wargeng who had not escaped. The men in the village were dead or they were herding the cattle to safety when the opposition's soldiers arrived.

The last Geng saw was the Arabs riding away howling at the sky and raising their rifles over their heads. A few of the SPLA soldiers followed them at a slower pace. Sometimes they stopped to take protection behind their vehicles, but still they followed, and shots were fired in the distance. Geng looked down at the smoke and through the smoke the weeping of the villagers. He waited for many minutes before he climbed down; he was not sure if they would return. His feet slapped down the trunk of the Kuel tree and he landed on the warm sand.

I am an old man. When I came back to the village I found Geng wandering among the terrible sights and singing a song I once taught him. Geng placed his hands over his face and he cried and sometimes he would bend down and speak to the dead. I took his arm and made him walk with me and several of the villagers who had survived – we walked in the setting sun to the next village. I promised Deng and his school friend Thuc Mawien Deng that we would return to Wargeng the next day. We would bury the dead and look for the people we love who are lost.

* * *

In the railway wagon smelling of oil the women wept and tried to hold each others' hands in the dark. One of the women was dead from her injuries – an Arab stabbed her with a knife when she tried to run – and now her two daughters lay with her in the middle of the wagon, wiping her cold face with cloths. Sometimes the train would stop for hours. Soon the sound of other woman and children would come: the sound of weeping and of men shouting in Arabic. The Arabs did not shoot at the women they had captured. They wanted to take them north. They wanted to save bullets.

Geng's mother and the other women were pulled out of the railway truck after several days. They could not speak for thirst. Many of the children were dead and the women who clung to life found it difficult to walk. The train had stopped in the desert. There was a farm there and many vehicles. The Arabs cut down some thorn trees and made a fence. The women and children of Wargeng were kept there with many others from villages along the railway line. A canister of water was given to them. Geng's mother spoke in whispers to Abuk, her friend from the village; they knew they were to become slaves. Abuk said they would be taken to the northern city. She said they would not see their families again. On the first night Abuk and her daughter were taken over the thorn fence with some others and put in the back of a vehicle. Abuk turned to Geng's mother as they pulled her out and she touched her face and asked that the Jesus would bless her and her son Geng. 'Your husband is with the Holy Lord and he watches you now,' she said, and then she went into the blackness.

There was a guard with the families and he beat them with the side of a machete and told them they were not human beings. At last the weeping stopped and the guard fell asleep sat on a wooden crate. Geng's mother picked at the thorn branches surrounding her; as the sun began to rise she saw that her hands were covered with blood and she had made a space to pass through. Making no noise, she crawled over the sand and then, at some distance, she rose to her feet and walked into the desert. She drank from a green river after walking for many hours. It is in God's hands, she said to herself as she looked to the sun for direction, and after many hours, she found the railway line. She sat on the rail and wept in her hands. If she followed it south she would reach the Fish River.

Geng did not go back to Wargeng the day after the massacre. When the others came back in the evening they said they had buried his teacher and many of his school friends. His mother was not there. The village was ash.

Two weeks later Geng walked to the railway line. When he got there he saw there was debris all around. He saw food containers and empty bags lying in the sand. He picked them up and saw they were covered in writing he was unable to read. He imagined it was English. Oil canisters and rubber wheels lay there, and empty bottles of Coca-Cola, bashed and dusty. Geng bent down and put his ear to the railway line. The metal was cool against his ear. He listened. There was nothing. He could see the railway line stretching for miles. It was like a spear. He kept his ear to the metal for a long time but he heard nothing and all he could see with his open eyes was the empty track until a heron came and perched on the rail up ahead. There was nothing else.

After some time Geng walked down the track until he reached Fish River. When he came down to the water he stopped in shock. Lying there, dead, with spread legs up on the sand and head and shoulders sunk in the water, was one of the Arab soldiers, flies buzzing over his remains. He was wearing some kind of uniform. A rifle lay beside him. Geng went down to the water. He pulled the dead man by his boots until his green-white face emerged from the water. There was a hole in the Arab's neck. His hands were black and swollen and there was a smell rising out of the body. As Geng pulled it from the water some creatures squirmed and escaped from his hair. The smell was very bad. The Arab's eyes were open and his eyes were not normal. Geng knew about dead bodies. We had taught him the things he must know. The Arab's blood had been attacked by the devils inside. He had been dead for more than a week. Geng lifted the rifle and poked the dead man's gut and saw that the soldier was soft.

He noticed there was movement in the pool. Geng sat on the sand with the smell of the rotting corpse high on the air and he watched these movements in the river and thought of what to do with the gun. He knew he would bring it back to me. I once told the child Geng Kuack Athiang that we storytellers must learn above all how to handle a rifle. He would bring it back. We have no freedom to throw rifles into green water. Geng's eyes went into Fish River: he could see that the movements were being caused by elephant snouts swimming just beneath the surface.

I told the child that we storytellers must now learn the words for everything under the sun. Elephant snout. In Dinka we say *Got.* In Arabic they say *khashm al banat.* In Zande they say *Tumbara.* In Shilluk they say *Ado Lakok.* In Nuer they say *Lentril.*

Got. Tumbara. Khashm al banat. Elephant snout.

The fish moved beneath the surface of the river in a day of our Lord Jesus two weeks and one day after the massacre of Wargeng. The fish pecked at the surface of the water and sent waves over the pool to the body of the dead soldier.

One day soon I will be another ghost weeping in the night. But the Jesus will comfort and protect me when I am no more. And Geng Kuack Athiang, the boy by the river and the railway with its spears of steel, will speak for all of us. He will speak. It will be his duty to speak as I am speaking now and you will hear him.

Geng's mother came in tatters to the new village as Geng stood against an acacia tree. When I saw her coming I ran with the boy and we laid blessings at her feet, which had carried her to us through the many broken villages of the south near the railway. She only left the railway track for water. And at the end, near the village, she could not drink the water of Fish River, for it was foul. Geng's mother had walked for sixteen days. Her son stamped his foot and sang for his mother. She wept into her torn clothes. 'I heard words I have never heard before,' she said, 'it was not an ordinary life but a life that is strange.'

Contamination

A NOVELLA IN REGRESS

IRVINE WELSH

For Robin Robertson

NOTE

Kumuara County, the towns of Hoki, Nambaro and Kroy and the Jamuri and Nazuri tribes are all products of my imagination. They don't exist in Sudan or anywhere else; they probably don't correspond to anybody's concept of the country, not even my own. I don't know much about Sudan: I was only there briefly to write a piece of fiction.

Bootleggers

In the slums of Nairobi a vengeful spirit was in the air. In a warehouse at the back of the meat-roasting district, three worried men had decided that it was time to leave town. Joseph, Marshall and Benjamin were urgently stacking their barrels and brewing equipment onto the back of the large truck they had rented. Jake, the driver whom they had employed to take them north, was in a highly agitated state.

– Hurry, he barked. – Time is short.

The decision to flee the city had followed the aftermath of the second major disaster for this gang of bootleggers. Their inaugural one, back in 1996, had seen them kill eight and blind six of their customers. Since then they had been very careful to fine-tune their brewing process, but subsequently the profit margins had fallen, even among the poorest consumers who could not afford the legitimate brews.

The word around Nairobi's slum areas and shanty-towns spread that the bootleg brew was not potent enough. The entrepreneurs had panicked and out of greed and desperation had taken action to extend their market share. This only precipitated their second major crisis. In the brewing process the men had added methylated spirits to their traditional blend of fermented corn and coconut juice. The effects, particularly on those who sampled the ale at the bottom of the barrels, were utterly devastating. Twenty-three drinkers died, and twenty-eight were left blinded for life.

Joseph and his friends knew that Kenya's laws against the manufacture and supply of illegal drugs, though strict on the statute book, were only sporadically enforced. The bootleggers could easily buy off the lawmen and minor officials, who were on poor salaries.

However, after the second spate of deaths, a group of local Christian women from the slums had declared war on the bootleggers. They had identified Joseph and his accomplices Marshall and Benjamin as the ringleaders of the enterprise and had harassed them everywhere in the local communities.

The bootleggers had retaliated ruthlessly.

One woman was badly beaten and another one was shot in the legs and then set on fire. Her injuries were bad, but not as bad as Joseph's, who had inadvertantly contrived, without noticing, to completely saturate the front of his own body with the spirit he then sparingly doused on the woman's legs. He was incapacitated with burns to his chest, stomach, thighs and genitals. As it was, the Christian women would not be deterred by the bootleggers' violence, and their campaign was given impetus by widespread local, national and international media coverage. One lingering image on CNN was of a tearful Marsha, a leader of the Christian women, contending emotionally, – God has taken our sons so that we might drive the demons from our community!

The media interest in the affair led to widespread pressure on the authorities, forcing them to take action, and they set up a special police task force to deal specifically with the bootleggers. So it was that Joseph and his men decided to leave Nairobi and head for the hard-living frontier town of Lokichoggio, a series of dwellings which had grown up around the Save Sudan base which served to bring international aid into rebel-held southern Sudan.

Benjamin, a wiry, excitable man, was especially delighted at this, being a native of Sudan and Kumuara County. Indeed, he was hoping to convince the others that it might be more prudent to cross the border and set up operations in Sudan itself.

– Lokichoggio is the place for us, Joseph contended. – It is an outlaw's town. Outlaws always need good, cheap brew.

Benjamin's large eyes widened, sucking in his colleague's attention. – It is also very dangerous, far more dangerous than Nairobi. Oh, my friend, the bandits they are terrible. And there are guns everywhere. I tell you this, we should press on as soon as we can and cross the border into southern Sudan. The girls will love our money, he held up a fistful of Kenyan shilling notes, – and our city ways, he rolled his large eyes and gyrated his hips. – Oh, they are so beautiful, you will see my friends, you will see!

– He will have little need of women for some time, Marshall, a tall, angular man smirked, looking at Joseph, who could not stop his hand involuntarily touching his raw genitals. In realisation, his face screwed up hatefully, and he mopped his sweating brow with a rag.

– You tell me there is a civil war up there, Joseph snapped choosing to turn on Benjamin, who had initiated this stupid talk of Sudan. – You say the country is governed by Muslims who cut off your hand if you drink alcohol. What will they do to us if we brew it!

Joseph was a slighter, shorter man than Marshall. He wore a thin moustache, which he was inordinately proud of. He was also the self-appointed leader of the group and Benjamin was slightly fearful of him.

Benjamin raised his hands in a placatory manner. – Yes, yes, yes, my friend, but my home in the Kumuara County is now very peaceful. The rebels are in control. They are not Muslim and they will welcome an enterprise like ours. We will be treated like heroes. I tell you my friend!

Jake the hired driver, full of fear and frustration and struggling with a crate, shouted at the arguing boot-leggers. He did not want anybody in Nairobi to find out he was working for them. – Hurry! Less talk! Time is short!

– Yes, Joseph agreed, – these madwomen will be on our trail soon. We will be going nowhere but the morgue or the prison.

They looked briefly at each other in wary acknow-ledgement, then recommenced their packing with great haste.

HEAT

In the Kumuara Province of southern Sudan, the small town of Kroy lay on the edge of the equatorial rainforest, just where it bordered on to grasslands which extended as far as the naked eye could see and beyond. At a deep well on the settlement's outskirts, Israel Kobache, an old warlord, who was clad in guerrilla soldier's camouflage clothes, wrapped a strong, bony hand around the pump. Then, as his underlings stood and watched nervously, he commenced a terse rhythmic action, pushing and pulling, hoping that this gesture and the dynamism of it would make the villagers who were gathering round view him as a man of action. The water took its time in coming and Israel's face screwed in tetchy impatience under a mask of moisture beads in the blistering sun.

Israel's hair was not just shorn but, contrary, to the custom of his people, was completely shaved. He regarded the grey, which naturally sprang from his skin, as a sign of weakness in a warrior. Nonetheless, the hair grew prolifically, and by noon would glint like metal-filings from his fine-featured, angular head, with a still taut skin remarkably free of creasing through lines of either laughter or worry.

So it was only in his eyes that you could truly gauge

the extent of the old warrior's years; a tired, dulled aspect to them evoked decades spent in harsh conditions of battle, under an unforgiving sun. These eyes were large, and of such apparent mass that it seemed as if they would fall like great stones from his head if he ever graced or deferred to bow it. Perhaps this, some of the Elders of Kroy were given to speculate, was why he never compromised in this manner. That head sat forward on an angled neck, which, with age's accentuation, now often gave the impression of being too weak to support it.

Israel's Lieutenant, Abraham, a tall, strongly built man of a taciturn front, whose darting, flighty eyes often hinted at a more calculating side to his character, held the vessel under the tap to catch the water, which spurted out in short bursts. Something briefly flashed in the edges of his vision and Abraham looked up and saw an eagle soar overhead, then glide and swoop, very much in its world, away from the human concerns below. Abraham felt a measure of envy with regards to the bird, and passed the brimming vessel to Israel.

The old warlord raised the clay bowl to his lips and sipped the water, letting the taste of it play on his palate, like a wealthy European in an exclusive restaurant might do, with some fine wine proffered at his table. Israel fancied he could taste something. Yes, there was a definite taint, possibly rust from the pipes, or perhaps even worse. A tumult rose in his breast and he spat the water out on to the dry, impacted soil. Turning to Abraham, he commanded: – I suspect contamination. Put a guard on all the wells, including this one!

Abraham saluted, barked affirmative and shouted at the sergeant, a tall, gauche-looking man named Anthony. He in turn sent a soldier, a young boy, over to the well. The boy looked almost ridiculous in his appropriated baggy, green, camouflage combat trousers, shirt and red beret. However, the large AK47 automatic machine gun he carried made it unlikely that any of the villagers, many of whom had borne first-hand witness to the rifle's power, would choose to comment on his attire. And his bearing and demeanour testified to the world that the youth most certainly knew this.

The old warlord stood erect, a belligerent set to his mouth, and Abraham mirrored this stance, keeping his own posture rigid. The old man was in one of his moods. Though exceptionally cynical of Israel's obsession with the wells, Abraham knew better than to voice his opinion. The old man was growing frailer in body, but he was as strident in attitude and as intolerant and truculent to any perceived flouting of his authority as ever. – I want you to question the villagers. Find out who has been hanging around by the well over the last ten days, with particular regard to any strangers, Israel ordered, and then turned away sharply.

– Yes sir, Abraham replied, as he watched the sloped shoulders but still rigid back of the old man head to the front passenger seat of his truck. The motor started and Israel's vehicle headed back into the village and to the clearing where he lived, which contained several small brick-built and thatched-roofed *tukuls*.

Back at the well, and happy that his commander was out of sight, Abraham raised the bowl to his lips and sipped. The water tasted fine. There would be another pantomime to go through again this week.

As he drank, Abraham looked up at the young guard by the pump. They held each others' gaze for traces of complicity, then on Abraham's initiative, exchanged quick grins. Abraham briefly wondered how the circumstances of the boy's recruitment into the army had differed from his own. In the hazy sunshine, he struggled to remember a time before war; it now seemed to belong not just to another life, but to somebody else's life. Yet he could still recall, through a fuzzier lens now, his days farming near the Kenyan border, trying to make an honest living, and being robbed at gunpoint by bandits, so many soul-destroying times. Then, one day, going into a frontier town to trade, he had been offered an AK47 assault rifle for the same price that he could have bought his intended purchase of a bag of grain. He'd thought about the men who had robbed him over the years. Not bad men mostly, just men like him; ones whose hearts had hardened in adversity until they made the simple calculation that a gun was a better investment than a bag of grain, for with the gun you could get all the bags of grain you wanted, and keep them. And a soldier never went hungry. The rebel army had grown up around such people, men, and some women, who were tired of being the victims of injustice, major and minor.

And he had become one of them.

Back in the shade of the *tukul*, in respite from the blistering heat, Israel, the old warlord, rested his weary flesh and bones on his bed. His thoughts were melancholy, as they tended to be when he was alone. His wife Rachael was gone, having succumbed two years ago to sleeping sickness. He had lost four sons: three in battle, another to the sickness, which had also claimed a daughter. That left only one son, Oliver, who was now a divinity student at a Ugandan Christian College. This younger boy, whom he scarcely knew, had had his education entrusted to Israel's late wife who had decided that she'd already lost enough sons in battle and because of this had sent her youngest one away.

The old warrior's extended family, the Jamuri tribe, was also in serious decline, their numbers falling yearly.

And then there was himself, now much older and mellower than when he had been feared and respected everywhere. Yes, he reflected he had been a great warlord, but now he was growing weary of the constant struggle between the in-fighting ragbag of the loose federation of liberation movements he belonged to, and the civil war with the Khartoum Government in the north. But even more so, he was tired of the constant local struggle between his people, the Jamuri and the neighbouring Nazuri tribe, lead by his great rival, Jacob Chidoze. It seemed perverse to remember that they were all supposed to be part of the same broad movement for the liberation of southern Sudan. So perverse, indeed, that they seldom even bothered to try.

Israel and Jacob had fought tooth and nail in the playground as children in southern Sudan's most prestigious school in Rumbek, a centre which most of the warlords from the various liberation movements and old tribes had attended. And they'd battled since, ceding and reclaiming territories from each other; costing lives, spilling blood, seizing land, cattle and property; murdering, looting, raping, burning.

Nominally, the dispute between the tribes was over a small strip of savannah, which contained the village of Hoki. This long-contested territory was now in Jacob's hands, and had been for a few years. In reality, the tribes just fought because they always had, or at least ever since the disastrous redrawing of the African map by the white man. The effect of lumping together weakened and fragmented groups of different cultural and linguistic traditions to suit the economic and strategic interests of white imperial powers had been, as intended, devastating for African unity. Now the institutionalised divisions remained, and were cast in the cold metal of the arms trade.

For generations this fighting had gone on, even when

the two tribes were supposedly united under the SPLA banner against the government in the north. With the discovery of the oilfields further south of the Jamuri and Nazuri's homelands, the Kumuara Province had lost strategic value to the Khartoum Government. With no Arab attacks to unify them, and the militarisation of their culture now embedded, the warlords were keen to turn on their older adversaries; each other.

The two old warlords played politics to curry favour with the senior SPLM Commissioners, who ruled most of the liberated parts of southern Sudan. They would engage in increasingly audacious acts of war against Government forces, often taking their own young children out of schools and sending them to fight for their rebel armies. To show the vibrancy of his forces, Jacob Chidoze, Israel's antagonist, had recently sent 40 Hoki-based Nazuri soldiers to join a major war party in the oilfields. Luke Chediah had questioned the wisdom of leaving security so threadbare in the occupied zone, but his Commander had dismissed his concerns. – We need to keep in with His Excellency and the politicians. They will be delighted that, thanks to us, they have made the county quota for this expedition. That miserable coward Israel cannot spare any men from his ragbag, plague-carrying band of misfits he dares to call an army. He would never dare attack Hoki!

As the Kumuara region became more peaceful, Israel and Jacob's factions would attack Government installations at the garrison town of Juba and send incursions south to blow up oil pipes, roads, bridges or railway lines, trying to outdo each other in prestigious victories. But mostly, the Jamuri and Nazuri warlords fought each other.

But Jacob Chidoze was wrong about Israel. Although he was sick of the fighting, his pride and, as he saw it, strategy, dictated to him that he would launch one more attack to win back Hoki. And even in contemplating this, he was aware that he could set in motion a whole new disastrous chain of events. Trying to shake off his despondency, Israel summoned an elder named Paul, who was an old friend and confidant, to assist him as he washed and shaved. Paul helped Israel fend off the grey, soaping his skull and face, and drawing the old razor over it. – You must be nice and clean *bukarami,* for there will be many young women coming to see you today!

– Ah ... the old warrior almost smiled at the thought. His friend Paul was a gregarious and outgoing man and had a licence with Israel that very few others were granted. – ... you tease an old man, he coughed and shook, causing Paul to nick his leathery scalp. The cut was not worth mentioning though, and any blood would soon dry in the heat. The two men almost came close to banter, before Israel felt a coldness spread over him, and Paul was dismissed. There were pressing matters to be concerned with.

Rank

Across the grassy plains, and over a red river in the village of Nambaro, Jacob Chidoze, Israel's great rival, shot a grin, the dazzle of which his young protégé, Luke Chediah, thought could have brought down an Arab aircraft. – Now we must go into Hoki and see the holy man, he smirked. Luke contemplated that grin, and the mischievous, portly figure who transmitted it. The protruding teeth had always been there, but the stomach, like the capacity for mischief, seemed to have expanded greatly of late. We have a clown for a leader, Luke considered fleetingly, shocked suddenly by the opprobrious treachery of his own thoughts.

Jacob, though, was far too immersed in his own

considerations to sense any contempt from his apprentice. The Catholic Church had reopened in the disputed town of Hoki, and he was going to visit the new priest whom the Christian Brothers had recently installed. – It might be amusing, he smiled at Luke, who stood at ease, though only in the sense employed by military men. – Men of peace are always good sport, he continued, – always battling in vain against the natural state of man. What do you think, my silent young friend?

Luke shrugged. – I am a soldier, General, he said with what he thought would pass as a dumb diffidence.

The General grinned once again. – My motives, though, are as strategic as they are sporting. It is as well to check on this priest, for they can be troublesome.

Luke nodded and left the *tukul*, leaving the General to finish getting himself ready. Jacob put on his most ceremonial uniform; it carried a medal sold to him by a Ugandan trader, which, the man said, had once belonged to Idi Amin. Though he knew this was unlikely, it polished up well, and lent his uniform a dash of glitter. He exited his *tukul* with a swagger, signalling to Luke as he strode across the yard towards his jeep.

Two child-soldiers with Kalashnikov rifles climbed into the jeep behind them. Jacob was always pleased to see youths in uniform, carrying their guns with pride. Too many young people in the Nazuri seemed tired of the adventure of war and spoke out for education, healthcare, peace and development. Jacob would shun such elements and attack them as disloyal. The enemy had, after all, spilt their blood for as long as anyone could remember. How could they accept that?

Father Roache was a white Rhodesian who had studied in Ireland and Australia with the Christian Brothers. After working in a mission in Harare in the years following Zimbabwean independence, Roache sought a new challenge and had begged the Brethren to let him open a school in southern Sudan. The struggle to solicit agreement had taken so long, with so many false starts and disappointments, Roache scarcely believed that all his politicking within the Brotherhood had come to fruition, even when he was sitting in the caravan plane heading for the town of Hoki.

Hoki had been chosen, not merely because it had no existing educational provision (most towns in Southern Sudan met that stipulation) but as it was already furnished with a schoolhouse building, adjoined to the Catholic Church. Furthermore, it was a building which miraculously remained almost undamaged by the civil war.

Jacob drove down the bumpy road to Hoki, a town almost equidistant between Nambaro and Kroy, and the prize he and Israel had fought over for years. As they pulled up outside the main square, Jacob decided to go on a brief walkabout, in order to take the nods, smiles and handshakes of the locals.

The market of Hoki was on its own a teeming shantytown of ramshackle huts, stalls and pens. A chaotic traffic of children, goats and chickens ran around its dusty lanes, avoiding collisions as if by radar.

Traders relied on eye contact and smiles rather than verbal exhortation to catch customer attention. The goods on sale ranged from subsistence foods to what could in neighbouring East and Central African countries be considered mere trinkets or junk; pieces of ribbon or cellophane toys, which nonetheless provided the colourful inspiration to fire the imagination of many impoverished villagers.

Satisfied that all was well, Jacob headed for the yellow-brick church building and the new priest.

Father Roache was a tall, bespectacled man in his late fifties, who gave the impression of athleticism only lately gone to seed. He had a large hooked nose, and an uncontrollable fringe of still-sandy hair, which flopped around, off-setting only slightly his general image as a serene man of great calmness and restraint.

As Jacob Chidoze arrived at the church, the new priest warmly welcomed the Commander, before informing him of his plans to re-open the school.

Jacob immediately considered that this development would need to be very carefully monitored. The priest might be one of those types prone to spreading sedition. With the flush of tyrant's blood bubbling in his veins, Jacob reasoned imperiously that perhaps this priest should learn that he had no voice, that he was not in a position to make plans, not in a position to even *talk*. Only Jacob Chidoze, full of his vainglorious bluster, could do that in Hoki, or any of the Nazuri lands. Not the defeated old syphilitic buggerer of young boys, Israel; certainly not that weak pen-pusher His Excellency the High Commissioner of the local SPLM; not the white aid workers; and certainly not a common priest. As they sat down at the table in the chapel vestry for tea, Jacob was determined he would have both the first and last words. – I am, he began, in a manner so obviously sarcastic as to be way beyond playful irony, – completely fascinated by matters ecclesiastical, particularly if I may say so, Father Roache, related to your own calling.

The priest meekly smiled back at him.

– Ah yes! Is it not so, Jacob continued, rising from his chair and sweeping his arms around the old building, its roof still damaged and letting in a thick ray of sunlight at the bell-tower end, – that the soldier and the priest must both, of necessity, be obsessed with the concepts of life and mortality?

– This is so, but ... Roache began, only to be cut off by the ageing warrior.

– Ahhh! But I know what you are going to say, Father! Forgive my interruption, but when one is schooled in the mess, one must fight as assiduously for airtime in social situations as one must for victory in battle, the General continued, as the priest nodded with a tight smile. – Oh yes, and also, please: pardon my buffoonery. War is an art that must be undertaken with great seriousness, unlike life itself, I find. I refer, of course, to the area of life free from war, for its trivia and foibles constitute my playground. Which leads me to often speculate: is the definition of war, then, not life at its most intense, its most real, when it compels us to treat it with such severity? But I talk too much, Father, much too much, and to my shame without either managing to convey to you my sense of your own paramount importance in the process of this war, for every army needs God on its side in order to be victorious, does it not? After all there is a saying: 'Only religion and strong drink can ease the pain caused by religion and strong drink', and when I think of that dilemma, Africa most certainly springs to mind. Oh yes!

Father Roache maintained a dignified silence throughout this bombast, which was even starting to embarrass the chisel-faced Lieutenant, Luke Chediah. The priest took off his gold-framed glasses and polished them on the sleeve of his shirt. – You make interesting points, General. They merit further discussion. Perhaps you will do us the honour of dining with us tomorrow night?

Jacob was about to accept, when he considered that the church meal might be base and simple to his tastes. – You must dine with me, in the mess at the compound, he barked, then gave the priest a lavish wink, – as the food is prodigious. Aid workers, soldiers ... the mischievous despot dropped his voice in a conspiratorial manner, – and clerics, they must all be looked after, eh? Let us say eight o'clock tomorrow evening. I will send a car. Now I bid you good day, my Holy Father, and with that Jacob turned and clicked his heels and exited, followed by Luke and the two soldiers, before the priest could raise his voice to offer acquiescence, contradiction or even request clarification.

As they clambered into their jeep, Jacob and Luke noted a dirty stray dog, with clumps of its fur missing, lying panting under the shade. On seeing them it shot to alertness and started barking, in loud, strained heaves.

When the motor sped off, the hound charged after it for about 40 yards, then stopped abruptly. – One day I will shoot that foolish old devil dog, Luke Chediah said, his face immobile, as if it were chiselled from marble.

PAGAN MAN

The arrival of the new priest had raised some high-ranking eyebrows in Hoki and had been the subject of much speculation around the Kumuara Province in general. However, the man of whom both the old warlords in the region were most wary was decidedly not a man of the cloth. Far from being a Christian, the local Witchdoctor, the *Biza*, was a dedicated pagan, based near the disputed town, by the Kua pass, close to the river. The *Biza* was often openly contemptuous of both Jacob and Israel, his caustic asides inevitably following some pronouncement made by one or other warlord. – It is not possible to stop two young goats butting each other. It seems as if it is the same with old ones, was an observation he was prone to making.

Both Jacob and Israel claimed to be dismissive of the Witchdoctor, but in private, each of them occasionally sought the council of the *Biza*, and very often put great stock by his prophecies. For his part, the Witchdoctor relished this power over the men, and he had carved out a good niche for himself as a seer, healer and prophet in Hoki and its surrounding areas.

The Witchdoctor's story was that many years ago, he had a dream, in which some anointing spirit had told him to leave his own village in the south, and follow the river to a point where the trees on either side overhung and touched each other. In obedience, he made this calamitous journey and at such a juncture was the town of Hoki. At this terminus the *Biza* claimed that the spirit had instructed him to trawl the bed of the river and take its gifts as his own. This meant that he picked out some stones and shells and the bones and skull of a small dog. It was these treasures, unlikely as they seemed to non-believers, that would comprise the Witchdoctor's toolkit. The skull of the dog was tied like an amulet round his neck and draped across his chest. This, with his head topped by a frayed hat stitched together from strips of cowhide, and wearing nothing else but a loincloth and the painted markings which covered his torso, ensured that the *Biza* cut a distinctive figure in the village. He kept his stones, bones and shells in an Adidas holdall, an impressive bag, which bestowed great status in the village. This was coveted enviously by more than one senior soldier, who all feared to requisition it in case they should be cursed by the Witchdoctor. The bag had been wheedled by the *Biza* out of a particularly superstitious Norwegian aid worker he had befriended.

The Witchdoctor's account of his appearance in Hoki, now over 17 years ago, was, of course, contested by less charitable souls. The alternative claim was that he had been drummed out of his own village for the theft and slaughter of a neighbour's goats.

During his residency in the town of Hoki, the Witchdoctor had become obsessed with resurrection. All his life the *Biza* had believed that he had been here in previous incarnations. Often in the extremities of dreams and visions he had an inkling of those past lives through the fleeting, unsatisfactory sense data accrued in such states. At his most aroused phases he could *feel* the phantom elations and pains, and the loves and losses of those antecedent incarnations. The *Biza* had a thirst for learning in this area. He was prone to heightening his sensory information base through the slaughtering of animals and the taking of women, his method of seduction little more than cynical blackmail, talking of curses that may befall his intended partners should they fail to acquiesce to his demands.

Another practice the Witchdoctor regularly undertook was self-burial in the soft, clay soil by the river. There he would lie under the Earth, free from the sun's scorching heat, cooling off his naked skin, breathing air in a soft rhythm through a hollow reed, thoughtful and contemplative, until a preternatural sleep would eventually envelope him. It was only then that he felt the crushing weight of the mortal soil on his bones, and through his skin, the absorption of the alluvium of the remains of ancestors left in the land. And in his trance, which grew steadily from comfortable to suffocating, he could implacably feel, as if aeons had passed, future generations trying to heap layer upon layer of their spent mortality on him. Sensing that he was now too far down into the bowels of the earth to dig himself free from its hold, he could feel himself being assimilated by the red silt around him, sucking out his energy, his minerals, taking him for its own. Then, when the foreboding, asphyxiating panic seized him, he would dig himself out in a fearful frenzy; feeling reborn, alive, as his chest heaved to take in the sudorific, hazy air. Washing the mud and slime from his body in the cool river he would feel the drum of his heartbeat steady and the stiffening in his loins diminish as his breathing settled.

And the *Biza* knew that he would, in some way, go on forever.

THE JOURNEY

The truck tore up the highway, the shantytowns of Nairobi's outskirts long gone, giving way to the open road and the lush, tropical pastures on either side of it. The bootleggers were happy to be away from the city, Benjamin especially, who felt he had been making excellent headway in persuading Joseph and Marshall that they should set up in Sudan, at least for a while, until the fuss in Kenya died down. Joseph was reticent about the war, but was having to concede that getting out of Kenya for a while, just disappearing, might be a very good thing. Marshall was completely unaware that there was a war on in Sudan.

Benjamin realised that they themselves had received more media coverage in the last week, due to the bootlegging disaster, than the war in neighbouring Sudan, which had claimed the lives of millions, had in the last year. There was no real way that most people in Nairobi could possibly know what was happening up there.

At the wheel, Jake the driver, who had only been commissioned to take them as far as Lokichoggio, was getting more and more cantankerous. It seemed that, as every hour rolled by, the burly man would look at his wristwatch and moan: – We are not making good time; I am losing money!

– Ah but my friend, look at the hills, the beauty of them, Benjamin implored him, as they emerged from a thicket of forest to be confronted suddenly by a series of rolling, verdant hills. In Benjamin's eager mind, they represented a sanguine exodus from the dangers of the city and the ochlophobic jitters it induced in his country sensibilities.

– Infested with bandits and cattle rustlers, Jake snorted in disdain, pulling out his gun from under his seat. – Sometimes we have to fight our way into Lokichoggio!

From the back of the truck, a concerned Joseph caught this exchange and Benjamin looked round in his seat to catch his partner's eyebrow raise as Marshall shuffled a deck of playing cards. Twisting round further, the Sudanese man set about quietly reassuring his companions. – In Lokichoggio we can sell our wares and head into southern Sudan with a pocketful of Kenyan shillings. Then we can drive across the country to my home county, which is so beautiful, my friend, oh ... you will see. We have all sorts of trees and bushes and grasslands. And the girls ... Benjamin's eyes grew larger, – ... oh my friend, you will love it so much. They are so gentle and sweet, not like in Nairobi. And they will love you, with your city ways and your clothes and money. Oh my friend, what a time we will have!

Joseph shut his tense red and blue eyes and tried to think of girls, their curves, softness, hair and lips, but the stiffening in his pants was accompanied with the terrible pain of stretched, inflamed tissue. His ardour cooled, but his mind was fevered enough, and all he could see through it was trouble ahead. As he watched Marshall deal the cards, he glanced at the back of Jake's chunky, shorn head, touching the pistol in his belt. Trouble. It always came, everywhere. Well, he would be ready when it did.

THE WARRIOR'S SON

Back in his *tukul* in the town of Kroy, Israel was preparing for one last assault to take Hoki from Jacob

Chidoze. He sensed that this would be his last campaign as a warrior, his final insurrection. Abraham had told him that Hoki only had a minimal security force now, as 40 men loyal to Jacob had been detailed to go north on an SPLM mission to the oilfields. Furthermore, their crusade's chances of success had been greatly enhanced by his troops' procurement of a cache of grenades. His lieutenants had been briefed, and had expressed confidence in the venture, yet the old man was uneasy. Something in the preparations had been missing. And so Israel had sent for his remaining son, Oliver, demanding that the boy, barely known to him, must be at his father's side for this final day of reckoning.

A few days later the boy arrived, unsure of why his father had sent for him. For his part, the old man beheld the meek, shy and serious young man in front of him, dressed in a light-grey linen suit and carrying a bible and a suitcase, and could scarcely hide his disappointment.

Israel thought again of the four sons he had lost; three gloriously to war and one, sadly, to sleeping sickness: cruelly taken before the boy had been afforded the opportunity to fall in battle. To Israel, the daughter who had perished by the same illness was really an irrelevance. He could fondly behold his wife Rachael's face in his mind's eye, see the strong faces of each warrior son, but the impression of his daughter seemed to blend into that of assorted nieces, or other village girls. This strangely comforted Israel, seeming to him to vindicate his sense of himself as a warrior.

So it was that his sole surviving son had returned from Uganda at his father's instruction. Oliver was a tall, handsome man, but of such a cerebral and religious bent, and so closeted by the institution he attended, that vanity was completely unknown to him. Additionally he was highly absent-minded, and as can often be the way with such people, he would stare at somebody for a long time but not actually *see* them. Allied to this, Oliver was cursed with very poor eyesight, which compounded this tendency to glare at someone, without episcopating any connection.

Oliver had made a life for himself in Uganda; not simply the only one he knew, it was the only one of which this dedicated young man could ever conceive. His sorrow at the death of his mother Rachael, a couple of years ago, was still highly palpable to him, and being back in the town of Kroy for the first time since her funeral made him feel very uneasy.

His father had always been away at war, and was for Oliver a distant and remote figure. The son had always found it difficult to establish a rapport with Israel, who seemed to entertain the ridiculous fantasy that Oliver would follow his father and elder brothers into the rebel army and become a warlord. Israel, for his part, did not realise that this was as far from his son's mindset as could be imagined.

Rachael had taken responsibility for Oliver's welfare, realising that spending some of the family war bounty by getting her youngest son an education in Kampala at the Catholic College for Men was the best investment she could make. A devout, tender woman, who employed her shyness and diffidence to great tactical effect, Rachael capitalised on the old warlord's tendency to cede to her all matters of the household, including the education of the children. Save, of course, that of military issues.

The three oldest sons had fallen in battle and Rachael was determined that warfare would not claim Oliver. There was a big age gap between him and the others, so that while the rest were away fighting, she was rearing the child and his sister in relative peace. When he was old enough, and after his sister had perished from the sickness, Rachael sent him to the Catholic school in Kampala.

The school operated a strict regime, as was customary for institutions run by the Christian Brothers. With the pettiest manifestations of rebelliousness often punishable with severe beatings, Oliver, always a dreamy, speculative boy, tended to live inside his own head. Contact with women in Kampala was out of the question. The idea that most of the students would go on to the Catholic University to train for the Priesthood was firmly rooted in the culture of the institution.

This sheltered, religious background in a son he didn't know would have disconcerted Israel enough. However, on his return to Hoki, something both perfectly ordinary and completely fascinating happened to Oliver. Women would habitually misconstrue his absent-minded gaze and think that this good-looking young man was staring boldly at them, with the thoughts of a seducer or a lecher burning in his brain. They, in turn, would stare coyly back, twirling their hair and smiling effusively, displaying rows of white pearly teeth to his blank sweep. Of course, Oliver would finally notice and think how kind and splendid and friendly the town girls all were.

However, his standing around in blissful innocence, blanking out the rants of his father, while his mind wrestled with theological matters, was a state of affairs not destined to last long. Mary Boadiah was a local girl of great beauty; of mixed blood, light-skinned like the Jamuri, and tall, and with the fine, chiselled features of the Nazuri tribe. She was accustomed to being admired and propositioned by the town's men, and used to them following up their appreciation with action. Mary felt that she was being severely teased by the old warrior's son, and the point soon came when she could bear it no more. Taking her opportunity when she spotted

Oliver alone at the Kroy marketplace, she engaged him briefly in conversation, then practically dragged him down to the riverbank where she put her hand to his genitals. The electric shock he felt fusing between brain and belly jolted the divinity student out of his personal psychic space and into the material world around him.

The virgin boy, aroused by the promiscuous girl, then discovered to the surprise and great delight of them both, that he had great innate skills as a lover, which he proceeded to deploy to the full. Mary could not believe that Oliver had never partaken in this sort of endeavour before, and from then on spent as much of her free time as she could in pursuit of him. Oliver was far too enamoured with his own new powers of seduction and lovemaking, and the exhilaration and ecstasy which they gave him, even to consider speculating on their origin. But from then on in, he went through almost every available and willing girl in the Kroy side of the Kumuara Province.

Of course, Oliver's antics soon came to the attention of his father. Israel, busy as he was with his own plans to retake Hoki, had turned a blind eye, and said nothing to his son. This state of affairs did not last. One afternoon, as Oliver prepared to meet Mary by the river, Israel entered his *tukul* and caught the boy preening himself. What was worse was that he kept on doing this, completely undisturbed by his father's presence. The old warlord could not conceal his annoyance. At such a grave time of preparation for battle, a son should be by his father's side. There was no point in him having sent for the boy to come home, if all he was going to do was chase women. – You come back here from the school in Uganda, and you show no interest in the art of war. All you want to do is to love the girls by the river. You will grow sick and weak with love! It is the sexual diseases that have ruined our people!

Oliver knew about the Jamuri's problem with venereal disease, how the medical aid workers had said that it was rife and it had constrained the fertility of the tribe. Now there was also the growing crisis of AIDS to contend with. While intellectually he could understand all of this, it meant absolutely nothing to him emotionally. Life-threatening disease, paradoxically, was part of life itself, he reasoned. Better to live a short time this way, than in the slow, living death of denial. His Catholic teaching on this issue went by the way as Oliver exhibited the zeal of the convert. After years of celibacy he was completely seduced by both the concept and reality of carnal pleasure. – We are a race of lovers, of romantics. If our destiny is to be extinction through the making of love, then let it be so, he responded flippantly to his father, holding up his arm to examine the pink of his shirt sleeve.

Israel was almost incandescent with fury. He moved to the mouth of the *tukul* and grabbed his rifle, his hands trembling on its barrel. – We are a race of warriors! We take the pleasures of our bounty from the spoils of war, no more, no less. Reckless love is a reward for victory on the battlefield, not an end in itself! Look at Chidoze's prodigy, the boy Luke Chediah: he is a warrior! You are my only son, and you too must be a warrior!

– Yes father, Oliver said, unable not to think of Mary, or Martha or one of the others, helpless to stop a lazy, depraved smile moulding his lips.

That he had produced a serial lecher caused Israel great chagrin. – The buffoon Jacob Chidoze mocks me! We must retake Hoki and liberate its people from his tyranny!

– Father, most of the people in Hoki are from the Nazuri tribe. The ratio is two Nazuri to every one Jamuri, Oliver said dreamily, thinking about whether the lime green shirt might not be more suitable.

An outraged cough exploded in the old man's lungs

and his large eyes burned like coals. – Only because Chidoze drove our people out! They will get back their land!

– Are there any left to give it back to?

The old man looked enraged. He turned back to the entrance of the *tukul* and gazed out into its yard, trying to control his breathing.

Oliver worried that he had gone too far. The old fellow seemed to be hyperventilating. – What I am trying to say, father, he began in tones of conciliatory appeal, – is that it is obvious that we cannot govern by consent in Hoki, not without displacing large sections of the settled Nazuri.

Israel turned and looked witheringly at his son. Now the feeble-hearted boy was sounding like His Excellency, or one of the local Commissioners. And this from the mouth of a young Jamuri man with warrior blood running in his veins! – Only by taking Hoki can we control a buffer zone to keep the homelands, to keep *Kroy* free and secure! There is even contamination of the water supply here! This cannot be allowed!

– But ...

– It has been decided!

Oliver tried to summon up enthusiasm, but all he could think of was further honing his powers of seduction and his lovemaking skills, then heading back to Kampala, or even on to Nairobi. The priesthood, he now considered, probably wasn't such a good idea. – Yes father, he smiled, but he was disengaged, thinking only of the curves of Mary Boadiah and anticipating heading down to the river to meet her.

Abraham appeared at the door of the *tukul*. Israel nodded to him, then turned back briefly to the trancy Oliver and mumbled something scornfully before heading away. Oliver straightened his shirt and fastened its second-from-top button. His face set into a broad smile as he heard the old man's truck start up and tear away.

EDUCATION

Father Roache considered himself fortuitously blessed by coming to Hoki. Not only did he have the schoolhouse, attached to the church, but also the schoolmistress who was currently based in Kroy came from this town, and she was a devout Christian. In fact, she had become the priest's greatest ally, mobilising many helpers to prepare the church for reopening. Through her duties in Hoki, she also had contact with the aid development workers, who were delighted to supply the materials and support to help set up the school.

Valerie Nuando was a strikingly handsome woman, who had ran the gauntlet of extremes. She had ballooned into fatness through childbirth, and wasted back to nothing in famine. Now at 35, Valerie seemed to set into a full-bodied *status quo* which suggested a youthfulness that defiantly ridiculed her circumstances. Valerie wore glasses with lenses that often seemed a bit too thick, and she had unruly hair which no scissors, comb or wax could master. These features gave her a permanently intense, even startled bearing that she didn't fully deserve.

The impression was held steadfastly though, because those aware of Valerie's history knew that she had known unspeakable terror, even for a part of the world which at times it seemed was almost defined by that state. Five years ago, Valerie had been burned out of her home when Hoki had been razed in the last major battle between Joseph and Israel's men. Her eldest son had followed Valerie's husband into the rebel army at fifteen years old, and both were killed in the combat. On her way to a neighbouring community for shelter and sanctuary, she and her daughter and one other son were set upon by a group of men in uniform. They were neither Israel nor Jacob's men, but Ugandan mercenaries. They dragged her into the woods and beat and raped her, leaving her for dead. When she recovered, she found her 12 year old son shot dead, lying by her side. Her daughter, Shola, 13 years old, was gone, kidnapped by the mercenaries.

Through all this horrible injustice Valerie's belief in God never seemed to waver, nor did her conviction that education and knowledge were the greatest weapons in combating the treachery, militarism and hatred that scared people's hearts and stopped them from moving beyond retribution.

The only family she had left now was her youngest son, Robert, who had thankfully been at her sister's when the carnage had started, and the orphan, Moses, a friend of Robert's who had become like a second son to her. Along with the church and her teaching, the boys were her life, and she was steadfastly resolved not to lose them. The pair often stayed with her sister, Grace, in the relatively peaceful town of Ristade, some fifty miles north-east of Hoki, although the schoolteacher liked to have them by her side. Valerie herself had elected to stay in Hoki, even though she was Jamuri and it was now mainly Nazuri, having been in Jacob Chidoze's hands for years. She had always stayed in the hope that she would get some news of her kidnapped daughter, Shola, and prayed that one day the girl would return.

Valerie was one of the few inhabitants of Hoki of whom the *Biza* was wary. He had always been worried about this strong, proud woman who, as a by-product of her own terrible decrements, seemed to have lost all fear. She walked strong and tall through the village, her contrasting righteousness and quiet grace making the power brokers, politicians, warlords and seers, with their own grandiloquent bombast, feel decidedly uneasy. The Witchdoctor was no exception.

Once, a few years back, the *Biza* had spotted Valerie down by the river and had attempted a clumsy seduction. She had repelled his advances by bending back his fingers, breaking two of them in the process. Screaming curses at her, he cast up the retributive powers of every malevolent spirit he could think off.

– You are too late, she observed coldly, gathering her washing in her basket and leaving the enraged Witchdoctor cursing and dancing in pain by the orange-hued river.

Now, working with Father Roache in Hoki, making the reparations to the Church while still cycling four times a week to teach the school in Kroy, Valerie Nuando was finding some kind of peace and fulfilment.

The priest was painting a wall of the vestry, and Valerie moved her bicycle out of the way in order to give him more room. She regarded the vehicle. – We are making good progress. I may have to give up this bike soon! Valerie said, enthused at the prospect. She'd miss her Kroy students when she took over here, but the journey there was dangerous and she had been grooming a clever young man, called Abel, to take over from her in the Nazuri village.

THE PEACE

It was June in the town of Hoki and the thick, dense mango trees hung over the rusty clay-soiled square. Stacks of cemented bricks, the top ridge like broken teeth, formed a platform from which the local officials could address the people. Around the square bountiful grasslands spread outwards towards the dwellings. The tallest building in view, though not as tall as the Anglican church which was concealed by the trees, was the Mosque, with its spire visible over all the other low-rise buildings from all points of the square. The Mosque was not operational, having been burnt out nine years previously. The few local Muslims who had not fled north stayed indoors, too fearful to venture outside for prayer.

Father Roache and his volunteer helpers were still cleaning out the old hall by the yellow-bricked church, in preparation for the opening of the school. As darkness started to fall, the priest reminded himself of the dinner appointment he had at the rebel camp.

The local rebel military and political administration had built their camps next to the United Nations NGO's Save Sudan aid camp. This had been Jacob Chidoze's first move when he seized the town five years ago, and had proved a tactically sound undertaking. Any aggressive incursions into Hoki, be it by Arab bombs or Israel's militia, now ran the risk of catching international aid workers in the crossfire. Indeed, it was often Jacob's boast that since he had taken Hoki there had been no Government air strikes on the town. While most townsfolk knew that this reflected the region's strategic decline with Khartoum's change in policy priorities, following the discovery of the extent of the oil reserves to the north, they enjoyed the relative peace and were happy to subscribe to Jacob's vanity.

Around the edge of the town, palm trees rose in tiers, as if sprinting with each other in a race to the stars, wearing their big hats of floppy green leaves. In their midst lurked Israel and his warriors.

The battle

Earlier in the day, back in Kroy, the Lieutenant Abraham had come to Oliver's *tukul*, and spread a uniform of combat trousers, boots, shirt, beret and Kalashnikov on his bed. – You are to wear these and to come with me, he said, almost gleefully, to the young man.

– I cannot! Oliver replied in horror, backing away from the gun. – I am not a soldier!

– Your father's instructions were explicit. Tonight we take Hoki, the Lieutenant told him, staring at Oliver's present attire, a red shirt with VODAPHONE emblazoned on it. Abraham took an immediate fancy to it, as it represented a football club that he decided he supported.

So Oliver was forced to go along with the invasion party. As well as the gun, which he carried awkwardly, he was given a grenade. Israel had come into a stock of them, procured for him by a group of Ugandan merchants. As they marched into town and the first of those grenades was lobbed at a party of Jacob's soldiers who panicked and fled, the Commander himself was entertaining the priest in the compound.

– As a Christian Father, you must surely believe in the concept of the just war, Jacob grinned, sniffing at the red wine in his glass.

Father Roache nervously cleared his throat. – I believe that there are some times when a war may be said to be just but ...

– Exactly! Jacob thrashed the table, causing the glasses and plates on it to shake. – It is what I have said all along. It takes a just man to designate a just war ... , and he sneered and spread his hands out, as if to look around for applause, – ... just so!

– Yes, but ... Roache tried to cut in, but Jacob Chidoze raised a finger to silence him.

– Of course, it is our leadership which has brought peace and security to this region, he said grandly, just as the first shattering explosions sounded from outside. Jacob spat out some of his wine and stood up. – What is that?

The soldiers looked around in panic and fear. They knew *what* was happening, they just could not think of the who or the why.

More explosions were heard, and they seemed to be getting nearer. A heavy rattle of gunfire started up, then intensified; the priest felt a spasm of guilt that his first thought had been for the health of the almost-restored church building, rather than for his flock, and sent off a quick prayer for forgiveness at this impropriety.

Jacob ran to the exit of the camp, but Luke approached in great haste, telling him that their small force in Hoki was being vanquished. The Save Sudan camp next door had guaranteed his party sanctuary, followed by safe passage back to the Nazuri territories.

– But ... but ... Jacob Chidoze spluttered, wildly discomfited, – where are the others? Ronald ... Alexander ... all the Hoki men?

Luke nodded sternly. – They are either captured or dead. Israel's men took us completely by surprise. Remember, he said in accusation, – we only had a reduced force in Hoki. Forty of our best men are north, blowing up Arab pipelines.

– Yes, Jacob moaned uncomprehendingly, – but how could we not get a force down from Nambaro?

– We did, but we were repelled. They have grenades.

– Grenades! Jacob gasped. – But how?

– We cannot say. Traders, I would suspect, probably from Uganda, Luke curtly informed him.

Jacob's eyes bulged in horror.

Luke turned around and looked at the skeleton force in the compound. – We have eight men here, including yourself. Do we fight them to the death, General?

Jacob could not stop his mouth from flapping open. The food he'd eaten queasily twisted in his guts. – Grenades, you say ... no, we must live to fight another day. Let us take our aid friends up on the agreement of sanctuary and safe passage! Quickly!

Luke made no attempt to disguise his contempt, and the old man felt too sick and shocked to counter. Father Roache watched the old warrior, completely deflated, being led away into the adjacent Save Sudan aid camp. It was here, where, under Israel's agreement, he and his officers would sit impotently in the compound and listen to his own forces being driven from Hoki by his great rival.

Outside in the town, Israel's forces marched through, securing all areas as their rivals took flight. The old warrior himself got out of his truck, and watched as several women attempted to put out a blaze at the Catholic church. Israel commanded some soldiers to help them. He went over to apologise to the women. – This runs contrary to my orders. Reparations will be made and those responsible will be punished.

– Reparations are welcome, but punishment is not needed, a woman retorted. To his surprise Israel found that he recognised her. She was the schoolmistress, the one who taught in his own village of Kroy, and she was burning with anger. – Can you not see that there has been enough punishment already? Valerie Nuando added truculently. – Open your eyes!

– You are our teacher! You should not even be here, he sniffed.

– I live here, she informed him, – and I will never be driven away by two stupid old men!

There was a terrible silence as the old warlord looked at the schoolmistress. Every eye from the soldiers in the car was on him, dripping tears of eager anticipation. In a split second, he looked into her soul and saw no fear, and saw that she was staring into his. The woman had thus seen what Israel had never allowed any man to, and she could not be allowed to live. The warlord felt his hand go to his holster.

– What is happening? Is everyone alright? It was the voice of the advancing priest, and now all the eyes were on him.

Israel relaxed his hand on the gun. The moment had gone. His rage settled with the smell of explosives, kerosene and burning; the scent of victory filling his nostrils and the buzz of carnage feeding his soul. His gaze at the schoolmistress softened slightly. Who was this woman? She came to his town of Kroy from Hoki, a good six or seven miles, just to teach their children. She was Jamuri? Yes, he thought so. Yet she chose to live here. His mind flipped a little again, and he turned to Abraham, urging: – Check the water supply here. That is vital! And as he climbed into the vehicle, he kept staring back at Valerie. The truck pulled away, with her steadfastly holding his gaze all the way, until she thought she could just see his large eye-whites fading in the dark.

Oliver was on patrol with Anthony the sergeant and he looked over at the women working on the church, passing vases of water, trying to douse the flames which licked at its wooden annex of a schoolhouse. One of them was an attractive young girl, whom he just had to speak to. He decided to ask Anthony if it might be acceptable to ask her name. There would be more girls here in Hoki. Perhaps this war wasn't such a bad thing.

He was a few yards away from Anthony and about to make the remark to him, when the sergeant's eye flew outwards of its socket and Oliver felt a stinging rip in the side of his face. Watching in a silent terror as blood gushed from the open hole in Anthony's eye socket, he saw, from the periphery of his vision, two soldiers cut a sniper down from a tree in a hail of bullets. The assassin had shot his father's sergeant through the back of the head. The bullet, flying out of Anthony's eye socket at the front of his face, was the same one that grazed Oliver's cheek. The warlord's son, the awkwardly uniformed student of religion and love, dabbed his own face and felt and saw the blood on his hand, as the soldier fell stone dead in front of him. At this, the warrior's son felt his own legs buckle and the hard, clay ground rise up to his face.

A VICTORY FEAST

In Hoki, Israel, the old warlord, had decided to hold a fiesta in the village square, to celebrate the return of the town to the Jamuri. His Excellency the High Commissioner of Kumuara Province had been invited and after a bit of soul-searching, had decided to attend. The tall, bespectacled politician was annoyed at himself, as Israel's surprise victory was a consequence of his advocating the Hoki Nazuri's incorporation into an SPLA squad for a mission in the oilfields. However, it had been merely a request and Jacob should not have granted it if it had left him short. The feuding old fools; the fat warlord and his folly, the thin one with his reckless adventurism.

Although he wanted to be, and particularly to be seen as, neutral in this dispute, His Excellency had the career politician's dismay of any serious interruption in the *status quo* which didn't unambiguously enhance his own position. Jacob's defeat by Israel had both annoyed and concerned him. It was prudent, though, to be on the winning side, and more to the point, he simply couldn't resist the opportunity to make a speech.

The chairs had been lined up under a wooden canopy on one side of the square. On the other, a burnt-out and broken-down bus, cannibalised for spare parts, was full of children, some of whom sat precariously on its roof to watch the processions.

In the shade, under a tree, the volatile stray dog, thin, wiry and scruffy, tore at the decaying flesh of a dead calf. Three boys with sticks gathered around and chastised the growling animal, which would not relax its grip on the carcass until several blows forced it to beat a retreat.

It was hoped that people from neighbouring villages would come into Hoki but only a few sycophants from the outlying areas did so. Most of the Kroy zealots who had followed Israel into town were soldiers. Nonetheless, the turnout in Hoki of the local Jamuri was good, as there had been a promise of roasted meat. The old warlord had thought it prudent to sanction the slaughter of a good number of head of the captured cattle from the local Nazuri farmers who had chosen to flee. Israel had reasoned that anyone running must be an opponent, and if their cattle were slaughtered, and their homes burnt, then they would have no reason to come back into the area.

Though itching to speak at the rally, Israel found it prudent to let His Excellency the High Commissioner go to the podium first. While the old warlord had a soldier's contempt for the politician, he would have to work with the High Commissioner and it served no purpose to alienate him. It was, in the event, considered a major triumph by His Excellency, who had elected to dress informally in blue cotton slacks and a cream shirt, that he had managed to speak at lengths without betraying the slightest hint of partisanship. Indeed, the politician contrived to scarcely reference the battle that had just taken place, an amazing feat with the Catholic church roof still smouldering in the background.

Only the more welcome smell of roasted meat and the promise of the feast kept most of the villagers present through the speech, although many had still opted to slope off. While His Excellency went on, the

Biza surreptitiously crept up to Israel. – Great Warlord, he whispered, – in the light of your wonderful victory I was moved to spend all day by the river consulting with the spirits, both the righteous divine and also those denizens of Pandemonium. They have assured me that there will be no reprisals from your rival on this day, nor will the Arabs drop any bombs on the square. The feast will be a great success. Great warlord, the spirits are with you!

– Thank you, most wise and gracious *Biza*, Israel said. This news was hardly contentious or earth-shattering, but Israel was in a triumphant mood where any support or endorsement was to be welcomed.

The *Biza*'s face crinkled in delight and he bowed his head and rubbed his hands together slowly. – I wonder, great and magnanimous one, if in return for such information, I may be so bold as to request the bounty of two goats to add to my very humble stockherd?

Israel sighed, then turned to his Lieutenant Abraham and said: – Arrange for the *Biza* to have two fine goats.

Abraham in turn nodded, and instinctively looked around for Anthony before feeling a jolt in his chest as the recent fate of his sergeant came back in shuddering recall. His wandering glance fixed on one soldier who led the grateful Witchdoctor from the platform.

Eventually Israel got up to speak, with the *Biza*'s praise ringing in his ears and the church roof still smoking in the background. – We want peace, for the Jamuri *and* the Nazuri! he declared steadfastly to enthusiastic cheers. – But those who follow Jacob Chidoze do not. And we are warriors! We are proud! We want peace, he repeated, – but we are warriors, he added again, trying to gauge which statement was getting the loudest, most heartfelt applause. Still insecure, and in a state of mild dissonance, Israel looked around at the faces in the square and blowed one more time. – We want peace ... but we are warriors! Always intellectually striving for a pragmatism which his absolutist nature ensured usually eluded him, he said, with as much enthusiasm as he could muster: – Let us now eat!

The assembled townsfolk cheered as one.

At the feast the old warlord saw the teacher and felt a sting of trepidation, given their last encounter. In as close to a spirit of benign reconciliation as he could ever hope to muster, he cautiously approached her and asked of her ideas for the teaching of the children. Valerie told him earnestly of her plans to work with the new priest to set up a school in Hoki. Israel's brow furrowed. – I am an educated man, but the people here have long been simple. This thirst for knowledge is in some ways admirable, but I am concerned that to educate poor people is to do them no service. Discontent will follow. I am anxious that they learn the ways of the Jamuri.

Valerie looked at Israel and again the warrior was forced to note that this woman's stare had a coat of steel he wished he could detect in many of his soldiers. – Which ways might that be? she enquired.

– Well, we are a warrior race, Israel said, almost apologetically.

Looking around at the smoking church, where the billows twisted upwards in the dry air, she caustically informed him: – I do not teach war, although I admit it is not a subject which is hard to learn here.

Israel nodded. – That is true, he considered in delighted approval.

Valerie looked at him, and coolly said: – You say you are for the Nazuri as well as the Jamuri. Well, there are 40 Nazuri soldiers who live in this town. What happens when they try to return from their mission?

– If they are Chidoze's men, then their families will

relocate to his lands in Nambaro. Many of our people from here had to go to Kroy, five years ago when they were driven out by the very same people! Israel argued stridently.

– So when does it end? Valerie asked.

– It ends here. Hoki belongs to us, Israel said defiantly, thinking about how many grenades they had left, and hoping that they'd be able to get more. He moved away from the schoolteacher, feeling once again disconcerted by her unbending presence.

Oliver, in the meantime, had recovered from his shock and was enjoying the festivities, save the odd nervous glance up to the trees. He was mightily relieved that he never had to fire a single shot. Abraham saw him stroking the cold barrel of his rifle and smiled at him. Oliver smiled back. – It was easy, eh? the conscript son of the warlord said to the Lieutenant.

– This time, Abraham grinned.

Oliver looked at the broad-shouldered lieutenant, and thought about Anthony, who fell before him, not much more than a boy really, but a veteran in this environment. – There are boys here who know how to strip a rifle before they know how to strip a girl ... His glance over the square had caught two village girls who were dancing – ... Can this be right?

Abraham gave the younger man a fellow lecher's look back. – There is time for both, he said, and they moved across the square in concert, smiles radiant.

NORTHBOUND

The lorry hit another pothole on the badly maintained road and Joseph toppled forward, the burned skin on his thighs and belly nipping, causing the gangster to let out an undignified squeal. The barrels and equipment, tied onto a frame, which ran the length of the inside of the truck, shook and rattled. Marshall, in the back with

Joseph, rose and went to check that everything was still secure. Content that no valuables had worked their way loose, he shot a glance back to the stoical head of Jake who was driving steadily as if nothing had happened.

Nairobi's bootlegging gang were becoming more uneasy, realising that they were heading north up to Lokichoggio; making this potentially hazardous trip via the beaten, bandit-ridden track in the rented lorry and in the company of a driver they knew little about. Benjamin was chatting to Jake in the front with gregarious enthusiasm, seeming oblivious to the fact that when the driver did deign to respond, it was only with the most minimal and very occasional of grunts.

– We are lucky to have respite from his Sudanese farmer's tongue, Joseph said to Marshall from the mattress in the back as the latter dealt yet another hand of cards.

Marshall said nothing in reply, but, as was his habit, touched the raised white lettering on his top, which spelt **SHARP**. They would all have to stay sharp, he thought, and he touched it again for luck, enjoying the puffy texture of the rubbery plastic on his finger tips. Above this impressive bold lettering, there was a small crest on the breast of the garment and Marshall supposed it was the manufacturer who had produced the sloganed shirt. He had been compelled to buy one from the marketplace after he had noted several youths admiring a similar top on another boy.

At one stage they were followed by a police vehicle with Marshall and Benjamin only relaxing a little when Joseph explained that the law enforcers were actually present to escort them through bandit country, rather than to search their cargo. Jake the driver confirmed this, and at the stop-off point Joseph and Benjamin laughed and joked with the policemen and offered them cheap cigarettes. Marshall did not like the rest areas: they made him nervous. He would have kept that Jake driving round the clock if he could, rather than pull into those grimy roadside shacks, with their stodgy food, snickering truckers and arrogant policemen, where insects flew suicide missions into crackling neon lights.

At one such halt Marshall whispered in annoyance as Joseph and Benjamin passed more cigarettes to two policemen who sat down to enjoy a break. – You waste our cigarettes on those curs, he complained.

– Kindness creates blind spots, Joseph retorted, and Benjamin beamed in agreement, heading up to the counter and examining the food on offer.

Marshall did hear this comment, which was meant mainly for his ears, although he was primarily now concentrating on the two police officers. The easy laughter of the lawmen made him nervously remember that the crude identikit mock-ups of them that had been displayed on that television show. And he considered they probably decorated many police stations, some of them, no doubt, way beyond the confines of Nairobi city.

Yes, it was just the sort of laughter, that nervous, hyena-like chatter, which so often preceded treachery. Then he glanced over at the driver, who was wearing a smart FILA shirt. That man Jake could not be trusted. He had refused to take them until the price was upped, then all his concerns about the police and Christian women suddenly vanished. Now all he talked about was his need to get back to Nairobi quickly, and about how much money he was losing. A man who worshipped money to that extent usually cared little about what he had to do to get it. If there was a reward for their capture, and there possibly was, this Jake fellow would waste no time in turning them in. Then there was the tools of their trade, stacked in the back of the truck; the barrels, tubes, valves, taps, thermometers, piping, filters and the large containers of methylated spirits.

Rubbing the embossed white lettering on his chest for luck, Marshall resolved to stay sharp. Pulling Joseph aside as a whistling Benjamin heaped rice and fish onto his plate from the buffet, Marshall said: – Do not create your own blind spot through kindness.

Joseph looked slightly put-out, but then stole a long, cold glance over at Jake and nodded affirmatively.

MODERNISATION

Luke Chediah had long decided that power, in uncertain times and in a terrorised land, could only lie in extreme ruthlessness. In an impoverished desert county to the north of Kumuara Province, Luke had watched his own family slaughtered by a band of horsemen from the north. He himself was taken north, to a desert town and sold into slavery to a merchant and his family.

Luke grew to admire the ruthlessness of his captors, their righteousness, and the strength and vigour of their belief. As a captive boy, he was often given to thinking, if only Christians could punish the infidel and the blasphemer with such zeal. And punish his captors he did, before escaping back south to participate in more terrible events that defined his life.

Since then Luke Chediah made it part of his personal project to modernise his faith, considering that it was the only way that it would be able to keep pace with the dynamism of those in the north. Otherwise they would eventually be the dominant force and the Africans would be the poor relation, right across the entire continent, as was the case here in Sudan.

What was needed was a militant calling, relevant to the needs of Pan Africanism. This revisionism, this turning of the other cheek, it only gave succour to the weak and indolent. That was the problem with too many African Christians: they wanted to bask idly in the love of Jesus without first having had their faith tested by the wrath of God. And Luke Chediah saw himself as an agent of that God, just as much as any disease or famine, where his own psychopathological nature was a basic part of a plan constructed by the Lord, in order to make him an instrument of His will.

During the period of his capture, escape and subsequent walk through the desert, Luke had first heard the voice in his head. It had been persistent and maddening enough in the confines of his lonely, locked room at nights, but became an irresistible force under the blazing sun above him and the scorching sands which tortured his feet. There were times when he thought that this voice was just the steely resolve of his own will, buttressing itself with some recalled biblical learning. Other times he was convinced that it was the voice of God himself.

Now this voice was telling him to be merciless. In his past battles, Luke had developed a warrior's mantra, which he recited to himself over and over again, to drive home his vengeful desire. As a rule of thumb, he resolved that for every one of his people killed by an Arab, ten of them would fall. And the same principle would now apply to rival tribes or rebel groups. Their common African heritage or religion would not save the Jamuri or any other tribe who dared cross him.

There could be no tolerance, either, of failure or mediocrity from within their own ranks. Jacob Chidoze had been a good warrior, but had grown weak and bloated. In fact, his once-endearing buffoonery had now almost descended into lunacy, to the point where he was nothing but a liability to his people. His disastrous complacency in sending the Hoki loyalists north to the oilfields and leaving them so depleted had resulted in the unpardonable loss of that town. Yet the old fool would endeavour to hang on, possibly for years. But it was time he was gone, the voices told Luke. Decisive action was needed, not just to retake Hoki, but to destroy the Jamuri once and for all. Israel, the old warlord, it was said that his brain was rotting away with syphilis. He and his plague-carrying tribe would not survive much longer. And the young warlord resolved: it would be Luke Chediah who would wipe the old sodomite and his people off the map, for the good of Africa, before they obliterated the whole continent with their foul, Satanic diseases.

But first there was the other old man to deal with, namely his Commander, the lunatic, Jacob Chidoze.

LUNATIC

Jacob had instructed the driver-cum-guard that Luke had assigned to him to take him straight home. He didn't know this man, but in the absence of his lieutenant, this soldier was getting his ear bent by the shocked and outraged Commander. – Our brave Hoki men are fighting the Arabs in the north. And while they are gone the coward steals their homes and drives away their women and children!

As they veered off the road and approached the group of *tukuls*, the guard, a man named Alexander, felt the side of his face twitch nervously, but he remained silent. The van stopped and they climbed out. Jacob looked around the clearing anxiously, then headed into a *tukul*, followed by the silent soldier.

In the hut he tore off his jacket with the medal on it, exposing his girth through his white shirt. – How can we be sure of anybody's safety? Israel Kobache is a madman! There is no telling what such men may do ... no telling at all ... a civilised dinner with a man of God ... he moaned. – Luke will see to it ... Jacob glanced around, but there was no sign of his deputy, who he assumed must be following in the other car.

Instead his young wife emerged from another *tukul*, her belly swollen with child. She smiled at Alexander, who felt a strange chill. Jacob turned and his face lit up. – Ah Clara, my lovely Clara! he exclaimed, and he moved over and embraced the woman who, the Guard uneasily noted, seemed genuinely delighted to have her husband back unharmed. Jacob made placatory noises at her and patted Clara's lump, displaying a great and ostentatious tenderness. This truly shocked Alexander. He had always viewed Jacob as a despot, if one prone to mad outbreaks of great personal charm. It was this side, though all too infrequently glimpsed, which appeared to suggest other possibilities for the ageing warlord. Now, in this hour of his greatest humiliation, they suddenly seemed to scream it. With his tunic discarded, he now looked like a friendly rich old man, happy with his lot, particularly his young wife.

The ageing warlord caught Alexander's eye and smiled, his eyes crinkling behind his gold-rimmed specs and his lips rolling up to an almost implausible extent, exposing his protruding teeth. Alexander thought it was like the sun coming up, and he well suspected that the old chap knew it.

He felt sad about his treachery, as Jacob dismissed his wife, who departed with a grace that failed to hide the concern etched on her face.

Jacob turned back to Alexander. – Where is Luke? We must tell them, he implored the soldier, his voice rising to a high squeak in plea, as if Alexander had the power of judgement – ... tell them of the injustice and the pain that this warmonger Israel has caused! And he took an urgent couple of steps close to the guard, causing his heartbeat to rise in unease. – We must tell them of the greatness and justness of the Nazuri ... there were no bombs that fell on Hoki under my rule! Because they knew of our justness! No bombs ... Jacob blubbered, his eyes filling with tears.

For the first time, Alexander was close enough to smell the alcohol on his Commander's breath, and he realised that Jacob was drunk and maudlin. The Nazuri Commander was rendered once more detestable in the young soldier's eyes; his drunken tears, his mood swings and his outpourings of besotted sentimentality. They were the murmurings of a selfish, spoiled child, who in attempting to appear human, only underscored himself as a psychopath.

– Where is Luke? the Commander yelped. – Go and find him!

And Alexander was happy to exit, head into the truck and drive away.

The old Commander felt a sickness in the pit of his stomach, and it spread up towards his heart. What would he tell his comrades, the brave men of Hoki who would soon be returning from the oilfields?

As Alexander's truck wound down the hill past their vantage-point in the bushes, Luke turned to a fellow conspirator and said: – That was his last guard, sent off on an errand somewhere. Wait here, he commanded the other two men, both of whom were delighted to obey.

SUCCESSION

Luke believed that the old man deserved a warrior's death, but unfortunately circumstances dictated otherwise. At least it would be done quickly and mercifully. This much he owed to Jacob Chidoze, the man who had taken him, a lost orphaned boy, found wandering in the desert, under his wing. His ruthlessness in this matter would be a direct tribute to the training the old warrior had given him.

However, when his prodigy entered the house, Jacob would not face him, would not look him in the eye. This unnerved Luke, but he took it as a sign from God, as he had done when, all those years ago, he reached that crossroads in the desert and took the turning which led him to run into Jacob's forces, an occurrence which saved his life. Now he saw this reticence to mean that the old man was ready to go, indeed, wanted to be put out of his misery. Within that blighted, blimp-like body, bloated with decadence, did a warrior still lurk? No. Events at the camp after the fall of Hoki had proven otherwise.

But part of Luke desired to hear one last defiant speech from Jacob's lips, about how Hoki would be retaken and the syphilitic hordes of the Jamuri repelled from this land. As he withdrew the pistol from his belt, Jacob did not move. Luke gazed across at the woman the old man had taken for his second wife, her stomach swollen with his heir.

Then the old warrior saw Luke glance at Clara, his pregnant wife. Sensing everything in that glance, he turned to the protégé in appeal. – No *bakuremi*, not Clara, he pleaded.

Clara screamed, but the young warrior's lip tightened; there could never be compassion nor explanation, only action. He pulled the trigger on his handgun and shot the General twice, once in the face and once in the stomach. Then he shot the fleeing woman once in the back. She fell over and crawled on her swollen belly to the door. It took another two bullets to finish her.

Shaking violently at the force of the intimacy of such a kill, Luke panicked when he heard a groaning coming from the side of the bed, and turned to see an apparition rise before him. Open-mouthed, the young soldier almost dropped the pistol and turned and ran before realising what this was, then broke into a loud, nervous laugh. The old man's face was shot off, a bloodied shapeless mass, but he was trying to get to his feet. Luke shot him once again, in the throat this time, and Jacob, raised on to his knees, waved his arms in the air; gurgling, choking to death on his own blood which coughed out like a fountain from where Luke fancied his mouth should be. And it was the old warrior's last bizarre performance; a crazed, bloodied dance of death, which encapsulated the strange pantomime of buffoonery and bloodlust, of frivolous sport and horror, that had been Jacob's life.

Perhaps it had been a fitting death after all, Luke contemplated, as he left the *tukul*.

His two henchmen, who had been standing back in the bushes, approached warily, looking around the still, deserted yard.

– They have killed our leader, Luke said gravely, for they *had* killed Jacob, the Jamuri; they had destroyed him by inflicting that humiliating defeat on him. Pulling the trigger was a merciful act and just a point of detail that the people did not need to know about.

The henchmen nodded in stern enthusiasm, as if endeavouring to assure the new master that their complicity in the propaganda was as thorough as their participation in the deed.

As they prepared for the acting performances of their lives, Luke felt euphoria rising in his breast: his heart thumped and his head spun as triumph's intoxication all but overwhelmed him. It was so powerful, Luke briefly feared for his health and questioned whether his constitution was vigorous enough to stand what he saw as his destiny. The force subsided to manageable levels, allowing the new warlord to savour his ascendancy. Jacob was gone now, the old fool was history! Yet thanks to Luke, his triumphs and victories would live on now, as his oafishness would be forgotten, his glory unsullied by any further displays of his facetiousness. When the Hoki Nazuri soldiers came back home in a vengeful mood, they would not now hold him to account for the disastrous loss of their home town. Luke pompously saw himself as the custodian of Jacob Chidoze of the Nazuri's reputation. This however was in the past, and all that counted was the future. – Now we must prepare for war, Luke snapped to accomplices, who were more than happy to endorse this contention.

LOKICHOGGIO

The four men had found spartan accommodation in Lokichoggio, in a crumbling shack of tin and wood, which boasted the sign 'hotel'. It was, however, adjacent to the huge Save Sudan UN base, and the security guard, for a few Kenyan shillings, had allowed them to park the lorry outside the base where they could keep an eye on it.

Makeshift bars and shops lined the streets of this lawless frontier town, which had grown rapidly in size and functions since it became the base to service international aid into southern Sudan.

– I will be glad to leave this place, the pudgy Jake said, sucking on a bottle of cold Tusker, enjoying, as much as his nature and circumstance allowed, a hand of cards on the porch of the hotel with Marshall and Joseph. Every so often his monitoring eye would stray over to where the lorry was parked.

Benjamin's eyes were wandering, too, as he was on the look-out for women, but very few seemed to pass. Yet hard-faced young men, who would meet his empathetic salesman's smile with flinty, death's-head stares; they, however, seemed to be particularly abundant. And Benjamin felt his soul freeze and his eyes avert quickly for the third or fourth time in half an hour as another hard stare met his gaze. – Oh my friends, this is such a bad place ... he whispered.

– Their strength comes from the whiff of your fear in their nostrils, Joseph said. – You must simply look those curs in the eye, then they will skulk into the shadows like beaten dogs.

– But I dare not ... the gentle trader said.

Joseph looked contemptuously over to Benjamin, who said nothing, only narrowed his eyes slightly as if bracing himself to receive a blow.

A silence followed, which was broken by the unlikely voice of the driver. – I will be happy to be out of here, Jake repeated, then cursed and threw in his hand.

– My friend, Joseph said, addressing him. – I am aware of the bargain we made, and also of your desire to return home, but ... might we not convince you to take us on into Sudan? I am led to understand that the Kumuara Province is only two days' drive from here.

Jake laughed at this proposal; a cold, mechanical sound, devoid of mirth or grace. – You rascals really are beyond compare! First I help you to escape from Nairobi, then I get you up here through bandit country, to this shabby frontier hovel. Now you want me to cross a border into a country, which, your friend tells me, he looked over to Benjamin, – has been at civil war for seventeen years? No thank you. I will return to Nairobi and I will drink and sing, if the mad churchwomen and the police and the bandits spare me. This is a long enough list of adversaries and I have no wish to add rebel peasants or dirty Arabs to it.

Joseph looked the driver in the eye. – What if we were to offer you the sum of one thousand shillings?

The driver looked straight at the bootlegger in disbelief. – You are surely joking?

Joseph pulled some money from his belt. It was more cash than Jake had ever seen.

He lowered the wad of notes under the table. – Half now, the rest when we get to Kumuara County and the town of ... he turned to Benjamin – ... what is the name of the town?

– Kroy, and it is only two days' drive my friend, a delighted Benjamin sang. – You will see!

The expression on the thickset face of the lorry driver never altered for a second, but Joseph felt the notes under the wooden table being tugged from his hand. He kept his own grip very, very tight, however, and his eyes gawked into the driver's.

Beads of sweat began to form on Jake's forehead. – I will drive you for two days. Then you get out the lorry and I turn back, wherever we are, he said.

Marshall looked at Joseph, who smiled at the driver, but still kept his vice-like hold on the money. – The bargain is made, he said, still looking Jake steadily in the eye. Then he released his grip on the notes.

That evening Benjamin and Marshall had decided to go and explore the town in search of female company. As the tenderness of his burns made such interaction impossible, Joseph had been designated to stay in the hotel, in order to keep an eye on Jake. The driver, in turn, was watching out for the lorry parked across the road beside some Save Sudan vehicles. Whenever Jake caught the eye of one of the camp security guards he had bribed to watch the truck, the man would smile at him, point at the vehicle and give him the thumbs-up. In this town, such a gesture was as likely to worry as it was to reassure the recipient, and Jake was no exception.

Lotte, the woman who ran the hotel, served them up

with a welcome meal of goat and vegetable stew with rice and bread.

After the food, Joseph was looking enviously at Marshall and Benjamin, who were making a great show of changing and preening themselves in their room, as he himself sat looking out the window at the parked lorry.

From outside they heard a gunshot ring out, just as darkness started to fall. This was the cue for a cacophony of gunfire to commence, crackling loudly into the night.

Benjamin opened the door and saw an unconcerned Lotte emerging from the kitchen. – What is that? he asked, trepidation in his voice.

– Someone has been held up and robbed, and all the others in the vicinity fire off their guns so that the bandits know not to come to their house. It is silly, everybody in Lokichoggio has guns! You think that they would realise this by now and save the ammunition, Lotte explained, shaking her head at the folly.

As Benjamin's large eyes glared in fear, Marshall shrugged. – It looks like it is cards again, my friends, and he reached for the deck on the old worn table, picked it up and started to shuffle.

INCUMBENTS

In what seemed like no time at all, through the whisperings of ragged children, washerwomen, market spivs and imperturbable farmers, the news of Jacob's death filtered from Nambaro through to Hoki and on to the Jamuri heartlands of Kroy. Many Jamuri tribespeople engaged in open celebration, and some troops fired rounds into the sky. Israel, though, was far from happy. The passing of his great rival, an occasion which ought to have afforded some jubilation for the old warrior, instead induced within him a lugubrious low and a terrible sense of foreboding.

With the disputed lands conquered, Israel contemplated why his first reaction to his old rival's death should be one of such ambivalence. First, there was the circumstances of Jacob Chidoze's death, with both him and his wife found shot dead, in their own home. While the Nazuri troops immediately blamed assassins from Israel's Jamuri, the old warrior knew, as he fancied did many of Chidoze's tribe, that his murderer came from within the ranks of his own people. His mind spun with the implications. The SPLM officials might get involved, suspecting his hand in this, accusing him of precipitating a major intertribal conflict, which could only benefit Khartoum.

Also, if Jacob Chidoze had not been safe from his own, how could he, Israel Kobache, really be sure of his own position? His thoughts once again to that water supply.

But the main reason that Israel was so uneasy with Jacob's death was that the ageing warlord would almost certainly now be succeeded by that headstrong fool, Luke Chediah. That boy was from another age, far more ruthless than his demised mentor, much less prone to observing the joint protocol which had evolved between the two tribes as custom and practice and which served as a rudimentary set of rules of engagement. The Chediah boy was schooled in the era of guns, would use them for any reason, and the consequentialism of the gun was devastating on local society. Israel thought, with a burning indigestion in his guts, how for younger men the bullet was considered the first resort thing, for even minor tribal skirmishes at the level of petty theft and hooliganism, such as cattle rustling. He recalled wistfully the old days of spears and bow and arrows, the real art and skill of the warrior, where the casualty rates were low and there was not the potential for such petty thuggery to precipitate a full-scale war.

However, the most disturbing factor from his own point of view was that Israel was now realising just how much he himself had mellowed and wearied with age. The taking of Hoki had failed to raise his sap as it would have back in the days of old. In fact, as he strolled around Hoki town square barking instructions to troops, he was already with some dreadful presentiment; considering worriedly the consequences of breaking the *status quo*, of having to defend this town and its ungrateful inhabitants. Now he had Luke Chediah to contend with, and the young Commander would soon be bolstered by the return of his soldiers from the north.

Israel thought about his own remaining son. Oliver was, like many of the younger people, sick and tired of the fighting. And indeed, he considered wearily, why should they not be? Why could he himself not try to make his mark as the man who brought peace to his region?

No. It was too fanciful a notion.

His opponents would never settle for it. Now it seemed that he had no choice but to fight, unless His Excellency or others in the SPLM could arbitrate. It was possible that they may have some kind of a hold over young Chediah.

TARGETS

In the town of Nambaro, the young warlord, Luke Chediah, was poised to make the public declaration. In a large room in the town hall, he had gathered his advisers round. – I will tell the people that for every one of our men killed in Hoki, one hundred of our enemies shall die!

Akibo, the political man in Nambaro, intervened. He

was of mixed Jamuri–Nazuri stock, and well rated by His Excellency and the other officials in the county. This gave him a power in the town, and he was a trusted counsel to Luke on strategy matters. Shaking his head firmly, he told Luke: – This is not an achievable target and to make a public declaration to the effect serves only to undermine your authority.

The young warrior thought about this, and reconsidered the numbers in question. It *was* rash. It was the sort of mad declaration that the old buffoon would have made. – What about ten?

– I still think that is excessive, Akibo the strategist nodded gravely.

– Four then, Luke Chediah almost sulked.

One of the respected elder soldiers, a man named Thomas, nodded in the negative. – Four does not have the emotional power in the delivery of the speech as ten.

– I agree, Luke said eagerly, now worrying a little that he was coming over as weak and indecisive. – It must be divisible by ten.

– But eight of our men have died. Does Israel have eighty men to kill? Another senior officer quizzed.

Luke felt the anger rising within him and was about to shout down the soldier when he saw Akibo, the strategist and potential Commissioner, shake his head vigorously, standing his ground against the military man. – This surely depends on semantics. If we say ten of their men, it's not achievable. If we just leave it at ten, full stop, with no elaboration, then all is good, he smiled.

– Yes! That is it! Luke agreed heartily, looking around, daring anyone to challenge him. They all nodded with enthusiasm at this compromise.

So it was that Luke made the speech to the crowded square in Nambaro, summoning up the departed spirit of

Jacob Chidoze, and stating that for every one of them killed in battle, ten of their opponents would be slaughtered like pigs.

SUDAN

In only a few incorporeal moments, even to Benjamin's tuned, appreciative eye, which greedily drank the scenery, the red clay desert and its dried-out riverbeds seemed to transform into lush, green grasslands. His homeland was as glorious as he had remembered it, yet paradoxically strange and disorientating. He was certain that Kroy lay along this road, but it had been a long time.

Marshall was not at all happy. They had needed to bribe some Kenyan army guards to let them cross over the border. After that they had another uncomfortable and nervous sleep by the roadside. The place was deserted, it was eerie, and the only sign of civilisation they came upon was a ruined village, long since abandoned.

The following morning they saw another truck heading up the road towards them. They were forced to stop as the road was so narrow at this passage, and so partly dismantled by the recent rains, that they could not have passed each other without great care, even at slow speed.

The occupants of the other truck were traders, up from Uganda. The two groups of men immediately struck up a hustler's rapport and the bootleggers paid the traders to vouch for them in a nearby village, to where they escorted them in order to buy food.

There were a few rebel soldiers present in the village, but they seemed to look upon the bootleggers with little interest. Joseph felt bold enough to approach one of them, offering him a cigarette, which the man accepted with thanks, and asking where Kroy was.

– Kroy is not too far from here, the soldier told him, receiving his proffered light with gratitude.

– But how far? Joseph asked with a thin smile.

– I do not know. I have never been there. They tell me it is close, the soldier shrugged, disengaging now that his needs had been met.

Cornseed idiot, Joseph thought, with a mildly affectionate contempt.

They enjoyed a meal of goat soup and rice, then stocked up with provisions, despondently unimpressed with the basic nature of the goods on offer. There was some fruit and bread and corn biscuits, which would tide them over on the last leg of their journey. They bade farewell to the traders and got back on the road, Jake the driver still grumbling, making what had become his habitual ominous noises about turning back soon.

After a passage of time the foliage heightened and densened and the trees rose in towering layers as the road narrowed abruptly. Soon, they were unable to proceed further, hemmed in by vegetation with the road becoming a churned path that denied all attempts to force access. – This road used to go further than this ... it has all changed. It is five years since I was home, Benjamin mumbled apologies, under Joseph's hostile glare which burned his neck, and in face of Jake the driver's curses.

Joseph was apoplectic, looking at Benjamin as coldly as a viper as he squeezed out his words through ground teeth. – There is a war on here, you idiot! This area has quite probably been bombed, evacuated, occupied. How far is this Kroy place we are going to?

Benjamin felt a shard of fear debilitating his thin body. It was so long since he'd fled from south Sudan, back in the days when he was a young trader. Domiciled in Nairobi's poorest shantytowns, he remained a country boy at heart, and had always entertained the hope that circumstances in his homeland might improve. That they could actually deteriorate was not something that had crossed his mind, not until now. – Not far, he said in almost breathless tones of appeasement.

Jake the driver turned around in his seat and looked crossly at them. He opened the door of his cabin. – We cannot go further. I will help you to unload, then I will go back. I must now have the remainder of my fee.

Joseph pulled out the revolver and shot him twice in the chest as Benjamin screamed like a fretting banshee, so much so that Joseph thought his partner had been struck by a bullet's ricochet. Jake the driver looked incredulously at the blood pouring from his two bullet holes, and gave an angry and disappointed sulk of self-hate, his last thought on Earth being to acknowledge how foolish he had been to trust those devils. Then he fell out of both the seat and the cabin and went crashing to the hard, impacted earth. Joseph and Marshall quickly jumped out the lorry after him, and went through his pockets, taking their cash advance back.

– Kick the robbing pig into the ditch, Joseph instructed.

Marshall looked at him as he'd forgotten something elementary. – But first let us remove his clothes ... he said.

Joseph looked at him in glum exasperation, then shrugged and looked up to the cab of the truck. – Quick! he shouted up at the static Benjamin, still shivering with fear in the cab, – you must help us!

– But ... Benjamin trembled, – you have killed him!

Joseph shook his head impatiently, like a tired parent trying to explain something important to a small boy. – There is a war on, with the Arabs. Also you say that the tribes in this part of the world fight each other. So let him be one of their casualties.

Marshall was already struggling with the driver's deadweight body, trying to remove Jake's FILA T-shirt. It was covered in blood and had two bullet holes in it. As he had expressed such great interest in the shirt, this made him livid. He had even said earlier to Joseph that he would be prepared to smash the driver's head in, or to strangle him, so that the garment would not spoil. This was useless. Peeling himself from the body, he felt the anger surge through him. He turned to confront Joseph, that pig who had done this selfish deed deliberately. – You knew that I wanted that shirt, you terrible rascal. But no, you could not in your heart bear for Marshall to have something that you would not have!

Joseph met Marshall's eyes slowly and shrugged. – I just took the best opportunity to send him to the better place, he said in a pointed challenge. Then he placed a propitiating hand on Marshall's shoulder, which his colleague's eyes followed to its resting destination, before glancing back to Joseph who contended: – The shirt is nothing. There will be more shirts. Come!

Marshall's anger subsided a little. – What about the truck? he asked.

– We sell the truck to the rebels, Joseph said smugly.

They did not have long to wait.

With great stealth and the silence of death in the night, a group of men, clad in the ragbag, military-style garments of rebel guerrillas, emerged from the lush cover of petiole and were all around them as soon as the bootleggers had registered their presence. The soldiers carried automatic weapons, which were most definitely not pointing at the ground. The men, Benjamin recognised, bore the marks of the Jamuri tribe, which he himself came from.

Joseph only knew Swahili and English. He decided he would try some of the latter, first hissing at the frightened Benjamin to keep quiet. Then he faced this broad-shouldered impassive man, who, standing like a huge rock before him, seemed to be very much in charge. – Ah, my friends ... he began, – we are merchants, who aspire to be brewers and make beers for the people's festivities. We are but simple traders, good African men from Kenya. Our lorry is of no further use to us. Please, let us donate it to your movement in return for safe passage to the good town of Kroy, where we plan to set up our operation.

The commanding soldier glanced down at the burly driver's body. The pool of blood from it was already tacky, drying out under the heat. – What about him? he asked, turning to an another trooper and smiling. – Is he a merchant, too? he queried, his expression then deathly cold again when he turned back to face Joseph.

– A thief, a rascally thief, who tried to steal our equipment; apparatus needed in order to set up the brewery here for the benefits of the people in your province. Here, in this fair town of Kroy. For African men, sir, for Christian men like your good selves. We move our operation up here to provide facilities for the brave people of southern Sudan who resist the terrible Arab tyranny, and this rogue tries to steal it from us. He pointed down at the chunky body, lying prone on the earth. – We only aspire to make beers for the people, sir, he repeated, failing to disguise his mounting desperation.

The soldier betrayed little emotion during this tirade, save for a raising of one eyebrow in response to the 'beer for the people' reference, and a faintly affirmative nod about the donation of the lorry. – Licence is required from His Excellency for any such activities in this county, the soldier said, and before Joseph could elaborate, the rebel leader then turned to the terrified Benjamin. – You are not a Kenyan, he contended, pointing at the tribal scores on his face. – You bear the mark of the Jamuri!

– No ... I ... am from here, but many years ago, Benjamin said fearfully in his mother tongue, – but yes sir, I am a proud Jamuri.

The soldier looked searchingly at him as Benjamin withered inside and blinked nervously under the heat of that incessant gaze. Then he said something in a local dialect to which Benjamin responded, and they chatted easily for a bit, both smiling at the end of the exchange, as were Joseph and Marshall, without having understood a word of what was said.

The Chief Soldier extended his hand to Joseph, who was happy to shake it. – I am Abraham, he introduced himself as he glanced at the equipment in the back of the truck. – You are brewers you say, he smiled broadly, counting his good share of luck. You had to be suspicious of everything as a first impulse, but as a second, it was essential to see the opportunity in it. – Brewers is good, he said warmly. – The beer here is imported from Uganda and sometimes even Egypt and Kenya. It is not affordable for the people, he said, with a sadness Joseph instantly recognised as contrived.

Abraham explained to the bootleggers that the rains had started and the big river was swollen. The bridge had been bombed several years ago, but the river was crossable by foot at one stretch close to Kroy. They would help them take the barrels and the brewing equipment over.

The big lieutenant barked a command and Joseph's heart sank as the soldiers, like a swarm of locusts, stripped the truck of its contents and headed off into the bush. Each of the brewers had a suitcase full of his personal belongings, and only Marshall managed to grab his, before a soldier picked it up. – Do not let them out of your sight, Joseph whispered at Marshall and Benjamin, as they endeavoured to follow the fast-moving troupe. Marshall soon grew less enamoured with the suitcase; it was impossible to make progress with its weight. Indeed, he was grateful, if a little embarrassed, when a smiling, wiry, youthful soldier took it from him, lifting it effortlessly on to his shoulders. The boy looked about half his size. He resolved to reward the youth with some Kenyan shillings; if, of course, he saw the blasted thing again.

It was a hot and desperate journey and Marshall annoyed Joseph by unwittingly pulling back a highly strung branch he as passed, then letting it go where it thudded into the scar tissue of his colleague's burnt lower stomach. Joseph cursed and shouted something, but was forced to keep moving. – Come! Come! Abraham would regularly exhort, as they struggled, even without a load to carry, to match the experienced bush-guerrillas for speed of movement. After an exhausting hour, they felt the ground under their feet begin to slope, and they found themselves emerging into a clearing by a great orange river.

Abraham was preparing the men to cross, a manoeuvre they had embarked upon many times but one which made the bootleggers somewhat anxious. Benjamin realised that his memories of the river were either of a dried-up path, or a benign, slow-moving flow of clay-red water, used for washing clothes and bodies. Now it had swollen in the rains into a far more unruly and turbulent adversary then he could ever recall.

The soldiers were experienced in such matters, however, and they operated with great stealth and discipline. They produced a set of ropes, which they started to thread through each other's belts in order to form a human chain. As chance or design would have it, Benjamin was first in line without even realising it. He had stayed close to Abraham, talking to the soldier about people in Kroy they had both known, enquiring as to their welfare, or otherwise, as had too often proved to be the case.

– I ... I ... he stammered, as the troops pointed him in the direction of the water's edge.

– Go now, Abraham said, beaming like a kindly priest. Joseph looked at him and nodded with anxious encouragement.

With the look of a condemned man, Benjamin tentatively waded into the river, half expecting to be cut loose and swept away and to hear the gleeful, twisted laughter of the others singing in accompaniment to his cruel demise. His heart raced to his mouth as he felt the powerful currents pulling at him. Taking one step too many, Benjamin cried out, suddenly feeling the riverbed pulling away from under his feet like a rug. Joseph, next in line, cursed and steadied himself, bracing for the wrench that pulled him forward towards his floating friend as the sinew in the legs and arms of all soldiers behind strained to keep him anchored. Benjamin flapped and struggled against the current for a bit, but was able to feel his feet sink into the clay-like mud of the riverbed once again. – Watch, he shouted back in warning, – it gets deep for a stretch, his tone effecting a defiant casualness which belied the extent of his fear.

Although Joseph was taller than Benjamin, after a bit he too couldn't feel anything under his feet. His heart skipped a few beats as he was whipped up like a toy in the swirling waters, but the men behind him held firm, as did Benjamin ahead. With Joseph safely over the worst, Benjamin now had an additional anchor and Marshall, Abraham and the rest of the men and the barrels and equipment were brought over one body or piece at a time.

The suitcases were almost last, and Marshall thought that the soldiers might be able to transport them, by some means, over the water level. But no, they were crudely threaded through the rope by their handles. Benjamin and Marshall glanced disconsolately at each other as the cases bobbed in the river. Each man tried to make a mental inventory of his contents, attempting to ascertain what sort of damage the water might cause.

After walking for about 20 minutes, they came upon some *tukuls*, then more. The dwellings continued to concentrate and they were in the town of Kroy. The rebel soldiers took them down a path to a clearing, which had two empty *tukuls* in it. – This is where you will stay for now, Abraham said, – until we can arrange to see Chief Israel and His Excellency, the High Commissioner for the Province of Kumuara. You and your equipment will be safe here.

Then the army departed, leaving the bootleggers alone, and in such alien surroundings. Marshall opened his suitcase. The clothes were a little wet, but not too bad. Benjamin checked the contents of his case, tutting gently as he took out some wet shirts and draping them over the thatched roof of a *tukul*. He stood back and gave a satisfied grin. – There. They will soon dry in this heat.

Marshall, though imitating his actions, was nonetheless highly frustrated and agitated at the turn their fortunes had taken. – We have lost our lorry and our driver. We are in the middle of nowhere, and surrounded by maniacs with guns, some of whom are only children, Marshall scoffed, casting his eye around the site, empty, save for what they'd brought with them. – Is this what we left our homeland for?

Joseph said nothing, but fixed Benjamin in a rapacious stare.

Benjamin was happy to be back and this time did not let the hostility of the others disperse his good cheer. – We have the patronage of the local commander and the High Commissioner. We will be well looked after and respected. Come, let us go into the town!

Joseph and Marshall looked at each other and shrugged wearily. Benjamin and Marshall then annoyed Joseph by insisting on changing into white shirts, which they had dried out in the sun. As dusk fell, the men walked into the town, wearied by their excursions, and headed into the market square. Although the traders were closing down, it looked as if it would be busy in the daylight hours. The situation wasn't all bleak, Joseph conceded to himself; the air felt fresh and sweet in his city lungs, and he looked at the others with delight as their ears registered music. It came from a spartan bar around the edge of the square. Best of all, both the Kenyan bootleggers were pleased to find that their Sudanese friend was right about the village girls. Some young women, alone or in giggling groups, looked them up and down and flashed synthetically coy and demure smiles. – It is like a discothèque in Nairobi, Marshall observed approvingly, as they instinctively headed towards the bar.

This validation was the sweetest music of all to Benjamin's ears. – See my friends! We will have all the best women. Give them dresses and they will sleep with you! We have high status here! For some, a hairclip or a ribbon is all it takes!

The watering hole was as basic as it could be; four bare walls, a bar, some wooden tables and benches. Behind the bar sat an old refrigerator, which was crammed with bottles of imported beer and soft drinks. African music rattled from an old cassette tape deck stuck on a corner table.

Only a few people were present in the bar, traders or

officials being the only ones who could afford the luxury of a beer. This was a great encouragement for the would-be brewers, although the exclusion of women meant that most of their wooing would have to be done in the marketplace. Joseph, who was dressed casually, was inwardly cursing Benjamin and Marshall for their attire of white shirts and ties setting them apart from the locals. It was folly to stand out, in a place like this, at least until they knew the situation.

And Benjamin was happy to be home at last, although nobody he knew as a youth seemed to be around. Nonetheless, he was coming back to his old town from the big city, and as a success. – My friend, what did I tell you! It is going to be so fine, Benjamin enthused. – So, so very, very fine!

MINES

The following morning, on the outskirts of Kroy, a bicycle tore down the bumpy road of compacted red earth. It was the one the army had requisitioned from the schoolteacher after the taking of Hoki. Oliver was peddling frantically and chickens, goatherds and children scattered from his path. Eagles, seeming as numerous as pigeons in temperate zones, circled imperiously overhead. The sun was coming up from behind a fresh sheltering of foliage and fauna, which encompassed every conceivable shade of green. Passing the church where he knew that a famous bishop was buried, Oliver looked up into the huge tower, which was the biggest in the town of Kroy. Even larger than the now-abandoned Muslim mosque which, like its counterpart in Hoki, had been left and was burnt out when the Arabs fled north after the liberation of the area by the SPLA, many years earlier.

Oliver had an urgent appointment to keep down by the river. When he got there, his spirits rose as he saw

Mary Boadiah, wearing a bright yellow dress and standing serenely by its shimmering waters, her hands clasped together in front of her. But not for long, as she was soon rolling around on a grassy bank, locked in an embrace with the old warlord's youngest son.

– Will you always love me? Mary asked him, half-joking, half deadly serious.

Oliver replied in the manner to which he had become prone. – You are so beautiful ... we will be married and be together forever ... oh, my darling, you are divine, he mouthed deliriously as his hands ran over her lithe and supple body, the resultant sensual data accrued frying his brain.

They both knew the nonsense of those comments, of how they never seemed to exist outside of the embraces and caresses, but also how they had become such an essential accompaniment to moments such as these.

As they languidly and tenderly made love in the heat, the pink shirt discarded from his back, Oliver remembered the brightly coloured military map his father had given him. He'd absorbed its details earnestly, knowing where all the landmines in the area were. He thought of the danger of such devices of destruction, some planted only a few feet away from them. Their perilous proximity was very sexy to him, heightening the sense of arousal.

But in reality some of the mines were a lot closer, having shifted due to the rains.

Mary felt inclined to alter the pace of their love-making, and with that unpredictability of passion he loved in her, the girl twisted from under the young man, pinning him down and pulling herself on top of him. Then she started to ride him with a ferocious passion.

Oliver was completely enthralled now, but something was distracting Mary. The couple were being sniffed at by the mangy, stray dog from the town square, which had tentatively stalked towards them. Oliver was in such rapture, he did not even try to shoo the beast, but Mary, fearing a bite, tensed slightly in her last-ever movement, for there was a deafening sound and a flash of blinding yellow light. A splintering of bone was followed by a splattering of blood, which splashed across the rusty soil of the riverside, accompanied by a torrent of crumbled earth.

Abraham, who had just left the hungover bootleggers after checking that they had settled in, heard the explosion as he drove into town. He turned back to investigate. A woman, washing her clothes by the river, had been the first on the scene. She shook as she told the two soldiers that she saw the girl Mary Boadiah heading down to the river with Israel's son. – They have both been seen there, she told Abraham, – many, many times!

There was a huge hole where the explosion had taken place, and chunks of burnt corpse lay strewn about it, in no easily identifiable order.

Abraham looked over at his fellow soldier, a man called Kenneth. They shared the nervous, grim laughter of men who had seen too much butchery, either to indulge in the luxuries of turning away or squirming in its face. – What a way to going though: at least one would have to say that the Earth moved for them both! Abraham jested, as Kenneth slapped his thigh in appreciative response.

The soldiers guffawed a bit longer before falling into a stunned silence. – I liked that boy, Abraham said eventually, breaking the ice.

Kenneth nodded in a sombre agreement, then considered, – Who will break the news to Israel?

Burial

Israel had taken the news of Oliver's death badly. For two days he had sat on a stool outside his *tukul* moping, only moving indoors when the sun was direct, thinking over and over again about the idiocy of the boy. He must have remembered the military briefing and the issue of the map, yet he was stupefied by his carnal lust, which had blinded him to this tutelage. – He knew where the mines were, he was given a map! Israel said once again to Abraham, who was pouring petrol into the tank of a vehicle.

Abraham put the can down and stood calmly by his leader's side. – They shifted in the rains, he replied gravely, and for the third or fourth time that afternoon. Was the old man going sick and enfeebled in the head, he considered, or was it just grief? Whatever, he had a matter to air. With a slight cough, Abraham began diffidently: – This may be a difficult time, great warlord, but might I air a personal matter?

– Yes, yes ... Israel said distractedly. What had that foolish youth been thinking of? He had been given a map, a comprehensive map!

Recalling his time, back in a hospital in Uganda some years ago, Abraham recollected the football shirt worn by the team on the satellite television-transmitted game. – Your son, he had from his travels procured a foreign football strip which I have, over the last few weeks, come to admire greatly ...

Israel looked at Abraham with such an air of disgust that the lieutenant felt moved to hastily elaborate and explain himself.

– I mean, since your son's arrival here and his joining with our forces, I felt that we became friends as well as comrades, and that Oliver would have wanted me to have this item of clothing, which meant something to me.

Israel sniffed wearily in his grief. It was two days since his son's death. A suitable period of mourning had surely now passed. – Take it. Take the blasted thing. Take any of his belongings you desire. All I wanted was his heart and soul, to forge and mould in the heat of battle into its warrior destiny. Now they are gone.

– Thank you, thank you great sir. I will ensure that Oliver is given a hero's burial with full military honours, all the leading SPLM people will be ...

– Ha! Israel silenced him with a sneer, his eyes screwing up in the sun. – The people know the truth. My son was no warrior. He was weakened by the twin curses of religion and sex. Build a mausoleum here by my *tukul*, and I will remember what he *could* have been, should have and would have been, a hero who died in battle like his brothers.

Israel was now contemplating his problem deeply. The issue was one of succession. If he could father another son, and this time school it himself ...

Abraham nodded thoughtfully, trying not to show the excitement of his anticipation in adding the football strip to his wardrobe. – As you wish, sir.

The funeral arrangements did not go smoothly, however, as a major problem presented itself. This was the identification and status of the corpse.

It was difficult, under the devastating impact of the explosion, to determine exactly what constituted Oliver, as opposed to either Mary or the dog. Abraham himself could make out the boy's head, but it was burst open at one side, and the grey matter of the brain melded with that of Mary's whose cranium was ripped open at the top like a boiled egg. Picking through this mess would be a waste of time. So under Abraham's instructions, the soldiers, when confronted with a pile of bloody stew and bone, basically, apart from a few obvious stand-out parts, scraped the gory remnants into three piles; greater, medium and lesser. Then they sentenced the remains to three different graves, commensurate in grandeur with their scale and status.

CAMPING OUT

His Excellency was enthralled by the idea that a brewery would open in the Kumuara Province. Israel himself, though still shrouded in gloom at the death of his son, was also inclined to be positive about it. It was Abraham who had suggested that the bootleggers set up their operation in Hoki, instead of Kroy. He reasoned to the old warlord that it would be a way for him to cement his influence, by appeasing hostile locals who feared that everything worthwhile would be plundered from Hoki and taken to Kroy. Israel was happy to agree, his despotically controlling instincts telling him that beer, more than bread, kept the people happy and content.

And so the bootleggers were approached to relocate near to Hoki, by an old vehicle storage depot, which was constructed from rusty sheets of corrugated iron. Many such panels, though, had been pilfered over the years, leaving the structure looking a little threadbare and skeletal. The Kenyans accepted this and quickly settled in to their new environment, befriending many of the local market traders in their search for the materials in order to start the brewing process. Supplies of both corn and coconut were abundant, and the Kenyans had brought their own methylated spirits.

As had been the case in Kroy, the men attracted some attention in the town, simply by virtue of being outsiders with their colourful, relatively expensive clothes and also due to the Kenyan shillings that they were not averse to flashing around. Once again, both factors impressed the local girls, although Joseph, as leader, was keen to get on and get the brewery set up before they enjoyed the fringe benefits associated with their position as traders and manufacturers in the area. A low profile was called for, and he grew impatient with Benjamin and Marshall's ostentatiously amorous antics. However, the tender skin around his groin and belly was beginning to heal and his own temptation would surely grow, too.

Dancing

Israel had ensured that the young woman, Alice Farrante, had been well briefed by Paul, the village elder in Hoki. Alice was a young, slim girl, with fine features and a statuesquely graceful build, who was one of the minority of Jamuri stock in Hoki. Alice had been picked to partner Israel at the dance to celebrate the victory.

Israel himself had been thoroughly shaved by Paul for this occasion, at the private bar and barbecue behind the public bar on the main square. Here, at each round, which consisted of one song, five couples were asked to dance to taped music. The sounds were either African drum music, or Western songs, by artists such as Bryan Adams, Bryan Ferry, Phil Collins and Robert Palmer. Then, when every round had been completed and every one had danced with a partner, the floor would open to a free-for-all, and the party began in earnest. When the compère got up to announce the first five sets of dancers, after pairing four couples, he gave the name: – Israel Kobache, then added in a low voice, just in case there was any ambiguity: – commander of our victorious army, will dance with Alice Farrante.

Alice was one of the prettiest and most sought-after girls in Hoki, and a few young soldiers present had to stifle groans after the announcement. In this ritual, the male dancer had to go round the assembled company and seek out his partner. There was some embarrassment, for in the darkness of the night, the tables lit only by candlelight, the half-blind old warlord had to be almost led by the hand to where Alice sat waiting, striking up a bashful pose.

Unlike his old rival Jacob Chidoze, Israel was no dancer, stiff, awkward and clumsy in his movements. However, the taste of victory and the good cheer of his troops assured that his adrenaline was high enough to get him through the performance.

After the dance, Israel nodded curtly at Alice, and turned away, making his way back to his seat. He said to Paul the elder: – That one is good. She is pretty, but knows how a woman should behave. This afternoon I saw women kicking a ball in the square. What way is that for a woman to behave? I do not approve of women playing sport, no, not at all.

Paul smiled grimly. Alice was one of the football players at the exhibition games on the main square, thankfully now unrecognisable to Israel in her party dress. Nonetheless, he would have to brief her about the need to drop her footballing activities.

Paul, normally a happy and gregarious man, had been forced by the urgency of circumstance to take on a serious bent in his briefings with Alice. – Should the warlord find it hard to get, or maintain an erection, you must not laugh, joke or attempt to belittle him in any way. This will bring dishonour and disrespect to our people. No, it will be your liability if this fails to happen. I cannot even begin to say how important this is, Alice Farrante. You are making love for our people. The Elder rested his bony fingers on the young girl's shoulders. – Our future rests with you.

A strange mixture of revulsion and honour had stirred in Alice when it was announced to her after the dance that she was to be the chosen one. The status had briefly turned her head, following the heady atmosphere of the festivities and the victory for the Jamuri in Hoki. Now the old fear had resurfaced. – But he is so old ...

– Do not fear child ...

Alice had heard stories, albeit mostly from Nazuri friends hostile to Israel, but which nonetheless concerned her. – ... and his preference in his declining years is said to be for boys ...

Paul shook his head vigorously, and his eyes blazed in genuine anger. – Do not dare to repeat the nonsense and the scurrilous rumours spread by our enemies! Now collect your belongings and go to him, Alice Farrante!

The following evening Alice moved into the principal *tukul* in the old warlord's compound. It was night and she could not see the old man, only hear his shallow breathing in the darkness as she approached his cot. She feared for his heart, worrying about what would happen if she fornicated the old warlord to death, what sort of political or military crisis would be precipitated?

The old scoundrel was wide awake, though, and she thought of how he must have been watching her outline in the door of *tukul*, lit up by the moon and the stars. In spite of all his warrior's instincts telling him it was weakness, Israel almost felt the breath being squeezed from his old lungs in sight of such beauty. There was a flutter in his heart and a moisture seeped into his eyes. Then, lower down, just like a good soldier, something stood to attention and the old man was almost moved to send off a prayer of thanks to some higher power. – Come and lie with me, the warlord wheezily commanded.

Shutting her eyes, Alice Farrante thought of younger, fresher men, with taut skin, men who did not drool, and she started playing with herself discreetly, so that she might be ready to receive him painlessly when the awful moment came.

KILLER BEES

In Hoki, people knew a great deal of the injustice and cruelty of war, but they could still be shocked when nature chose to augment man's folly. On the road to Kroy a woman lay on the ground, although you only knew it was a woman from the cries of her children, as she was covered, almost completely, by rust-coloured bees. Everyone stopped, watching her groaning and kicking out slowly, as if in some sort of dream-disturbed sleep. Eventually, some people fetched rags, which they tried to light in order to smoke the African killer bees away from the woman.

The *Biza*, who had joined the crowd, casually observed this scene and made a pronouncement. – She will survive. The bees make a lot of noise but most of them are impotent after one sting, and he looked waggishly over at Israel, the old warlord, who was passing by in his army vehicle. The truck horn blared and the crowd moved to let the soldiers through before bunching up again. And now the crowd was growing in numbers as lighted blankets were waved downwind of the stricken woman. It seemed that everyone had stopped to watch the scene, apart from one body, which was coming straight towards them, lurching into town. And the crowd parted and shivered as this bizarre and repulsive thing, this hideous, mutant creature, staggered on past them, not registering them or their drama through its one large eye.

Even the Witchdoctor was temporarily rendered mute, as this skinny, ragged demon lurched away from them towards the town. One woman said to him: – What is it *Biza,* what is it?

All the Seer could do was cough without conviction: – This is a sign that the spirits are displeased.

Another rebel army vehicle following behind Israel's banged its horn and the crowd parted, like the bees under the smoke, the insects finally starting to peel off the prostrate woman. Then many of the villagers panicked and beat a hasty retreat, mindful of how the swarm of bees, as if they were a single entity, sought only one victim and attached themselves to that unfortunate person. One boy was battered against the oncoming truck's side and yelped like a dog, holding his hip in pain. The soldiers scarcely registered his plight. They soon left the crowd behind, but then were forced to slow down abruptly so that they would avoid colliding with the crippled presence, walking on ahead of them, taking up the whole road. The driver pushed the horn and shouted and cursed at the lumbering creature in front of them. When it turned to face them, he almost ran the truck off the road. It was a badly mutilated girl, and as she saw and registered their uniforms, she screamed, then with a speed so discordant with the structure of her crippled body, ran into the long grass by the track and vanished out of sight.

The *Biza* was correct: the heavily stung woman did survive. Scarcely anybody noticed, though, as all the talk was of the strange, wretched girl-creature who had come into the county. In his excited mind, the *Biza* tried to reconcile the girl's coming with a vivid dream he had had that morning. A persistent voice had told him, with great clarity, that a demon-child born of warriors would stalk this land and would repel the enemies before being lain to rest. While he was still unsure what the prophecy meant, he was determined to let everyone in the marketplace know about it.

Serpents

Marshall had been walking in the country grass with a girl from the village, whom he had met at the market. She seemed so pleased with the simple red ribbon he had given her for her hair, that the man from Nairobi, who had been compelled by harsh circumstance to make crime his life, for the first time actually *felt* like a thief. The amorous couple, looking for a suitable spot to settle down and enjoy each other, were disturbed when Marshall felt a bite on his ankle. He cursed and turned to see a snake slithering away. Examining his leg, Marshall saw the teeth marks and watched the area around them swell up before his eyes.

The girl looked at the wound. – Bad, she said. – The bite of the snake. Bad.

It was painful, but his ardour was such that Marshall ignored it, and carried on with his mission.

Later he returned to the rusting tin shack that they now called the brewery. In spite of his satisfied air, he was concerned about the bite, and, in superstition, rubbed at the puffed-out white lettering on his red top.

The next day Marshall found that the swelling had not gone down, and he began to feel sick. As he rose in the morning, Joseph and Benjamin were already up, and working on replacing some of the old corrugated iron panels with ones they had been given by the rebel army.

– I must find a doctor, he moaned. He turned to Benjamin. – What happens with those snake bites? Benjamin, you are from here: tell me what I should do …

Benjamin looked at his friend's ankle and shrugged. – Oh, I cannot say, my friend. There were no snakes here in Benjamin's time; the Sudanese man patted his own chest. – I have never seen one before.

Marshall squealed in fright as the panic rose in him. – How can this be! There must always have been snakes! Tell me what to do! I am sick!

Benjamin shrugged meekly, but Joseph was irked by Marshall's complaints, working hard as he was at setting up the brewery. – Sick? Sick he says! Phoo! We have no time to be sick! Not from the bite of a puny grass snake! We have to work! he barked, dropping his end of a sheet of metal and causing Benjamin, carrying the other end, to let go of his, his hands stinging as its sharp edge scraped them.

Joseph put his hands on his hips. The injustice of the situation vexed him greatly. Marshall and Benjamin spent most of their time in the market, gambling with the traders and fooling around with the village girls. – The work is mostly all down to me, though others will be quick to claim the fruits of the enterprise! Oh yes, they will! he complained bitterly.

– But I am unwell, this is not a matter for joking, Marshall appealed.

Joseph poo-pooed this again and was about to elaborate on the extent of his perceived injustice, when he heard the noise of a vehicle's motor running and its suspension jangling on the road. Turning, he saw an old jeep approaching them.

It was the old warlord Israel himself. He stepped out of the car, domineeringly greeting Joseph and Marshall. A man in a yellow shirt with steel-rimmed glasses, who had his hands behind his back and looked important, followed him.

Joseph had been enjoying the patronage of the old warlord and the local rebel army. He was delighted when they'd turned up yesterday with some more old sheets of corrugated tin. – Great warlord, he sang with obsequious cheer.

Israel, for his part, was keener than ever to encourage this enterprise. Nobody had anything like this in all of Sudan! Even, especially, the hated Arab Muslims in the north! The young upstart Luke Chediah had no brewery in Nambaro! Yes, the Nazuri had nothing like this and he, Israel Kobache, had generously bestowed it on Hoki's people, half Nazuri, half Jamuri. Of course, it had to be controlled and monitored to ensure that local people did not become weak drunkards. Discipline could not be eroded, but it was true that brew did engender contentment wherever it was introduced in the world. It was no bad thing for the people of Hoki to be content.

– How are things progressing? Israel enquired.

– Very well, Commander Israel, Joseph smiled fawningly. – We are almost ready to start gathering the harvest to brew our first batch of ale.

Israel's stony face remained impassive, as he took this news and then gestured to the man at his side. – Let me introduce you to His Excellency, the High Commissioner for the Kumuara Province, Israel said grandly, sweeping a hand towards the politician. Joseph wiped his own sweaty hand on his trousers again, before shaking with His Excellency. He then looked anxiously to the distracted Marshall, who then wearily extended his hand as Benjamin eagerly scurried over to follow suit.

– Ah, it is so good to meet you sir, Joseph brayed. – We were, of course, with most certainty, intending to see you about obtaining some form of licence from your Ministry in order to conduct our activities. But you see, great sir, that first we wanted to get the product right, in order to provide you with the samples you will require so as to make an evaluation of our skill as brewers and the social worth to the community of our product.

His Excellency nodded slowly, smiling like a Nile crocodile which had just enjoyed a substantial meal. It was truly a vindication of the success of his movement that businessmen were coming up *from Nairobi,* to set up an enterprise of this sort. The rivals on the regional council would be most impressed. – I will inform the

Commissioner responsible for these affairs and he will be in touch, His Excellency smiled, nodding and heading back to the jeep.

Israel moved closer to Joseph and dropped his voice. – His Excellency is pleased. But you must be fully operational soon. Anything you need, you ask Abraham. Anything, do you understand?

– Yes, thank you so much, great Commander.

Stepping even closer to the brewer and lowering his voice further, Israel hissed urgently, – And the water you use in the brew, check first with Abraham, to ensure it is from a supply where there is no evidence of contamination. This is of paramount importance, do you understand? He ground his teeth together and stared at the bootlegger like a prizefighter.

Joseph nodded in solemn agreement. – Oh yes, I will ensure that Abraham approves the water supply.

Israel nodded curtly, snapped at the other soldiers, and without the grace of the politician, headed back to the jeep. As it departed, he shouted back at the brewers: – Remember what I said!

– We must work harder, all of us, Joseph hissed at his associates. – We must be fully operational soon!

– But my leg ... I cannot gather coconuts and corn ... Marshall complained.

Joseph shook his head and spat in acid loathing. – Then we must recruit some villagers to gather the coconuts! I am setting up the brewhouse! Am I the only one who is prepared to work?

TEASE

As Valerie Nuando came upon the village square, she saw two wiry-looking men, unfamiliar to her, both dressed in relatively expensive clothes. They were leading a troop of women and young boys who were carrying sacks full of coconuts. One of the men, wearing khaki shorts and a red surfing shirt who looked like he was on holiday, smiled broadly as they passed her. He had Jamuri markings and Valerie also noted a gold ring on his finger. – Hello ... he burred.

– Hello, she replied, almost surprising herself with the flirtatiousness in her voice.

The man extended his hand. – I am Benjamin, and this is my colleague Joseph, he said, introducing a man who gave her a slow, hard smile and a nod.

– My friend is a Kenyan, Benjamin explained, as if excusing Joseph's lack of enthusiasm.

Valerie regarded them with a glint in her eye. – So you are the brewers I have heard so much about?

– Yes, Benjamin said, now starting to notice Joseph's withering stare. He stole up closer to Valerie and whispered: – and you are the schoolmistress. You work at the church. May I stop by later to talk to you properly?

Valerie raised her eyebrows and walked away haughtily. Then she looked back and said: – There is nothing wrong with talking, before turning again and continuing into the church.

Benjamin admired her full body, then turned to Joseph. – A real woman, my friend. The young girls, they look so fine and pretty, but there is nothing like a real woman.

– Enough, Joseph spat, and they rushed to catch up with and follow the procession.

Valerie got back into the church and began to prepare some food for herself and Father Roache, who was reading in the vestry.

After about an hour, there was a knock on the kitchen door. She opened it and the smiling bootlegger Benjamin stood before her. – What do you want? she asked him.

– Just to go for a walk with you ... down by the river.

How long had it been since she had been down by

the river with a man? Valerie laughed loudly at the thought. – You are no more than a boy, she smirked.

– Please ... Benjamin's eyes grew larger.

– I am a respectable Christian woman.

– I am a respectable Christian man!

Valerie laughed again. – I have heard the stories of you brewers and the girls from the village!

– If you cannot come down to the river with me, please step outside and give me one kiss, just one kiss.

Valerie looked around. It could not surely hurt. Just one kiss. And they embraced and shared a long kiss. She could feel something pushing against her thigh. She broke off the kiss.

– Please ... please come down to the river with me, Benjamin did a little dance of exasperation in front of her.

Valerie threw up her hands and laughed, shaking her head spasmodically. – Look at me. You do not want me, she said, then she grabbed one of her own breasts roughly through her T-shirt, and held it like it was a weapon, a boulder she was about to hurl at an adversary. – Those flabby breasts that many children have suckled!

– You say that I am a child. Let me suckle at them, too!

– No!

– One more kiss then, that is all, I promise. He pleaded so sadly, that she could not refuse this handsome young man. They locked into another embrace, and their hot tongues twisted like duelling vipers, and for a while Valerie Nuando was able to lose herself and take flight from the pain of the mortal world around her.

A nervous cough jerked them into the present. Father Roache stood in the doorway. – I'm sorry to disturb you ...

– Oh Father, forgive us, we ... Valerie began, buckling away and she started to cross herself, but she saw the gravity on the priest's face, a seriousness which transcended any worry she might have had as to his feelings about what he'd witnessed. Benjamin grinned humbly at the priest who ignored him.

– No ... no ... Father Roache began, bleating nasally, seeming to be in a strange trance, – Love must be taken where it's found. I believe that even more than ever after the sight I've just witnessed outside ...

And they were now aware of the crowd of townsfolk outside the church, who were silently watching as the deformed, mutilated girl, clad in rags, hobbled down the dirty path into the square. Her toeless feet bled and there were sores on her legs. The villagers who encountered her backed away in horror, for she had no ears, nose or lips. Just raw, black-rust and blood-red gaps which snarled in anger, where those features should have lain. And she only had one eye, one red, lidless eye, which she covered from the merciless sun by a finger-less flipper of a hand. With her lips cut off, the serrated-edged skin would have given her a permanent grin of clowning evil. But all of the girl's teeth had been removed, so all that was visible under the hole that was her nose was a monstrous black cavern, which dominated the lower part of her face.

Only one person recognised her and screamed in a strange mix of horror and delight so hybrid, so paradoxical that the warpedness of it sent a chill which ate up Benjamin's spine in the blistering heat.

The bootlegger beat a subtle retreat, vanishing into the crowd as Valerie Nuando ran to the zombified girl, passing through the fearful crowd of villagers, and held her in her arms, crying: – Shola, my Shola, oh dear Lord, what have they done to my beautiful little Shola, oh no, no ... The girl was physically halted in her stumbling trajectory by the barrier that Valerie's form imposed, but otherwise gave no reaction to having her progress impeded.

Then she glanced up with that one, crazed, suffering eye, and opened her lipless, toothless mouth. And the schoolteacher could see that only half of her tongue remained, the rest of it having been crudely cut out. In spite of this the girl made a noise, which Valerie Nuando believed was Mama.

FLOWERS

For five years Valerie had prayed for the return of her daughter. Now Shola was back, but in name only. What was returned to her was scarcely recognisable as the happy, outgoing, beautiful young girl who had been taken.

Valerie took Shola back to her *tukul* up by the river, where she wrapped the girl in blankets and watched her sleep. The sheets over the girl's head covered both the always-sightless red-raw socket, and the other one, which could not shut, doomed as it was to witness everything.

Then, sitting by the river, under the night stars, Valerie prayed and wept. The pain leaking out of her near exhaustion took her into a heavy, fuggy trance, and she stumbled back to her hut and fell into her daughter's arms and sleep.

Sleep spared her; in Valerie's dreams she saw the girl as she had remembered her; reading, drawing, playing by the river. But in the dream there was the ominous threat of something lurking in the bush, something terrible, and it was coming for them. But in the sleep she held on to her Shola, protecting her child from this perilous, predatory evil, with every fibre of her body and soul.

When she awoke into the horror of the red, rising

daylight, to the twittering and squawking of the birds, and the distressed mews of the thin, ragged feral cat which skulked around, she looked at her ruined child. And Valerie Nuando felt the crashing, sinking agony bend and warp the space in her chest cavity as she found to her unmitigated abhorrence that the evil had again left its mark on their lives.

FEVER

Over the next day Marshall's condition grew steadily worse. The pain had spread up his leg and he was running a fever. Abraham, on his frequent security checks round Hoki, had been watching him, registering the fact that the Kenyan's limp was getting constantly more pronounced. He approached the bootlegger, who blinked as the sun glinted off the soldier's rifle. – I have noticed your bad leg, my friend. You have fallen foul of the snakes, yes?

– Yes ... I was bitten on the leg, in the long grass, Marshall said hesitantly, raising his hand to his brow in order to give his stinging eyes, which throbbed in their sockets, some relief from the cruel sun.

– Ah, such a terrible thing, the soldier incongruously smiled, the whites of his eyes blood red. – There were very few snakes in this part of the country before the bombings. Now the vibrations drive them over here. Children are bitten as they play in the grass. This war, eh!

Marshall shook in sick understanding, the wish now settling into his mind that he had stayed in Nairobi and braved the wrath of the Christian women and the authorities.

– And there is no local medical hospital, Abraham explained, with a sadistic delight, as Marshall's face contorted in fear. – This cannot really be treated, only by amputation at the hospital in Lokichoggio. A terrible, terrible thing.

– But ... I cannot lose my leg! Marshall shrieked incredulously.

Abraham curled his bottom lip downwards, managing to convey a sorrow both deep, yet transparently insincere, for the terrible news he was bringing. – You will find it is either that, or die. But even life-saving amputation is quite an outside chance. You see, it would only work if we were to radio and apply for green light clearance. It is a Red Cross hospital and it is only really meant for the war wounded ... only an outside chance ... Abraham continued with relish, watching Marshall's eyes grow so huge it seemed now that the irises filled the sockets of his skull, – ... but for two thousand Kenyan shillings, I could try to get you green light clearance, and in a week they will come and take you away and amputate your leg.

– But ... there must be other things to be done!

Abraham ignored Marshall's plea. – If we make haste we may be able to get away with a below-the-knee amputation, he said, bending down and running his finger under Marshall's bony knee.

Marshall stepped back, almost feeling the phantom scalpel-cut in the soldier's blunt nail. Stuttering, and quaking with fear he whined, – But ... it is ... it is only the bite of a small snake! Can we not ... can we not cure this with medicine, or with ... with the help of the local Witchdoctor?

Now so immersed in his performance that he was starting to *feel* like an expert medical practitioner, Abraham gave a slow, resigned nod. – We have no medicines here, no hospitals. Nothing. You can trust yourself to the Witchdoctor if you choose, but the poultices and concoctions of a pagan fool will save neither limb nor life. On the other hand, I, for two thousand Kenyan shillings, can get the nurse to come out and make the assessment. If she agrees that it is worth amputation, she will take you away for the operation in Lokichoggio. If it has gone too far and nothing can be done, then she will leave you. Then ... he drew a finger across his own throat and made a choking noise, drinking in the bemused terror on the bootlegger's face. – So either way, there can be no guarantees. If the infection has not gone far enough and there are more pressing casualties, then she will leave you, until you become sicker so that amputation is necessary to save your life. Of course, the chances are that you will be dead by the time she comes back again, he shrugged, matter-of-factly. – It is an unfortunate situation, but a common one.

Marshall, now running a cold sweat, shook his head in disbelief and his voice went into a high, indignant whine, almost breaking in Abraham's ears. – But ... this cannot be ... it was only a snake ...

Nodding in a lazy, half-agreement, Abraham told him, – For sure, this could have been treated easily with medicines or a poultice earlier, but it is now way beyond that. Try such remedies if you will, but green-lighting you for an airlift will take perhaps as long as a week anyway, and, as I have told you my sick friend, you may already be dead by the time the nurse arrives. Therefore, I would advise you to give me the money and I will call them. You have little to lose and everything to gain.

Shaking with a fear he now fancied was raging fever, Marshall dug into his money belt and handed over the cash to a serious Abraham. The soldier counted it, occasionally glancing around to ensure their privacy, and said distractedly: – You are a wise man, my friend, a wise man in a place of great foolishness, and one who may yet survive this theatre of lunacy.

All the time, Marshall had the terrible sensation that Abraham was addressing himself.

Rituals

The inside of the *tukul* was half-flooded with an orangey-red, unreal enough to give away instantly its unearthly origins, as Alice heard the desperate, outraged crowing of the cockerel and opened her eyes into the early dawn. Then a whirring sound, almost mechanical, and of close proximity, registered in her brain. A huge, armour-plated beetle, the size of a man's fist, had somehow become entangled in the old, frayed and ripped mosquito net which covered the window just a few feet from her face. Aware with a sudden shudder exactly where she was, Alice turned with great care, so as not to wake the old warlord.

When she saw his leathery body, sitting bolt upright in the bed, she almost jumped out of her skin. Israel turned his head slowly and looked down at Alice, her naked shoulders and breasts swathed in the strange reddish glow, the light of the devil, he was given to speculating. The girl was useless. Nothing was happening with her.

The old warlord had been considering seeing the Witchdoctor again. He was worried by this strange prophesy, the word of which the *Biza* was relentlessly spreading around the marketplaces of both Hoki and Kroy. It surely meant that a future son of his opponent, Luke Chediah, would be the power in the region. In what should have been his greatest hour of triumph, Israel felt a mounting dismay that, in the longer term, things were looking worse than ever.

Alice, much to her relief, was dismissed, and Paul the Elder summoned. – The girl is of no use. Find another. One with bigger hips, he urged, holding his hands wide apart.

Paul nodded, made to move, then stopped. He began to reason haltingly: – We are now older men, my friend. It is not as if we can ...

He was cut short by Israel's glare. The warlord looked at his old friend and comrade with a brief surge of hate, only to find it quickly replaced by the flood of tired resignation. – Yes, yes ... then you must get me the *Biza*.

The *Biza* had been in Hoki's marketplace telling all about his latest prophecy and bragging to some doubtful traders about his influence on the victorious commander of the town. The traders took his boasts lightly, but this scepticism was to be dispelled when Paul and Abraham pulled up in a rebel truck. To the great shock of the Witchdoctor's cronies, Paul stepped out and addressed the *Biza* in tones of diffident respect: – Wise man, the Commander needs to see you immediately.

The *Biza*'s gap-toothed grin flashed through the marketplace as he climbed slowly into the truck after the elder.

Israel greeted the Witchdoctor with as much warmth as he could muster, leading him into his *tukul*. Lowering his voice, he said: – *Biza*, I need your help. As you know, with the passing of the years, the powers of a man may decline ...

The *Biza* thought about this for a few seconds. It ran completely contrary to his own beliefs and experiences, but he smiled and nodded in quiet agreement.

– ... especially in certain areas, Israel added, all the time scrutinising a silent Witchdoctor for signs of understanding. – Physical areas, he coughed.

While enjoying this, the *Biza* glanced outside at the serious faces of Paul and Abraham, who stood around looking grave enough to tell him that showing such enjoyment would be the most calamitous folly. – How can I help, Commander? he asked keenly.

– I have a young woman ... oh, enough of this. You know what I want. Your prophecy ... I must have a son. You know what to do, Israel barked.

The *Biza* seemed to deliberate for a few seconds, then nodded in slow affirmation.

Israel prompted further. – A spell, a potion perhaps. Do this, he commanded, and watched the Witchdoctor nod again, this time more emphatically.

The *Biza* promised that he would talk to the spirits and ask what should be done about Israel's problem. He was driven back to Hoki, where he elaborated on his influence in the marketplace. Several of the traders bought him cold beers from the bar, which the *Biza* consumed with a great relish. Later on, as the sun went down, he headed, quite intoxicated, back towards his home by the river.

On his journey down the Kua road, the Witchdoctor stumbled a couple of times and almost lost his footing. This was uncustomary, as he knew this path so well. Heading into the woods, guided through his drunkenness by the cool smells of the river, the *Biza* paused, contemplated something that amused him, and cackled loudly into the darkness. This guffaw was suddenly cut off, as the pagan was felled by a blow from the butt of a rifle before some men dragged him, groggy and screaming, through the scabrous woodland.

Feeling the ferns tear at his bare skin and the beery contents of his stomach separate from him, he slipped into a woozy trance somewhere just short of unconsciousness. Although too weak to resist or even protest, the *Biza* was aware enough to assume that he had been ambushed by Luke Chediah's men.

So it proved. After being dragged and pushed through the forest for what seemed like an eternity, he was bundled into the back of a waiting truck, which lay by the side of the road. Too weakened to curse his assailants, the *Biza* crouched in silence as he was taken to the young warlord's base at Nambaro.

After further torments, consisting more of threats than

actual beatings, fear and desperation moved the *Biza* to find his tongue, and he threatened to put a curse on Luke. – If I am not released and compensated for this outrage with two goats, the spirits will be displeased, and your eyes will be torn from your head by ...

– Do not threaten me with your nonsense, heretic, Luke snarled, silencing the prostrate, trembling, medicine man with a savage boot to his chest. – I am a Christian! He glowered and spat at the *Biza* who yelped in pain and decided there and then that he was absolutely terrified of this warlord and would not cross him. Sensing the older man's fear, Luke Chediah lowered his voice. – You serve me now, he said, in a proprietary tone, and one which the Witchdoctor had never heard from either of the old warlords' lips. Then the younger man smiled into the *Biza*'s large, terrified eyes. – Cheer up, old pagan; if you do my bidding, you will be rewarded with four goats.

The *Biza* was now totally engaged. His face opened up in a smile, only to have it crushed from him by the young man's vice-like hand, which with a swift motion of sudden violence, was gripped round his throat, constricting his windpipe.

The *Biza*'s head began to drift with oxygen starvation, and as the life was draining from him, he felt that familiar rising under his loincloth, just as the young warlord released his grip and pushed him to the dusty ground. As the *Biza* struggled to pull air into weakened lungs which felt as though they were full of hot coals, Luke outlined to him what the situation was. – But if you flout me, I will hunt you down and destroy you like a sick dog. Do you understand?

The Witchdoctor nodded slowly and fearfully.

– Now, why is it that you are visiting the old fool in Kroy? Luke asked, turning with a smirk to his colleagues, before adding more solemnly: – What is his state of mind?

The Witchdoctor told the young warrior about Israel's grief after the death of Oliver, and his desire to father another son, especially now, given the *Biza*'s own vision of the child of a great warrior wreaking terrible havoc on the enemies of his people.

– What nonsense is this? Luke spat in a stinging scorn, which shivered the Witchdoctor to the marrow. He was used to being either feared, or disdainfully ignored, but to be treated so contumely, with such active abhorrence, and by a hypnotically powerful young tyrant, was completely beyond his experience.

Managing to find his voice, the *Biza* croaked in protest: – This came from the spirits. They said that the offspring of a warrior would wreak havoc through this distressed homeland and banish the foes!

Luke, though, was now not even listening to the Witchdoctor, engaged as he was in counsel with his advisers regarding Israel's folly. – That old fool, Luke laughed. – That AIDS-spreading buggerer of young boys! Ha! He mocked, as his colleagues brayed in sycophantic concert. Akibo, the would-be commissioner, who had become one of Luke's most trusted advisers, whispered something in his commander's ear. The young warlord smiled and nodded in approval, then turned back to the *Biza*. – Let old Israel think that this conception is possible, he stated, then he dropped his voice and held the trembling pagan exhibitionist in his burning gaze. – Here is what you will do.

CURES

The shimmering orange disc of a sun rose from behind the thicket of lush tropical vegetation, its heat diminishing the river, giving the air round its bed a slightly vaporous hue and the taint of baked clay.

The Witchdoctor was up early, still a bit shaken and bruised from last night's encounter with Luke Chediah.

He took the herbal preparation he'd made on his return home yesterday evening, and washed some banana skins with it, letting it soak into them.

Concerned though he was about being stuck between a rock and a hard place, the *Biza* took succour from the fact that both warlords now sought his counsel. And his influence was surely spreading, as, in accordance with his growing status, he was becoming busier and busier. The boy Solomon, his helper, who was dressed in a ragged orange T-shirt and old blue shorts, came into the *tukul* and the child informed the *Biza* that someone was here to see him. Initially annoyed at this disturbance to his duties, the medicine man's attitude changed when the boy added: – It is a Kenyan man, a maker of brews, so they say.

The *Biza* had heard all about the bootleggers. They were the talk of the marketplace. Whatever happened in military or political terms, a brewer would always have power and influence. – Bring my Kenyan friend in!

Marshall, in a state of extreme agitation, limped into the *tukul* and sat down on a mat. Pointing at his bulging, reddened leg, he informed the *Biza* that a snake had bitten him. – Please, you must help me!

Bereft of any sign of emotion, the Witchdoctor patiently examined the wound. – I will, of course, require two goats in payment for the treatment, he said matter-of-factly.

– Can you cure it? Marshall asked in a desperate plea.

The *Biza* remained inscrutable. – It depends on the spirits, and what they say. He wagged a finger in front of his own stony face. – You see, sometimes they do not speak with one voice. That is what those who do not have the powers often fail to understand. Many can hear the spirits talk, but very few can work out what is meant by their utterings. But, of course, such consultations can only take place after the payment of two goats.

Marshall clasped his hands together in desperation. – I have no goats! Here, take those Kenyan shillings, he pleaded, digging into his money belt and thrusting notes at the medicine man.

The *Biza* raised his palms and turned his nose up at the money. – These are no good to me. Only goats! I need to build up a stockherd. You must go to the market and buy them. Only the sturdiest, mind you. In this task, he gestured over to his young apprentice who watched eagerly. – Solomon will help you. Now go!

Marshall looked at the boy, who promptly assisted him in getting him to his feet and urged the bootlegger to quickly follow. Struggling with his hindering limp and shaking body after the fleet-footed youngster, who skipped down the road and into town, Marshall saw the boy head for the crowded and bustling market. In the oppressive heat, flies seemed to swarm around his face and eyes, and he felt like he already stank of death.

Sick and stunned by the waves of nausea that rippled through him, Marshall suddenly felt the marketplace begin to spin around him. From the corner of his eye, he saw Benjamin, putting a ribbon into a bashful girl's hair, all smiles and joy, and this in the face of his pain and suffering! Marshall shouted something, or at least felt words clear from his throat, but somehow they failed to reach his mouth.

Then, just as he was almost totally consumed by an urge to charge over to Benjamin and rip his partner's throat open with the knife he carried in his belt, he felt a tug at his sleeve. Solomon's reappearance, with two young goats, restored some sense of perspective. – Come to my friend, the ragged boy said, pointing over at a smiling man by a herd penned into a small stockade.

Marshall was unaware of the rate, and in any case was too sick to bargain, parting with what seemed to him to be a lot of money. But he urgently needed to lie down, lest he weaken himself further and pump the infection round his stricken body. It was a long, torturous walk back in the blistering heat to the *Biza*'s, where the Witchdoctor had, in anticipation of his return, prepared three potions. Applying one to the wound, and another cold one to the grateful Marshall's sweating brow, and bidding him to drink the last, an almost clear, sweet elixir, the *Biza* then let the Kenyan collapse into a welcome sleep. As he began to drift into unconsciousness, he heard the medicine man say: – You will live, my friend, for you are strong and the spirits have willed it so. Yes, my Kenyan friend, you will live.

When he awoke several hours later, the Witchdoctor and his boy had left, the sun was going down and Marshall felt strong enough to blunder home. On the difficult journey in the twilight, the *Biza*'s reassuring noises about recovery were sweet music to his ears, and he fancied he could still hear the old pagan whispering encouragement, promising salvation.

Unknown to him, however, as he slept, Solomon, milking the goats, had asked the medicine man: – Will he live?

The Witchdoctor had shaken his head, sombre, yet at the same time smug. The bootlegger was a fool who had failed to take action quickly, and he was finished. – No. The spirits tell me that he is doomed, but it is best to let him live out his last days in hope. Hope is something we always need. To be able to buy such a gift for the paltry sum of two goats is the greatest bargain he will ever have made in his life, the *Biza* remarked, in munificent spirit. Then he cast his eye over the new additions to the herd. The white and brown male was aggressive, butting a previously dominant young goat. The Witchdoctor did an excited little skip of delight. – Ah, my young friend, what a fine eye you have for goats! Now you must take the herd for a walk while I meditate with the spirits and prepare for my visit to my great friend the old warlord.

So, while the bootlegger lay in a deep sleep, the *Biza* went back to see Israel. And in the privacy of his *tukul*, the Witchdoctor wrapped the reluctant old warlord's penis and scrotum in a sack made from oiled banana skins stitched together.

– What is this nonsense? the old man protested, as the *Biza* fastened the pouch by means of a string which went round Israel's waist and through his legs and between his buttocks.

– The skins must be from new fruit in order to bear new fruit. Keep this on for three days, then there will be no problem, the Witchdoctor sang. – Now, my friend, might I take the goats I was promised?

The old warlord looked gravely at the Witchdoctor. – Only when the girl bears the fruit of my loins.

– A bargain made cannot be reversed, *Masambi*. If the sacred contract is dishonoured, then the spirits feel cheated. The girl will bear only deformed idiots. The medicine man shook his head darkly.

Israel bristled for a second but then looked with something approaching fear at the gloomy, knowing smirk on the *Biza*'s face. It seemed to invoke the knowledge of some higher, greater, more terrible power than his own, and a demoralised Israel felt subdued by it.

– Give him his goats, the warlord shouted outside the *tukul* in the direction of Paul the Elder.

As he moved towards the exit of the hut, the *Biza* turned and smiled piously back at Israel. – Are you sure that there is no other problem? The seed of the Warlord may be potent, but the device ...

– What? Israel looked briefly out at Paul to see if there was complicity on his old peer's countenance. A cursory gaze convinced there was none, and he turned back to face the Witchdoctor.

The *Biza* almost sang in elaboration. – A couple of days ago a woman on the Kua path was attacked by killer bees. You know the African killer bee. Once it has stung, it is rendered impotent ...

– Enough! You mock me! Israel roared, like a scarred old lion, and the Witchdoctor was almost convinced by the power of the warlord's wrath to fear that he had fatally overstepped his mark.

– I meant no offence, great warrior ... I only sought to convey to you that I have spells for every need ...

– Go!

The *Biza* did not argue, beating a hasty retreat, but only after he saw the truth in the eyes of the warlord. In that rage, as fearsome as it was, there was also inertia and paralysis. Israel had hit his boundaries. On the other hand Luke Chediah had not yet learned his weaknesses, had yet to make that shuddering impact with his own limitations. The young man was the future, and he was the man the *Biza* would cultivate. Yes, Israel's tenancy in Hoki would be a very short one.

On the Witchdoctor's departure, the old warlord himself felt the loss of power that comes with age, and a terrible sense that wisdom had not been accrued quickly enough to come anywhere near compensating. He commenced a quiet but desperate speech to himself, one that he hoped to his own ears would sound statesmanlike and dignified. – I am the Warlord. Yet, my powers wane. Might not the warrior find peace? Might not the soldier, upon seeing the beauty of the butterfly's wings, become an aesthete? The flesh of the female, once so tempting and succulent to the senses of touch, taste and smell ... Oh it, now seems like the wrestling of a large, whip-corded, sinewy snake. For as the battlefield of the war is lost, so too is the battlefield of home, the war zone of the bedroom. And it, too, is lost to the younger, the fitter, the more ruthless ... Israel winced and shut his eyes. Somewhere along the line his speech had turned into a declaration of surrender.

ROUT

Convinced that Israel was demoralised and his forces weakened, Luke Chediah prepared to launch a counter-attack to take Hoki. Luke's army was now bolstered by the return of the 40 men, who had come back from their excursion with the main rebel army in the oilfields. The mission had been a success, there had been no casualties and Luke had gained great influence with His Excellency and the SPLM by graciously refusing to complain that this deployment had weakened his Nazuri forces and cost them Hoki. – Our internal squabble, he told the politician, – serious as it is, cannot be allowed to undermine the war against the Khartoum Government and the Muslims, he stated boldly to approving nods of the SPLM officials, who were very impressed by his commitment.

But to his returning Nazuri troops, Luke was singing a different song. The men had come back fired up from the success of their mission, they had blown up a major pipeline which would seriously halt the production of oil, and were enraged to find that their home town had been taken and their families banished to Nambaro in their absence. They wanted their land and their town back, and they wanted Jamuri blood. With both, Luke would be happy to oblige. Buoyant with confidence that he would be successful in his first major test as Commander, Luke marshalled his army and made his rallying speech in the marketplace in Nambaro. – For every one of our men who died in Hoki, ten of our foes shall perish!

His men invaded Hoki with great ruthlessness, the

native Nazuri of Hoki, in particular, fighting like demons. They began with a full-on attack from the east end of the town, where a prominent spy had revealed to Luke that Israel's fortifications were weaker, and pushed on towards the main square. En route, *tukuls* were burned or bulldozed, the chairs and tables outside them smashed and thrown on to blazing pyres. Many Jamuri tribespeople, and some Nazuris, ran for cover, and diverse numbers crowded into the church for refuge. Alice Farrante, purchasing fruit from the market when she heard the first shots and learned of the enemy advance, was particularly terrified. As Israel's consort, she feared that she would be raped and beaten by incoming troops. Sneaking into the woods, she took the river trail, and headed with fearful stealth towards the sanctuary of Kroy.

Along the way, as she waded waist-high in a section where the river, in spite of receding recently, had swollen over the path, Alice screamed in terror as an almost naked figure jumped out in front of her. It was the *Biza,* and this realisation calmed her only slightly. Alice Farrante greatly feared this man and believed in his powers, as she had seen an exhibition of them in her childhood as she played alone by the river. – You are the old warlord's woman, he grinned, in salacious excitement. Then his face suddenly twisted and his sharp eyes sparkled with mischief. – But why do you hurry so to get to him? Is he so good? Ha!

Alice bleated in indignant consternation. – No! Chediah's men have Hoki! All is lost! We must go to Kroy!

The *Biza* would not let her pass, however. His withered-looking, but strong and flinty fingers grabbed her chin. – Yes ... you must go to Kroy, to Israel. You must bear a son. But when I summon you, you will come to me. If you are with child, he will be happy.

You must be with child soon, but the seed has no relevance. Do you understand?

– But I ... Alice stammered, feeling the rank odour of dead meat on the medicine man's breath, completely mesmerised by the urgent evil that fused his eyes.

– Obey me, or feel the wrath of the spirits, he groaned, his erection pressing into her thigh.

Alice could not avert her gaze from those maniacal orbs of the Witchdoctor, remembering when she had first seen him by the river, all those years ago. – Yes ... yes ... great *Biza* ... yes ...

– Now go! The *Biza* released his grip and watched her depart in haste, first admiring her shapely calves as her naked legs kicked through the water, then the suppleness of her body as she scrambled up the bank. Under normal circumstances he would have taken her there and then, but the current situation was far from normal, even in southern Sudan. Great opportunities could arise.

And the medicine man too moved swiftly, but in the opposite direction, heading for the sound of gunfire. With great stealth, he crawled through the woods, approaching the Catholic church from the rear, staying clear of the fighting that was evidently taking place around the square, where the pattern of gunfire informed him that the men had dug in and were exchanging shots.

Though he was no military strategist, a cold logic told the *Biza* that the ones with the least men and ammunition would eventually beat a retreat. It seemed also reasonable to assume that this would not be Luke Chediah's forces, as they had initiated the attack and, indeed, had got so far as the square without being repelled.

His timid raps on the back door of the church resonated with the priest who opened up and let him in. The *Biza,* like a man possessed, stole past Father Roache, barely registering the priest's presence, let alone his kind actions. Instead he scurried up to the pulpit and began hysterically addressing the frightened crowd. As the gunfire sounds exploded outside, the Witchdoctor roared at them: – This is the revenge of the spirits! This is as I prophesied!

– Yes! It is true! One old trader shouted at the assembled, frightened ranks, and many then frantically jostled and roared to make their own endorsements heard. Another man remarked that he had heard the *Biza* claim a peaceful and prosperous future for Hoki, but the prevailing mood was such that his voice was drowned out in the great need for affirmation.

The ratification of the majority of the souls present spurred the *Biza* on. – It was said that a new power would emerge, a power so magnificent that all would tremble in its wake. And this power will be from the fruit of the loins of a tribesman of great strength. This was my prophecy! This! And so it has happened! Luke Chediah is the new power, and his offspring will rule this province!

Father Roache and Valerie Nuando stormed the stage, and dragged the hysterical Witchdoctor from the pulpit. – Enough! The schoolteacher shouted, – or you will go outside and face the guns of Chediah, you blasphemous, pagan oaf!

The *Biza* became more compliant after a grenade explosion shook the building, but still croaked defiantly at the terrorised people as he was led away: – I am the *Biza!* I will not be silenced!

Outside, the ferocious fighting raged on. Israel's men had run out of grenades and were being repelled by the more numerous and committed forces of Luke Chediah. One of Israel's lieutenants, Kenneth, was vexed that Abraham had not shown up with reinforcements.

Ammunition was running low and they were being over-run. There was no option left but to abandon the Square. He gave the signal to retreat. In spite of this order, two Jamuri zealots held their positions, refusing to back away or down their weapons even when being overwhelmed on all sides by Nazuri forces.

Inside the church, Father Roache screamed: – Keep that door shut! No man of war enters this house!

The people cowered on the floor, or huddled together in corners, as the noises started to subside into the night.

Then there was a ghostly knock on the door. Father Roache tentatively answered it. A group of soldiers stood before him. One powerful-looking young man he knew by sight came forward and smiled and bowed in front of him. – Greetings, Holy Father. I am Luke Chediah, the Commander of the legitimate SPLA forces in Hoki. We have banished the criminal occupation of the tyrant Israel and his men, and restored peace to Hoki, he said, gunfire shots and the odd explosion still ringing in their ears. – Now we require your blessing.

– I am always happy to bless peace ... Father Roache said, and then, watching Chediah's eyes blaze, added diplomatically: – and those who bring it to us. Come in, but lay down your weapons.

Luke squinted a bit, then glanced to his men, who nodded, standing guard, his party passing over their weapons before heading inside the church.

The Witchdoctor, on seeing Luke, burst into delirious rapture. – This is the man! This is the great warlord whose offspring will destroy our foes! Commander, it is I, your great friend, the *Biza*!

He was silenced with a glacial, terrifying glance from Luke, which the Witchdoctor felt strip away several layers of his soul. Pausing to focus on the frightened faces present, Luke then got up onto the pulpit and made a speech about peace and reconciliation, to nervous cheers. Then he dismissed the crowds, who crept tentatively from the church and nervously across the Square, which was fortified with soldiers. Some looked at the frightened townsfolk, clocking faces, noting the direction in which they headed off.

And the spirit of Luke's speech would be adhered to, but only after the prior pledge in Nambaro to the bloodthirsty troops had been honoured. So in a carnage that lasted through the night and most of the next day, the town of Hoki was once more ravaged. More than 80 men, women and children, most, but not all, of whom were from the Jamuri, were butchered, later to be buried in a mass grave by the river.

Now the villagers of Hoki were to be assimilated into the regime of yet another new warlord.

Meanwhile, Valerie maintained her sanctuary in the church, holding her son Robert and his friend Moses, as they huddled in a dark corner of the small vestry. Her daughter Shola was hiding under the blanket close to them, her one eye glowing in the darkness.

HEARTLANDS

As the sun rose in the town of Kroy and the cockerels began their screeching wars, a car pulled up into Israel Kobache's compound of *tukuls.* Three men stepped out, and one of them was His Excellency, the High Commissioner of the SPLM in the Kumuara Province.

Even as his men fought a valiant rearguard battle on the outskirts of Hoki, the defeated old chief, in desperation, had asked for a meeting with the governing power in the province. This move underlined Israel's disheartenment, ridiculed as it was by both friends and rivals as indicative of great weakness. For as he strode, back as straight as a rod of iron, through Hoki's empty market where only a few traders had opened up their stalls, Luke Chediah,

Israel's victorious young rival, laughed on hearing of the old warlord's disgrace. – When the old fool loses, he sulks like a child and cries foul! That toothless old baby, crying, hanging on to His Excellency's skirts! He imitated baby gurgling sounds to the delight and amusement of his troops and the civilian advisers who followed him through the almost derelict marketplace.

Back in Kroy, the defeated old warlord cut a broken, pathetic sight to the High Commissioner, who could not believe that he once respected and feared this man so much. It used to be that his very name made one tremble. Now look at him, the politician thought with a contempt he battled hard to conceal; a fool, out of time and nothing in the New Sudan. The truth was that His Excellency had only come out to Kroy in order to gloat quietly in witness to the old warrior's demise.

To the administrator's scornful ear, it seemed as if even the warlord's voice had developed a pathetic warble. – We are a warrior people, but there must be some regard for human rights, Excellency, the old man said in baleful appeal. – The type of atrocities perpetuated by the thug Luke Chediah tars all Africans with the brush of barbarians and lends succour to our enemies in Khartoum and further afield. This is not our African culture!

– Ah, that is true, the High Commissioner smiled grimly back at the old warrior. For the first time, he could see white-grey stubble coming through on the old man's head and chin. Old Israel was so obvious. Did he really think that in order to secure his support he only had to flatter the High Commissioner in this way by imitating the sort of comments he himself had made to Israel down the years? Did he honestly believe that his lubberly attempts at Pan-African rhetoric would impress?

His Excellency the High Commissioner moulded his

face into a sympathetic smile, reminding Israel of a doctor who is about to tell a patient that he is suffering from an untreatable disease. – All we can do at present is to send our officers to Hoki to investigate and prepare a report. I'll be blunt with you, however, Israel, my old friend: Luke Chediah's stock is high with the SPLM. He has sent many men to our army of liberation's excursions in the north, and promises to send many more. Before your capture of Hoki, it had been peaceful for years and acquired a *de facto* Nazuri status. While I myself have kept an open mind on this dispute, I tell you, my friend, there are many on the council who believe that your seizure of Hoki was morally dubious and of spurious legality with regard to the constitution we are striving to develop here in southern Sudan.

The old warlord shook his head sadly. He knew as well as the so-called High Commissioner, this jumped-up clown, this office boy, this puppet, that Luke Chediah could afford more men than he could, now more than ever with Hoki in his control, and that this was what would interest the rebel high command. His own forces were struggling to function, and now, after the loss of Hoki, could not even be confident of securing their own territories.

Now Luke Chediah and his Nazuris once again controlled all the disputed lands, and Israel's greatest fear hung across the battered old table in that short space between the two men. It was that Luke would press on, into the Jamurian heartlands and Kroy, and rout his tribe completely, eradicating them once and for all. This mad boy was crazy enough to do this, to break the protocol established by his own mentor and Israel's old opponent, Jacob Chidoze. For the first time, Israel was almost actively mourning Jacob, recasting him as an old rogue, a jocularly thuggish but an essentially honourable and amiable figure. Surely it was in the SPLM's interests not to let that upstart Chediah become too powerful. Israel was at a loss to understand His Excellency's motives. Why would he not want this maverick tamed? The High Commissioner rose and bade Israel farewell and left the *tukul*, as the old warlord succumbed to fear and allowed himself to shiver in the scorching heat. He had been in tighter spots before, but he was young and strong then. Now he was an old man who had no sons.

And practically no tribe.

Israel sat alone in his largest *tukul*, and contemplated his terrible circumstances. He was disturbed by a noise as, suddenly, Alice entered, frantic and tearful, and literally collapsed swooning into his arms. Israel was embarrassed at this ostentatious show of intimacy, as the girl sobbed about her flight from Hoki as Luke's men took over the town. Nervous in face of the pang of softness he felt, yet touched by her loyalty, Israel let a stiff hand brush over the girl's hair. – There ... everything is fine, you are now safe ... he said, trying to weave certitude into his voice. In fact, the warlord felt even more scared and despondent than ever. This young woman had impressed him as being of stronger heart than many of the men he had in the vestiges of his armed forces. Now she was reduced to a frightened child by Chediah's power.

– Oh, it was so dreadful, and I was stopped by the *Biza*, you know, Alice whined. – That horrible man ... I fear him so.

– The *Biza* is but a harmless fool ... Israel said in a weak reassurance, thinking about just how much he'd come to rely on that abstruse, mystical pagan of late.

Alice shook her head, as if seeing Israel for the first time. It was the white hair of his head and face that shocked her. This frail old man could not protect her. –

No, no, he is a monster of great power! He has lived many lives!

– That is nonsense, it is just superstition, Israel almost cooed.

– No ... I saw it with my own eyes, Alice explained, her face stiff with terror. – Many years ago as a child playing by the river, I saw the man dig himself out of the earth. He was reborn in front of my eyes! It was him! He has the power of reincarnation!

Israel gazed into Alice's petrified face, and he knew that she wasn't lying. Mistaken perhaps, confused even, but certainly not lying.

Recruitment

To Father Roache, the schoolteacher's daughter, Shola, had come to embody the ends of the transparent evil that gripped them. The priest was given to consider that when an environment became so brutalised by war, it provided the cover for the psychopath, not the soldier, to flourish. Some of the men with guns, how coldly they looked at him as he walked through the village.

The girl Shola responded to nothing, except the hugs of her mother. Often Father Roache beguiled himself by imagining she was paying him heed, as she would follow the Holy Man around as he lit the candles, her one eye entranced by the simple flame. But if he tried to make contact in any way, say by offering her the torch, she would back away and emit a high scream, which would not cease until her mother held her again.

Valerie would take Shola to the church under the cover of pre-dawn, and did not bring her home until darkness had fallen. The girl usually sat shivering or staring into space, rocking slowly in a silent world, awaiting the next hug. Either that or she slept, a blanket over her head to shut out the light from the lidless eye.

The terrors that lone eye had been forced to witness

were in evidence all over her body. Shola held those blankets to her with her flippers, would let nobody witness the full extent of the desecration. In the night as she slept, a tearful Valerie, muttering a prayer, would gently pull them up and in a slow, sweating chilled terror, examine the nipple-less breasts, mutilated genitals, sears and the welts all over her daughter's ruined body.

Shola's condition and her story had fascinated Luke Chediah, as he knew the men who had inflicted these sickening deformities upon her. The girl's injuries, unthinkable to many and unutterable to many more, were the trademark of a brigade of mercenaries who had fought alongside him for Jacob when they had first taken Hoki five years ago. The men had made an impression on the young soldier, who himself had been a youthful abductee. Harsh and boorish, they were madmen, not warriors, the disturbing glint of insanity ever-present in their eyes. Where were they now, he wondered, dead perhaps, or in Angola, or in any war zone where they could secure beneficence from whichever tyrant engaged their services?

Those doomed, mad devils particularly loved human bounty. They would kidnap war victims, usually refugees, particularly young pretty girls, and torture them, betting each other as to who could dream up the most nefarious practices. They would always ensure that the victims had to witness this, and that their life would not end; thus their presence would be a heinous testimony to the gang's depraved, flagitious, power.

With a cruel, almost tender precision, the mercenaries systematically dismantled their captives. It was said that one of their ranks had been a trained surgeon, a healer, though that was probably hearsay. What was beyond doubt was that the perverted, calculated intelligence they employed on such occasions, allegorised the acts of men who had lost all traces of humanity, or had been born deficient of it in the first place. And in war at its rawest, those twisted actors had found each other and a theatre to display their indulgent, pathetic, degradation, free from the civic and moral restraints sane men and women created to protect themselves from the outcomes perpetuated by such freaks.

But they were feared, and Luke would strive to be like them. And when they met him again, they would not see a green young soldier, but a great and merciless warlord, and they would bow to him, before he destroyed them.

Until now Luke Chediah had never had the opportunity to see one of the mercenaries' victims. This, he considered with a strange twist of emotion, was about to change. As he pulled into town in his jeep, he saw a woman emerge from the church to greet two young boys in an embrace, whom Luke recalled as the schoolteacher, the one who walked to Kroy to teach Israel's Jamuri. She would pay for such fraternisation. He signalled his driver to pull up at the corner of the market, where he could watch the proceedings.

The young warlord sat in his jeep for a moment, studying the woman, fascinated by her ostentatious display of affection for two boys who had followed her from the market, across the square towards the church. He wiped the back of his neck with a piece of material he pulled from his pocket. Who were those boys? Her sons? And where was the poor girl? He watched them vanish into the church, saw the sandy head of the priest briefly, as he opened the door to greet them.

A large, whirring insect thrashed against Luke's chest. He crushed it in his palm, flicked away the corpse and wiped his hand on his makeshift handkerchief, almost in one motion without flinching for a second, indeed, barely registering anything. So they were all there; the schoolmistress, the priest and the two boys. Luke's interest began to shift from the destroyed girl to the boys in the church; two healthy youngsters, who, in this place of fighting, should be men, should be soldiers. His Excellency and the rebel army needed more troops, as did he, for the final assault on Kroy, and the end of old Israel.

Luke waited until they had vanished into the building and shut the church door behind them. Then he climbed out of the jeep, his boot crunching satisfyingly on some small stones, and signalled to his soldiers.

When the uniformed men appeared in the church, Shola was the first to see them, her large eye heeding the makeshift combat uniforms, then the guns. Rooted to the spot with fear, the tongueless girl let out a tortured grunt of supplication. Registering what was happening, Valerie ran to her side, trying to comfort the young woman as she huddled in the corner. Moses and Robert backed away hesitantly as the troops approached them.

– Greetings, Commander, Father Roache said with a grace he hoped was not obviously forced, as he appeared hastily from the vestry.

Addressing the priest, Luke Chediah pointed over at Robert and Moses. – Those boys are fine and strong, Father, he said as the young men shivered, gazelle-like, in apprehension. – Now you must give them to me and I will make men of them!

Father Roache started to speak in protest, but Valerie had heard this before and, in panic, she ran over screaming: – No! No!

The young warlord beheld the startled-looking schoolmistress. – They are strong. The army needs them!

– The army has had all my sons! No more! No more! she howled at him.

Those women, they were so strange, he reflected, with incomprehension suffused slightly with the compassion one might have had for an enfeebled idiot.

– Not my Robert ... I beg you ... Valerie sobbed, falling on to her knees.

– Promises were given by your predecessor, Father Roache stated assertively, stepping forward to face Luke Chediah.

The young warlord looked imperiously on. – What promise can a man give in times of war? The *raison d'être* of the warrior is the war, and when its dictates impose themselves we are soldiers of Jesus marching into battle against the non-believers. For our people the only way to victory, the only way to peace, is to march with great zeal against our oppressors.

Valerie stood up, enraged at Luke's words. Her eyes blazed blood-red and took on a sick and desperate hue. – My son is all I have! Do not take him, I beg you! The foolishness of you men; you are blind! You see nothing!

Then Luke grabbed Valerie by the shoulders and shook her violently and thrashed her with the back of his hand, splitting her lip as she fell back to the floor. – It is you who sees nothing! He pointed down at her. – I see! I see!

Father Roache was over, crouching by her side, attempting to restrain Valerie Nuando who was trying to get up, to face the warlord once more.

The teacher.

Strange, but she was the first woman he'd met in this village. And that foolhardy priest, with his useless piety. They thought it was easy, to make the choices the warrior had to make. Let them see how easy; he would acquiesce to a point with their pleas. – I will take only one of the boys, he said coldly, glaring down at Valerie. – You must decide which one.

– No, no, not my Robert, Valerie pleaded again, rising to her feet, then looking at the terrified Moses. – My Moses ... no ... please, I beg you, no ...

The warlord pointed at Robert. – This one is your son?

Valerie looked at her boy, her last son, the image of his father as a young man ...

Luke took the glance as acquiescence. – Then I will take the other one, he shrugged, smiling at Moses, who stood wide-eyed and open-mouthed.

And now it was happening. Valerie was being forced to pick between Moses and her son. She stood rooted and immobilised in disbelief and shock.

The fearful impasse was broken when Luke nodded to two soldiers, who grabbed the fearful boy Moses and took him out and into the truck. Valerie made to go after him, but was stopped in her tracks by Luke, whose huge fist thudded into her throat, causing her to stagger back, choking, trying to force air into her lungs. – If you continue with those unpatriotic protests, we will take the other one, too! You have been warned!

Father Roache stepped forward and fastened his hand on to Luke Chediah's wrist. – I will be forced to protest to His Excellency the High Commissioner, he said, as Valerie, finding her voice spectacularly, roared alternate curses, pleas and prayers around the church, first directing her chants Heavenwards, then at Luke and his troops. To the warlord's disconcertment, he found that he could not shake the grip of the white priest from him. The old man had power. Instead, with his free hand he pulled out his pistol.

In an instant the priest thought that he would be shot, but instead Luke Chediah whipped the butt of the gun on to the bridge of Father Roache's nose. The Holy

Man's eyes flooded with tears as the pain seared through him. His grip growing limp, he staggered back as the blood flowed from him.

– Attend to the spiritual welfare of our people, Father. Do not attempt to prevent either myself or any of my men from executing their duties as soldiers, Luke barked.

Valerie, now attending to Father Roache, screamed another volley of abuse at Luke, who ignored her and followed his men outside into the jeep. Father Roache, still dizzy, once again held grimly on to Valerie, restraining her and simultaneously comforting her until she broke away and ran to the door, only to see the vehicle tearing off into the distance. In a strange and horrible trance of shock, Valerie went into the church and hugged Robert, then a still-shrieking Shola.

Electing to sit in the back of the truck, Luke smiled at the blank-faced boy, who kept his gaze straight ahead. Moses had been here before: he knew that stoicism was his only ally.

Luke was pondering on the actions of the woman and the priest. Brave, but misguided, like so many who protested both at home and abroad against the inevitability of war. They could debate philosophy about means and ends as much as they liked; there always came a time when you had to pick up a gun. And in the buzz of victory, the lunacy of war, emotions were coarsened and morals shed like a snake's skin. And what always emerged was something newer and slicker, but colder to the touch, something more treacherous and wicked.

Most of the warlords were the same, he considered, but they were lazy; happy with their small pile, their little zones of power. Luke, however, could not accept that, nor just lord it over his mentor Jacob's old rival Israel Kobache. He wanted nothing less than to liberate south Sudan, New Sudan, to lead it to total freedom.

TUITION

Moses had been taken to the barracks, which adjoined the Save Sudan camp, and was kitted out with a makeshift uniform of camouflage T-shirt, green combat trousers and red beret. Then he was handed an automatic rifle. – A good rifle, the sergeant informed him, – made in Britain, they say. Go on, hold it. It's not loaded. Take it, he urged the hesitant boy, get used to the feel of it.

The boy conscript picked it up. It felt good in his hands. His mind journeyed back to the painful massacre of his family, where he could see the crazed eyes of their killers. If he had had this gun then ...

Luke Chediah came into the barracks, and dismissed the saluting sergeant. He smiled at Moses. He sat down on a bunk and regarded this youth, who stood straight-backed to attention, staring right ahead, just as he had been told to. Such a fine boy, lean, strong and righteous. – At ease, he said.

Moses relaxed slightly.

Luke nodded to the bunk opposite. – Sit down, my young friend.

The youth sat down, his knees almost touching those of the adjacent warlord's.

– They say you are an orphan, Luke said to Moses. – I too was an orphan.

– Yes, my parents were killed before the liberation of Rumbek.

Luke nodded severely. – Yes, he said, then again, – yes. He then began to tell a tale, to which Moses, even if rank and authority had not compelled him to do so, would have sat and listened in total silence and with complete engagement. – My village was to the north of here, in a mixed Arab and African, Christian and Muslim town. Then the Khartoum Government began to preach their doctrines of intolerance to our way of life and the bearing of the local Muslims changed. The traders would spurn us, and the Arab boys who had been our friends openly mocked and taunted us. Then the horsemen came and took us all north to slavery. My parents were killed stone dead before my eyes and I was sold as a slave on account of my youth.

– I was sold to a family in Menzah, a harsh Arab desert town, to work as a houseboy for a wealthy merchant's family. They had a son, a young boy called Nifendi, who was spirited and rebellious. I lived off their scraps, but sometimes he would sneak me fruits, breads and meats to my room, and also books, which were a great comfort to me.

– The merchant, Azakbah, was a pompous man, and was always out on business. His wife and Nifendi would be alone all day with me and two servants, Jallow and Behrin, and a cook called Shanah.

– The strangest thing was that these people saw me as their prisoner, me, this twelve-year-old boy, when I was just waiting for my chance to destroy them. I could not escape for I had nowhere to go. Had I tried, I would almost certainly have perished in the desert which surrounded the town.

– One evening, I climbed over the wall, leaving obvious marks of my egress, then climbed straight back in again. I headed though, not for my own room, but for Nifendi's. With my dying mother's face in my mind's eye, I took a knife I had removed from the kitchen earlier and plunged it straight into my sleeping little helper's heart. He made no sound but merely opened his eyes for a second, though it appeared to me that he witnessed nothing. Then I took some things from the house in a hessian bag, some gold goblets and the like, and I climbed back over the wall into the street. I threw the sack into the back of a parked vehicle which was a refuse truck, then I walked back along the deserted streets in darkness and climbed back in through the window, tiptoeing to my room, where I had the soundest sleep of my life. Until it was disturbed in the morning by a woman screaming.

– Then things became interesting. The police were called and the parents were distraught, their beautiful little Nifendi murdered so coldly! I was addressed, of course, but the others testified that the little boy and I were friends, he brought me books and food.

– Ah my little Nifendi, such a lovely boy. The trader, who would have beaten his son to a pulp had he known of the assistance the lad gave me, was happy for the departed soul to be seen in this virtuous light.

– Suspicion of the murder fell on one of the servants, Behrin, who had shouted at Nifendi when the little fellow was caught raiding the kitchen, probably on my behalf come to think of it! The others had heard the servant, at the end of his tether, making the young scamp such a threat.

– His position was only alleviated when they found a vagrant who had come across the booty in the rubbish lorry and taken the goods intending to pawn them. A feeble-minded soul, he was arrested, tried and hung a week later. The execution did not appease the merchant's grief or sense of injustice. Blaming his staff for the poor security which made Nifendi's murder so easy, he proceeded to fire them all, reducing them to penury. Then he turned against his wife and began to beat her wickedly. And I watched; watched and enjoyed them all falling apart. That feeling of power over them, those ones who had wronged me. He stared at Moses. – Do you see?

– Yes sir, I do, Moses replied in earnest conviction.

– Yes, Luke laughed hollowly. – I ruled that household, a twelve-year-old boy, and the Arabs didn't even know it! My hand was only forced into further violence when the fat merchant got around to beating me. So one night I crept into his room and cut his throat as if he was a pig.

– Then I was forced to flee, to take that long walk into the desert and my certain death. For make no mistake, I would rather have died free under the desert sun than as a slave under Arab tyranny. God had something else in store for me, though, for I ran into my destiny in the desert, when I was rescued by a patrol of our men.

Moses could not stop his face breaking into a smile.

Luke put a hand on the boy's shoulder. – I am just like you, young soldier, our destiny is war. We must embrace it. It is the hardest and most thankless discipline, he said regarding the young man, who, if he did his job correctly, would one day slay him just as ruthlessly as he had destroyed Jacob Chidoze. – No, it is not easy. You will never be loved, for a true warrior is a loveless entity, for he can never be constrained by the burden love imposes. Even gratitude does not last, he smiled bitterly. – In the marketplace I feel their cold, scornful eyes on my back, clinging to me like cot-bugs. Then when I turn, I face only craven bows and smiles. It is the way I like it, though. I prefer their fear to their love. For fear, unlike love, never carries with it the message of deceit. Do you understand?

– Yes, I understand, said Moses.

Replacements

To his great consternation, the Witchdoctor was kidnapped once again. This time he was dragged from his home by two Kroy village elders and their sons, who wore no uniforms. They hid in waiting until a mourning mother he had been with had departed, then moved in on the drowsy medicine man, ripping him from a contented half-doze.

The still-lactating woman had wanted to know if the soul of her dead baby had gone to a peaceful place. The *Biza* assured her that this was indeed the case, as he plundered her mammaries, the contents of her mothering breast the payment for the reassuring consultation she had needed. He was still in a satisfied stupor, tasting the sweetness of her milk in his mouth when they were upon him.

On the way back to Kroy, through dangerous enemy-occupied territory, the Jamuri kidnappers were elated at their minor victory in avoiding Luke Chediah's patrols. In order to ensure that he didn't raise the alarm they had beaten the *Biza* badly. So badly in fact that Israel, always a bet-hedger where the Witchdoctor and his powers were concerned, shed a good pound in anxious sweat in the half-hour after being presented with his bloodied, stunned and prostrate figure.

After the *Biza* recovered sufficiently to orientate himself, he saw the old warlord standing above him. – You must give me a son! I need a spell!

Though in pain and distress and somewhat delirious, the *Biza* managed to moan. – The payment of goats will be ...

– No! No payment! Your payment is that you are allowed to live. You will be hunted down and destroyed if you do not do as I command!

The *Biza* looked up at the grey, whiskery old man. Israel was now way beyond frightened: he was so desperate he was almost unhinged, tottering on the brink of insanity. Something had to be done. This old man would and could send an assassination squad after him, of this the Witchdoctor was sure, particularly after the ease with which the old warlord's men had abducted him.

– I will give you a son, I will do this, the *Biza* croaked, and, suddenly considering that not to mention the last preparation may be construed as an admission that it was a ruse, decided to meekly quiz: – Have the bananas not worked for you?

– No! Israel roared.

The *Biza* cowered further away from the old warlord, but then managed to rally a little and fuse some conviction into his voice as he told Israel: – Then I will consult the spirits and give you a stronger spell, the strongest. You will have what you once had.

Israel resisted the urge to reveal the spasm of excited anticipation that flooded over him. Instead he nodded sternly, and gestured to his men who then took the shaken Witchdoctor away. *I will have what I once had.*

OUT ON A LIMB

As he sat in the back of the jeep driven by Abraham, Marshall felt his spirits soar and dip, almost in imitation of the plane above, which did a corkscrew manoeuvre before making a bumpy landing at the airstrip. The Kenyan bootlegger was in the back of the truck with others like him, some of them worse. All grew visibly more animated, as the nurse from the hospital was on the plane, and would now see them all to make an assessment. With any luck, Marshall teased himself with the thought, he'd be taken to the hospital over the Kenyan border and lose this poisoned leg before it destroyed him. But his spirits slumped as he listened to the groans and smelt the smells of the other wounded who lay alongside him. Having done a quick calculation, he reasoned that the number of men, women and children in this vehicle exceeded the number of seats in the small caravan plane.

Abraham opened the back of the truck as Marshall, shaking with fear and fever, climbed unsteadily out with the others where they sat on some small wooden chairs which had been lined up on a porch.

– Are you sure I will get on the plane? Marshall pleaded with the soldier.

Abraham shrugged in a distracted and disengaged manner, as if he had far weightier issues to consider. – As I said, I have green-lighted you, but the final decision is a medical one and rests with the nurse. He focused on Marshall with a broad grin. – So you must act as if you are sick ...

– But I *am* sick! I am dying! Marshall cried.

– How? How do I do this! Marshall squealed in pain.

– My friend, my friend, my friend, just be pleased that you are getting out in time. There is a new commander in these parts. Things may get worse. I suspect that you are the lucky one. Pray for your friends!

It was God, punishing him for the beating of the Christian woman back in Nairobi! Marshall ground his teeth together and recited a delirious prayer over and over in his head.

Sheena Moran began her inspection of the patients, looking each one over with a dispassionate eye; probing wounds, asking questions, nodding to an orderly with a clipboard and a watchful soldier. In what was an agonisingly long time from his nerve-shredded, fevered perspective, she got round to Marshall. – When were you bitten?

– Four days ago ... I think ... I ...

– Okay, she said curtly, squeezing at the lump in his leg. Then turned to the silent man with the clipboard who accompanied her. – Get him on. He'll need an amputation.

– Thank you! Thank you! Marshall burst into tears, and tried to kiss Sheena Moran's hand, which she pulled away, resuming her no-nonsense tour. – You are a saint ... he bleated, but the Irish woman had shut out his cries and was now talking to the next patient.

All the time, still in silent prayer, Marshall rose

unsteadily, hobbled across the pounded red soil of the airstrip and clambered into the first plane he'd been on in his life.

Resurrection spell

Now feeling that he was truly caught between irresistible force and immovable object, the *Biza* had no alternative but to begin his deepest consultation yet with the restless ghosts. While aware that disturbing them in such a wilful manner carried heavy risks, he also knew that in his present predicament he was in great jeopardy. Israel Kobache was a man of the past, yet events had shown the medicine man he could not rely on Luke Chediah to protect him, at least in his current abode. For the *Biza*, his location was of paramount importance; in order to practise his craft, he needed regular access to the river. Here, however, he would be vulnerable to the assassin's bullet. Yes, it was essential that he helped the old warlord.

So the *Biza* began the most extensive and dangerous preparation of his life. He sat chest-high in the river and meditated for a while, until the wisdom of the ancestors who had once plunged into its waters saturated him. Then he set about collecting herbs, berries, pods, leaves, barks and roots, many of them known to be poisonous. The Witchdoctor never destroyed the host plant or tree, careful to take only what he needed. Plant life could only provide so much, however, and for this concoction he needed one other ingredient. He trawled the grasslands with a heavy stick, until he came upon a snake, crudely and savagely battering the animal to death. Carrying its limp body around his neck, he took it home and cleaned it, removing its sacs of venom, which he added to the mixture he was boiling up.

After allowing the elixir to cool, he drained off the sediment. This potion would take him deep into the land of the spirits, and he was fully aware that he might not return from this terrible journey. The Witchdoctor also knew that if he did recur back into his human life on the completion of his quest, then his powers would be greater than ever.

Solomon was entrusted to ensure that he should not be disturbed, no matter how ill he seemed, or how crazed the hallucinations were. Sending the boy out of the *tukul*, he stood with the clay bowl full of the potion he had prepared. With trembling hands the *Biza* drank steadily, then lay on his cot and gazed outside at the stars. Soon he felt a powerful nausea in his stomach as he watched the tight muscles on his lean abdomen cramp in regular spasms. His head was dizzy as he looked up at the glistening sky. Sweating, the medicine man watched the room pull in and out of focus. Feeling the urge to vomit, he sat up and fought it; the elixir had to stay down and flow fully through him. The *Biza* held on, his hands gripping the blanket beneath him and the pull on it was the only way that he could ascertain that he was still on his bed and in the room.

He fell back on to the bed. After a torturous, fitful writhing which lasted for what seemed to him like hours and hours, he felt exhaustion's relieving tug, and he was ready to make the journey, drifting into the violent and crazed state of sleep he needed to be in, in order to encounter the spirits.

This first awareness that he was in another place came from the sense of tingling weightlessness in his body. Then voices crowded in around him, followed by a changing, shifting face which formed and then altered in a demonic flux, seemingly just a few inches from his own. First he could see Luke Chediah scowling, then this head approximated Israel; then Jacob, the priest, the schoolmistress, and, it seems, all the women he had known. Such glimpses, though, were fleeting, for as soon as he could identify one mocking, sneering antagonist, the head of this beast would reshape into someone or something else. Now, as a high-pitched sound seemed to tear through his brain, it was showing him the faces of truly grotesque, demonic creatures: beasts that had perhaps stalked this earth long before man. – Tell me what to do, he implored, but all that came back to him in response was aggression and the terrible threat of unspeakably violent torture. Then, in this fevered dream, he saw the foul countenance of a creature so vile, so ripped and twisted, and his bed seemed to move under him as he was torn from it, tumbling in a convulsing shock on to the floor.

He tried to look up, but this proved so difficult; his head was as if it were made of solid rock and his neck which supported it, like a mere handful of dry twigs. The *Biza* felt this skull of great mass lolling around, snapping back one way, then the other, as if it would break the neck and crash to the ground. He thought of his head hanging by a thread, so that he could see his roof, or the stars but only glimpse in a brief flash the monster that faced him. Grabbing his dome with his hands and feeling the weight of it in the muscles of his aching arms, the sorcerer straightened it up, training it, and his almost equally heavy eyes inside it, on what was crouching in the dark corner of his *tukul*.

And he saw it with a horrible soul-freezing clarity; a festering, stinking thing of skin and bone, looking out at him from one huge devil-red eye, an eye that had seen all the evil in this world. The creature said nothing, but yet he heard it, as a voice in his exploding head, shaping his own thoughts, defining them as its will.

Yes, and what this manifestation of the spirits was urging him to do was to consider the very last weapon in the armoury of the sorcerer, the taboo act of resurrection. Now the creature was coming closer, and its thin fingerless hand touched his cheek softly, feeling like a cobweb, the action having the effect of snapping him into another state, another place, back in the cot from which he'd fallen.

As the night wore on, the fever broke and the hallucinations faded. The *Biza* woke in his sweat-drenched bed, and shakily staggered down to the river where he lay out in a shallow pool of its waters.

After some bread, mango and water, he felt stronger and headed into Kroy and to the old warlord's house. When he shut his eyes he could still see the demons and hear their shrieks, though the image and sound were now fainter. He looked up at the eagles, swishing through the hollow sky, or looking down at him from their perches in the high trees with a towering hauteur. When he got to Israel's *tukul*, he found the place deserted. There was no sign of a permanent flight, no upheaval. It seemed to him, even in his highly disoriented state, that they may come back at any time.

The *Biza* cast his eye over the small, bricked, slanted-roofed temple which was Oliver's resting place. It would be better to perform the ritual now, completely undisturbed. From his pouch he poured a circle of ash around him. Then he let the mystic contents of the great orange river fall into the circle.

Still reeling as he was from the previous evening's ritual, it took the *Biza* only a short meditation to induce a trance-like state. Soon he could hear the sounds and feel the energy of newly disturbed spirits flashing all around him. It was a continuation of last night, yet in the early day and in fuller consciousness the spirits were further away from him. Nonetheless, the shrieking of both his ancestors and the pre-human forces present were terrifying to his jangling, febrile brain, and he was tempted on many occasions to open his eyes and break their tortuous hold on his psyche.

But the fear was passing as the spirits became soothed and talked in whispers; lulling caressing whispers, and for a moment he himself did not exist as a physical entity but became just another force, a current of air, intertwining with the ghosts around him; forces of a furious and demented power certainly, but ones which he had not encountered before, and which he could not decode with any certainty.

Suddenly spent, the *Biza* sprawled recumbent on the red clay soil; emitting sharp, shrunken, swinish gasps as he looked up at the shimmering sun, then lowering his glance, he watched the pole under his loincloth slowly subside.

Disturbed from a leisured recovery by the wheels of a truck grinding up the ragged road, the Witchdoctor quickly staggered to his feet and scuttled into the bushes.

FLIGHT

The aircraft rose up over the desert plains of southern Sudan, bound for the Red Cross Hospital in Lokichoggio. One of the wounded Sudanese rebel soldiers in the plane was a man, who had never been out of his own smoothly terrained county. Now he was seeing hills and mountains for the very first time. Having received no education and thus completely without terms of reference, this soldier, whose flesh had been ripped by bullets had lain serenely enough in the plane. Yet the same warrior screamed in terror at the sight of those mountains, convinced, as he was, that they would crash, that those silent, unforgiving red hills of northern Kenya would devour them.

His fevered cries woke a lightly dazing Marshall. The bootlegger stretched out in the back of the plane, breathing heavily. This shaking piece of tin was like a sidecar he once had on an old motorbike back in Nairobi! To think of such a thing flying through the sky beggared belief, yet here it was and he was in it, and it was his passport to salvation!

He met the terrorised eyes of the soldier and nodded at the frightened man with a light smile. The soldier's gaze seemed to feast on him for a second, before the man forced a grin in return.

Demons

The villagers feared the demented girl-creature. That monster with the large one eye which never closed; the scarred face and body, the lurched, crippled walk, and the silence of a ghost, terrifyingly punctuated by a demonic shriek from that large, black hole of a mouth. Along with everything else that this tormented people had been forced to endure, there was now a monster in their midst.

Nobody worried more about Shola than the *Biza* himself, who, growing in stature and influence with each passing day, regaled the townsfolk with further refinements of his vision. Embellishing the tale like the great storyteller that he was, the medicine man told all ears willing to listen of his dream that some deformed creature of the devil, born of a warrior, would wreak havoc in the area. However, the death of this creature would satisfy the spirits who would then show their appreciation by attacking the enemies of the people.

Though most of the villagers were sceptical of the tale, many still wanted the girl banished, if only because she reminded them all daily of the atrocity which could befall each and every one of them, their daughters and their sons. By day Valerie had kept the wretched young woman in the church, hidden from the townfolk's eyes, as much as she could. Yet Shola was prone to sneaking off and wandering away, particularly at night while her mother slept. The destroyed girl would go and turn her head skywards, and look at glistening constellations of the stars, perhaps wishing she could be up there with them.

When Valerie woke at nights with a juddering start to find the space beside her empty, her spirit would not be assuaged until she peered out the hut to see Shola gazing skywards. Often Valerie wanted the same as her daughter, to be up there, away from all this pain. Everything had gone. Luke had taken Moses.

Wrapping a blanket around her shoulders, Valerie moved over and looked down at the remnants of her child. Yes, her daughter was gone. In order to hide in a place of safety where the tortures, humiliations and mutilations to her body meant nothing, the girl had gone so far into her own head that she would never find egress.

No, Shola would never return, because to do so meant that she would once more have to engage with, and face up to, the unspeakable terrors that had befallen her. She would have to live through them again, not just for one day, but for all time, writ large as they were all over the ruined mess of her body.

Her daughter liked looking at the stars. Yes, she should be up there with them, Valerie thought, with an egregious, righteous fortitude; an emotion both humanly warm and insect cold at the same time. Praying for forgiveness, for deliverance, she took the girl's wrecked hand in her own and led Shola down to the water's edge. They went into the cooling river together, Valerie's arm around her daughter's waist.

Then the mother kissed the daughter on her forehead and allowed the scent of the spoiled young woman to fill her nostrils before shoving down hard on the girl's shoulders. Keeping a firm grip, she pushed Shola down to her knees. Then Valerie dropped to her own knees and held the young woman's head under the water.

Valerie Nuando couldn't really see that solitary eye, in the murky dark of the river, even with the slivers of moonlight rippling and bouncing on its surface. But there was only a mild, instinctive shaking as the water filled the lungs of the girl. Valerie, in her own mind's eye, saw her daughter's face, and it was smiling, with full teeth, lips, ears and nose, and there was not one eye in that beautiful head but two, and the stars glinted and danced in them. And the message they cast to her was one of gratitude and eternal love.

But through this contumacious baptism, Valerie's grip remained as staunch as ever on the shaking, thin body in her hands. That great temple of youthful beauty had been re-fabricated into an ugly prison by the evil ones, and now Valerie was releasing her daughter from it, so that Shola could play and laugh and dance again, in a better place beyond those stars.

And when it was over Valerie Nuando took her little Shola's lifeless, ruined body and carried it back to outside her *tukul*, where she dug tearfully for hours, before she had a hole in the soft clay soil which was deep enough to hold the remains of her daughter.

Then she sat up all night and cried and moaned and prayed for both their souls.

HOSPITAL

In the hospital in Lokichoggio, Marshall looked at the white spots on the dominoes he held, and down at the white bandage on the stump of his leg. The bandage was so white, he thought, with a funny sort of pride. Whiter than those domino spots, even whiter than the Sharp lettering on the top the soldier had taken from him in part-exchange for his life.

Unfortunately, he had lost the leg above, rather than

below the knee, which made adjustment to the prosthetic limb more difficult. It now sat by his side. It was heavy in the heat and he'd removed it, taking a welcome break from lugging it around.

Marshall had been surprised to find that most of the hospital admissions came from infighting between competing rebel groups rather than from engagement with the Islamic Government forces. Equally strange to him was that, in spite of this, soldiers of the different factions all seemed to get on with each other in the hospital, with little or no animosity in evidence. It was only here that they seemed to realise that they were all southern Sudanese together.

As a Kenyan, Marshall found himself readily accepted into the domino schools, which flourished in the compound. The staff displayed a dedication and commitment to others, so manifest that it frequently shamed him when he considered his own life and how he'd chosen to live it. Otherwise, the hospital seemed like a factory. It had a series of large, tented wards, with about 40 beds in each, 20 per side in rows. Amputations were done just below or just above the knee in exactly the same spot. Indeed, part of the hospital actually *was* a factory, with a prosthetics-manufacturing plant lying within the fortified and highly secured compound. The technicians measured from floor to knee and knocked up a customised plaster-based limb for each amputee. Marshall marvelled at the skin tone of the false leg; it was exactly like his own.

During his period of convalescence, patients kept pouring in to the 500-capacity hospital, at the rate of between five and 25 admissions per day. It wasn't just men; there were many women, victims of gunshot wounds, snakebites and pregnancies or childbirths that had gone wrong. For much the same reasons, many children were present in the hospital.

Marshall decided that there was no way he was staying here too long, and there was certainly no chance he would ever go back to southern Sudan again. Joseph and Benjamin could keep whatever profits the brewery generated. He would get back to Nairobi, even the wrath of the authorities or the Christian women was worth facing compared to what he'd been through, and then try to get some money together. Maybe then he'd move south, down to the coast, Mombasa perhaps, where he had some contacts, and where he might start again.

ENERGISING

The brewery Benjamin and Joseph had set up in a *tukul* near the Kua path on the outskirts of Hoki was finally operational. The men, from their isolated enclave, heard the gunfire and were aware of people fleeing. But they had no fear; the High Commissioner and the Commander of the rebel army were backing them. That was good enough for Joseph, who knew little of the politics of the region. These were explained to him in a direct way, however, when he heard noises and then suddenly saw Benjamin's head blown to pieces in front of him by a round of dum-dum bullets from an automatic rifle.

Luke's men had surrounded the compound and Benjamin had, in instinctive panic on seeing a soldier point a rifle at him, gone for the pistol in his belt, the one that Marshall had left behind. It was to be his last move. From about six feet away, Joseph watched his friend's head explode, showering him with blood and grey matter. The soldiers were all over him and trained their guns on the unarmed, paralysed Joseph, who unlike his friend had no time to lose his life by reacting stupidly. He watched in goggle-eyed terror as his friend's almost headless corpse kicked, twitched and excreted into stillness at his feet.

– That trader was a Jamuri, said the shooting soldier.

– One less plague-carrier to be concerned with! a rebel trooper roared in joyless laughter.

Luke Chediah's victorious troops could hardly believe their luck when they saw the bounty. They all grinned, then whooped, except Moses, the boy soldier, who kept a steely glint in his eye as he contemplated Benjamin's corpse, and the fear on the remaining brewer's face. The boy's reaction was not lost on his Commander Luke Chediah. He'd watched the young man undertaking his drill and exercises in the town square, admiring that steely devoutness he saw in the youth's bearing. Potential zealots were ideal, if they could be caught in time and properly trained. The boy would be taken aside and spoken to again; indeed, he would be groomed as Luke's apprentice.

Energised at the thought of being able to mould raw material in his image, Luke Chediah stole out of his jeep and inspected the haul. – Amazing. God is truly on our side, he smiled. Luke then ordered his men to load the barrels on to a lorry, which had been earlier hijacked from Israel's men. Joseph, looking on in great fear, immediately recognised it as their old vehicle from Nairobi.

Even through his terror, Joseph's gangster heart and gambler's instincts still remained to the fore. Now he was wondering how to play this. He thought that he should mention this outrage, that they had the backing of His Excellency and Israel, but perhaps they were not Israel's men. The sounds of the gunfire had indicated to their ears that the fighting had been intense; perhaps, as they'd speculated, the old man had been ousted. No, it was better that he would try to offer help. Whoever they were, they needed him to brew the ales. Those simple Sudanese cornseeds were just farmers playing at being soldiers, indulging in fantasy with their guns. Yes, they were dangerous, he couldn't bring himself to look at Benjamin's corpse, but they would be his serfs once he gained their trust. Thinking of a way to ingratiate himself the Bootlegger contemplated the barrels full of the beer they had brewed, and pleaded to Luke Chediah: – This has not been tested yet.

The young warlord took out his pistol. – Neither has this, he said grimly, silencing the Kenyan by emptying a round into his stomach. As Joseph fell to the ground, Luke added: – But it works perfectly, does it not, he quizzed in arrogance, replacing the gun in his holster to the babbling laughter of the soldiers.

The bootlegger lay bleeding on the ground, his eyes rolling in pain up at the harsh, unrelenting sun, his miserable agony underscored by intermittent squeals which leaked from him like the dark blood, as his life slowly drained away.

Turning to the beer, Luke tapped on one of the full barrels. – Tonight we celebrate our victory! he declared with great zeal, the cheers of his men ringing in his ears.

Theft

Israel was shattered at the rout of his forces in Hoki, which had reduced his army to a small rump. Paranoia and despondency seared from the old warlord. Fearing assassination by Luke's men, Israel moved from *tukul* to *tukul* in Kroy and the surrounding areas. Young Chediah was surely coming for him, and his tribe would perish. That was to be his epitaph; the last ever chief of the Jamuri, the man who led his people into extinction.

Then, returning to his own home from a security round with his men, he noticed mounds of earth on either side of his son. Oliver's grave. The old warrior's heart thumped as he approached the tomb. – The grave has been desecrated! he croaked.

Then he almost went into a seizure, for it was far worse than that; they had taken his son. Oliver's body had gone!

Israel went to his *tukul* and sat brooding for most of the day. Eventually Paul the elder could bear this state of paralysis no more. He entered his old friend's hut. – What is to be done? the elder asked Israel. The old warlord shrugged at his companion and said nothing.

Paul turned and left him, the elder now concerned more about the future of Jamuri tribe than ever. The once-great warrior's fear of the final insurrection by Luke Chediah could not have been dispelled by the arrogant desecration of his son's grave, obviously by the young warlord's men, from right under the father's nose. Israel literally slept only a few yards away! This atrocity was greater than any Paul could have imagined in his harshest nightmares. The vile scoundrel had removed his son's body! It was gone!

Inside the shaded hut, Israel's brain buzzed and his weak frame shook as he considered, why, when Luke could have easily tracked him down and executed him, had his young foe gone to the trouble of doing this? The answer was simple. He was showing Israel his power. He did not want the old warrior destroyed but rather to have him live in fear of the most demonic force, that of his young rival! And this great fear would be a testament to the power of Luke Chediah and the Nazuri as Israel would be compelled to live his life, or what was left of it, in a frightened and bitter exile.

CAKE

Father Roache had risen early, and after examining his swollen nose, washing and dressing, he made his way to the kitchen. The priest, a habitual early riser, was surprised to see that Valerie Nuando was already there, working at the large kitchen table. – Good morning, Valerie. You're early today.

Valerie turned around to face him. Father Roache swallowed hard as he contemplated her eyes; they were showing him a large, overwhelmed soul. – Shola has gone, she whispered.

– Oh no ... how much more, the priest moaned, his hands going to his head, almost as if in a strange advocacy of despair to God on her behalf.

– She disappeared the day before last, Valerie explained. For the first time Father Roache saw that the schoolteacher looked frailer, more withdrawn. She seemed faded, diminished in spirit. – Nobody knows where the poor child has gone, she said, then in a gesture which struck him as strange, she put her hand to her mouth, – I have asked everyone ... Something erupted in her chest, coming out as a cough, rather than a sob, and she turned back to her work.

The priest put his hand on the teacher's shoulder, who grabbed it in both of hers. Then after a pause, Valerie loosened her grip and went back to her labour.

– What are you up to here? Father Roache asked, in forced cheer.

– I am baking a cake from cornflour for your birthday, Valerie told him.

Roache had forgotten that it was his birthday later this week. Valerie had asked him a while ago, a casual enquiry he had thought, and he was touched by her kind intent and overwhelmed by the fact that it hadn't been forgotten, even when she had grave matters on her mind.

– That's so kind ... but you must ... we must ... Roache said, the words sticking in his throat.

They were disturbed by a heavy knock on the door. At first Roache fancied that it might be that amorous brewer who had been hanging around and he would shoo the fellow, as Valerie didn't need a rogue like him, especially at the moment. Then he thought that it might be news of the vanished girl. In fact it was the last person he wanted to see.

Father Roache opened the doors and stepped back in shock as Luke Chediah entered the church, and by his side was Moses. Valerie looked out from the vestry and saw him. Despite being lost in her grief for Shola, and the terrible secret which was tearing her insides out, she could not look at the young boy. When eventually, her guilty eyes did meet his, she saw in them no judgement, only the same rancorous frost with which they now greeted the rest of the world. From her perspective, it was as if his soul had been ripped out. She turned away quickly and went back to the kitchen and hung her head in a bottomless pit of sorrow.

The priest, though fearful of Luke Chediah more than ever after facing the butt of the warlord's gun, had been considering his strategy. It had been wrong to grip his arm, to make physical contact. He understood that the man was a Christian and reasoned that he may be more amenable to his influence than his predecessors. It was important to try to build some kind of relationship with this warlord. – You must forgive us, Father Roache began, in some kind of explanation to Luke for their evident lack of enthusiasm at his visit. – Valerie's daughter has gone. We cannot find her.

Luke gazed at the priest, the swelling on his nose, a little surprised at the man's openess. – Ah, that unfortunate girl, he said, with a concern which almost seemed genuine. – She has suffered so, and so unjustly. I will tell our men to watch out for her, of this I assure you. However, I am also sorry that our paths crossed in conflict last time. In a spirit of reconciliation I have come to invite you to a celebration the army are having in the old bar tonight, Father.

– Thank you for your kindness, but we have a lot of work to complete here, the Priest said, as warmly as he could.

– As you wish, Luke Chediah smiled, picking something from his teeth with a small splint of wood. Then, as he departed, he added: – We will keep a lookout for the girl.

In the kitchen, Valerie Nuando heard this conversation, and she could feel part of her essence sliding out from her, leaving behind what she imagined was little more than a cadaver, herself now similar to the remains of the daughter she had just buried. She held up her hands and almost choked at the sight of the red clay, pieces of which, despite much scrubbing, were still clearly visible, embedded under her nails.

BLIND

Thin wisps of smoke continued to billow skywards from the remnants of burnt-out settlements in Hoki, as many from the resurgent Nazuri tribe took angry revenge on Jamuri neighbours. In some cases this came from a real sense of righting past injustices. Others, though, reacted in this way for the pettiest of old grievances, or merely through surrendering to the triumphalist hysteria and the general mood of violence. Many of Israel's men had fled into the jungle, and Luke's forces were still in hot pursuit. On occasion, the sound of gunfire from their running battles could still be heard in the town.

In addition to the direct atrocities, the conflict produced other disastrous outcomes. One man, a farmer named Ben Magiah, was badly lacerated, having been mauled by a leopard, which he disturbed skulking in his *tukul* when he came home drunk. The beast lay dozing, and it was only a few feet from his sleeping wife and baby son. Without television, books or schools for the best part of 17 years, Ben had never seen any representation of a leopard before, so, confronted with a beast beyond his emotional vocabulary, screamed in panic. The big cat rose quickly and, seeing that the farmer was blocking its egress, it jumped on him, tearing him badly on its way out. Elsewhere, the displacement of snakes continued, with many men, women and children receiving bites in the night, which invariably resulted in the loss of either life or limb.

Such matters did not concern the young warlord Luke Chediah, who was in a triumphant mood. In a few days his forces would march into the town of Kroy, the home of Israel Kobache, and what they could not kill they would plunder, and what they could not take they would burn. The Jamuri would be no more. When they got to Kroy, the captured women and children would be sold into slavery. His Excellency was nothing; he had been bought off, and would turn a blind eye simply due to the guarantee of men to fight the Arabs, which he knew would take him up to the county quota that the SPLM leadership had demanded.

However, it was now appropriate to reward the tribesmen with a celebration, as they had fought so hard and valiantly to win back Hoki. And now they had the liquor, confiscated from the Kenyan rogues who had set up their brewery in that clearing in the jungle, on the outskirts of the conquered town. Things were looking up. The adrenaline of victory surged through Luke's veins. The troops were saying that he was a great warrior, and indeed, other rebel leaders were taking note. One prominent warlord in a large province to the north had already sent a messenger with a letter of congratulations.

As the soldiers prepared for the celebrations, young Moses sat outside the makeshift rebel outpost in the square, cleaning his gun, polishing it with a rag. Lost in thought while undertaking this task he once again, as had become his habit, considered ruefully how if only, for the sake of his family, he could have had this gun sooner; back then, when the Government soldiers came.

Now he too was a soldier, and a good one, many of them had said it. Indeed their great leader Luke Chediah had called him his 'new blood' and had taken a special interest in his development. Valerie Nuando was a good woman, she had taken him in and given him love. But love had never repelled any foe, and her own family's fate was proof of that. And was it not she who had called him her son, 'just like Robert'? How noble to his ears such words had been at the time, and how he'd received them with such hope and gratitude. Now he could see what a fool he had been to let her nonsense soften his heart, to temper his own circumstance, his own experience. What an idiot he was to deny this reality for her pious platitudes, when she'd been so quick to deliver him into the hands of his real destiny, the man who truly understood his past, the warrior Luke Chediah.

Moses considered the relationship of himself to the warlord. What exactly was it? Not merely that of master and apprentice, for the trade of warrior in a zone of war was such an all-embracing one it defined of necessity not just the lives of those two parties, but strove to do the same with every other human it crossed. Therefore, he considered, the elder warrior is a man who takes your soul and will into his soul and will. On choosing, or being chosen, by your elder, you yield your own will to him in complete self-renunciation and total submission. You may be chosen for this terrible ordeal, as he was, but its endurance always requires your assent. The apprentice hopes that in exchange for bearing this hideous ordeal, after an extended period of trial he will conquer himself and finally achieve self-mastery, and, through a life of obedience, total freedom, that is freedom from himself.

Now the boy soldier watched his comrades, hearty in victory, rolling the barrels of beer across the square towards the bar in preparation for tonight's celebration. Luke Chediah's jeep pulled up and the warlord stepped out, only to be approached by an obsequious *Biza*, who was watching the barrels with undistinguished glee. – Ah great warlord, there is to be a festival for the people, yes?

In the middle of the square, in front of all the assembled groups of people, now tentatively appearing again in the town, Luke arrogantly impelled the *Biza* in the chest, toppling him over onto the dirty earth. – Get out of my sight, you stinking old idiot! This beer which you so greedily covet is for *my* soldiers, for heroes, for fighting men! It is not for filthy, weak-brained old pagan clowns!

And the warlord's boot crushed the prostrate Witch-doctor's ribcage, causing him to make an undignified squawk, as the laughter of the soldiers filled the air. Luke Chediah considered whether or not he would spray this terrified pest with the contents of his pistol. Then he turned to young Moses who was watching impassively, and said: – No, I'll keep this fool around a little longer. His antics can be fairly amusing at times.

A few of the men from the market stalls had witnessed the *Biza*'s humiliation. None though, even his most stalwart enemies, would indulge in the luxury of ostentatiously enjoying it, viewing the proceedings, as they did, through the lens of their own fear.

– Watch how he cowers, Luke said to Moses, putting an arm round his young comrade's shoulder. – Watch and learn, young warrior.

Young Warrior. Moses remained impassive and his

face stayed inscrutable, even as he felt that his heart might burst open, swelling as it did with a golden pride. It was said by his forefathers that the warrior who fought under the sun became of the sun. Now, for sure, he could feel a fiery globe burn in his heart, forging in him the constitution of the warrior.

As the men pulled the barrels into the back of the old bar, the somewhat smoky sense of dusk falling was heightened by the smouldering of trees, bushes and huts around the town. Crickets, phantom in the darkness, began their mechanistic, petulant cacophony, breaking the deathly stillness that had fallen on Hoki.

Then the celebrations began and raucous laughter rang from the back yard of the bar on the edge of the square. Luke Chediah examined the tapes that were lying around. He looked at the Western ones, and took a Phil Collins cassette and crushed it under his boot. Turning to Akibo his adviser, he said: – This is the kind of thing which destroyed Christianity in the white man's world. These are their new gods. It means nothing, and can only be enjoyed by people who have nothing, who lead meaningless lives. Let the whites keep their trinkets for their own people, to keep them happy in their polluted, diseased, crime-ridden cities, for the African has had his fill of them! He was about to mete out the same treatment to the other Western cassettes, when he was distracted by an aide who brought him another message; this time a congratulatory telegram from the head of a neighbouring state.

The alcohol was served up, and the music played louder as the soldiers mopped back the bootleggers' fare. The troops heartily approved of the brew; it was strong and heady stuff. Luke Chediah supped from his cup, and wondered whether he may have been a little hasty in executing the brewer; he could have made more of this stuff. But as the drink flowed, a strange mood descended on the gathering. The tapes alternated between the building crescendo of African drum music and Bryan Ferry and Bryan Adams. One rebel man started to weep, and his neighbour, with a dizzy head, asked him what was happening. Another man shot a volley of bullets into the air, as Bryan Ferry crooned 'Avalon', and looked strangely at Moses. – You like the gun boy? Have a drink! Be a man!

– Perhaps later, the boy soldier warily replied, moving away from his table and to a seat in the corner of the bar. He looked over at the top table, where Luke sat with his lieutenants. Akibo, the political man, and the warlord raised their glasses in a drunken toast.

No, Moses was the only one who did not drink that night and he watched the growing madness around him develop slowly and implacably into a terrifying insanity.

A few yards away, inside the church, Valerie's soul was in torment. She lay kneeling at the altar, lost in a fevered void between hopeful prayer and recriminative thought.

I have taken the life of my child.

Thou shall not kill.

Vengeance is mine, sayeth the Lord.

But she hadn't killed Shola, she'd freed her, delivered her ... and now, oh the terror of it, the horrible sickness of it, she was sounding exactly like the warlords, applying their own vile, twisted rationale to her awful circumstance. Yes, she thought, they had won, they had contaminated everything, and made her one of them. – When will I see, dear Lord, she begged, her large eyes burning heavenwards. – It is so hard to keep the faith. Give me a sign. Please, give me a sign.

And as she heard the screams and howls start in the night and grow louder and more desperate, Valerie was moved to open the church door and go outside to investigate. The cries were the horrendous shrieks of lunatics and were becoming sicker by the minute. Valerie felt that some evil calamity was about to take place and sat down on the step and prayed with a desperate fervour.

As the schoolteacher's silent song of mercy went towards the stars, the dark madness swept through the fevered brains of the drunken soldiers inside the bar. At first the men had joined in a rabid chant of victory, raising fists in the air in concert with a drumbeat. Then fear crept in to one, then more sets of those monomaniacal eyes, and spread like a dreadful virus through their midst, inspired by the onset of physical symptoms; sickness, dizziness, irregular breathing and the terrifying rattle of the heart in the chest. Suddenly one man, without any warning or in face of any provocation, turned an AK47 on two of his own; peppering them with bullets, their blood staining the walls of the brick outhouse behind them.

In shocked realisation at what he'd done, he dropped his gun and ran over, hugging his bloodied, dying comrades, weeping hysterically. The others scarcely noticed this, all now beginning the descent into their own private hells. The music and chanting became horrendous sick shrieks of agony and madness. They were now completely crazed; a human torch stormed out into the village, screaming, the unfortunate soldier having set himself ablaze. Luke, the young warlord, lurched forward a bit, then fell from his stool to the ground. In panic, he scrambled barely upright in an instant, and then tried to open his eyes so as to navigate. But the pounding of his head was worse than the most terrible headache he had ever known, and Luke realised that he could not see, and roared to that effect. – I am blind, I am blind ... he staggered past his screaming, tearful troops, out into the square, heading sightless, towards the church. – Oh help me! I am blind!

Valerie Nuando finished her prayers and sat outside on the step, and was in ecstatic delight, as it seemed that they had been answered. Luke Chediah was staggering towards her, – I am blind! he was screaming at her, his arms open.

– Jesus be praised! Valerie roared, getting to her feet. The rascal had seen the light! If this man, this tyrant, could admit to his blindness, then there *was* hope. She opened her arms wide to receive him. – Oh Luke Chediah, it is so good that you now recognise this truth ... may God forgive you for your sins! May he forgive us all!

The young warlord sobbed, his skull a crucible, his brain burning inside, like a molten mass. Valerie smiled. It was as if he couldn't even see her ... – I have done something terrible ... at the feast ... something terrible ... he moaned.

Valerie's tiny hands latched on to one of his large ones like two small predators attacking an immense but mortal creature. – I too have done something terrible, she cried. – My Shola ... oh, you must make your peace ... we must both make our peace, she said, and she helped to guide the stricken warrior into the church.

Weekenders

GILES FODEN

NOTE

All the characters in this story are fictional, even those whose names readers might recognise. This story was written before the terrorist attacks on the USA on 11 September 2001, which at the time of writing some are attributing to associates of Osama bin Laden.

CAPTAIN Hassan Majoub, a pilot in the air force of the Islamic Republic of Sudan, strapped on his throat mike. Then, as so many times before, he eased himself into the seat of the Antonov. The mike was a little tight. It had been his uncle's birthday at the weekend and the family had slaughtered a sheep. That, and the kisra bread and boiled okra he had consumed, had thickened his neck a little. Or so it seemed.

Still, it had been a good feast, an altogether pleasant weekend in fact. It was comforting to spend some time with his wife and their new baby child. He had convinced himself that his son would be the most handsome and brilliant young man in Khartoum. All Sudan indeed.

His eyes flicked over the Antonov's grey-blue instrument panel. Apart from the GPS, it had the same fixtures – bakelite knobs, rubber-topped levers, analogue meters – which its Soviet technicians had originally put in, back in the 1960s. It was, he conceded, something of a crate, but it got the job done and was easy to maintain. That was important in Africa.

He pressed the ignition. The heavy engines coughed, coughed again, then kicked into life. He let them run for a little, then taxied out into the middle of the runway. After he had made his final checks with the tower, he pushed forward the throttle. The Antonov began to lumber along, rattling and screeching. The noise grew deafening as the plane picked up speed, shaking alarmingly. Even now, with years of flying under his belt, it amazed Hassan that these old things could leave the ground.

But – there it was, and suddenly, a jabbering old

goose turned swan-like, gathering height every second. The shaking and rattling died down somewhat. A familiar, soothing feeling of buoyancy swept through the pilot. He could relax now.

Captain Hassan was flying to south Sudan, a region under the control not of his government in Khartoum, but of the so-called Sudanese People's Liberation Army, or SPLA. There was little if no cloud cover and the bright, open sky gave him a feeling of total awareness. After a couple of hours, he could see the towers and gantries of the oilfields. The west. Bentiu region.

Speaking into the throat mike – its little sensors picking up the vibrations of his vocal cords – he gave notice of his position to a military helicopter flying below him in the direction of the oilfields. That was his dream, to get a job flying one of those. The helicopter pilots were occasionally paid extra when a new area of exploration needed troops delivering to it: each well had to have a cordon of security. Now and then, too, he had heard, these gunship pilots earned even bigger money for clearing those villages which had the misfortune to be situated directly above wells. But he wasn't sure whether he could bring himself to do that, quite. Yet he didn't doubt that the revenue from the oil was a boon to his beleaguered country.

He continued his journey south, feeling the rumble of the engines as they rippled through his body. Sometimes he wondered if what he was doing – a bombing mission over SPLA-held territory on the Uganda border – was a very useful way of prosecuting the civil war. All it did was cause widespread fear among the civilians. He rarely seemed to be given military targets as such. Nonetheless, those civilians were the support system of the SPLA and other anti-government militias, and eroding that support was a central part of his mission.

He looked down over the parched, exhausted landscape, criss-crossed by sunlight and shadow. The wide brown stripe of the Nile displayed itself beneath him. He could also see, here and there, the circles of cane fencing round villages and cattle stockades. These weren't the big cattle camps, just family herds. He had been into one of the big camps though, once. A hundred thousand cattle all in one place. It was quite a sight, and quite a smell. He had flown in with the army to pick up a number of beasts for meat. Some trip that had been. It was no joke flying with 60 head of cattle in the cargo hold, kicking about in the wooden stalls. And it had been months before they had got the stink out of there, too.

Now and then Hassan would recognise a position as he flew, glancing at the modern GPS system that, with screws and wires, had been barbarically attached to the Antonov's antiquated instrument panel. Looking down, he would see the pockmarked ground where he and his crew had loosed bombs on previous sorties. Not for Hassan the advantages of the laser-guiding; he had to rely on the GPS, and that made his work an imperfect science. Because of this he always released the bombs at the same grid reference.

Occasionally there was resistance from the ground: a surface-to-air missile fired by the SPLA had once missed him by the narrowest of margins. He had called in MiGs to strafe the position. Some of the MiG pilots were Libyan, others Russian mercenaries, looking for work after the end of the Afghan war and supplied to African governments by a man named Sergei Kepitsa. He was a Russian aviation fixer and arms dealer, a former KGB officer and pilot. Now he expedited things for people and governments all over the continent. Once a familiar face in Khartoum, he was now based in Uganda, so as to be closer to the opportunities offered to a man of his talents by the wars and diamond mines of Congo and Angola.

Sergei, whom Hassan had met through flying circles, still had a presence in northern Sudan, retaining a branch office in the capital. This was smart, as it enabled him to work for both sides. His pilots flew for the SPLA and the Khartoum government. Both sides desperately needed pilots and were prepared to overlook this playing of a double game. Sergei himself, and his employees, were only too happy to take their money.

Hassan had heard that Sergei sorted out problems for the CIA, too, these days. It was said to be he who had brokered the deal between Khartoum and the United States which, two years back, saw the fundamentalist leader Osama bin Laden expelled from Sudan. Hassan's own uncle, who was a cabinet minister under President Bashir, had been involved in all that.

He had told the Americans that it was better to let bin Laden stay, where they could keep an eye on him. And so it had proved: only a few days ago, the bin Laden organisation had blown up the American embassies in Kenya and Tanzania, with horrific casualties. Hassan had seen pictures of the injured on CNN back in the officers' mess at his base. They had made his gorge rise. One was of a severed hand, with a ring still on the finger. The pilots – all men who had shed blood themselves – had watched in horrified silence. It was all very different, Hassan reflected, from their reactions to what had filled the screen over the previous few weeks. The spectacle of President Clinton trying to wriggle out of charges of sexual impropriety had caused great hilarity among his fellow officers.

The world was all very tangled up, thought the pilot, adjusting an aerilon. Now that his own government did want good relations with the Americans, the US wasn't interested. At the birthday feast, his uncle had told him that intelligence operatives had picked up two bin Laden people in Khartoum on Friday and offered them to the Americans. But neither the CIA nor the FBI had taken up the offer.

Hassan ripped a Benzedrine tablet from its foil and popped it in his mouth. He had crossed over into SPLA territory now, and had to keep his wits about him. He considered something else his uncle had told him: that US special forces trained SPLA fighters in camps in Uganda and Eritrea. That made him angry. It wasn't right.

Even their former President Mr Carter agreed that it was wrong. He, like Hassan himself and his uncle, could see that people in Sudan wanted to resolve the conflict. The biggest obstacle was US government policy. The US was committed to overthrowing the government in Khartoum and had basically promoted a continuation of the war. A good deal of the $20m of military equipment – including radios, uniforms and tents – that it had shipped to neighbouring countries would find its way to the SPLA, in preparation for the great offensive against Khartoum.

In the meantime, however, Hassan had his own offensive to deliver. He had reached the position over the dusty little town of Yei where he always released the bombs. He hoped the bombs didn't hit the hospital this time. It was a function of releasing the bombs at the same grid reference and nothing to do with any particular desire he had to damage the hospital.

On a sortie a few months ago, that had happened and it had caused quite a fuss. Even the Americans had got involved, condemning 'in the strongest possible terms, these indiscriminate bombing campaigns against civilians'.

It was all just words, Hassan said to himself.

Hypocritical words. Like the American secretary of state who praised SPLA leader John Garang as being 'very dynamic' – whereas in reality Garang's people were a murderous gang of pillaging Dinkas routinely diverting food aid from famine victims to combatants.

The pilot gave a little burp, checked the GPS, then pulled the lever which would unleash his cargo. Shush, shush, they went as they fell through the air.

As chance would have it, Sergei Kepitsa was on his way to Yei at the same time as Hassan. Crew-cut, shiny-nosed, he was driving up from the Uganda border in an open-top four-by-four. The purpose of his visit was to sign a contract with the SPLA leadership to supply them with arms. The tally comprised four anti-aircraft guns, eight 122mm propelled cannons, two anti-tank rockets, 16 anti-aircraft missiles and 20,000 mortar bombs – which came to a tidy sum.

Sergei had flown up to the border in one of his own cargo planes and driven the Landcruiser out of the back hatch. He couldn't risk flying over the border and landing in Yei. A foot soldier with exactly one of the anti-aircraft missiles he was intending to supply could too easily mistake him for a north Sudanese bomber – for the likes of Captain Hassan, in fact.

Sergei smoked as he drove along the bumpy road. He was feeling pleased with himself. It was a good deal he was about to make. Things were working out well. He was already a rich man, and this would make him richer still.

Formerly political officer in a MiG squadron that had seen service in the Russian occupation of Afghanistan, after his discharge he had returned to his home city of Vilnius, where he signed up as a pilot with Aeroflot. On the eve of the fall of communism he had seen his chance. Under the guise of saving the local fleet from the predations of Lithuanian nationalists, he had rounded up all the pilots of Russian extraction in the area. Together they had simply stolen half the local Aeroflot fleet, relocating first to Khartoum, then to Johannesburg, finally (when the South African authorities got a bit edgy) to Uganda. There, with friends in high places, he was able to get comfortable, installing himself and a number of associates more or less permanently in suites in Kampala's best hotels at a total cost of some $2,000 a night.

The original source of his wealth wasn't Africa at all, but Afghanistan. An old enemy, another mover behind the scenes, Osama bin Laden, had put him in touch with the country's new Taliban leadership. The Russian organised a number of covert or 'ghost' flights above countries which would not have allowed aircraft from Afghanistan to overfly them. These flights were usually carried out by IL76s operating out of Sharjah in the UAE, although Kigali in Rwanda and Entebbe were also used.

The Taliban contract, for which Sergei was paid in gold, enabled a massive expansion of the Russian's operations, allowing him to enlarge his fleet and to put money into various schemes of his own. Numerous aircraft were registered under different names across the various sites of the company's operations, including Let 410s, Yak 40/42s, IL18s and TU154s and an AN24 – the same type of plane that Captain Hassan was using, right now, to bomb Yei.

The bombs missed the hospital. Well, they missed the row of tents the hospital had become since the last time. The original building was wrecked. Paulo, a young Dinka boy (he had Catholic missionaries to thank for the name), heard the bombs whistle as they fell. It was a sound he knew. What it meant was he had to run. He dropped the empty food-aid sack he had been fashioning into a sort of kite and ran towards the river. As he ran, he wished that he could somehow become liquid – that the ground could open up and he melt away into its crevices.

The river was the next best thing. Throwing himself in, Paulo submerged himself totally. Even there, in the stinking water, he felt the shock waves ... .

It was a surgeon at the hospital, a custard-haired Norwegian called Tomas Følling, who pulled Paulo out of the water. The boy was unconscious, and hardly recognisable. Fragments of shrapnel had torn off half his face. Følling carried him straight to the tents, and placed him on a truckle bed. He called the nurse, and she gave the boy a large injection of morphine. Følling calmly began debriding the wound.

Any ordinary surgeon would have then begun sewing up the ruined face as best he could, in the knowledge that it would be terribly scarred. But Følling was no ordinary surgeon. Baring the boy's thigh, he began slicing skin from it to replace irreparable areas of the facial epidermis. This, too, he did calmly, although inside he was burning with the fierce anger of the righteous. Not so much on behalf of the boy – like many surgeons, Følling had a highly developed capacity for detachment – but because he knew this latest attack meant Khartoum had targeted the place. He swore to himself that he would do something to protect it. Whatever was necessary. He looked at the boy's face. If these grafts took, he would be able to complete the operation by next weekend.

Sergei Kepitsa was just on the outskirts of Yei when he saw Hassan's bombs drop and the flames lick up. He saw, too, a reasonable portion of the town's 80,000 inhabitants rushing down the road towards him, terror in their eyes.

'Fuck,' he said to himself, in Russian, and stopped the Landcruiser next to a painted sign declaring: 'Action not words – Yei district is a beneficiary of Norway Crisis Aid.'

He opened the glove compartment and slipped off the safety catch of his automatic pistol. You never knew what could arise when this sort of thing happened. He'd had no problems with the SPLA roadblocks on the way. His papers had the imprimatur of the highest authority in that organisation. The guards had, in any case, been forewarned of his visit. But ... frightened civilians, well, they were a menace.

Sergei was annoyed. The bombing of the town was highly inconvenient. He had been trying to set up this deal for months. He only needed the signature of Garang, the SPLA leader, and it would all be sorted out. Well, nearly. He had neglected to tell Garang that he had not yet got false end-user certificates for the weapons, which were US-made and could only be exported from that country on apparently legitimate pretexts.

He wondered whether to turn round and head back to the Ugandan side of the border, and wait for things to die down. Then he thought, what the hell and drove straight at the oncoming crowd of people, which parted like a herd of cattle.

Quarter of an hour later, he was in the centre of Yei, to see a man with hair the colour of custard lift a young Sudanese boy out of the river. The boy's face appeared to be a bit of a mess. Sergei asked an SPLA guard where Garang was to be found, only to receive the dispiriting news that the leader was on an operation in the Bentiu region. Sergei was furious. After all the effort he had made to keep the appointment, the only man whose signature would seal the deal had gone off blowing up oil wells. It struck Sergei that it was a bit rich to expect oil companies to grant you revenue streams in your own territory while you go sabotaging the same company's wells in your enemy's.

He wondered whether it was worth waiting around. Probably not. He decided to go and have a soft drink in a bar before heading back – a Sprite was what he fancied, a nice cold, fizzy cold Sprite. He walked around the town – still burning in places near to the bomb craters – but unaccountably there didn't seem to be many suitable hostelries open right then. The one place that was, didn't have any Sprite. In the course of his wanderings, his desire for that particular brand had increased, and he turned up his nose at the innkeeper's offer of a Fanta or Coke. He carried on strolling about among the ruins.

Finding himself next to a line of large, old-fashioned green tents – they reminded him very much of those the Russian army had used in Afghanistan – he poked his head round the entrance to one. What he saw nearly made him faint. Although he had seen many a grisly sight, and killed dozens of people himself (God knows how many he had killed indirectly), there was one thing Sergei Kepitsa couldn't stomach, namely a surgical operation. The yellow-haired man he had seen earlier was busy reconstructing the face of the young Sudanese boy he had pulled out of the river.

The reason for Sergei's horror was simple. During his time in Afghanistan he had been badly wounded in the crotch, suffering a laceration to the penis and scrotum. The army doctor who – cutting and trimming, stitching and darning – had patched him up might as well have had the hands of a farm labourer, so lacking was he in dexterity. The consequence was that what now hung between Sergei's legs was something like a mangled piece of bacon.

Thus his horror of the surgeon's art. Yet like all horrors, Sergei's phobic condition also had an element of fascination to it. For wasn't it the case he was always hoping to find the surgeon who, a master of his art, was going to put him right and restore his manhood?

With his nurse by his side, the surgeon was lifting a thin layer of skin from the boy's leg. Sergei watched, spellbound, as the Norwegian lifted up the piece of skin: it looked like the petal of a delicate rose. It seemed crazy to be performing such a complex operation in a makeshift field hospital, downright dangerous in fact.

'Can I help you?' said the nurse, turning to pick up an instrument from a stainless-steel kidney dish.

'No, no,' Sergei said, retreating as she held up the terrifying implement.

The surgeon himself took notice of him now, pulling down his face-mask and walking over.

'Kindly explain to me what you are doing here?' he said, in a strong Scandinavian accent.

'Nothing,' Sergei said, horrified by the film of blood on the man's gloves. 'I was just going. Well, if you could tell me your name?'

'My name is Følling. Now go away at once unless you want to have a death on your hands.'

As he walked back to his jeep Sergei turned the name over in his mind. It seemed very familiar.

He drove out of the blasted town and into the country, to begin the long journey back to Uganda. The abortive arms deal flitted in and out of his mind, alongside an image of the surgeon. What was it he had heard about this man? It was just on the edge of his memory.

The cab smelt of dust. Sergei lit a cigarette and began muttering to himself as he drove through the stunning sunlight. The wasted trip irritated him intensely. The preparations and journey itself had taken up most of his weekend. It would be night by the time he got back to

Kampala. Fuck, he whispered, letting the smoke drift out of the corner of his mouth, fuck.

That went on for a good few ks. He watched the kilometres roll by on the dial, cross-checked with the clock, with the speedo. Time and space in a vehicle in Africa, measured by numbers. No: by the passing of scrub and hut-roof, by the vibrations of the engines and the heat coming up through ... by ruts and holes mainly, by the shock and the shock and the shock of a ruined road.

He tried to stop thinking about the unsigned contracts beside him on the seat, and the man with the knife and bloody gloves. He tried to think instead about a woman with a silky mouth and very long legs: Aissa, the Somali girl he'd installed in one of his suites at the hotel in Kampala. She was one of the most gorgeous women he had ever seen, but from his point of view she had one distinct advantage over other women. Blinded at a young age by a landmine explosion in the course of her country's interminable conflicts, she didn't recoil in horror from his mangled manhood. This was the reaction of most women, even those whom he was paying very well indeed.

He passed another sign advertising Norway Crisis Aid, and suddenly the missing piece of his mental jigsaw fell into place. Følling was famous, the Albert Schweitzer of his time! He had been on the cover of *Time* magazine and that was what Sergei had been remembering when he had first seen the doctor. The point was that Tomas Følling wasn't just any doctor. He was Norway's most brilliant plastic surgeon. Or had been until, sick of cutting the skin of rich women, he had thrown it all in to go and do relief work in Sudan. Maybe Følling was, after all, just the person he needed.

The skin on his crewcut scalp crinkled as he smiled. The day, which had faltered so badly in the non-appearance of Garang, was starting to look much brighter. But he would still have to explain the delay to Jack Queller, the CIA man who had promised to help him get the end-user certificates. It would cause problems if they weren't able to fix on a date for the transaction, as Queller had to find an equivalent deal for another country if the certs were to be issued.

As Sergei expected, Queller was not happy. Before leaving for Africa he had sourced a set of papers which could easily be duplicated, and thereby slipped under the nose of the relevant Congressional committee. Once he had ended the call, the veteran spook, who had only one arm – the other had been shot off on a hillside in Afghanistan – put his head in his single hand.

As if he hadn't got enough to deal with. He was in Dar-es-Salaam as part of the FEST (Foreign Emergency Search Team) sent in the wake of the bombing of the US embassies, there and in Nairobi. There was no doubt he was the right person for that job: it was Osama bin Laden himself, the man behind the bombings, who had caused Queller's arm to be shot off ... the closing incident of a long period in which bin Laden had been, as the SPLA was now, the beneficiary of arms paid for by the CIA.

That was in the fight against the Soviets, in Afghanistan. Everything was different now. Everything was screwed up. Sometimes it blew Queller's mind what a tangled world it was that he existed in. Even for someone like him, someone with a good deal of the information at his fingertips, it was bewildering, awesome.

Like just this morning, for instance, when news of the air strikes came in. The State Department Ops Center hadn't forewarned him, of course, even though he had supplied much of the intelligence which had lead to the strikes. Sergei had laughed his scuzzy, shaven head off when he had told him that.

Queller wondered whether another of his operatives, Miranda Powers, had heard about the strikes yet. He had sent her across the water to the island of Zanzibar, to follow up on a bin Laden lead – some suggestion that one of the terrorists had come from there. He dialled the number on his mobile where it lay on the desk. They made them too small these days and it was hard for him. He had to hold it still by pressing his stump on the edge of the fascia. Then, with that only hand, he picked it up and listened for the dialling tone. But all he heard was the wah-wah of a busy satellite.

The person Queller was trying to ring, Miranda Powers, was in the TV lounge at the Macpherson Hotel, Zanzibar. Her partner, Nick Karolides, was in shorts and T-shirt on the sofa beside her – and President William Jefferson Clinton was on the television again. But this time, even though the President's *mea culpa* was still as fresh in the wind as the Macpherson's jacaranda, he wasn't talking about Monica Lewinsky. He was talking about helping people hurry to the life eternal.

'We have convincing evidence these groups played the key role in the embassy bombings in Kenya and Tanzania,' he said, in a statement from Massachusetts. 'Terrorists must have no doubt that in the face of their threat, America will protect its citizens. Today, we have struck back.'

'Christ,' said Nick.

'Shush,' said Miranda.

'That was the President speaking from his holiday retreat at Martha's Vineyard,' intoned the announcer. 'In the wake of his Grand Jury ordeal, he was weekending there with Hillary and Chelsea. Now he has cut short his visit and is returning to Washington. We hope to bring you coverage from the White House shortly of a briefing he will give on the strike.'

They listened to the backgrounder, and watched the graphic displays. It might have been full of technical wizardry, but, in terms of human cost, the missile attacks to which the President and the announcer were referring were less effective than the embassy bombings.

At Zhawar Kili Al-badr, a complex of three camps associated with Osama bin Laden near Khost, in Afghanistan, 21 people had been killed and 30 wounded.

At the Al-Shifa pharmaceutical factory at Khartoum in Sudan, said to be owned by the terrorist leader, 12 people had been killed and dozens injured. Some, the camera showed, were still being dug out from beneath the rubble. But the facility thought to be there, for the manufacture of VX nerve gas, had been 'functionally destroyed', said National Security Director, Sandy Berger.

The Sudanese government and independent sources were already protesting that the factory hadn't been making Empta, the chemical precursor to VX. It had, they said, been making cough medicine, antibiotics and simple analgesics (aspirin and paracetamol), as well as veterinary drugs for animals. The factory also produced medicines for diabetes, ulcers, tuberculosis, rheumatism and hypertension, supplying 70 per cent of the drug needs of a country beset with war and disease.

US officials countered that they 'could find no evidence' of all this. What they did have was a CIA soil sample from the factory, a sample containing Empta, they said.

Sudanese officials were also quick to point out that they had expelled bin Laden in 1996 after requests from the US and Saudi Arabia, sending 100 of his followers with him to Afghanistan.

'We can now bring you the President in the Oval Office.'

'Good afternoon. Today, I ordered our armed forces to strike at terrorist-related facilities in Afghanistan and Sudan because of the immediate threat they presented to our national security.

'I want to speak with you about the objective of this action and why it was necessary. Our target was terror. Our mission was clear ... .

'Their mission is murder. And their history is bloody ... .'

'Oh my God, they have bombed?' said Da Souza, coming into the room. The hotel's Goan manager stood next to the sofa with the white arms of his suit stretched out in front of him like those of a supplicant.

'Shush!'

'Our forces targeted one of the most active terrorist bases in the world. It contained key elements of the bin Laden network's infrastructure and has served as a training camp for literally thousands of terrorists from around the globe. We have reason to believe that a gathering of key terrorist leaders was to take place today, thus underscoring the urgency of our actions.

'Our forces also attacked a factory in Sudan associated with the bin Laden network. The factory was involved in the production of materials for chemical weapons.

'The United States does not take this action lightly ... we will persist and we will prevail. Thank you, God bless you and may God bless our country.'

'That was the President, who will now be resuming his long weekend at Martha's Vineyard, after making phone calls to other world leaders to garner their support for the strikes.'

Later in the day (during which Miranda and Nick had the manager bring them pizza and beer), it became clear that bin Laden himself had been nowhere near the camps when the missiles fell. He was, said his Taliban protectors, 'alive and well'. According to one report, he had left the camp an hour before the strike. Others were saying he hadn't stayed there for months and that other terrorist groups were renting the military-style complex off him. Whatever the case, bin Laden had been on the qui vive ever since the embassy bombings, an unnamed security source in Pakistan said, and had started moving from base to base.

'The word,' vouchsafed the CNN reporter quoting the source, 'is that he is now at an opium farm south of Jalalabad. It is not at all certain that any of the members of his organisation have been killed. Back to you, Peter.'

'Thanks, Wendy. Now over to William Cohen at the Pentagon,' cued the anchorman.

'We have taken these actions to reduce the ability of these terrorist organisations to train and equip their misguided followers,' the US Defense Secretary said in his briefing.

'Those who attack our people will find no safe place, no refuge from the long arm of justice.'

As he spoke, Miranda realised that Queller's views must have rapidly become official US policy. They must have picked up further Al Qaeda people while she had been away. Pointing the finger at bin Laden himself, with respect to the Sudanese plant, Cohen added that the terrorist leader had 'contributed to this particular facility'.

She went outside the room to call Queller on her mobile, suddenly realising that with all her confusion and happiness over Nick's arrival, she had quite forgotten to inform him about it. Nick himself continued watching as CNN switched to a feed from ABC, which had a scoop.

'I have never met him,' the owner of the Khartoum

factory, Salal Idris, said of bin Laden when questioned by a reporter from the network, which had tracked him down at his house in Saudi Arabia. 'I have never dealt with him. I have never knowingly dealt with any one of his agents.'

'The satellite is screwed,' said Miranda coming back in and hooking her shoulders under Nick's brown arm on the sofa. At their feet, pizza crusts sat on red-smeared plates, next to green bottles of Becks.

'Have I missed anything?' she asked.

'I dunno. I can't get a handle on it.'

That, at least, was true. What a tangled web it was, that Nick Karolides and Miranda Powers were trying to get their heads round, flushed with love as they were, on a Thursday afternoon in Zanzibar, in the month of August, in the year of 1998. These were moments of history they were witnessing, determination, chance and entropy all at work, and the spectacle was so confusing and bizarre it was like looking through a steamy window, only to find another behind it, and another, and another.

You could polish the window till it was thin as tissue-paper and you still wouldn't see through. There was no going to the cause. There was no understanding in it, this endless etcetera of events which led from dead Russians in Afghanistan, via this and that and the other, through dead Americans in East Africa, to – if one was to put one's finger on a consequence of particular regret – a baby bursting like a plum on a road on the outskirts of Khartoum, caught in the blast-wave of a Tomahawk missile.

A lot of work went into that. Over the previous week, progress reports from the investigation into the bombing of the embassies had been flooding into the White House situation room from all over the national security apparatus. Everything, from interviews with suspects to trawls through telephone intercepts and satellite surveillance tapes, seemed to point to bin Laden. Jack Queller (CIA) had indeed been vindicated in fingering bin Laden so early. Even Mort Altenburg (FBI) agreed with him now – to the extent of saying he had thought so all along.

Consumed as he was with his own problems, President Clinton met in secrecy with six advisors to discuss a counterattack. The group included, in all probability, Security Director Berger and Secretary of State Madeleine Albright, as well as General Tom Kirby from the Pentagon. The group decided that Sudan and Afghanistan were the targets to go for.

The planners worked round the clock. Once the targets had been pinpointed by a number of the US government's 24 global positioning satellites (GPS), the weapons units of six US navy warships and a submarine locked on to the co-ordinates. Two of the ships were in the Red Sea; the others, including the submarine, were in the Arabian Gulf. They were, assortedly, part of the USS *Abraham Lincoln* Battle Group, the USS *Dwight Eisenhower* Battle Group, and the USS *Essex* Amphibious Readiness Group. The sub was the USS *Columbia*.

The next stage involved logging the co-ordinates of the targets into the autonomous tracking systems of 80 Tomahawk cruise missiles. Then it was just a matter of waiting for General Kirby to relay President Clinton's final executive implementation order, which was delivered – earlier that weekend – over an encrypted line from Martha's Vineyard.

Once the holiday order had been given, initiating the vertical launch systems of the various vessels was a matter of diverse hands turning diverse keys and buttons. It was all as safe as could be. For all these keys and buttons were as cross-checked and balanced as the government under whose auspices the operation was taking place. And the hands were strong hands, at the ends of strong arms, rolled with khaki, and attached to cross-trained bodies topped with shaven, right-thinking heads, some wearing caps.

In such a way, navy weapons officers detonated the solid booster explosive charges which lifted the Tomahawks away from their silos. The missiles rose straight up at first. Then, the optimum altitude having been reached, the casings fell away. Tail fins and wings were deployed, pushed out of slots in the sides of the missiles by automated servo motors. Tiny rockets on the sides of the missiles changed the angle of thrust. Then the turbofan propulsion kicked in. Once that happened, the missiles ceased to be projectiles and became something more like small robotic planes, just over six metres in length and half a metre in diameter.

Four-score strong, they descended to a lower altitude, to avoid radar detection. Silver specks, cigarette-sized in the sky, they left vapour trails like, on nursery walls, children's crayons do. But the vapour did not last, you could not tell, it was gone as soon as childhood, too.

For as Security Director Berger observed, the point of using Cruise was to avoid 'giving the show away'. On TV screens worldwide, in a hotel lounge in Zanzibar, on an opium farm in Afghanistan, in the officers' mess of the Sudanese air force, he explained after the fact that 'the primary motivator here was maintaining operational secrecy'.

On the Tomahawks flew, guided by the GPS transmissions, carrying their 1,000-lb titanium warheads to the targets, within a 1,000-mile range, to an accuracy of 12 feet. The missiles continually realigned themselves by comparing time and location signals transmitted by atomic clocks in the satellites with their own onboard clocks and computers. From these calculations they extrapolated the ever-decreasing distance to the targets and made adjustments accordingly, also taking into account the shape of the underlying terrain and the prevailing weather patterns.

Detonation was simultaneous with impact, from side on or (in which case the missiles were programmed to make a parabola in the last minutes of their journey) directly above. At the factory in Sudan, observers reported three massive explosions. Walls were blown out, steel and concrete thrown over the compound. In the Afghan camps, command and communication facilities, weapon and ammunition dumps and training areas, such as shooting ranges, were destroyed. Checking over satellite photographs made after the blasts, CIA analysts reported 'moderate to heavy damage'. No mention was made of a baby bursting like a piece of fruit someone dropped on the pavement.

> *It was a terrorist university, and what it taught was death. From the outside it looked like an ordinary factory, but deep in its underground bunkers they were making deadly nerve gas. Keep tuned to CNN for updates on the US missile strikes on Afghanistan and Sudan.*

Miranda and Nick learned more as the reporting gathered pace: what a great educator is television! As afternoon wore into evening, and evening into night, the channel introduced coverage of how the Tomahawks had been received. In the countries where the missiles had fallen, important officials gave their views in greater depth. The strikes were 'a gross violation of human rights' declared the Taliban Foreign Ministry in Kabul.

The screen showed thousands of Afghan protestors

stoning the empty US embassy in the city. Then switched to Khartoum, where a similar scene was taking place, with crowds climbing the fence of the embassy building (which had also been evacuated, several years ago) and setting light to the American flag which still flew there.

'Down, down USA!' howled the protestors.

'This is a terrorist action,' said President of Sudan, Omar el-Bashir, more soberly. 'This aggression targets Muslim and Arab people. They have no right to strike Sudan without any vindication or evidence. Clinton and America will have to pay.'

As to the question of whether or not the Khartoum plant was being used to make nerve gas or other chemical weapons, he remarked: 'Putting out lies is not new for the United States and its President. A person of such immorality will not hesitate to tell any lie.' He went on to call the beleaguered President 'a war criminal of the first degree'.

Elsewhere in the Arab world, the reaction to the missile strikes was no less outraged. In Syria, Radio Damascus announced that 'it was impossible to justify such actions because they violate the sovereignty of nations and the sanctity of their land, as well as gravely endangering the lives and property of innocent people'. The terrorist group led by Ahmed Jibril accused the US of 'state terrorism' and 'hatred of everything Arab or Islamic'. 'It is a conspiracy against the Muslim world,' said Qazi Hussain, leader of Pakistan's Jamaat e-Islami party.

'Lewinsky's dress is no longer the preoccupation of the world after Clinton has discovered Osama bin Laden's *salwar kameez*,' declared an editorial in Beirut's *Al Kifah Al Arabi* newspaper, referring to the baggy Afghan tunic and trousers favoured by the terrorist leader.

'We will join the jihad!' shouted demonstrators on the

streets of Karachi. They, too, were burning American flags, and effigies of President Clinton to boot. For good measure – the cameras went close up on this – they stamped the burning embers into the pavement.

The US government responded bullishly to the criticisms, even saying this might just be the start of a whole wave of bombings. 'In life, there is no perfect security,' explained Undersecretary of State, Thomas Pickering. 'There may be more such strikes. We will act unilaterally when we must, in order to protect our citizens – but we invite other nations of the world to stand with us in this battle.'

Some Western states did back the strikes. 'I strongly support this American action against terrorism,' said Tony Blair of Britain.

Others didn't. The Al-Shifa plant had two prominent signs to it on the road out of Khartoum, and there was nothing secret about it, many diplomats in the city maintained. 'One can't, even if one wants to, describe the Shifa firm as a chemical factory,' said Werner Daum, the German Ambassador to Sudan.

'I condemn these bombings,' stormed Russia's President Yeltsin.

Officials from the Organisation for the Prohibition of Chemical Weapons came forward to say that, as well as nerve gas, Empta could be used to make fungicides and anti-microbial agents. It was also linked to a process for softening plastics.

Professor R. J. P. Williams of Oxford University's Inorganic Chemistry Laboratory contradicted Security Director Berger's claim that Empta is definitively 'a chemical used in the manufacture of VX nerve gas and has no other commercial distribution'.

'Types of the compound, an ethyl-methyl-phosphorus derivative, can be bought on the open market,' said the Professor. 'If every laboratory which has such a chemical is to be bombed, then it is goodbye to many chemistry departments in UK, USA and all over the world. The public must know the facts about the chemicals concerned in order to feel that terrorist targets were attacked and not innocent parties.'

Other Western scientists pointed out that VX gas shared some of the chemical constituents of cherry flavouring, as used in boiled sweets or cough syrup. As for the physical evidence, the soil sample, the Empta compound wasn't stable in soil, they said.

Foreign executives who had visited the plant joined the chorus of disapproval. 'I was courteously received and shown round every area in March,' recalled British businessman Peter Cockburn, disputing State Department despatches that said the plant was a secured facility. 'I recognised it as a normal factory for the production of simple pharmaceutical products – syrups for humans, powders for goats and camels. Just who are the terrorists in this case, and why is the British government supporting acts of incomprehensible barbarity?'

Through the offices of the UN, Sudanese diplomats submitted to the United States a $40-million bill for repair of the factory. It was revealed that the operative who had clandestinely collected the contested soil sample had been subjected to repeated polygraph tests to ascertain whether he had carried out his mission as directed. Sudanese officials said there was very little soil on the site anyway, 'just concrete and steel and lino and carpets'.

'I can't talk now,' said Queller when Miranda finally reached him, the following morning.

She kept him on the line to tell him about Nick.

'What? You've found him? When?'

She told him.

'What the hell have you been doing since then? This isn't some kind of jaunt you know, you're not a pair of weekenders.'

Miranda took a breath, then simply said she hadn't been able to get through.

'Stay there. I'll come over as soon as I can. What's that place you're at again?'

'The Macpherson Ruins Hotel. Outside of Stone Town.'

During the next day, in that very place, the TV remained on whenever the generator permitted. There was to be no more lovemaking for the weekenders, though there was more pizza and beer. And chicken curry and coconut rice. Over the tin roof above the sofa, bush babies would thud across, making the aerial dish wobble and, in electronic concordance, the picture too. Da Souza would come in from time to time, put down their food and drink on an old tin tray marked Property of Union Castle Shipping Company: Southampton–Madeira–Cape Town–Zanzibar–Aden.

Assuming his posture of supplication, the manager would stay and watch for a while.

'Very bad,' he'd say. 'Very bad. They will do, and the others will do, and they will do, and the others will do again. And soon we shall all be dead!'

When Da Souza left, the wooden-framed mesh door would creak on its hinges, and the warm, jacaranda-scented air streamed more briskly in through the screen. Time passed no less swiftly, and still the reporters and the anchormen, and the witnesses and the commentators and the experts chattered on.

'Let's go for a swim,' said Nick, eventually. 'Before it gets dark.'

Under a reddening sun, they went to the room and put on their costumes, then walked slowly down to the beach, with towels over their shoulders.

In the lounge, the TV played on unwatched. Then

died as the generator went out with an unearthly moan. At that moment, more or less, CNN happened to be reporting big news. How Osama bin Laden himself had apparently sent a message to London's *Al Quds Al Arabi* newspaper, saying that he had vowed to make further attacks on 'Crusaders and Jews'.

'The battle has not begun yet,' the message continued. 'The response will be with actions and not words.'

Over in Sudan, Captain Hassan Majoub was watching the broadcast, furrowing his brow as he looked at the fuzzy picture of bin Laden. He was in a stupor, he could not speak, he had lost his son. His baby son who had burst like a plum in the shockwave of a Tomahawk missile.

Another person was watching the picture, too – what is television but a great unifier of peoples? It was Sergei, of course. Sat on the edge of the bed in the most expensive hotel suite in Kampala, he was staring serenely at the screen, a cigarette between his lips as Aissa's worked dutifully over his open thighs.

Khartoum–Kampala–Dar-es-Salaam–Zanzibar. One of the few persons in this story who hadn't seen CNN lately was a young Sudanese boy called Paulo. Firstly, the only satellite dish in Yei had long ago ceased to work. Secondly, the custard-haired surgeon's brilliance seemed not to be working in this case.

The grafts Følling had made for Paulo's face had not taken. Now, as the boy lay on a truckle bed in the tented hospital, a blond head was bent over him. It wasn't Følling's. It was that of the nurse, who was changing the dressing over his eyes and forehead. She was tough, but a field hospital in South Sudan is a long way from Oslo. What she saw, then, as she removed the yellow-and-red stained bandages and the grafts were exposed to the air, almost brought tears to her own eyes. There was a terrible smell, too. Septicaemia had set in. There would be no chance of a second operation by the weekend, not as Følling had hoped.

Paulo gave an inarticulate moan. The nurse finished replacing the dressing. Hoping she had not made it too tight, she looked out of the doorway of the tent, to where the evening sun was casting golden shadows on the land – conjuring them up from trees, from stalks of millet, from the single jacaranda whose blooms shrieked like a disgraceful guest at a funeral. At sundown any place might have potential, but the nurse knew that people were starving not so very far away. She wondered, when she got back to her own country, how she would measure this experience. How she would tell them about it. Only her boyfriend would understand. But then he was in Sudan himself, working for one of the oil companies. He wasn't one of the others, the home people, those who hadn't seen places where leisure and comfort were the rarest of experiences. She glanced at Paulo, then walked over to the opening of the tent.

It would get cold later in the night and she best let down the door flaps. With her back to the sleeping boy, she undid the ribbons. Shush, went the canvas as it unrolled on either side, shush.

Getting It Wrong, Getting It Right

VICTORIA GLENDINNING

'ARE you excited?' someone said, as we prepared to leave.

Excited ... I'm not sure that is the right or respectful word. We are going to a land of war, hunger, disease.

But yes it is exciting to be off into what the aid agencies call 'the field'. The phrase has an adventurous ring, with missionary and military overtones.

The military element at least is apt enough. South Sudan is a war zone.

With ambivalent feelings and some apprehension, in the last week of November, off we go. To Africa.

Like most of Africa, south Sudan is pullulating with NGOs. If you're not familiar with the aid industry you may not know that an NGO is a Non-Governmental Organisation (even though government funding is often involved). It's an aid agency, a voluntary organisation, what used to be called a charity. NGO staff are paid, though not a lot. There are thousands of NGOs, mostly from Europe and North America, working all over the developing world. New ones are set up every day. Some of them are tiny. Some of them are huge, and run as efficiently as successful businesses. UNICEF, as an agency of the UN, is not strictly speaking an NGO, but it operates in a similar way, and is the lead agency for Operation Lifeline Sudan, (OLS), in which over thirty NGOs are also involved.

In Nairobi, Kenya's capital, I meet a Rational Man, a Celt who has worked in industry in Africa for most of his adult life. I like him a lot, so I listen.

NGOs are politically naïve, he says. Each aid agency has its own agenda – women, or children, or water, or trees, whatever. They don't address the wider issues. Their staff are in it for the adventure, and to make themselves feel good about themselves.

Well, that's not a crime, I think. Any more than preferring to work in your own country is a crime, and God knows there are wrongs to be righted and child deprivation here. Remember Mrs Jellyby in *Bleak House*, mercilessly satirised by Dickens for neglecting her own unfortunate children because she was always so busy campaigning for the unfortunate children of a distant land. Charity begins at home, they say.

Charity may begin at home, but it doesn't have to end there.

And I guess there have always been people who, for whatever reasons, want to get as far away from home as possible, and to do something worthwhile and exciting in foreign fields where the weather is hot and they can go around in shorts.

The only thing that bugs me a bit about habitual expats, when they are British, is that they tend to rubbish Britain, or rather England. The England they have in mind is the stultifying one they grew up in. (Most adolescents find their world stultifying.) The expats don't know how England has opened out, and don't want to know. They mostly bang on about the iniquities of the English class system, while – in spite of the hardship and even danger which they may face – all their cooking, laundry and housework is done for them neatly and silently by black or brown people who are not paid a great deal. Even aid-workers temporarily in the field, and hangers-on like myself, get this privileged treatment. You could argue that the aid-workers could not do their job if they also had to run their domestic lives. But that is the argument men used (to women) for generations. It makes for a seductive disjunction.

In the big, busy OLS compound at Lokichoggio in Kenya, we are briefed by security officers in preparation for entering south Sudan. We already each have passes issued by the southern rebel forces. They are date-stamped Nairobi. Any southern group with any clout has its base in Nairobi, even though Kenya recognises the Khartoum government – officially, anyway.

There are four security levels for personnel involved in Operation Lifeline Sudan. Level One means 'normal' – peace and tranquillity. That doesn't exist at the moment in south Sudan. Forget it.

Level Two means 'medium', Level Three means 'tense', Level Four means 'Grab your "quick-run kit" and take to the bomb shelters or evacuate'.

Most of south Sudan is permanently at Level Two, unless the Antonov from the north makes a raid unexpectedly and drops bombs, in which case you're at Level Four before you know it. Even so, a lot of south Sudan is calmer than this part of Kenya.

Lokichoggio has its problems. The OLS compound has 52 security men working in three shifts. Here we are up by the Sudanese border, a thousand kilometres from Nairobi. Seventy kilometres down the road is a camp of 60,000 refugees from Sudan, Somalia, Ethiopia. In the countryside all around, the cattlemen carry arms. The town has grown from 1,000 to 35,000 in ten years. Labour disputes with employees in the compound can turn nasty; there is local animosity about all the food-flights disappearing with their goodies out into Sudan. To leave the compound after 8pm is to invite attack. Cattle-rustling and highway robbery are a way of life, almost a game. On the most dangerous sections of the long, long road to Nairobi, vehicles may not proceed unescorted.

The pocket-sized Security Aide-Memoir for UN and

NGO staff tells you what *not* to do if your group is taken hostage. 'Don't whisper among yourselves. Don't look your captors in the eye.' That's useful. I would do both those things, automatically, getting it wrong. Most people would, don't you think?

South Sudan is silent. It is silenced. In this whole vast territory there is no newspaper, no radio station, very few landline telephones. The railway that runs from north to south is controlled from Khartoum and escorted by hordes of armed Arabs on horseback who are allowed to loot and kidnap in lieu of payment. The south Sudanese are cut off from their own remote areas and from the outside world. They are terrifyingly isolated. Because of the lack of communications, what goes on here is not often reported in the world's press.

That is why we have come.

I, with my companion, split off from the main group and fly over the Kenyan border, deep into South Sudan, 600 km north-west, as the crow or a Cessna Caravan flies, to an airstrip outside the town of Rumbek. It's hotter here than in Lokichoggio – about 35°C.

Rumbek is an important town in these parts, though a small one by our standards. It was totally wrecked by Khartoum government forces in 1986. The inhabitants fled; the town was abandoned and deserted. Only in 1997 when the rebel SPLA took it back did the people begin to return. The town and its environs have, in the past, been landmined. It's still not sensible to walk far off the road.

'Do both sides sow landmines?' I ask.

Pause.

'I suppose so.'

But because we are in the south, seeing and hearing what they are suffering, it is easy to be convinced that

Southerners and the rebels who fight for the freedom of 'New Sudan' are the good guys, and the government in the Muslim north the bad guys. UNICEF can't think like that. UNICEF helps the children of both south and North. UNICEF doesn't take sides. UNICEF negotiates access across war zones with the Khartoum government. Air access to certain areas is denied from time to time, without reason. One could speculate that it is bombing raids, but it could equally easily be movement of troops, people or food.

That's interesting. Couldn't we warn those places we aren't allowed to go to that something might be up?

No. I've got it wrong. UNICEF can't use this information, partly because they do not always know why access is denied and they could easily frighten a community for no reason. But more particularly because it is not part of the operating agreement they have with the government and it would be making a political stance. If either side in the conflict suspected that UNICEF was handing over information to the other, it would be disastrous for their humanitarian operations, and there is no way that local populations could be warned without it getting back to the military authorities.

Some of the worst things that happen in south Sudan, anyway, are unpredictable, perpetrated by militia who abduct and enslave. Slave-taking is not new: it has been going on since slavery was the accepted practice, though it was suppressed in the colonial period. Part of General Gordon's mission to the Sudan in the 1880s was to crush the slave trade (and look what happened to him). Our own Baroness Cox, a member of the House of Lords, collects up money from Christian charities and in person takes wads of dollar bills out to Sudan, to pay for slaves and return them to their families. Either she is a heroine, or she's getting it wrong, or both. It is arguable that, in some sense, she may be subsidizing the slave trade.

In and around Rumbek, lumps of twisted, rusted ordnance, tanks, trucks and the odd field-gun, lie crookedly where they were abandoned or shoved to the roadside. The roads, as everywhere in south Sudan, are uneven and terrible. In the rainy season they become impassable mud sluices. But now, when we walk, and even when we bump-bump-bump along in the UN Land Cruiser, the dry red dust gets everywhere on our skin and hair and clothes.

There are lots of potholes about four feet across and three feet deep, in the streets and in the marketplace. Bomb craters. In the main street, buildings of dried-mud brick lie in ruins. *Tukuls* – the round thatched huts of ordinary people in the villages – have been put up between and among the ruins, and there are 'suburbs' of *tukuls* where Rumbek peters out into the countryside. Transhumant cattlemen make their encampments outside the town and bring their milky-white long-horned beasts into the market.

Some men carry guns openly on the street – they may be members of the SPLA, or they may be cattlemen or farmers. Guns are a status-symbol, 'like cellphones' says Sid. (I'll come to Sid later.)

The men and women are startlingly good-looking. It goes without saying that the children are irresistible. Both sexes are typically, in adulthood, very tall and thin, with small, cropped, perfectly poised heads, and a careless kind of elegance. Men walking in pairs – young or old, it makes no difference – lope along loosely linking hands. Big trees have benches under them, in a ring, to serve as classrooms, magistrates' courts, meeting-places.

Under a tree in the middle of a bare area surrounded by buildings in various states of collapse sits a headmaster. He is writing a letter to the parents of a pupil who cannot afford to pay for their child's food. Many children have displaced parents, or no parents. If no one pays for their food, they have to leave. Wrecked tanks lie around like broken toys that no one has cleared away. The headmaster's table is a high iron trestle, another relic of war. His briefcase, into which he carefully places his letter, is a dirty green plastic bag.

The headmaster is a hero, or an angel. His name is Gabriel. He receives no salary. He has 420 pupils, four of whom are girls; there will be more girls coming up from the primary school, if only because an educated girl can command a higher bride-price. There are 21 teachers, only four of them trained and permanent. The others come in when they can spare the time from their work in the fields.

They follow both the Kenyan curriculum and the 'Old Sudan' curriculum, neither of which is satisfactory. The headmaster would like to key into the Ugandan system, and have his boys take 'O' and 'A' level exams so that they could go to university in Uganda. There is no third-level education at all in south Sudan. The university at Juba, the capital of the south, was closed down when Juba was captured by the government troops.

When we take a photograph of the headmaster, one of his staff moves forward, tactfully, to remove the dirty green plastic bag out of camera range.

Whatever sort of school is this?

It was one of the few secondary schools in south Sudan, founded by the British in 1948, with books and teachers provided by the British Council. In the school's heyday, Rumbek was a prestigious seat of learning, and this wide campus accommodated 1,600 boarding pupils, with playing-fields, and a lab, two chapels, and a library with the works of Dickens and Shakespeare. The present headmaster was a pupil here.

In 1986, when the government forces from the north – 'the Arabs', as they always say here – attacked and took over Rumbek, and the population fled, the school became their barracks. In 1997, when the rebel SPLA recaptured the town, they took the buildings over in their turn. Much of the school has been demolished or destroyed.

For 15 years there has been no educational activity in the region, and no teacher training. A lost generation.

When they finally reopened the school last year, one of the buildings was discovered to be full of unexploded landmines and bombs – three tonnes of material. Sid (yes, I'm coming to Sid) organised a workgroup to carry them away, bury them and detonate them. UNICEF has also provided the school with pit latrines and a grinding-mill for meal.

There's another and very special kind of school in Rumbek. On the outskirts of the town is an SPLA barracks, and close to it a huge bare compound. This is the Deng Nhial School for demobilised child-soldiers.

The child-soldiers are used to visitors; this school is 'news'. They crowd round us, some smiling and some wary, hoping for little handouts, keen to be photographed, dressed in ragged, filthy T-shirts and shorts, either too big or too small for them.

A 13-year-old, erect and assertive, demands my attention. He speaks quite good English:

'I want to be a doctor. The teachers here don't know any of the things I need to learn. How can you help me? *When* will you help me? And I need clothes.'

They all tell us they need clothes. To get new ones, they work for a bit of money to buy something in the market. UNICEF, or even you or I, could organise a shipment of clothes to these children. But that would make the child-soldiers an 'élite' group, I am told. I'm getting it wrong. What about all the other children in other schools?

They put their small hands in ours. They look remarkably healthy. One very little boy has a whitish deposit over the whole surface of his skin and head. Has he got some skin disease? No. It's just a thick layer of dust.

The SPLA and the SPLM have undertaken, in a letter to Carol Bellamy (executive director of UNICEF), written on the day of her visit to the school in October 2000, not to admit any more child-soldiers and to demobilise those they still have. UNICEF provides educational materials, sports equipment and primary health kits. There is a dire shortage of books and pencils. The headmaster would also, he tells us urgently, like a mechanical grinder, because the boys don't like pounding meal, traditionally a woman's job. (And also because the Rumbek boys' school we have been to has already been given one; it was proudly demonstrated to us. Bit of rivalry here.)

The headmaster himself is ex-SPLA. There are about 450 children, the youngest ones less than seven years old. They get just a primary education, even though they will be able to hang on here until they are 18. Most are boys, though there are a few teenage girls. The girls worked in the officers' houses and were 'for the soldiers' – presumably abused.

The very youngest boys were never trained as soldiers, but employed as batmen. Many of the children were either brought in by their families during the famine and fighting of 1997–8, or turned up on their own at the SPLA barracks after the SPLA won Rumbek back. They needed food and shelter and had nowhere else to go, and their parents were dead, or captured, or lost. Other children come from up north, in the devastated areas near the oilfields, and don't want to go home 'because of the fighting', they say. (Schools on the front line are mobile, under trees, on the run.) Their families, if they still have families, don't know where they are. That didn't seem to bother any of the kids who talked to us, but then you can't tell.

The children sleep in open-sided *tukuls* clustered round the edges of the compound, which they build themselves, and they cook their own food in small groups. Because they lived in barracks before, says the headmaster, they are used to institutional life. They need more rules and regulations than ordinary children. They have seen bad things – bombings and killings – and they have been trained to be killers. Many of them are pretty bright; they are impressed by the authority of educated officers, and want to be like them.

'Discipline is the task. The boys reminisce about their experiences but it's not encouraged,' says the headmaster. 'The aim is to wash the past from their minds.'

I wish you could meet Sid. Everyone calls him Sid, though his real name is Siddarth Chatterjee. His accent reflects the fact that he was educated at an English public school – Rugby – and at Lincoln College, Oxford. He served with the Paras for 16 years, including in Bosnia and in Iraq. So, he's tough. He's made a little golf-course and practises golf every day, and goes for runs. He's also smart and sophisticated, a man of the world who keeps his personal politics out of sight 'except perhaps in a drawing-room in London or New Delhi'. He has a flat in Nairobi for his time off, and a home in the hills in India, with a private menagerie. He's unfailingly charming except when one of his staff fails to come up to scratch, and then he barks. From outside his office door, we hear him barking. You would not want to get on the wrong side of Sid.

Sid runs the compound as if it were a military camp. The effects of his discipline are apparent. The bare earth is swept clean of leaves and litter, and everything paintable, including the edging-stones, is painted white.

Sid has also had flowers planted round the huts. There is no pastoral care at the school for child-soldiers, and it is Sid who expresses concern for their psycho-social needs, their premature adulthood, and possible return to innocence. Sid is an occasional poet and a considerable prose stylist, a lover of music and of wild animals, something of a mystic, certainly a romantic. He tells – very well – the story of how he sat by a beautiful blonde on a plane and proposed marriage to her as they waited for their luggage by the carousel, without even knowing her name. (She accepted. They married. The marriage did not last very long.)

So there are two sides to Sid. There are probably more than two.

Each hut in the compound is labelled, on a neatly painted bit of wood stuck in the ground, with the name of a south Sudanese town as well as a number. Mine is 'YEI 13'.

Unlucky number, unlucky name. The Tuesday before we arrive in Rumbek, the Khartoum government inflicts a surprise bombardment on Yei, which is about 300 km south-south-east of Rumbek, near the borders with Zaire and Uganda.

The bomb falls on the busy marketplace. Those who run for shelter when they hear the Antonov coming rush back into the marketplace to help the wounded and to salvage their possessions and stalls. Then the plane comes round again and more bombs fall, causing worse carnage.

This horror does not hit the headlines in the outside world. News from south Sudan does not filter out – through Nairobi – for several days, by which time it is no longer hot. Anyway, this is just one of 33 such incidents, involving 250 bombs, between July and November 2000. Rumbek itself was bombarded in July, while a workshop on the child-soldiers was in progress.

We hear the details about Yei from a Roman Catholic bishop, Erkolano Ladu, who happened to be there last Tuesday. He saw severed body parts and shreds of flesh scattered all over the marketplace. Some victims were nowhere at all – blasted to smithereens.

'It's sheer terrorism,' says the bishop.

On a slab, he saw, lying beside the body of his mother, a live, open-eyed, but motionless child, about a year old:

'Completely traumatised.'

There are 12 Catholic bishops in Sudan, six in government-held territory and six in the South, in the 'liberated areas' as they say. The southern bishops are holding their Eucharistic Conference in Rumbek, with lots of bustling, animated priests – mostly Sudanese – and representatives of religious NGOs.

We get an audience with the bishops. The Bishop of Rumbek, their chief spokesman, is Italian. Since the Catholic Church sees the conflict, unambiguously, as a religious war – black African Christianity versus the northern Arabs' state religion, Islam – the bishops are shamelessly partisan.

The bombs, they tell us urgently, fall on hospitals, schools, markets, not on military installations. The Church runs schools and hospitals. The most prevalent diseases treated in their 30-bed Rumbek hospital (opened in 1998) are malaria, TB, polio, snakebites, tetanus and syphilis. Not much AIDS, yet. That is the one and only benefit of south Sudan's isolation, and given the increasing traffic with Uganda it can't last for long.

The bishops tell how they act as a 'mosquito' to the Khartoum government, and lobby the UN not to admit it to the Security Council. But politicians everywhere must respect official sovereignty. They work with Khartoum; and other African countries all have their own agenda. The Egyptians, for example, don't want an independent, Christian south Sudan because of the importance to them of the Nile which flows through both north and south. Egypt, like Libya, is a Muslim country.

'This is a devilish war. What is taking place is genocide. Why does the international community not involve itself here, as in Kosovo or Sierra Leone?'

Because, I say, communications are so slow and difficult. There are international journalists in Nairobi, but not here, so the stories rarely get into the world's newspapers. There are no journalists here because south Sudan has no strategic importance for the West. Every nation's geopolitics is ruthlessly self-interested.

And it's complicated. Even if the northern government and the SPLA made peace, there would be half a dozen other rivalrous rebel groups – some of them, would you believe, armed by the north, in order to foster faction – who would not agree or abide by the peace. Nor would it affect the endemic tribal warfare which rends the south.

It's even more complicated than that. The ethics of armed intervention do not bear examination. The Sudan is officially one nation; the north, in its persecution of the south, is not illegally invading a foreign territory. The Islamic Khartoum government is probably not exercising brutal control against the wishes of *most* of the people it governs. And the United Nations was founded on the principle of national self-determination and the integrity of sovereign states.

But the champions of armed intervention in foreign conflicts – chiefly the USA and Britain – now argue, *when* it suits them, that human rights are more important than state sovereignty. This is the new imperialism.

Yet what 'we' did, in the bombing of civilians in Belgrade and Baghdad, could be construed as war-crimes. I was in Cambodia recently, where they are beginning to arraign the surviving Khmer Rouge commanders for their war-crimes.

Perhaps the British should have partitioned Sudan before they left. Perhaps it wouldn't have made any difference: think of the unhappy history of partitioned Ireland. 'The Church is the people,' says one of the bishops in Rumbek. Yes, again. But beneath the Christianity the old religions of south Sudan prevail – animal sacrifice, spirit beliefs, witchdoctoring and tribal scarring – and, less significantly, extraction of the lower front teeth – initially they say for fear of lockjaw, now just an unlovely (to us) convention.

The compound has its own generator, and Sid has every aid to communication known to man. He lets us use his office to send emails. I tap out a message to K., my husband:

'Today I talked to six bishops and three rebel commanders.'

I meet the SPLA commanders in the half-light of a *tukul* on the edge of the child-soldiers' school. They sit on one side of a low bench with a folded brown blanket on it, and we on the other. One wears fatigues and a big smile; he does most of the talking. This is Commander Piang Deng Kuol. (Apparently he is absolutely brilliant at Scrabble.) The second, Alternate Commander John Lat, is in ordinary clothes and has an intellectual air. The third, who joins us later, is an older man, Commander Alias Waya. He defected from the government military eight years ago to join the SPLA.

Commander Alias Waya has presence, and a reputation, and status, but I suspect he is yesterday's man. He says nothing at all for a long time. He just sits there looking gloomy, his head turned away to one side, while Commander Piang talks. In the end I turn to him:

'Sir, you have not spoken to us.'

He rouses himself and asks – as had the bishops – why it was that no one in the West publicised and supported the armed struggle in south Sudan. I said – as I had to the bishops – that it was because of the bad communications with the outside world and because south Sudan had no strategic importance for the West.

'It is because they think in the West that the SPLA is Communist,' he said.

'I don't think so.'

The SPLA is grotesquely ill-equipped in comparison with the government forces. They have radio telephones but no national HQ, no ground-to-air missiles, no Antonov planes. They are determined to recapture Juba, the capital of the south, from the Arabs.

'We will retake Juba. But it will be a moral victory only; it will bring down on us terrible retaliation from Khartoum. The Arab world will move in to help the north, and the south will be punished.'

They seem fatalistic.

UNICEF's main project in Rumbek County is the establishment of community centres. The aim is to establish one for every 1,000 people, at a cost of $45,000 per centre over five years. The plan is that the people themselves will take over the running and maintenance.

We go to visit the first and recently completed centre at Cueicok, driven by Sid in the Land Cruiser with demonic insouciance along a road so bad that even he takes half an hour to go ten miles.

How on earth does Sid know when we have got to Cueicok, or anywhere at all, or when one village or *payam* begins or ends, when the flat landscape of trees and scrub all looks exactly the same, and there are no signposts where tracks intersect, and no signs of habitation?

Sometimes we pass people walking on the road, carrying things. A dog appears from nowhere and runs ahead of the car, running faster and faster, not having the sense to swerve to one side, looking round in terror at its pursuer, the roaring Land Cruiser with its menacing aerial. I am afraid the dog's heart may burst.

We pass a rusting, jagged truck on the side of the road, blown up by a landmine when the SPLA were advancing from this direction to liberate Rumbek. A shrub has grown up through the broken belly of the truck, and pours clusters of fragrant pink and yellow flowers over its shrapnel-riddled sides.

We arrive somewhere. It's Cueicok. The community centre was built by local people under Sid's mercilessly energetic supervision. They had to clear the site of landmines first. It consists of a school of two classrooms, open at the sides; a medical centre; a water-pump; a meeting area, and a playground, all enclosed within a compound. The people who constructed it are there to greet us and show us around. They seem very pleased, and crack sly jokes about Sid's ruthlessness as a taskmaster.

Clean drinking-water is an absolute priority for the children's health. We go to see another water-point, not part of a community centre and seemingly in the middle of nowhere. An amiable woman demonstrates the pump for us. Our guide says:

'Five thousand people live around here.'

'Where? Where?'

I look around, mystified, at the flat expanse of scrubby bush on every side, extending as far as the eye can see, apparently innocent of hut or *tukul*. During the fighting, the people moved their homes away from the tracks down which the tanks came, into hidden places. Maybe they will creep back. Cattle people have to live far apart from one another anyway, to have space for the animals to graze.

At the end of the day we reach the old waterhole, all that there was in this area before the water-point was made. It is a swampy, cattle-trodden, clearly filthy patch of shallow water in a hollow of low hills. As the sun goes down, the clods of mud and cowshit at the edges of the swamp cast purplish shadows. There are long-legged waterbirds, and a scattering of small children bringing goats to drink, silhouetted against the sun – an unspeakably ancient and weirdly beautiful scene. It is absolutely quiet. This is the old, spellbinding, eternal Africa.

Thinking about the international community's lack of concern for south Sudan, I tell myself that self-interest is not a crime. No one would survive without it. No one would get any lunch.

People aren't only motivated by self-interest, I thought, alone in my hut in Rumbek. I mustn't get this wrong. There is also the desire or perceived obligation to 'make a difference'. Anything anyone attempts in this direction is bound to be tainted by all the human faults and errors of governments, institutions and individuals. What do you expect?

UNICEF will not help the families of those tribespeople in places where there is fighting – Nuer v Dinka, Dinka v Dinka, whatever. It's too dangerous.

Only when they stop fighting can aid agencies move in, to assess their needs. Meanwhile there are 'peace and reconciliation' conferences set up for tribal chiefs who have no notion of a life without conflict. Some of the chiefs and warlords were at the boys' secondary school together in Rumbek in the old days. That means they know each others' strengths and weaknesses. Fighting is what they have always done. Fighting is what they do. It's not peace that they want, but victory.

We tried to gatecrash, respectfully, the current 'peace and reconciliation' conference of chiefs and were seen off by the convener, a thin European lady with upswept grey hair and dangling earrings. The proceedings were very sensitive, she said, and private.

We could hear one of the chiefs speechifying eloquently in his own language inside the hut. They make very long speeches, the lady said. You have to hear them out or they feel aggrieved. She was in a hurry to get back to them. She sounded like she was having a great time, and the chiefs, too. We sloped off.

The chiefs will come to this conference, just as the SPLA will attend workshops on the Rights of the Child and other topics on which UNICEF and the aid agences set such store. Aid is the big carrot. Is it a bit like Victorian ladies of the manor visiting cottagers, and dividing people into the 'deserving' and the 'undeserving' poor?

But as my companion reminds me: 'Funds are limited.'

Yet the international community, which means the rich West, if it had the will, could at a single stroke wipe out the worst of the child deprivation in South Sudan. It could fund all 400 community centres planned by UNICEF in this area. Schools could be equipped and clinics set up for almost no money in Western terms. Then we could leave them to it, so as not to promote the culture of dependency.

Why is it better to do it piecemeal, with difficulty, spinning out the agony and the dependency? Because the population must be educated slowly into taking responsibility? Because throwing serious money at the problem would put the aid agencies out of a job, out of thousands of jobs?

In any case the rich West will not do anything of the sort. Self-interest, again. There is no strategic importance for the West in south Sudan, I say to myself for the tenth time.

The people of Rumbek are moving along as best they can. Rumbek is alive with start-ups. Juanita's Millennium Bar has just opened, though Juanita doesn't have much in stock to drink.

On the edge of town, five married women have got together and built a 'hotel' with their own hands. It's called Panda Hotel, and consists of a group of *tukuls* with two or three beds – also built by the women – in each. It has taken them two years, and has just opened. Food is cooked and eaten outside, under the trees. They want to get a licence so they can have a bar.

The deputy manager of the hotel is particularly long-limbed, lovely and languid. Her skin is like black silk. She seems very tired. I think she may be anaemic. She looks about 22 and tells me she has nine children. Girls are married here so young and immature that 50 per cent die in childbirth. Maternity care, and clean birth-kits, are priorities for UNICEF as for all the health-oriented agencies. These five women have 30 children between them. The whole idea of the hotel is to make enough money to buy primary education for the children.

In the market area we meet Chol and David, the Richard Bransons of Rumbek, smiling and prosperous in their co-op, the Rumbek Grain Trading Association.

They deal in groundnuts and sorghum from a warehouse behind the office. They built their premises, subsidised by grants, with materials trucked in from Uganda. A lot of people from Rumbek went to Uganda when the town was occupied by the Arabs, and are now returning and planning businesses.

Along the street is another co-op, importing – also from Uganda – all kinds of household goods: trays, kettles, pots, clothes, building-materials, cafetières, sewing-machines. (The cloth of the djellabahs worn by Rumbek men also comes from Uganda, and is made up locally. At the moment the prevailing colour is holly-green; not long ago it was blue.) All Rumbek's entrepreneurs tell us their chief problem is the cost of diesel for the trucks back and forth from Uganda, and south Sudan's currency, which is not much good abroad. They have no sentiment about Sudanese money. They still deal between themselves in old Sudanese pounds; the official currency, the currency of the enemy, of the north, is dinars. Both are soft as butter. They would be happy to adopt Ugandan shillings.

Standing in the sun outside their grain store, David says to me out of the blue:

'I have one true friend who is English.'

He tells me his name.

'I know him, too! We used to work on the same paper. He is my friend, too!'

It seems the most astonishing coincidence, at the time, even though our friend is a long-time friend of Sudan, as I knew. David writes a letter for me to take back to England (where, of course, he himself has never been), and sends one of his employees out to buy an elegant, hand-made, copper-stemmed pipe from the market, as a present for his true friend in England.

Our Richard Bransons are quite optimistic about the economic revival. But the rebel commanders tell us that the north is bombarding precisely those towns which show visible signs of reconstruction and development. Hence the bombing of Yei. Evidence of economic life spells their doom.

The rebel commanders don't believe Khartoum will give a damn about that. The rebel commanders say they themselves will go on fighting for as long as it takes, all their lives if necessary. Fighting is what they do.

When I get back to London I go to the annual general meeting of an NGO which runs projects to improve the lives of people living in countries bordering the Sahara, and in which I have an interest because of the close involvement of K., my husband. The guest speaker, John Hayley, a management guru from Oxford Brookes University, plays the devil's advocate: 'Who needs NGOs?' – incidentally expressing uncomfortably well the unease I myself had had about aspects of the aid industry.

He gives the case against: aid agencies are paternalistic and neo-colonialist; not fully accountable; self-perpetuating; myopic and politically naïve; not always cost-effective; often badly and weakly managed; bad at collaborating with one another in spite of the rhetoric to the contrary; dependent on official funding, so potentially just contractors; risk-averse.

I remember the Rational Man in Nairobi. What, he said, if aid is interfering in a system which doesn't work and shouldn't be kept going? Should people in inhospitable, backward and poverty-stricken areas of the earth be encouraged, or condemned, to remain where they are, by small improvements in their standards of living? We could be trapping them in a situation where no one should be. What leads to freedom is development. Aid should perhaps be hung on housing, in and around towns, to help people move away from subsistence farming.

'But you wouldn't want us to destroy the culture of the *tukul* and the cattle, would you? Destroy an age-old traditional way of life? Do we want to do that? Do we have the right?' That's what someone said to me in Rumbek. I don't know the answer.

History moves along, says the Rational Man. It's all process. Everywhere, there are pockets of peace and flowering, and then everything all falls apart again. This is normal, organic. We shouldn't strive after unrealistic solutions we aren't prepared to pay for and see through. When you try to imagine the millions of children in Africa who live in conditions of near-nothingness, to aspire to 'the eradication of child poverty' is not just grandiose rhetoric, it is plain barmy.

Even if it were to be done, as Matthew Parris wrote shortly before I went to south Sudan, it would no longer be a matter of 'fiddling at the edges or sending in small teams to help':

> Entire civil services would need to be reconstituted, legal systems reassembled, tax-gathering functions reconsidered and rebuilt, roads and sewers relaid, health services, armed forces and police reorganised from scratch.[2]

The Empire once again, perhaps. Don't even think about it. We will go on meting out our aid, funding 'projects', fiddling at the edges and sending in small teams to help.

Maybe that's not such a bad thing. John Hayley, in the talk I heard, also provided the positive answers to his question 'Who needs NGOs?'

Aid workers have 'small fingers', and are flexible, he said. They are willing to work in arduous and dangerous conditions, in close participation with communities. They are direct intermediaries between donors and recipients, and their non-political 'observer' status gives them a unique perspective on possibilities for development. Above all, they have integrity, and are 'value-driven'. This question of values is becoming increasingly important as I go deeper into south Sudan's problems and open my mind to what is happening on the ground.

Meanwhile the Rational Man says human beings are aggressive animals and will fight for their own survival. Face up to this, he says. The respectful thing, the honest thing, is to acknowledge where our self-interest lies.

There will always be bad men whose self-interest becomes damaging. Some of them may be people in offices, thinking up projects to secure the survival of their own jobs and organisations. Set-ups such as the UN and the World Bank are so large and diffuse that they can only function by consensus within the group; there is enormous institutional inertia, decisions are opportunistic, and no individual is ultimately accountable.

Having your heart in the right place is not enough, says the Rational Man. OK, so you have to defend the weak against the bullies. But how? Why didn't we just take out Milosevic? Why don't we just take out Saddam? Because it suits us not to. They are key players in the game we and they are playing.

So we prefer to bomb their territory and kill hundreds of people whose names we do not know.

Who profits from this? I do know the right answer to that. The international arms industry.

Sid identified south Sudan's three 'challenges' as the

disastrous economic situation, intertribal warfare – and the increase in available arms.

Those who with deep sincerity organise conferences about 'peace and reconciliation' between warring tribes and groups might be better employed directing their energies towards the third of these challenges, the increase of available arms. As it is they are behaving, perhaps, like ostriches.

In many places, by the way, the ostriches, like the elephants, have disappeared from Sudan, wiped out by war. Now there are only hyenas and vultures, and puff-adders. And killer-bees.

The latest issue of *CAAT News*, the newsletter of the Campaign Against Arms Trade, is waiting for me at home. It reports on the globalisation of the arms industry: 'Most major weapons projects are collaborative efforts between companies in several countries and rely on procurement by all the participating countries to get the project started.'

The UK is one of six countries which in July 2000 agreed on a new system 'for the transfer of components and the completed weapons between the participating countries, as well as exports of such weapons beyond them'.

Children are disproportionately affected by armed conflict – killed, maimed disabled, traumatised, separated from their parents, orphaned. Anti-personnel weapons are anti-children weapons. The ease of acquiring small arms exacerbates the situation.

'Small arms have probably extinguished more young lives than they have ever protected' says Carol Bellamy, UNICEF's executive director.[3]

If arms were not readily available, the war between south and north Sudan could not be prolonged or escalate. The Khartoum government is supplied by

China, Libya, Iran. The SPLA gets help from Iran, too, but not much. It's not quite true to say that arms-manufacturing countries, including the UK, sell arms to absolutely anyone. But with this new global agreement, it'll be impossible to keep track of what originates where.

The rich countries, knowingly or not, already end up arming both sides in regional conflicts and then throw up their hands in horror, holding conferences about 'peacekeeping' and 'conflict resolution', when the arms which they have manufactured and marketed are put to the precise use for which they were designed.

The USA is still manufacturing landmines which get round the agreements of the Ottawa Convention. Prosecutors in India continue to investigate allegations of corruption in connection with an arms deal involving the Swedish araments firm Bofors.

So the globalised arms industry surreptitiously ships its products round the world. Meanwhile we feed someone in south Sudan today who may well die of starvation later. We heal a young man's shrapnel-wounds so that he may return to fight again.

The surgical hospital run by the International Committee of the Red Cross in Lokichoggio, which we visit on our way back, has two planes which pick up anyone needing surgical treatment in southern Sudan including the badly wounded from both sides in the Sudanese conflict, and from intertribal wars in the south. A lot of these are children, who lie silently in bed wrapped in bandages, or hop around the hospital on one leg. With 500 beds, this is the largest field hospital in the world.

They say they are always in need of blood for transfusions, so I give some blood. I see the bag of my blood being popped into the freezer like a bag of frozen peas. Maybe it will do some mangled child a bit of good.

A bereaved mother says to one of the doctors in this hospital:

'Why did you cure my son so that he could go out again and get killed?'

But who would not rather have one more year of life, one more month, one more day?

I have seen, in Ethiopia, an old woman painfully climbing the steep track back to her village in the burning heat with a bundle of twiggy firewood on her bent back. She does this every day; and every day, as the arid slopes become stripped of scrub, she has to go further to find anything worth carrying home. Nothing deters her. The wood is for the fire which will cook the family meal. What is important to her is that her children and grandchildren should eat. Today. Then again tomorrow. Life for life's sake, day by day. Who is to put a limit on that?

The management man at K.'s AGM had talked about aid agencies not being 'cost-effective'. Nothing that is really worth having or doing is cost-effective in the world's terms. It's a question of values. At home I talk to K., who says that the world we live in is geared to profit and materialism and selfishness. Its values are reckoned to be the only common-sense virtues. Someone, K. says, has to maintain the reverse values.

So what counts are the living conditions and personal experiences of every single individual person, as intense and urgent in south Sudan as in our own towns and villages. It's better to do something than nothing, that's for sure.

The Rational Man would not agree. Nothing, according to him, is often the *right* thing to do. It delivers no 'feel-good factor', so it requires discipline.

K. and I go to an Advent service in Southwark Cathedral, near where we live. Holding lighted candles in the dark church, we sing the hymn beginning

Thou whose almighty word
Chaos and darkness heard
And took their flight ... .

Every verse ends with the words 'Let there be light'. When we came to the last verse –

Move o'er the water's face,
Bearing the lamp of grace,
And in earth's darkest place
Let there be light –

I, who love to belt out hymns I know without thinking too much about the words, cannot go on. South Sudan under the blazing equatorial sun is earth's darkest place. Let there be light. Let there be light.

The trouble is that light and darkness, in the sense of good and evil, don't come in separate packages like day and night. They co-exist, battling it out. There's something seductive about the third-century Christian heresy called Manichaeism; the Manichees based their dualistic theology on the idea that the devil, the Prince of Darkness, had invaded the Kingdom of Light and succeeded in mixing up all the particles of light and darkness. Man's task is to separate them out again and to set free the light. Two bits of news from Rumbek reach me a couple of months after Christmas – one dark and one light.

The first is a desperate email from the Italian Bishop of Rumbek, Caesar Mazzolari, whom we met out there.

He reports at first hand the consequences of terrible fighting that erupted in early February between the armed Arab horsemen who accompany the trains from the north, raiding and plundering as they go, and the southern rebel forces, the SPLA. Corpses of horses and combatants are buried in shallow graves, which when the rains begin will become exposed, and precipitate an epidemic of cholera.

Worse still, around a million people around the railroad area and across a swathe of land 200 km by 300 km have been displaced, their villages burnt out by the combatants. The raiders from the north took their cattle. They have lost absolutely everything, and are existing in makeshift camps and shelters in deserted areas with almost no food, water, or utensils. 'Their situation is pathetic,' writes the bishop, 'and it is clear that the international community is not aware of them ... These people are on the brink of death.' This is darkness visible.

The second message is dated Rumbek, 27 February 2001: 'In the largest effort of its kind ever undertaken in southern Sudan, the United Nations Children's Fund (UNICEF) announced today that it had airlifted more than 2,500 child combatants out of conflict zones and into safe areas where a rehabilitation and family-tracing process can begin.'

What a feat! The SPLA, to their credit, released the children in accordance with the written pledge they made in October. UNICEF used two planes operated by the World Food Program, which flew the children to reception centres where UNICEF set up water-points. Those children for whom no family members can be traced will be looked after long-term, in the care of institutions like the Deng Nhial school we visited in Rumbek. That's going to take some organisation, and funds. 'Our first priority was to get these children to a place of safety,' says Dr Sharad Sapra, head of UNICEF's operations in south Sudan. 'Now our goal is to give them an education and some time to recover.'

There are probably another 9,000 child-soldiers still with various armed groups in South Sudan. But this recent operation, as Dr Sapra says, shows what can be done. 'We are more inspired than ever to convince military leaders in this conflict that children have no place in armies.' You can say that again. The airlift story is more than just a gleam of light: it's a sunburst.

Meanwhile, on a day-to-day level, the work goes on in Rumbek. Sid says that what the people in south Sudan need most is information. They are at least 200 years behind the developed world and have narrow perspectives. The thing is not to seek actively to change them, says Sid, but to give them a choice.

This may not always be possible. How, for example, in the absence of refrigeration, can it be demonstrated to the south Sudanese that there are better ways of preserving milk than by mixing it with cows' urine? Theirs may be the 'appropriate technology' for the lives they lead.

Nevertheless, 'Very small things make a big difference,' says Sid.

Take the UNICEF oxcart project. Oxen aren't traditionally used as draught-animals by Dinka or Nuer. Nevertheless, Sid has a basic box-like cart made, and harnesses two oxen to it. At first the oxen are as shocked as their owner, but settle down.

The locals may not yet have reinvented the wheel satisfactorily – the UNICEF cart lurches along on wavering discs of solid wood – but they now know that they can, if they want, transport in one single journey what normally takes ten journeys. They may not choose to do it, but they've got the choice.

It was Sid who said to us: 'It gives my life a spiritual

dimension, working here.'

I'd asked my companion over our evening beers in the compound at Rumbek, why she worked for a development agency, doing what she does. She acknowledged most of my quibbles about the illogicalities and intrusions of aid, and replied:

'I've got to be somewhere. This is where I find myself.'

Writing this down, I see for the first time that her answer has a double meaning. I don't know if she realised that, and I shan't ask her. It's a bit like the story told to me about the ex-Merchant Navy man who used to run a hamburger stall in Newcastle. He's jacked the whole thing in and gone off to Calcutta, where day after day he produces forty breakfasts for forty street-children.

'What on earth is the point of that?' everyone said. 'In Calcutta alone there are hundreds of thousands of beggar children, and in the whole of India ...'

'Forty breakfasts are forty breakfasts,' the man replied. 'Besides, it's what I can do.'

* * *

'It is necessary only for the good man to do nothing for evil to triumph.' To hell with governmental departments and their budgets, to hell with nation states and their strategies and their self-interest, to hell with public men in suits discussing conflict resolution at conferences in luxury hotels. Let's not get this wrong. They aren't the international community.

The international community is ordinary people, it is each one of us. We can sit around nitpicking about getting it wrong and getting it right till the cows come home. That way, we don't have to do anything at all.

So what can we do?

'Funds are limited, ' as A. said. We can do what we *can* do, either on the spot or from thousands of miles away, without fuss – our equivalent, in whatever form, of the forty breakfasts.

History and politics will look after themselves. Children can't.

NOTES

1 For good articles on the ethics of intervention see 'Wars of intervention: why and when to go in', *The Economist,* 6–12 January 2001; and Simon Jenkins, 'The new order that splits the world', *The Times,* 31 January 2001

2 Matthew Parris, 'Here are some thoughts for Mr Blair to consider before he takes up the white man's burden', *Spectator,* 9 December 2000

3 Quotations from *CAAT News,* November 2000. The address of Campaign Against Arms Trade is 11 Goodwin Street, London N4 3HQ. www.caat.org.uk

Epilogue

W F DEEDES

YOU have just finished reading our impressions of this beautiful country, tormented by conflict. In our different ways, we have tried to convey a portrait of its luckless people, the pain they have endured and the cruel consequences – especially for their children. Why is Sudan like this? What has gone wrong? We end this account of our travels with a few cold facts ... .

Historians will find it difficult fully to chart the agony suffered by the people of Sudan over 40 years of intermittent civil war. Fighting has gone on too long. The political shifts have been too obscure. The territory is so vast; Sudan is the biggest country in Africa. It is a land that has known no lasting peace since the Anglo-Egyptian condominium of 1899–1956 ended, the country secured independence and its turbulent history began.

Starting as a parliamentary republic, it came under military rule in 1958–64, then returned to civilian rule for five years; then from 1969 until 1985 was ruled by a revolutionary council under Colonel Gaafar Mohoammed El Nimeri. A third military coup in June 1989 brought Brigadier General Omar Hassan Ahmad al-Bashir to power. After presidential and legislative elections in 1996, he was elected without a serious contender and with 75 per cent of the vote.

The conflict is still widely seen as one between an Arab/Muslim north and a mainly African/Christian or animist south. But it is not entirely a religious war. It is also about land and resources. It is about attitudes. Countless peace initiatives have begun, shown promise and then vanished into the desert sands. It is reckoned that some 1.4 million of Sudan's 27 million population have died from this war, 300,000 of them in the war-induced famine of 1988, and thousands more in 1994. At least twice as many have fled the fighting and lost their homes. Many of the population have been perpetually on the move. Sudan's people belong to that sad multitude in the world 'who expect no harvest and possess no home'.

It was the imposition by Khartoum of Islamic sharia law in 1983 that made the conflict harder to stop. Colonel John Garang, leader of the Sudan People's Liberation Army (SPLA) in the south, has been fighting for secular democracy ever since. But wars of this kind, if they go on long enough, splinter into factions, as this one has done. The original cause becomes obscure. Then the world ceases to understand what is going on, or greatly to care.

The death roll would be higher, the anguish greater but for an initiative taken ten years ago by the United Nations. At a small airbase on the border of Kenya and Sudan, it established Operation Lifeline Sudan (OLS) coordinated by the United Nations Children's Fund, and involving 43 non-government organisations. From this base in Lokichoggio, relief is flown to areas in southern Sudan including rebel-hell regions and those areas allied to the government. The work is backed up by many of the world's non-government organisations.

From dawn to dusk planes fly from Loki to deliver food, medicine and other essentials to those caught up in this interminable civil war. It is, as those who have joined these flights will know, hazardous work. The relationship between Khartoum and the NGOs is complex and uneasy. In August 2000, believing the UNICEF planes were being used to fly arms to rebels, Khartoum actually sent its air force to attack the UN planes as they unloaded food and medicine on rebel-held airstrips in Southern Sudan. For a while, UNICEF had to suspend flights.

From another flank, UNICEF and the non-government

organisations engaged in this work have been accused of 'prolonging the war'. Supplies for the starving, it has been alleged, have been taken by soldiers. Instead of having to till the soil and reap the harvest, men have been left free to fight. The charge is best answered candidly. Amid the turmoil of Sudan, it would not be surprising if 1 lifeline to the homeless and the starving had not sometimes been misused by military forces. The strength of OLS lies in delivery to the needy on both sides. War has brought suffering to the north as well as the south. If UNICEF were not even-handed, Khartoum would not permit the planes to fly.

Flying on these missions with OLS, I have once or twice been close to tears. There was a scene embedded in my memory which took place a year or two back not far from Yei in Eastern Equatoria. There in blazing heat, mothers brought their babies to be weighed and measured for supplementary feeding. Most of them had walked miles from their homes. I found them sheltering under a tree, awaiting their turn at a tiny medical centre. There the babies were being assessed on a weight for height formula. Supplies were short. So many had to be turned away. The mothers then had to gather up their babies and set off empty-handed but uncomplainingly on the long journey home.

For some years, Khartoum suffered diplomatic isolation. The UN imposed sanctions on the National Islamic Front after Sudanese agents attempted to assassinate Egypt's president, Hosni Mubarak, in 1995. Accusing Sudan of harbouring terrorists, America imposed further sanctions, and gave military help to Sudan's neighbours. Some of the weapons were passed over to the Sudan rebels. African governments supported the rebels. Arab governments, who held aloof from Sudan for supporting Iraq in the Gulf War, suspended Sudan's membership in 1993 for failing to pay debt interest.

What recently caused the world's attitude to Sudan to undergo a change – and made the war nastier – was the finding of oil around Bentiu in the region of Western Upper Nile. The hunt for oil began in the mid-1970s. It was President Omar Hassan Ahmad al-Bashir who brought oil into the north by adjusting the boundaries. It was the Talisman Energy Inc., Canada's largest independent oil and gas company, which helped to make the oilfields profitable. A 1,000-mile pipeline has been laid between Heglig and Unity oilfields and Port Sudan on the Red Sea coast. As the oil started to flow in 1999, Sudan's economic prospects looked up. So did Sudan's foreign relationships. Oil has drawn international business back to Khartoum.

But oil has also intensified conflict. Alarmed by the extent of its own involvement, Canada sent a mission of inquiry to the oilfields that reported early in 2000. It was forced to admit what those of us who have visited the region already knew: oil has led to an enforced displacement of population. 'It is difficult to avoid the conclusion,' one passage in the report ran, 'that a swathe of scorched earth is being created around the oilfields.'

'For Talisman,' it admitted even more critically, 'so very much seems to be explained "as an intertribal problem," but displacement has gone on and on and is still going on, and in Ruweng County it is hard to deny that displacement has been for some time because of oil.' That was an understatement. As those of us who have seen burnt-out villages around the oilfields know, there has been more than displacement. 'Two things are certain,' said this report of Canada's assessment mission. 'First, the gunships and Antonovs which have attacked villages south of the river flew to their targets from the Heglig airstrip in the Talisman concession. This is known to the Nuer commanders defending these villages and is part of why they say they will target oil facilities.'

They know also that oil revenue is being used to buttress the war against the Sudan People's Liberation Army. This was once admitted by Hassan el Turabi, ideologue and founder of the National Islamic Front. That oil helps to build up Sudan's military strength has since been admitted by government officials. That is why the conflict has become fiercer and the 1,000-mile pipeline has been blown up three times.

As oil provides an increasing share of Sudan's budget and Khartoum strives to become a major oil producer, the oilfields are fiercely protected. In the fighting thousands of local people have been driven from their homes and some have been killed. Seemingly deaf to international protests, Western and Asian oil companies have hastened to the feast. The Western interests cover their backs by working on their image. One group has hired an American public relations firm and has created a 'social responsibility unit'. Not for the first time, oil is proving a rapid solvent of international ethics.

Earlier oil exploration was concentrated in Western Upper Nile. Now a huge area of Eastern Upper Nile is involved and civilians are being driven out to make the region safe for oil exploration. With supreme irony, this is a process which is drawing Khartoum back into the world that once shunned it.

Whenever this conflict ends, it will take more than a generation to restore the country to anything like normal life. Much of this work will fall to today's children, many of them robbed of their education by war and constant movement. Therein lies one of the challenges to UNICEF, for it will be for UNICEF to conjure up books and paper and pencils, to assist in the resurrection of Sudan's battered schools. As some of us have seen, when conflict ends, UNICEF knows how quickly to ease children back into schools without windows.

The hope must be that this generation of Sudan's

children can be equipped to lead their country back to a better life than their parents and grandparents have ever known. This book dwells on the past and the present. But it should also be seen as a contribution to the future; a very small beacon of hope for innocent children from whom so much has been taken, and on whom so much of Sudan's future now depends.